Lies

A native of Dundee, Marion Todd studied music with the Open University and worked for many years as a piano teacher and jobbing accompanist. A spell as a hotel lounge pianist provided rich fodder for her writing and she began experimenting with a variety of genres. Early success saw her winning first prize in the *Family Circle Magazine* short story for children national competition and she followed this up by writing short stories and articles for her local newspaper.

Life (and children) intervened and, for a few years, Marion's writing was put on hold. During this time, she worked as a college lecturer, plantswoman and candle-maker. But, as a keen reader of crime fiction, the lure of the genre was strong, and she began writing her debut crime novel. Now a full-time writer, Marion lives in North-east Fife, overlooking the River Tay. She can often be found working out plots for her novels while tussling with her jungle-like garden and walking her daughter's unruly but lovable dog.

Also by Marion Todd

Detective Clare Mackay

MARION TODD
Lies to tell

First published in the United Kingdom in 2020 by

Canelo
31 Helen Road
Oxford OX2 0DF
United Kingdom

Copyright © Marion Todd, 2020

The moral right of Marion Todd to be identified as the creator of this work has been asserted in accordance with the Copyright, Designs and Patents Act, 1988.

All rights reserved. No part of this publication may be reproduced or transmitted in any form or by any means, electronic or mechanical, including photocopy, recording, or any information storage and retrieval system, without permission in writing from the publisher.

A CIP catalogue record for this book is available from the British Library.

Print ISBN 978 1 78863 820 3
Ebook ISBN 978 1 78863 749 7

This book is a work of fiction. Names, characters, businesses, organizations, places and events are either the product of the author's imagination or are used fictitiously. Any resemblance to actual persons, living or dead, events or locales is entirely coincidental.

Look for more great books at www.canelo.co

Printed and bound in Great Britain by Clays Ltd, Elcograf S.p.A.

5

For Ally, Euan and Alicia who, between them, moved house three times during the writing of this book.

Thanks for that!

Friday, 15 May

Chapter 1

Wish you were here!

DI Clare Mackay stood in front of the kitchen window in Daisy Cottage reading the gaily coloured postcard in her hand. Outside in the garden a group of noisy hedge sparrows were cheeping while three starlings were clearing every scrap of food off the bird table. With only a month to midsummer the sun was high in the sky already, warming the Caithness flagstones below the kitchen window, but Clare saw none of it. She stared at the postcard. *Wish you were here.* What the fuck did that mean? She turned it over in her hand again and scrutinised the picture on the front. Where was Provincetown anyway? Somewhere the buildings were painted with bright, cartoonish figures, obviously. She read on.

> *Spending the day here with friends from the university. Such a fun town.*
> *Fancy coming out for a holiday? You'd love it!*

It was signed simply with

G xxxx

'Damn you, Geoffrey Dark,' she said, tugging open the fridge and taking out a punnet of grapes. She put these down beside a bowl of granola and picked up her phone. She tapped Provincetown into Google and clicked on the Wikipedia link.

'Cape Cod,' she told Benjy, the English bull terrier sitting at her feet, awaiting his breakfast.

He wagged his tail in response and Clare took the hint, lifting a bag of dried dog food from the foot of the larder and filling his bowl. Benjy fell on the food and Clare returned to her perusal of Provincetown. As she read, her phone dinged and a message flashed across the screen. DCI Alastair Gibson. She clicked immediately to read it.

> Pick you up from station car park at 8:30 a.m.
> Al

Clare stared at the message. Had she forgotten something? Some arrangement they had made? The DCI wasn't her biggest fan – was there something wrong? A complaint, maybe. She tapped a reply.

> Sorry, sir. Team meeting in St Andrews at 9.
> Can we reschedule?

She watched the screen, seeing that he was typing again. And then it arrived.

> I've cancelled your meeting. See you at 8:30.
> A

He'd cancelled her meeting? What the hell was going on?
She tapped back,

Something wrong? Am I for the high jump?

The reply came almost immediately.

Nothing like that.
A

Clare stared at the screen. Clearly he wasn't inviting more questions. If it wasn't a disciplinary matter, what was so important that he had taken it upon himself to cancel her team meeting? She glanced at the clock. Seven thirty. She whistled to Benjy, picking up his lead from a hook on the wall. 'Come on, you,' she said. 'Quick walk.'

She opened the kitchen door and stepped out into her garden, pulling the door closed behind her. The sparrows, panicked by her sudden appearance, flew across the garden while the three starlings simply hopped onto the fence, observing her progress down the path. As she walked, Clare avoided looking at the borders either side of the flagstones. It was a typical cottage garden, plants spilling over each other either side of the path. Roses, lavender, lupins and heathers were bursting into bloom and the scent from an early flowering honeysuckle was attracting bees. The path meandered down the garden, past a shed painted in a soft green, towards a wooden infill gate, the timbers silvered with time. As Clare walked, Benjy running ahead of her, she picked her way over the thorny shoots of brambles, encroaching on the flagstones. She really needed to spend some time out here, before the garden got out of hand. The problem was she knew nothing about gardening. She vaguely recalled seeing some garden tools hanging on hooks in the shed when she had moved in, but she hadn't taken the matter any further than that. Benjy was at the gate now, waiting patiently, and Clare quickened her pace. Perhaps she could find a gardener, she thought, lifting the latch on the gate and pulling it open.

She stepped out onto a track that led through the woods behind Daisy Cottage. Benjy shot off to snuffle in the undergrowth while Clare strolled along, enjoying the warmth of the sun where it shone through the trees. After ten minutes she whistled and Benjy came running back to her.

'Short walk today,' she told him. 'The DCI's after me.'

The little dog trotted obediently behind her and she opened the gate for him, picking her steps carefully over the brambles, back to the kitchen door.

She decided against her usual work suit, reaching further back into the wardrobe to find a new jacket and trousers she had bought in the spring sales but not yet worn. She had an uneasy feeling about that message from the DCI. What was so important that he had taken it upon himself to cancel her meeting? They had worked together just once, almost a year ago now. She couldn't easily forget that time when a hit-and-run driver had been picking off seemingly random victims, and DCI Gibson had been brought in to oversee the investigation. He had doubted her competency from the outset, but she had won him round and they had parted – well, not exactly friends – but colleagues with mutual respect. Clare hoped fervently she was not going to have to win him round, all over again.

She stepped into the trousers and zipped them up. Turning to check her profile in the mirror she admired the cut. She couldn't normally afford to buy from Jigsaw but she was glad now that, whatever awaited her, she would be well-dressed to receive it.

Her phoned dinged again. Chris, this time. Her DS.

> You in hot · water? DCI's cancelled the
> meeting.
> Wot's that about?

What indeed. She tapped back:

> No idea.
> Text me if anything comes up.

Chris replied with a thumbs-up and she tucked her phone
into her workbag. Benjy was stretched out beneath the
kitchen window, basking in the sun that was now filling
the room. She ruffled his head, picked up her water bottle
and headed out to the car.

Chapter 2

Clare pulled into the station car park at twenty past eight and backed into her usual space. There were a few cars already parked in front of the low, red-brick building but no sign of the DCI's sleek Jaguar. A gaggle of schoolkids wandered languidly past, eyes glued to their phones. Clare took out her own phone to check work emails for any clue as to what was going on. Nothing. A sharp toot made her look up and she saw to her surprise that the DCI had arrived in what she thought was an older Ford Focus. Clare grabbed her bag from the passenger seat and stepped out of her car. As she clicked the remote control to lock it, she smiled. It was two weeks old already and she still wasn't used to having it. She ran her hand along the bonnet then turned and climbed into the Focus.

'Morning, Al,' she said to the DCI. 'Where's the Jag today?'

The DCI clearly had the same ideas as Clare, dressed to impress in a fine dark grey suit. The jacket hung from a hook behind his seat, the *Giorgio Armani* label visible. His tie was knotted tightly at the neck and his shirt cuffs were held by a pair of plain silver cufflinks. He pulled out of the car park and into Pipelands Road, avoiding another group of schoolkids, stravaiging across the road. 'Erm, bit of a tale there.'

Clare wasn't sure whether to pursue it. Instead, she said, 'So, not that I don't appreciate you picking me up this morning, but what's so urgent that you cancelled my meeting?'

'Not now,' he said. 'You'll see when we get there.'

She stared at him. 'Get where?'

He hesitated. 'Clare – if you don't mind, let's just wait till we arrive. Everything will be explained then.'

She continued staring but he wouldn't be drawn. A couple of red-gowned students started to cross the road in front of the car, apparently unconcerned about the morning traffic.

'Take your time, why don't you?' he muttered, adding, 'What's with the red gowns anyway?'

'Tradition, I think,' Clare said.

They drove on past the historic West Port, a seventeenth-century sandstone gate with semi-octagonal towers, and joined City Road. At North Street he turned left, heading out of town, past the iconic Old Course Hotel and the world-famous golf course.

As they neared the sign for Balgove Steak Barn, the DCI said, 'Ever eaten there?'

Clare looked up the drive that curved round to the barn. 'Yeah. It's pretty good, actually. Quite literally a barn though. Can be cold at night. But they have heaters and blankets.'

'Not fine dining then?'

'Oh, the food is excellent. But it's not a dressy place, if that's what you mean.'

They lapsed into silence, the tree-lined golf links giving way to lush farmland with a view across to the Angus hills in the distance. After a few awkward minutes Clare said,

'What's wrong with your car? Surely the Jaguar garage have better courtesy cars than this?'

DCI Gibson cleared his throat. 'Actually,' he said, 'this is my new car.'

Clare gaped. 'This?'

'It's a good little runner. Economical too and a decent boot.'

Clare racked her brains. Had she missed something? Al Gibson was definitely not the Ford Focus type of guy. He was more your designer suit and Jaguar sort, courtesy of his DCI's salary. She looked round the interior of the car. It was nice enough. The kind of car her parents would drive. But it was a basic model. None of the finer touches she recalled from the last time she was in his Jaguar. 'It's erm, it's – nice. Yeah, nice car.'

He threw her a grateful smile which puzzled her even more. This car – and the designer suit jacket hanging in the back. It didn't add up.

They were nearing the roundabout at Guardbridge and Clare wondered if he would head north to Dundee. Bell Street in Dundee was one of the larger stations in the area. Perhaps they were going to a meeting there. But he carried on, heading west towards Cupar.

'Still not going to tell me where we're going?' Clare asked.

'As I say, you'll see when we're there.'

Clare decided if she couldn't draw him on their destination she'd have a go at the Ford Focus. 'So, the car – you trading down to save the planet?'

There was a pause. Then he said, 'Not exactly.' He seemed to be struggling for the right words.

Clare waited and then he spoke again.

'Alison and I...'

She saw his face flush and she waited for him to speak – to order his thoughts.

He ran a finger round his collar, as if to loosen it. 'We've, erm, decided to separate.'

Clare could have kicked herself for not recognising the signs. With the shifts and long hours working on major incidents, it wasn't unheard of for police marriages to founder. 'Oh God, Al. I'm so sorry. I really am. I wouldn't have mentioned the car if I'd realised.'

He replaced his hand on the steering wheel and glanced at her then away again. 'It's fine, Clare. We're sorting things out. The Jag – she was fond of it. And I'm trying to hang onto my pension.'

Clare racked her brains for something to say. Until today, her relationship with DCI Gibson had been strictly professional. He had kept himself aloof from Clare and her team and she was disconcerted by this rare glimpse into his personal life. She had been to his house, of course. His twice-yearly treat for the troops. Mulled wine at Christmas and a barbeque in the summer. She could never quite make up her mind if it was for the benefit of the cops or if he just wanted to show off his house. It was an elegant Victorian property in the leafy Grange district of Edinburgh and he had the wife to match. Alison Gibson with her thick hair and well-cut clothes was every bit the DCI's wife. Probably fancied herself as a superintendent's wife, come to that. Clare pondered what might have gone wrong between them. One of them playing away? The DCI didn't seem the type but you never could tell. Clare wasn't sure about Alison. Finally, she said, 'It can't be easy. You've been together a while now.'

'Almost twenty years. It's our twentieth wedding anniversary next month.' He flicked another glance at Clare. 'Won't happen now, of course.'

Clare shifted in her seat, feeling for the knob to adjust the angle, more for something to do than anything else. She'd never had this kind of conversation with the DCI and wasn't sure how much she should ask – if anything. He saved her the trouble.

'The house will have to go, of course. Neither of us can afford to buy the other out.'

Clare didn't know what to say. The house was so lovely. No expense spared. Full of richly patterned curtains, thick carpets and – oh –that kitchen! She remembered Alison saying they'd had it custom-made by a kitchen designer in Edinburgh's Stockbridge. 'Oh Al,' she said, at last. 'Your lovely house.'

He shrugged, slowing down as they reached the village of Dairsie. 'It's only a house, Clare. Bricks and mortar.'

Clare reckoned things must have been pretty bad to evoke this reaction. If it had been her house, she'd have wept buckets over it. 'Can't have been easy, though,' she said.

'Suppose.'

'Is it on the market?'

'Sold.'

Clare was shocked. Normally the gossipmongers would have had this news all round the Force. But she hadn't heard a peep. 'So soon?' she said.

'It's a good house. Lots of interest and we got way over the asking price which helps with finding somewhere else.'

'I suppose that's something. When do you move?'

'End of next month.'

'Must be a wrench.'

'Not now,' he said. 'It was an awful thought at first. We'd put so much work into it, Clare. Made it just the way we wanted it. But then Alison moved out and took half the furniture with her. It didn't really feel like home after that.' He checked over his shoulder then pulled out to pass a tractor. 'I'll be glad to leave.'

So Alison Gibson had moved out. Clare wondered if she had gone to be with someone else. The DCI hadn't mentioned her having a new partner. For his wife to move out of her lovely house, she must have had a pretty good reason.

'Where will you go?' she asked.

He smiled at her. 'Aberdour.'

'Aber-where?'

'It's a lovely wee village. North edge of the Forth.'

Clare was surprised. 'Not Edinburgh?'

'No. I reckoned I was better getting out of the city. Clean break, you know?'

Clare nodded. 'I suppose. Means you have to cross that bridge every day though. You're back in Edinburgh now, aren't you?'

He cleared his throat. 'Erm, actually not for much longer.'

'You're not leaving the Force?'

'Pfft. I wish. Can't afford that now. But I have asked to be based in Fife. Once I move house, you know?'

'Oh!' The exclamation was out before Clare could stop herself. 'I mean...'

'Don't worry,' he said smiling for the first time that morning. 'I won't tread on your toes, Clare. You've no room for me anyway.'

'So – where?'

'Dunfermline, probably. It's a good-sized station. I'm sure they'll find me a broom cupboard somewhere in the building.'

Clare thought it more likely some poor inspector would be shifted to the broom cupboard to make room for the DCI. But she said nothing. They were approaching Melville Lodges Roundabout now. She wondered which way he would go. South to Edinburgh, probably. But why? Where was it they were going? She searched her memory, trying to recall if there were any strategic meetings planned. Perhaps it was counter-terrorism. But if so...

He cut across her thoughts, evidently deciding a change of subject was in order. 'Are you following the Phil Quinn trial?'

'The firearms haul? Yeah, I caught the news last night. Seems to be going okay...' She glanced at him and saw his lips thin. It was a moment or two before he spoke.

'There's such a lot riding on it, Clare.' He swallowed then went on. 'Months of work.'

Clare watched him. She couldn't recall ever seeing the DCI look so anxious about a case. So uncertain. 'But you have all the weapons – that warehouse.'

He nodded but didn't smile. 'It was quite a haul. Guns, knives, bomb-making equipment.'

He glanced at her and, from his expression, Clare had the impression he was seeking reassurance. That he needed someone to tell him it would be okay. 'That's a whole lot of gear off the streets then,' she said.

He glanced over his shoulder and pulled out to pass an orange-clad cyclist. As he pulled back in again his hand went to the gear level to move it into sixth gear, apparently forgetting the Focus only had five. He clicked his tongue in irritation then fell silent.

Clare eyed him for a moment, trying to gauge his mood, then said, 'What's his defence?'

'Phil? I reckon he'll implicate Paddy Grant.'

She racked her brains. The name was familiar but...

'Paddy was Phil's right-hand man,' he explained. 'My guess is he'll say it was Paddy's doing. That Paddy went rogue and he couldn't control him.'

'Think the jury will believe him?'

'Dunno. I mean, to us, he has gangster written all over him. But juries...'

Clare considered this. He had a point. She'd had a few cases herself where she'd known for sure that the accused was guilty yet the jury had returned a *not guilty* verdict. But surely, in this case... 'Is there DNA?' she asked. 'On the weapons you seized?'

'Nope. He's too clever for that. No prints, either. He doesn't get his hands dirty, our Mr Quinn. He has plenty of guys to do that for him.'

'Big operation then?'

He nodded. 'One of the biggest we've seen – in the past ten years anyway. There's a bunch of his lads on remand, awaiting trial. If we can put Phil away we've a fighting chance of convicting the whole lot.'

Clare mulled this over. She had heard the talk; heard cops saying the DCI had jumped the gun, arresting Phil Quinn.

Again.

She thought back to a couple of cases recently where he'd had his fingers burned. Meticulously planned operations, yet somehow the main perpetrators had managed to stay one step ahead, disappearing before they could be arrested. Admittedly he'd broken up a county lines drug operation, netting a fair quantity of Class A; but the four a.m. knock on the door had come too late. The guys they had really been after – dealers who had flooded Edinburgh with their drugs – they had melted away like snow.

No one had blamed the DCI – not out loud at least. But there had been mutterings – questions about his fitness to lead such high-level operations.

Clare glanced at him again. His knuckles were white on the steering wheel and she realised just how much he needed a result from this case. 'Any sign of Paddy Grant?'

'Nope. Probably out of the country by now.'

Then Clare saw the hint of a smile.

'But we have the wife.'

'Phil's wife?'

'The very same.'

'She's going to testify?' Clare was surprised.

'So she says.'

'Bit unusual, isn't it? A wife turning against her husband?'

'I suppose.'

'What's in it for her?'

'Immunity. She's been no angel herself, over the years. There was enough evidence in the matrimonial home to charge her with *Possession with Intent to Injure*. And, given the haul we've recovered from the lock-ups and the warehouse, there's no way she didn't know what was going on. But my guess is we wouldn't have found her prints or DNA on any of the weapons either so the Fiscal agreed to her testifying in return for immunity.'

Clare gave a low whistle. 'So she's dropping him in it to save her own skin.'

'That's about the size of it.'

'Is she in custody?'

The DCI shook his head. 'No. Prison's too dangerous for her. Phil could easily get someone to warn her off.'

'She in a safe house, then?'

'Yeah. Round-the-clock surveillance. Only for another week or so. She's due to testify next week. Wednesday I think. Hopefully she'll give us enough for a conviction and we can set about auctioning some of the stuff we've seized.'

'From their house?'

'Yes. Jewellery, TVs, iPads and a huge campervan. Should net a few thousand quid for the community.'

Clare digested this as the DCI drove on. They passed the junction for the M90 motorway, continuing along the A91, and she turned her attention to the passing scenery.

'It's an attractive road,' she said. 'Don't think I've been along here.'

'It's the Hillfoots Road. Skirts round the foot of the Ochil Hills. Ben Cleuch ring a bell?'

Clare frowned. 'Maybe. I've been up a few hills but I honestly can't remember.'

He laughed. 'You weren't navigating then?'

'Nope. I just make the sandwiches and trail along behind.'

They drove on for a few miles then the DCI took a right, leaving the main road. He slowed down as they bumped along a forest track.

'Sorry. Suspension's not great on this thing,' he said.

But Clare wasn't listening. She was looking round to see where they were going. The trees bordering the track were dense and their route curved round, hiding the main road completely. They drove on for what Clare estimated must have been a mile or so through thick forest until suddenly the trees cleared. She stared as they approached a high concrete wall which sloped outwards from the ground up. It looked to be at least twenty feet high with an overhang that would make it difficult to climb. It was topped by a circular metal tube. Clare studied this. Why would anyone build a wall and top it with such a thing? And then it dawned on her. The tube was there to prevent anyone using a grappling hook to scale the wall.

A knot was forming in her stomach. What was this place and why the hell had they come?

Chapter 3

A steel gate set into the high wall was opened and they drove through into a yard where another high wall faced them.

'What the hell is this?' Clare said, her voice low.

'This,' the DCI said, 'does not exist.'

She looked at him but he said no more.

A uniformed officer in a Kevlar vest waved them over to the side and the DCI parked where the officer indicated.

'Best leave your phones in the car,' the DCI advised. 'They'll only take them away. Bag too,' he added.

She stared at him. 'What if there's an emergency?'

'This takes priority. Oh, and bring your ID badge.'

They stepped out of the car and the DCI handed the keys to the uniformed officer. He led them over to a gate built into the second concrete wall. As they walked, Clare took it all in. She could see little above the outer wall except tall evergreen trees but there was no mistaking the cameras, so numerous they must be covering every inch of this yard and the walls surrounding it. As the gate was opened their badges were scanned by a female officer.

'Shoes please,' the officer asked.

Clare flicked a glance at the DCI but he was already unlacing his brogues. She stepped obediently out of her own black mules and handed them over. The shoes were put through a scanner then handed back to them.

'This way,' the officer said, indicating an airport-style security gate.

Clare went through first and a buzzer sounded.

'Over here,' the officer directed and she proceeded to scan Clare with paddles. Her wristwatch was found to be the offending item and they moved on through another security door. A long corridor seemed to slope gently downwards but the absence of windows made it difficult to be sure. Motion sensor lights flicked on as they walked along and the occasional flash from small red lights told Clare there were more cameras, probably sunk into the ceiling.

Finally, they stood before a heavy oak door with a digital keypad. The female officer tapped in a number and stood back to let them enter. Then she closed the door behind them, leaving them in a windowless room. It was austere, with magnolia walls and a basic industrial carpet on the floor. Clare looked round the room. Not a single picture adorned the walls but in each corner of the ceiling were small cameras. She turned away from them and surveyed the rest of her surroundings. Half a dozen chairs were arranged round a low coffee table on which sat a jug of water and a stack of plastic cups. A woman rose from one of the chairs as they entered. She was, Clare thought, about the same age as her. Not quite as tall, perhaps, but wiry and fit-looking. Her dark hair, threaded through with highlights, was cut short at the sides and back, and swept up on top in a pompadour style. Her woollen dress was delft-blue and set off with a silver dragonfly brooch. Her black patent leather boots had a fine heel and looked expensive. Her studied appearance was somehow at odds with the starkness of her surroundings.

She held out a hand and smiled warmly. 'Gayle Crichton.'

Clare scrutinised her for any sign of an ID badge that might indicate who or what Gayle Crichton was but she couldn't see one. 'Clare Mackay. DI at St Andrews.'

'Yes, I know who you are,' Gayle said. She turned to the DCI, her smile still fixed. 'Al,' she said, and he inclined his head in response. The introductions done, she indicated the chairs. 'Please sit. Can I pour you some water?'

Clare nodded. 'Thanks. And may I ask how you know who I am? And why I'm here?'

'All in good time.' Gayle picked up the jug and poured three cups of water, passing two across the table. Then she sat down, smoothing her dress. 'So, Clare, first of all thank you for coming all this way. As DCI Gibson knows, it's vital we meet here, in this building.'

Clare glanced at the DCI and he gave her a brief nod.

Gayle went on. 'The reason you are here – by which I mean here, in this particular location – is that the building is entirely secure. Had you been left with your mobile phone, for example, you would have seen that there is no signal. Not anywhere within these walls.'

'That's not so unusual,' Clare said.

'No indeed. But security here is on another level, Clare. The outer walls of the building are two feet thick with steel mesh built into the concrete. No doubt you realised, as you made your way to this room, that the building is partly sunk into the ground. The surrounding walls are capable of withstanding an impact from a forty-tonne truck and they are designed to be as blast-proof as is currently possible.'

'It's a bunker,' Clare said.

'In a way, yes. But the building is in daily use. It's not for emergencies.'

'Might I ask what it's used for?'

'Not really. All I will say is that it is used for the most covert of activities; those where normal security is not sufficient.'

Clare looked at the DCI. 'And you knew about this place?'

'Not much. Only that it existed. I wasn't given the location until this morning.'

Clare's mind was in a whirl. What the hell was going on here? She reached for her cup and drank, moistening her lips. 'So, now that you've explained the security, will you tell us why we're here?'

'Of course.' Gayle moved a stray hair back into place then she regarded Clare, the smile gone. 'Before I go any further, I will remind you – both of you – that you have signed the Official Secrets Act. As such, if anything discussed today is leaked beyond these walls, you will immediately be arrested and face the full force of the law. Is that clear?'

Clare ran her tongue round her lips again. 'Of course.'

Gayle turned to the DCI, an eyebrow raised, and he gave a brief nod.

'Then allow me to explain,' she said. 'I am what is known as an ethical hacker. Are you familiar with the term?'

Clare's brow creased. 'I think so.'

Gayle saw Clare's expression. 'Basically, I have studied how hackers operate. How they gain access and, having gained access, how they set about exploiting it. Usually it's my job to be one step ahead of the hackers, assessing the vulnerability of new systems. But, from time to time, I am called in where breaches have already occurred and this is one such occasion.'

Clare and the DCI exchanged glances. Gayle watched them for a few moments then went on.

'I am under contract to Police Scotland to investigate a serious security breach. I cannot give you details. Nor can I tell you how I propose to carry out my investigation. But I do need your help.'

Clare blinked. 'My help?'

'Yes, Clare. I'd like you to help me.'

Clare frowned. 'But I don't know much about computers. My DS...'

'No, it's you I need. Not your computer knowledge; and it goes without saying that your DS will not be privy to this conversation. Yes?'

Clare hesitated, then said, 'Of course. So...'

'What I need,' Gayle said, moving her seat closer to Clare, 'is an office at your station. Somewhere I can work uninterrupted.'

Clare looked round the austere room. 'But surely here...'

Gayle shook her head. 'No, here won't do. I need to be out among the cops, monitoring their traffic, seeing what comes in and out. In a busy station, I might attract attention. But in your station – well, I'm pretty sure your staff believe what you tell them.'

'But what am I supposed to tell them?' Clare asked. 'How do I explain your presence?'

'That's easy. The official line is that I've been hired to develop a new communications system and that I need somewhere out of the way where I can work in peace. You have an office I can use, I presume?'

Clare mentally ran round the station. There was an interview room they didn't use very often. 'There is a room that might do. It's pretty small though. No window either. But it does have a data point.'

'Don't worry about that,' Gayle said. 'I'll set up my own network access.'

Clare flicked a glance at the DCI and he gave a slight nod.

'DI Mackay will be happy to assist you, Gayle.'

'Excellent. Now, Clare, I understand you are good friends with one of the Technical Support staff down at Glenrothes.'

Clare's eyes narrowed. How the hell did she know that? And what else did she know? She swallowed. 'You mean Diane?'

'That's right. Diane Wallace. Clare, under no circumstances are you to discuss anything we have said today or anything relating to my presence in St Andrews with Diane.'

Clare's expression clouded. She'd known Diane for years. There was no one she trusted more. 'Mind if I ask why?'

'It's like this. We don't know if the security breach has come from an outside attack or if there is an internal leak. And, I'm sure I don't have to spell out to you that, whether internal or external, this kind of breach would require a high level of IT skills.'

Clare stiffened. 'I can tell you quite categorically that Diane is one hundred per cent reliable. I'd trust her with my life.'

'Clare, with respect, you can't say anything of the sort. Now I'm not suggesting that your friend is implicated. But the fewer people who know about this the better.

I must have your guarantee that you won't discuss this matter with anyone, particularly Diane.'

Clare looked mulish.

'Or I'll have your warrant card,' Gayle said.

Clare turned to the DCI.

'Detective Inspector Mackay will do as you ask,' he said to Gayle, glancing at Clare. 'Won't you?'

Clare's lips tightened. 'Of course.'

'Obviously,' Gayle went on, 'should any of your colleagues in Tech Support become aware of my investigations, you will plead complete ignorance.'

'Saying what?'

Gayle smiled broadly. 'Just act normally. Thank them for flagging it up to you and say you'll have it checked out at a senior level. That should hold them for a few days which, I hope, will be long enough for me to complete my investigations.'

Clare was not convinced but she was starting to realise she had no choice in any of this. 'Okay.'

'One more thing,' Gayle went on. 'And this is particularly important.'

They waited.

'Until my investigations are complete, I will not know how and from where the information is being leaked. You should carry on police business as normal but you must make no reference to my investigation within the walls of the station, on your phones, in any car you use and even...' She broke off for a moment. '...even in your own homes.'

'You're not seriously suggesting—' Clare burst out.

'I'm not suggesting anything, Clare. Only that the less you mention this matter the more secure it will remain.' She scrutinised their faces. 'Are we agreed?'

They both muttered their agreement and Gayle rose, all smiles again. 'Then I need detain you no longer. Thank you both for your time. Clare – I'll see you on Monday morning.' She moved to the door and pressed a button on the wall. Seconds later the door opened and the female uniformed officer appeared.

'I'll escort you back to your car,' she said.

They followed her in silence, Clare more conscious on the return trip of the incline in the corridors. Out in the yard, between the two concrete walls, she drew in a deep lungful of air and looked up and over the outer wall towards the trees beyond, only the tips of them visible. She was so glad to be outside again. Out of that place. It was so – weird. As they walked back towards the car, she whispered, 'Even this car?'

'Even this one,' the DCI replied, clicking the remote control. 'Fancy an early lunch before we head back?'

'Definitely.'

Chapter 4

They drove out of the enclosure, back onto the track and through the trees. Neither of them spoke until they emerged onto the road again. Clare was in no doubt that Gayle had been deadly serious in her warnings not to discuss the security breach in any cars or buildings; but even normal conversation seemed out of the question. Eventually, Clare broke the silence.

'An early lunch, then?'

He nodded, his face impassive. 'I know somewhere, about five miles from here.'

They drove on, the tall conifers giving way to farm-land. A few miles further on they saw a brown AA sign for a garden centre. The DCI indicated and pulled off the road and into the car park. 'This do?'

Clare clicked her seatbelt off and opened the door. 'Anywhere,' she said.

They walked, still not speaking, passing through the sliding doors at the entrance.

The DCI indicated a sign for the cafe. 'It has an outdoor seating area,' he said and Clare nodded.

At the self-service counter they ordered coffees and paninis which the smiling waitress said she would bring out to them. The DCI led Clare through the cafe to an outdoor area with wooden picnic tables and chairs. He indicated a table furthest from the door and away from the other diners. Clare sat down and he took a seat opposite.

'Phones off?' Clare suggested.

The DCI reached into his pocket. 'Good idea.'

With their phones powered off, Clare opened her mouth to speak then, out of the corner of her eye, she saw the waitress approaching. 'Food's here.'

The waitress put a tray down on the table. 'Enjoy,' she said, heading back indoors.

Clare picked up a spoon and began stirring her coffee. When the waitress was safely out of earshot, she said, 'So – what just happened back there? I mean, did you know about this, Al?'

He hesitated. 'I knew there was something up, but not much more than that. I was told it was strictly confidential and that I was to bring you with me this morning.'

'Did you know about that place?'

He shrugged. 'You hear things but I didn't really know what it was. What it would be like.' He looked up. 'Bit of a shock, to be honest.'

'I'll say. Like something out of a *Bourne* film. What do you suppose goes on there? Who even works in a place like that?'

'No idea. Sometimes I think we're better off not knowing.'

Clare bit into her panini and began chewing. After a minute or two she spoke again. 'You reckon there is a leak?'

The DCI glanced round as the waitress reappeared with an empty tray and began clearing the table next to them. They munched on until she had left then he said, 'What else could it be? I mean, these ethical hackers don't come cheap. Sounds to me like they reckon one of our own is leaking information.'

'Well it's not Diane. I can tell you that for sure.'

'Yeah, maybe so. But you can't tell her about this, Clare. You'll end up on a charge, if you do.'

Clare sighed. 'I know. I just hope this Gayle person gets it sorted out quickly. The team aren't daft you know. They'll suss something's going on.'

The DCI shook his head. 'Can't happen, Clare. It's your job to make sure they don't suss anything, as you put it.'

'Easier said than done.'

'Look, Clare,' he said, 'I'll keep in touch. I'll pop in every few days. On some pretext. We can go for a walk and chat over any difficulties. But nothing inside the station, mind. Treat every room, every office and every car as if it's been bugged.'

Clare sat back in her chair. 'It's ridiculous, Al. I don't believe it.'

'I'm finding it a bit far-fetched myself, to be honest. But that wasn't a joke this morning. Far from it.' He took out his phone and clicked to switch it back on. 'Let's forget it for now and enjoy being out of the office.'

Clare took in her surroundings. He was right. The cafe was next to the outdoor plants area and there were shelves full of bedding plants in polystyrene boxes. Perhaps she should take some back for her garden at Daisy Cottage. But that made her think of how overgrown it had become.

The DCI saw her expression change. 'Something wrong?'

'No, not really. I was just thinking of my own garden and how I've neglected it. I'd love to take some of these plants back to brighten it up, but I wouldn't know where to start.'

He surveyed the plants. 'It's a bit early for some of these. Alison always left it until the start of June. You can get a late frost up here in May, you know.'

'And that's bad for the plants?'

He laughed. 'You really don't know much about gardening, do you?' He picked up his cup and drained it, dabbing at his now frothy moustache with a napkin. 'Get yourself a gardener, Clare. It'll save a lot of work.'

'I suppose.'

'Or – I could come round and give you a hand – if you wanted.'

Clare flushed. 'I don't know, Al. I mean, you've a lot on your plate just now.'

He smiled. 'Not really. But the offer's there if you want it.' He let this hang in the air for a moment, then said, 'So, you've heard the sorry tale about my car. Tell me about yours.'

Clare couldn't help returning his smile. 'Oh, the car,' she said.

'It's a pretty flashy model. Mercedes, yeah?'

'Yup. C-class Coupé.'

'Nice. So, did somebody die?'

'Eh?'

'Did you come into a fortune? It's not a cheap car.'

Clare didn't reply.

'Sorry,' he said. 'None of my business.'

'No, it's fine.' She forced a smile. 'I just felt like treating myself. I have the car loan from hell but so what? I mean, we work hard, don't we?'

'Mm-hm.'

'And it goes like stink.'

29

He laughed. 'I didn't have you down for a petrol head, Clare.'

'I'm not really. Just wanted…' She lowered her eyes. 'I wanted something that made me happy. Something just for me.' She hadn't meant to say that. Especially to the DCI. But it was out now.

He watched her for a minute before answering then said, 'Mind if I ask you something?'

'Suppose.'

'Your sculptor friend…'

'Geoffrey.'

'Yes, Geoffrey. Is it – I mean, are you still together? Tell me to mind my own business if you want.'

Clare raised her eyes to meet his. 'No, it's fine. I don't mind you asking. Truth is, he was offered a job in the USA. Too good to turn down, really. He asked me to go but – well, it just wasn't possible.'

'Why the hell not?'

Clare looked at him, surprised at his reaction. 'Oh, I couldn't. I mean there's my cottage, my dog – and then my sister and her husband. Their little boy – he's autistic; and he's my godson. They need my support. I couldn't go, Al. Too many ties here.'

'And so he went?'

'And so he went.'

'Is he coming back?'

Clare shrugged. 'Dunno.'

'Are you still in touch?'

She sipped at her coffee. 'Yeah, now and then.'

'And, do you want him to come back?'

She was prevented from answering by his phone which started to ring. He fished it out of his pocket and squinted at the display, shading it from the sun with his other hand.

'Sorry, I have to take this.'

Saved by the bell, Clare thought, a little relieved. The conversation had been making her face up to things she'd rather have kept buried. Did she want Geoffrey to come back? Now there was a question.

The DCI put the phone in his pocket and scraped back his chair. 'We have to go.'

Clare rose. 'What's up?'

'Wait till we're out of here.'

They walked quickly back through the cafe, past the checkouts and out into the car park. He stopped in an empty space and checked all round, then said, 'Phil Quinn's wife...'

'The one who's in witness protection?'

'Yeah, Tamsin she's called. Well her location's been compromised. We have to go and pick her up.'

'Now?'

'Yup. And not a word about it in the car. If there's the remotest chance it's bugged, someone might get to her before we do. I'm not losing the trial at this stage. I've put too much work into it.'

They rejoined the A91, driving in silence until they came to the junction with the M90. The DCI took the motorway, heading north. Twenty minutes later they were sitting in a queue approaching the Broxden Roundabout.

'I hate this bloody roundabout,' the DCI said. 'It's always like this.'

'Should have come off at junction ten and gone through the town. It can be quicker.'

'Now she tells me.'

Chapter 5

They cleared the roundabout, eventually, and drove on until they came to another one, controlled by traffic lights. The DCI drummed his fingers impatiently on the dashboard waiting for the lights to go green. Eventually they were moving again and he turned right onto a long road, peppered with car dealerships.

'Obviously the place to come to buy a car,' Clare observed. 'Where are we going?'

'Look out for a sign for the grammar school. We take a left there.'

Clare looked out of the window, past the glass-fronted buildings advertising zero per cent finance on car deals. She thought of her sleek Mercedes, parked back in St Andrews. Definitely not bought with zero per cent finance, judging by her monthly repayments. But it gave her a thrill every time she saw it and it was an absolute dream to drive. It wasn't like her to be so extravagant. Probably a response to Geoffrey going off to Boston. Perhaps if he hadn't gone she wouldn't have bought the car. She'd still be driving her old Renault Clio. But maybe – just maybe – she would be happy.

'Some navigator you are,' the DCI said, slamming on the brakes and indicating left at a roundabout.

Clare muttered something about being distracted as the DCI swung the car round and into a housing estate. They drove on, past the grammar school, finally turning off into a newer development. With a glance at the satnav, he slowed down, crawling on through a succession of streets, finally pulling in beside a detached two-storey house, finished in a cream render. The curtains were closed and he jumped out of the car, pulling his lanyard with its ID badge off his neck.

Clare followed him, looking up and down the street. It was quiet, apart from a couple of young women pushing prams. At the far end she could see a DPD delivery van executing a three-point turn in the road. She watched the driver bump up on the kerb then down onto the road again as he drove towards them. She followed his progress until he had passed and was safely out of sight. Glancing up and down the road again she saw nothing other than parked cars. Satisfied there were no vehicles observing the house she followed the DCI up the garden path and waited as he knocked on the door.

'This is one of our safe houses?' she whispered.

'Not so safe, as it turns out.'

The letterbox opened and he passed his lanyard and badge through. A minute or so later the door was opened by a young man in jeans and a T-shirt who Clare assumed must be an undercover officer. He stood back and they entered the house, closing the door quickly behind them. For the second time that day Clare found herself in a building where no daylight was admitted. The artificial light came from a bare bulb hung from the ceiling. It was a harsh light, casting shadows up the hall, and it did nothing to enhance the flecked beige carpet and white walls. A staircase lay ahead to the left and a hallway to the right. A door at the end stood open and Clare could see it led to a small kitchen. A faint odour of fried food and cigarette smoke hung in the air and she tried not to think of the panini she was still digesting.

The officer led them through another door into a small sitting room, sparsely furnished with a two-piece leather suite, a couple of tables and a TV on a glass stand. An electric fire, styled to resemble a wood-burning stove, was against one wall with a mantlepiece above. An ashtray filled with dogends sat on the mantlepiece next to an empty coffee mug. A wheeled suitcase stood ready in the centre of the room and its owner sat on the edge of one of the leather chairs.

So this was Tamsin Quinn. The woman who was married to one of the biggest importers of illegal arms in Scotland. The woman who, next week, would stand up in court to give evidence against her husband, in return for immunity from prosecution. Clare wondered how much she knew about her husband's activities. Enough to convict him? And how would she react to being cross-examined with her husband sitting just a few feet away? Was Tamsin Quinn tough enough to see it through? Clare certainly hoped so. It wasn't just Al Gibson's judgement that was in question. The case had blown the backside out of the overtime budget and it hadn't gone unnoticed.

She appraised Tamsin and guessed she was about fifty. She could be younger, of course. Maybe the strain of the last few weeks in protective custody was showing on her face. She took in Tamsin's leathery complexion, a hint of yellow in her eyes, and decided it was more likely due to a combination of fags, booze and foreign holidays. Her skin was certainly dark and rough-looking. Her hair was a cascade of dyed blonde that hung in layers, past her shoulders, a style that seemed too young for her face. The dark roots at her crown did little to help. Clare thought her face was plumper than the rest of her and she suspected Tamsin had a Botox addiction. She wore a black crocheted top and dark blue jeans, tucked into high-heeled boots. On her hands were several rings with large stones, and her wrist hung with metallic bangles that tinkled as she moved her arms.

She regarded Clare and the DCI then her glance flicked back to the young officer.

'It's fine, Tamsin,' he said. 'I know these officers. They'll look after you.'

Tamsin said nothing but rose from her chair and put a hand on her suitcase.

'I'll get that,' Clare said, heading for the door. 'Hang fire here, while I put this in the car, then we'll be on our way.'

Tamsin watched Clare as she wheeled the case towards the door, but she said nothing.

Out in the hall, Clare stood the case against the wall and ran lightly up the stairs. She opened the first door she came to and found it was the front bedroom. Moving to the window, she put her eye to a small gap in the curtains and peered out into the street. She stood, her eyes trained on the property directly opposite. In the downstairs room she could see a figure moving back and forward, as if pushing a vacuum cleaner. The curtains on the other windows were drawn back and Clare thought it would be difficult for anyone to be watching the safe house, unobserved. She then focused on the houses on either side and could see nothing at all. She ran back downstairs and opened the front door, leaving the case in the hall. She went out to the car and round to the driver's door facing back towards the house. She stood for some minutes, pretending to fiddle with the lock. In reality she was scanning the houses to the left and right of the safe house for any sign that someone was watching. When she had satisfied herself she was not being observed she went back indoors and brought out the suitcase, stowing it in the boot. Then she returned to the house.

Tamsin was pacing the room now, her arms wrapped round herself. 'What if they're out there – waiting for me?' Her voice was low and gravelly, the kind of voice Clare used to hear when she was a young cop, manning the Hogmanay celebrations in Glasgow's George Square. There was always someone ready with a song, giving it laldy. Amazing what a few drinks would do. Suddenly everyone was Bonnie Tyler, belting out the big numbers in spite of their forty-a-day habit. But Tamsin wasn't belting anything out today. There was a tremor when she spoke that belied her hard-as-nails appearance.

Clare gave what she hoped was a reassuring smile. 'I've had a good look outside. There's no one, Tamsin. We'll get you into the car quickly and we'll be out of here in seconds.' She turned to the officer. 'You'll finish up here, yeah?'

He nodded. 'Aye, don't worry. Not much left to do now.'

The DCI went to the window and opened the curtains a fraction to peer out. Clare sized Tamsin up. Her blonde hair was a dead giveaway. 'Do you have a hat?' she said.

Tamsin shook her head. 'No, but my coat has a hood.'

'Tuck your hair in then and pull the hood as far forward as you can. Oh, and one thing more...'

'Yeah?'

'Not a word about this in the car. We'll discuss everything once we arrive at your new digs.'

The young officer raised an eyebrow but Clare simply tapped the side of her nose in reply.

'Coast clear now,' the DCI said.

Clare eyed Tamsin. 'Ready?'

The woman nodded and Clare led her to the front door. The DCI went ahead and opened the door for Tamsin to climb in behind the driver's seat. She moved swiftly, her head down, and he closed the door behind her. Clare jumped into the front passenger seat and they were off and out of the street within seconds.

'Keep down,' Clare said to Tamsin. 'Just until we're sure there's no one tailing us.'

Tamsin didn't speak but lay down across the back seat.

'Take a left,' Clare said, as they emerged onto the main road. 'Trust me – it's quicker.'

He followed her directions through the centre of Perth until they were driving alongside the river. As they stopped at traffic lights, Clare's eyes were everywhere. A dark blue Transit van had been behind them for a couple of miles now. She adjusted the vanity mirror on her sunshade and squinted at the van.

'Anything?' the DCI asked.

The van began indicating left and Clare focused her attention on the road ahead. 'We're fine. No – don't take the bridge – carry straight on.'

Their route bordered the river on the left for almost a mile while the hotels and office buildings to the right gave way to a large grassy area. As the road curved away from the river their surroundings became more industrial. They passed the entrance to the harbour and Clare directed the DCI up towards the main road again. Within a few minutes the sign for the M90 motorway loomed up and

Clare turned round to Tamsin. 'Soon have you in a new place.'

Tamsin forced a smile and Clare turned back to the DCI. 'Know your way from here?'

He rolled his eyes. 'Just about.'

'Did I save you from getting stuck at Broxden again?'

'Yes, you saved me from getting stuck at Broxden.'

'Thank you, Clare,' she suggested.

'Don't push it.'

Chapter 6

As they entered St Andrews, passing the Old Course Hotel again, Clare wondered where they were going. When the DCI turned up City Road and onto Bridge Street she realised he was taking them back to the station. As he drew into the station car park, Clare glanced across at her car. Someone had parked alongside it, too close for her liking, and she made a mental note to shift hers at the first opportunity. The DCI opened his door and stepped out, indicating that Tamsin should stay put. Clare followed him out of the car and closed the door.

'What now?' she asked.

He indicated the red-brick station building. 'There's an officer from the Serious Organised Crime squad waiting in there for you. He has the details of the safe house. He'll fill you in.'

Clare looked at the DCI. 'Are you telling me there's a safe house here in St Andrews? On my patch, and I know nothing about it?'

The DCI glanced into the car. Tamsin was watching them and he moved a little away. 'Clare, they are everywhere. And the fewer people who know about them the better.' He checked his watch and turned back to open the door for Tamsin. 'I need to get back to Edinburgh.'

'Wait,' Clare said, putting a hand on his arm. 'This officer – what's his name?'

The DCI took out his phone and tapped in the pass-code. 'Steve Robins,' he said. 'And that's all I know, Clare.' He jerked his head at Tamsin who climbed out of the car.

Clare opened the boot and took out Tamsin's suitcase. Across the car park a painter's van was parked and three men in white boiler suits were in the process of setting up their ladders near the staff door, to the side of the building. *Typical*, she thought. *I've been asking for the paintwork to be done for weeks and they choose today to turn up.* She would have to take Tamsin in the front, past the public enquiry desk.

'Come on, Tamsin,' she said. 'Let's get you inside. And keep your hood up.'

Inside the station there was a small queue at the desk. Clare's uniformed Sergeant Jim Douglas was speaking to a young lad – a student probably. He was dressed casually in jeans and a dark blue puffer jacket. He seemed ill at ease, flicking glances left and right. Clare watched as he ran a hand through his dark curly hair and she wondered if he might be a junkie. Then she decided he probably wasn't. He lacked that pinched look she had come to recognise. But there was definitely something odd about his behaviour. Thankfully, Jim was adept at dealing with all sorts and she was confident he would soon have the young lad sorted. Sara, the uniformed constable, was sitting in front of a computer, tapping away at the keyboard. Clare was glad to see there was no sign of her DS, Chris West. Given what she had been told that morning about a possible security breach, it was a relief not to have to explain Tamsin's presence to Chris. Tamsin was looking all around. Her hood had slipped off her head and she put a hand up to smooth her hair. Clare was about to head for her office when a tall man in a suit appeared at her side.

'DI Mackay?'

She recognised immediately that the man was a plain-clothes officer. He carried a black leather attaché case and he wore the favoured CID uniform of a dark suit with a plain tie. None of the fancy, designer ties favoured by her ex, Tom – a solicitor in Glasgow. Tom even had one ruinously expensive tie that was hand-painted silk. Clare had often teased him that he was trying to outdo Jon Snow, the newsreader, famed for his quirky ties. Funny she should find herself thinking about Tom at that moment. Was that another consequence of Geoffrey heading off to Boston?

She regarded the man before her, now. CID officers never knew when they might be called to the scene of a tragedy, or be required to give a news interview with little notice. As such, sober suits were the order of the day and this was most definitely a sober suit that stood before her. She smiled back at him. 'Yes.'

'DI Steve Robins. Serious Organised Crime squad. I believe you were expecting me?'

Clare glanced at Tamsin. She had attracted the attention of the queue who, having nothing better to do, were sizing her up. 'Look, let's go to my office,' Clare said and Steve Robins nodded.

She led them to a door, punched in a code then went into the rear of the station. In the office she pulled out chairs for them and moved round her desk, taking a seat opposite. And it was then that she remembered Gayle Crichton's warning against discussing Gayle's own investigation within the station. But did that apply to Tamsin and her whereabouts? Someone certainly had found her in Perth. Could the security leak Gayle was investigating be linked to the discovery of Tamsin's safe house? Better safe than sorry.

'As long as we're in the station,' she began, 'I'd like to keep discussion of the specifics to a minimum. For security reasons,' she added. She thought Steve Robins might question this but he said nothing. He lifted his attaché case, placing it on top of Clare's desk. Then he flicked open the locks and withdrew a long white envelope.

'This will explain all you need to know,' he said. 'You have a safe here?' he asked looking round the room.

Clare indicated a small metal panel with a keypad, set into the wall.

'Once you've read the contents,' he said, handing over the envelope, 'store it securely. Change the combination daily.'

Clare took the envelope, thinking that the day was fast taking on a surreal quality. She opened it and withdrew a small sheet of paper. It contained the address of a property in the town and the name of the Family Liaison Officer who would support Tamsin. She was pleased to see it was Wendy Briggs. Clare had worked with Wendy on a previous case and knew she could trust her. Or could she? Was there anyone she could trust, now? She scanned the address and raised an eyebrow.

'It's a busy street,' she said to Steve Robins. 'Will it be secure enough?'

He nodded. 'The busier the better. Makes it easier for us to keep an eye on it without attracting attention.'

'You'll have someone nearby?'

'Yes.' He smiled at Tamsin. 'You won't see us, Mrs Quinn, but we'll be there so don't worry.' He turned back to Clare. 'I'll give you my card, just in case of emergencies.

And I'll make sure they have your photo, Inspector, in case you need to call in to see Mrs Quinn. Anyone else attempting to enter the flat will be intercepted.'

Clare acknowledged this but said nothing. 'Anything else?'

'Just this…' Steve reached into the case again and withdrew a small Nokia mobile phone with a charger attached. It was an older model, the keypad below the screen. 'DI Mackay's mobile and the station number have been added to this phone. The Family Liaison Officer will give you her number too and, worst case, call 999.'

Tamsin took the phone and stared at it. 'I didn't know you could still get these,' she said. 'It's not exactly state of the art.'

Steve Robins laughed. 'No, I'll grant you that. But it's a phone and it's vital that you don't use your own mobile. It must be switched off at all times.'

Tamsin gaped. 'What? Not even text messages? I can't use it at all? It has all my contacts in it.'

'Tamsin,' Clare said, 'with the right equipment, you could be traced through your mobile, even if you don't make any calls. It's only for the next week or so. Just till you've given evidence. Once that's behind you, it won't be so much of an issue.'

'Actually,' Steve interrupted, 'you won't be using your own phone again, Mrs Quinn. We should have it deactivated by the end of the day. Once the trial's over, you'll have a new identity and a new life.'

Clare tried not to react to this. Tamsin's evidence must be crucial and damning for them to go to this much trouble. Suddenly, the importance of keeping her safe dawned on Clare. It was going to be an anxious few days. She glanced down at the piece of paper in her hand. 'Should we go then?'

Steve Robins rose. 'The sooner the better.'

The safe house was actually a two-bedroomed flat in busy Market Street, above a shop selling what Clare called *tartan tat* to tourists. The street was broad at this end, cobbled with a dried-up fountain in the centre. Steve Robins nosed the car into one of the diagonal parking spaces in front of *Luvian's Ice Cream Parlour* and put a parking permit on the dashboard. They emerged into the street, busy with mums wheeling toddlers in pushchairs and red-gowned students going between lectures. A party of tourists was collected round the fountain where a guide with an American accent was explaining its history. Clare and Tamsin followed Steve across the cobbles – Tamsin wobbling on her high heels – to a dark green door which he opened then stood back to let them enter. Clare went first and was faced with a steep flight of stairs. She climbed these and, at the top, found another door with a Yale lock. Steve threw a set of keys up to her and she opened the door onto a short hallway with doors leading off, left and right. Two of the doors led to bedrooms, simply furnished but, crucially, with Venetian blinds on the windows. Another door led to a sitting room with a small kitchen beyond. The bathroom was behind the last door and Clare was glad to see a shelf with basic toiletries.

'We've stocked the fridge up too,' Steve was saying. 'You won't need anything for a few days. But, if you do, let Wendy know. She's your Family Liaison Officer.' He checked the time on his phone. 'She should be here any minute now.'

Tamsin was opening and closing cupboard doors. 'How long will I be here?' she said, her voice small.

'Depends,' Steve said. 'We're hoping the trial will be over this time next week. You'll have to stay here at least until the verdict is in.'

Tamsin turned to face him. She opened her mouth to speak, then moistened her lips. 'And Paddy?' she said, her voice barely above a whisper. 'You caught him yet?'

Steve's face clouded. 'Not yet. So it's vital that you keep that phone off and stay back from the windows.'

Tamsin was quiet for a moment, as though processing this. Then she spoke again. 'You think he'll try and get to me?'

Clare eyed Steve. 'I think—' she began but Steve cut across her.

'No point in soft-soaping it, Tamsin. It is a possibility. But it's one we're ready for. We have people watching this property now. So you do your bit and we'll do ours.'

The doorbell rang, the shrill tone breaking the tension and making Tamsin jump. 'That'll be Wendy,' Steve said and he went to let her in.

Tamsin's face was drained of colour, her eyes wide.

Clare moved to pat her on the arm but she barely seem to notice. 'We'll keep you safe here,' Clare said. 'Try not to worry.'

Tamsin looked at the room and began walking round, taking it in. She moved towards a watercolour on the wall above an electric fire. It was a view of the town from the West Sands. 'I used to come to St Andrews, you know.'

Clare was glad to see her starting to relax. 'Really? On holiday?'

'Yeah. My granny lived in a village a few miles away. Balmullo. Know it?'

'I do. Nice wee village. On the way to Dundee.'

'That's the one. We used to come up and stay when the air base at Leuchars had a display. Great to see all the fast jets, Red Arrows – that sort of thing. There was a hill at the back of Balmullo. We'd climb it to watch the planes.' She wrinkled her brow, trying to remember. And then her face cleared. 'Lucklawhill,' she said. 'I remember it because we scattered my mother's ashes there.'

'Oh, I'm sorry,' Clare said but Tamsin waved this away.

'Don't worry, Inspector. A few years ago now.'

'Call me Clare.'

The door opened and Steve Robins came back into the room with the Family Liaison Officer behind him. Having shown Wendy in, he said his goodbyes and headed back down the stairs. A few seconds later they heard the sound of the front door banging shut behind him.

Wendy Briggs smiled warmly at Clare. Clare regarded her and thought she had lost some weight since the last time they had met. Her grey flannel trousers fell from the hips and her fitted pink blouse enhanced a trim waistline. Her blonde hair was tied back in a simple style which suited her.

Clare rose and went to greet her. 'Wendy, great to see you. You're looking so well.'

'WeightWatchers,' Wendy said. 'Had to do something, Clare. I'm off to the sun in a couple of months.' Then she looked past Clare to Tamsin, now perched on the edge of a chair. 'You must be Tamsin. I'm Wendy. Very pleased to meet you.'

Tamsin shot a glance at Wendy but didn't reply. Then she turned to Clare. 'So many new faces today. I don't know who to trust.'

Wendy moved past Clare and sat next to Tamsin. 'Well you can trust me, Tamsin. I promise you that.'

Tamsin looked at Wendy. 'It's Paddy, you see. Paddy Grant. I'm afraid of him.' She let her shoulders droop. 'I'm afraid of what he'll do if he finds me.'

Wendy nodded. 'Yes, I understand that. But you'll be safe here, Tamsin. We know Paddy Grant. We know what he looks like, what he drives and, although you can't see it, we have people watching this flat, day and night. You have to trust us. Will you?'

Tamsin hesitated, then she said, 'Yeah, okay.'

'Good. Now, I'll be here for the rest of today, see you settled in and we'll have someone across the road all night, just to make sure you're okay. Then I'll be back in the morning. And you have Clare's number?'

Tamsin nodded.

Wendy rose again. 'I'll take it from here, Clare,' she said. 'I'll give you a call later.'

Clare didn't reply but jerked her head for Wendy to follow her.

Out in the street, she waited for a car to rumble past on the cobbles then she led Wendy across to the fountain, now absent of tourists, and perched on the rim, scanning the street as she spoke. 'Wendy, I need to tell you something but you'll have to take my word for it, okay? No questions.'

'Okay...'

'If we speak on the phone, please don't make any reference to Tamsin's location.' Her eyes went involuntarily to the windows of Tamsin's flat. 'The same goes for back at the station. I can't tell you any more than that, but Tamsin's last safe house was leaked and I don't want the same thing happening here.'

Wendy searched Clare's face for any sign of what was going on and when none came she said simply, 'Okay, Clare. You can rely on me.'

'Thanks, Wendy. I needed to hear that.'

Chapter 7

The station was quieter when Clare returned. The painters were packing up for the day, loading ladders and batons into their van, and the unmistakable smell of paint hung round the station. Sara was out on patrol and Jim was in the front office, keeping an eye on the desk as he caught up with paperwork.

'How's it been, Jim?' Clare asked.

'All fine, thanks, Clare. The usual nonsense.'

'Chris?'

Jim avoided her eye. 'Er, not sure, actually. He's maybe...'

'Knocked off early?'

'Aye, well, maybe.'

'I'll send him a message,' Clare said. 'Wind him up.'

'Well you didn't get it from me.'

'Okay, Jim. I won't rat you out.' Clare suddenly remembered the young man who had been in the station when she arrived with Tamsin. 'Jim, there was a young lad in earlier. Dark curly hair. Seemed a bit uneasy.'

'Aye.' Jim rubbed his chin. 'Swiss lad. Not quite sure what to make of him. He said he wanted to report his friend missing. I started to take down the details then he asked for the toilets and that was the last I saw of him.'

Clare considered this. 'Did he say how long his friend had been gone?'

'Two or three days.'

'Mm. Is he a student?'

Jim nodded. 'They both are. The missing lad's studying physics, I think. Probably on a bender, Clare. Or holed up with some lassie his friend doesn't know about. I've got the details here if you want them.'

'Please.'

Jim moved to the computer and navigated his way to the report on the missing student. 'I'll send it to the printer.'

Clare suddenly remembered Gayle Crichton and she pondered how to broach this. 'Jim…'

'Aye?'

'There's a woman arriving here on Monday morning. Gayle Crichton.'

Jim groaned. 'Not another one come to tell us how to do our jobs?'

'No, not quite,' Clare said, recalling Gayle's instructions. 'She's setting up a new communications system but she can't get peace to work where she is. She's asked for a quiet office somewhere out of the way…'

'…and so she's coming here?'

'Yes. I wondered – Interview Room Three?'

Jim smiled. 'Leave it with me. I'll make sure it's cleared out for her. She'll be wanting a computer, I'm guessing.'

'No, she'll bring her own laptop. If you could just give it a quick tidy. I'll send an email round telling everyone to expect her.'

The printer began to whirr and click. Clare wandered over to pick up the printout then took it into her office, sitting down at the desk. She checked her watch. Almost five o'clock. She ran her eye over the partly completed report. The young lad with the curly hair was Marek

Schmidt. He had given his address as Kinnessburn Road. Clare racked her brains then remembered it was just off Bridge Street. It couldn't be more than half a mile from the station. She wrote a note on her pad to check it out then she read on. His friend's name was Johannes Muller, and there the report ended. That must have been the point at which Marek Schmidt had left the station. Clare pondered this. A young lad who had come in to report a friend missing then bolted needed further investigation. She stifled a yawn. The strange events of the day were catching up with her. She shook the mouse on her computer, keyed in her password and ran an eye across her email inbox. There was nothing urgent. She typed a quick email to all the station staff letting them know about Gayle and pressed send. That done, she logged off and powered down the computer. It was time to call it a day. She closed the window blinds then picked up her jacket and headed out to the car park, stepping gingerly past the wet paint.

The sight of her car, shiny and sleek, brought a smile back to her face. Clare clicked the remote control and the doors unlocked with a reassuring clunk. She eased the car out of its space and headed back to Daisy Cottage and her dog Benjy.

—

She was welcomed by Benjy who brought her the remains of a yellow duster she had left on a bookcase. She held it out for him to see and he responded with furious wagging of his tail. 'Honestly, Benjy,' she said, throwing the duster in the bin.

She wandered into the kitchen, leafing through the mail to see if there was anything of interest, but it was mostly bills. There was an estimate from a joiner for some odd jobs she needed done around the cottage with a Post-it attached stating he was booked up for the next couple of months and to give him a call if she wanted him to put it in the diary. She ran through the list of jobs on the estimate and concluded only a couple of them were urgent. The hinges on her garden gate were threatening to pull away from the post and there was that gap in the sitting room floorboards that the wind whistled through on cold nights. A nursery rhyme from her childhood days came back to her:

For the want of a nail…

She decided it would be better to try and find someone else to do these jobs before they ended up as major repairs.

The usual scribbled note from her neighbour Moira confirmed Benjy had enjoyed his walk and that she'd be round at the same time tomorrow.

'What would we do without Moira?' Clare asked Benjy who was chasing his tail round and round the sitting room. She put the letters down on the kitchen table and her eye fell once more on the postcard from Geoffrey. Suddenly, she was outstandingly tired. She stepped out of her shoes, kicking them across the floor and opened the fridge. A cottage pie from M&S stood alone on the shelf and Clare made a mental note to get some shopping in over the weekend. She pierced the film with a fork and set the microwave to high. Then she took a bottle of red from the wine rack and uncorked it, pouring herself a large glass. As she waited for the pie to heat she tapped a quick message to Wendy. The reply came back just as the microwave pinged. Clare opened the oven door and the aroma of the pie began to fill the kitchen. She checked her phone and saw that all was well. Wendy had left Tamsin watching TV, safely locked in for the night. Clare spooned the pie out onto a plate and, carrying plate and glass to the dining table, she sat down to eat. From eighty miles away she could sense her mother's disapproval at her microwave meal. But then her mother hadn't been career-minded, staying at home to look after Clare and her sister while her father had gone out to work. Always a home-cooked meal on the table. Six o'clock every evening.

'Ach well,' she said to Benjy, who was lying contentedly on the fireside rug, chewing a rubber bone. He wagged his tail at the sound of her voice but carried on attacking the bone.

The pie eaten, Clare poured herself another glass of red and moved to her desk to power up her laptop. She opened her emails to see if there had been a message from Geoffrey but there was nothing. She had a vague idea he might be on a spring break but maybe she was wrong. She clicked to open Facebook. No notifications. She moved to Geoffrey's profile and saw there were six new photos. The first two were of a tall granite tower and he had added a caption indicating it was *The Pilgrim Monument*. She flicked quickly past these, onto the next few photos – Geoffrey smiling in a faded blue T-shirt and shorts, Geoffrey with a group of friends, Geoffrey sipping from a beer bottle. His smile was so broad and familiar that her heart lurched at the sight of him. If only she had accepted the invitation to go to Boston. She might be in these photos, alongside him in a sundress, sipping beer with the Atlantic Ocean for a backdrop. She zoomed in and scrutinised the group in the photos. Males and females. Arms around each other. She studied the woman who was next to him. She and Geoffrey were standing quite close. They were bunched up for the photo but she couldn't see their arms. Were they tucked round each other's waists? Clare reached for her wine glass and took a slug. Had Geoffrey – who she thought she loved and who she had thought loved her – replaced her with a younger, blonder model with teeth like a toothpaste advert? She found she had a lump in her throat and she took another drink from her glass. Tears were pricking her eyes now and she clicked back to her own profile. The laptop pinged and a red number one appeared at the top of the screen. She had a friend request. She clicked to see who it was and it took a moment to register.

Al Gibson.

She had a friend request from her DCI. DCI Alastair Gibson who, that very morning, had told her he was in the throes of a divorce. If anything, Clare was amazed he even had Facebook. He was far more your LinkedIn type of guy. Her hand hovered over the Accept button then she hesitated and topped up her wine. Rather than accept him, she navigated to his profile but he had chosen maximum privacy and she couldn't see much at all.

'Oh, what the hell,' and she clicked to accept his request. Carrying the laptop over to the sofa, she placed her wine on a nearby table and settled down to browse his profile. Benjy jumped up to join her on the sofa but she was too focused on Facebook to scold him. She was surprised to see how sporty Al Gibson was. There were photos of him in a rugby scrum, standing in a wet suit on the edge of a loch, crossing the finish line at the Loch Ness Marathon. And there were family photos too. An elderly couple Clare presumed were his parents and another man and woman, so like him they had to be his brother and sister. Clare had only a vague recollection of Alison Gibson but it looked as if all photos of them as a couple were missing. She moved to his Friends List and searched for *Alison*. No results. It obviously hadn't been an amicable split if he'd rubbed her completely out of his life.

The laptop pinged again and Clare saw she had a private message. It was him.

> Hope you're okay after today. Bit chal-
> lenging. ☺

She pondered this. In all the years she'd known the DCI he'd been – well – standoffish; a bit superior. But then, after those hit-and-run murders last year when he'd been the Senior Investigating Officer, he'd softened a bit towards her. But she'd still thought it stopped short at mutual respect. A professional working relationship. And now here he was sending her private Facebook messages. It was all a bit odd. She mulled over her response, finally typing:

> Yes, I'm fine, thanks. Got it all sorted in the
> end. X

Dammit! She'd automatically hit the X, sending him a kiss. The way she ended messages with her sister and close friends. Was she better ignoring it? No, she couldn't. He'd read her message now and was typing back. Quickly she began typing:

> Oops sorry – hit the X by mistake. Meant to
> send a smiley face.

And to emphasise this, she sent a smiley face after the message. He had stopped typing now and had read her second message. There was a pause for a minute and then he too sent back a smiley face. Clare wondered what he had been typing when she had said the X was a mistake. Hopefully not an X in return. She logged off quickly hoping he would see she was offline and she shut the laptop down for the night.

'Better get to bed before we do anything else wrong,' she said to Benjy and she opened the back door to let him out for a last pee.

Saturday, 16 May

Chapter 8

Clare had forgotten to turn off her alarm on Friday night and it sounded as usual at half past six on Saturday morning. She reached for it, groggy from the wine and finally succeeded in switching it off. She squinted at her phone to make sure it was Saturday then scrolled to see if she had any messages. None.

She put her phone back on the bedside table and buried her head under the duvet again. But the May sunshine was peeping through the curtains and lighting up the room. She had deliberately chosen this room for her bedroom because it would catch the morning sun but now, a month from midsummer and desperate for a longer sleep, she was regretting this decision. In the end she gave in and by just after seven she was sitting at her kitchen table in an old tracksuit munching on toast and butter. She flicked idly through her phone, checking on the news, the weekend weather, and then she opened her emails. She scanned past the usual junk messages and her heart rose. There was an email from Geoffrey. The subject was

Hey You.

'Hey to you too,' she said to the email. She fetched her laptop from the sofa where she'd left it last night and powered it up to read the email more easily. The message took a minute or two to open and, when it did, Clare saw it was full of photos, similar to the ones he'd shared on Facebook.

It was a lengthy message, chatting about work, his classes, how different the students were to the Scottish ones, his trip to Provincetown – *Did you get my postcard? What about those buildings? Aren't they fab?!* – and his friends there. His new friends in Boston. Names Clare didn't know and, frankly, didn't want to know. They were all too bloody smiley and tanned. Clare's suntan from last year's holiday in France had long since faded. But this lot were straight out of a holiday brochure. She read on:

> Term's almost over here. Not sure of my plans – a few options to consider. But I'd like to fit in some travel.
> Maybe go north from Boston. Fancy joining me?
> You must be due some leave and you'd love it here.
> Think about it, Clare. I'd love to show you round.
> Better get to bed. Late night at a harbour bar.
> Love to Benjy,
> G XXXXX

Love to Benjy? Was he having a laugh? What about love to her? Clare bit into her toast and chewed on. She thought back to the DCI's question yesterday:

Are you still together?

'I'm damned if I know,' she said to Benjy. And she rose to clear away her breakfast dishes.

Later, having washed up and showered, she made a list:

> *Benjy – walk*
> *Food shopping*
> *Phone joiner*
> *Phone Jude*
> *Find a gardener*

And then she remembered Tamsin. She picked up her phone and tapped a message.

Sleep well?

The reply came a few minutes later.

Not really. But I'll get used to it.

Not surprising, Clare thought. She tapped back.

Wendy should be with you soon.

Tamsin sent back an *OK* in reply. Clare decided not to respond. It was her weekend, after all, and if Steve Robins was to be believed, there were plenty of cops keeping an eye on the Market Street flat.

She whistled to Benjy and, picking up his lead, opened the back door. He came trotting out after her and she stood for a minute, enjoying the morning sun. It was going to be warm and she thought again of Tamsin, stuck in that flat on this lovely May morning. She surveyed her garden. It had been well laid out at one time, with deep borders down either side and fences behind. Smaller borders spilled onto a path of the same Caithness flagstones that sat beneath the kitchen window. There was a long strip of grass that had been well-tended when Clare had first viewed Daisy Cottage but now she could see that, while she had cut it the previous week, she'd forgotten to trim the edges and they had grown long and untidy.

The previous occupants had left some terracotta pots, a variety of shapes and sizes, weathered with age. But looking at them now she saw they were choked with chickweed. She reached down and pulled at a clump and it came away in her hand, sprinkling earth at her feet. Her brown bin where she put garden waste was full now with grass clippings and she fired the clump of weeds over the fence into the woods beyond. She remembered the polystyrene trays of plants for sale at the garden centre where she and the DCI had eaten lunch the previous day. They would have added a splash of colour to the pots. But she didn't want to think about that lunch – about their meeting with Gayle Crichton. Gayle and the unsettling prospect of what her investigations might uncover.

She looked back at the borders. The weeds were taking over at an alarming rate and she determined to find a gardener before it got any worse. The DCI had offered to help but she wasn't sure about that. She had felt a bit uncomfortable on Friday, listening to him talking about his divorce. Maybe best to keep him at arm's length, until things had settled down. 'Maybe Moira will know someone,' she said to Benjy. He wagged his tail at the mention of Moira. Moira meant walks in the woods and Benjy liked that.

'Well you're stuck with me today,' she told him and, locking the back door, she headed down the path and out through the gate at the end. Benjy scampered off to explore the wood and Clare strolled on behind, the fresh air helping to clear her head. The wood was alive with birdsong and there were patches of bluebells and cowslips attracting honey bees. It was a perfect morning for a walk. She came to a tree stump and sat on the edge for a minute while Benjy snuffled in the undergrowth. She took out her phone and opened Facebook. There were a few notifications but nothing that interested her. With one eye on Benjy, she navigated her way to Al Gibson's page and saw that he was doing a parkrun that morning. *Probably one of the Edinburgh runs*, she thought, wondering which would be the closest to his house in the Grange. She had done a few of the Glasgow parkruns when she worked there but never Edinburgh.

She returned to her perusal of his page.

Hoping for a PB, he had commented.

Clare wondered what his PB might be. He was taller than her. Bigger boned, too. Not built for distance but he wasn't overweight either; and with all those photos of him in wetsuits and cycling gear, she thought he was probably quite fit. Maybe he was a fast runner. She stood up from the tree stump, whistled to Benjy and carried on round their usual circuit. It had been a while since she'd done a parkrun. But Craigtoun Park was just along the road. She checked her watch. Ten to eight. She had time. She quickened her pace and Benjy followed suit, running ahead of her.

By eight fifteen she was back in the cottage. Benjy settled himself on the kitchen floor as usual to enjoy the morning sun while Clare hunted through drawers to find her parkrun barcodes. Eventually she unearthed them in the zip pocket of her running shorts.

The St Andrews parkrun was popular and the car park was filling up when Clare arrived. The park, originally part of a large country estate, was a magnet for families, with its large stretches of grass, miniature railway, boating lake and play areas. It was popular with park runners too and a large group had already gathered round the start, some jogging on the spot, others chatting. There were serious runners among them, judging by their attire and the chunky Garmins round their wrists, while others were preparing to jog holding onto three-wheeled prams and dog leads. The sun was high in the sky now and there was little wind so Clare peeled off her hooded top and tied it round her waist. As she began stretching her legs she heard a familiar voice.

'Hello, Clare.'

She turned to see Diane Wallace, decked out in a fuchsia-pink vest top and navy shorts, her thick dark hair scraped up in a high ponytail. Diane, her good friend and colleague from the Tech Support office in Glenrothes. The same Diane that Gayle Crichton had warned Clare against speaking to about the security leak. Despite their friendship, Clare was momentarily flustered. 'Oh, Diane!' she said, wondering what else she could say.

Diane grinned. 'Bet you didn't expect to see me here.'

'Er, no. I mean I've not been for a few months…' Clare said.

'Oh, it's not my usual, Clare. I tend to go to one nearer home. Lochore Meadows. But I fancied a change. I've heard it's a good course here. Just the one short hill.'

Clare's mind was racing. Was it a coincidence? Diane turning up here the day after Tamsin Quinn was taken to a safe house in St Andrews, and two days before Gayle Crichton was due to start her investigations? Was there even more to it than Gayle had said? Could Diane be working for Gayle and Gayle's warning not to speak to her a test of Clare's discretion? Or was Diane, with her superior technical knowledge, actually part of the surveillance team guarding Tamsin?

And then she gave herself a shake. She was getting carried away with the whole thing. She'd known Diane for years. Since her days at Maryhill Police Station in Glasgow when Diane had been seconded there. But, if Diane wasn't working with Gayle – wasn't part of her investigation – how long would it be before she realised something was going on? She was so sharp. She would spot any unusual activity on the network straight away. Was it worth taking Diane into her confidence? And then she recalled Gayle's warning: 'I'll have your warrant card.'

As much as Clare knew that Diane was completely reliable, Gayle didn't strike her as someone to mess with. She put these outlandish theories to the back of her mind and gave Diane a smile. 'Yeah, it's a good course. The hill's not too bad. Three circuits and a bit tacked onto the end.'

Diane smiled. 'Sounds good.'

Clare returned her smile. 'I'll have to come down your way one day. Try out the Lochore course.'

'I'll hold you to that.'

She racked her brains for something else to say. Something noncommittal. She wanted to avoid the subject of work but it was what they had in common and she decided it would seem odd not to mention it. 'How's work?'

'Don't ask.'

'Busy as ever then?'

'Clare, you've no idea. I've been a member of staff down for three months now. Apparently I'm getting someone on Monday but it'll take weeks to clear the backlog. You know what it's like – the jobs keep coming; and everything's urgent.'

She carried on chatting but Clare had stopped listening. *Someone new starting on Monday.* Was this Gayle Crichton's doing? Was she putting a spy in Diane's camp? Or was there some other reason the vacancy in Tech Support was suddenly filled, after months of Diane asking?

'Honestly, Clare,' Diane was saying, 'it's beyond a joke these days. I've even offered to do Saturday mornings to try and clear my feet but they say there's no money for overtime. They still want the results though.'

Clare tried to put thoughts of Gayle Crichton to the back of her mind. She gave Diane what she hoped was a sympathetic smile. 'It's pretty much the same with us too, Diane. It's fine when there's a major incident. They throw money at those. But sometimes we struggle just to keep up with the routine stuff. And don't get me started on the paperwork.'

'Ach, it gives us something to moan about.'

Clare suddenly remembered. 'Diane, how's your mum these days?'

Diane sighed. 'Not great, Clare, to be honest. She really needs residential care now. But there are so many hoops to jump through before we get to that stage. I can probably get her into one of the local authority places. But, for all the time she has left, I'd rather she went into one of the private homes.' Diane stood on one leg, pulling her ankle up behind her to stretch her quads. 'I'll probably have to sell her house to pay for it,' she said. 'I've not told her yet but it'll break her heart.' She let her ankle drop down and swapped to stretch the other leg.

Clare looked at Diane, unsure what to say. Diane's eyes were bright and she seemed close to tears. 'Oh Diane, I'm so sorry.'

Diane gave a little shrug. 'Ach, it'll get sorted out. One way or another. The doctor says Mum might not see another year so I'll maybe ask the bank if they would give me a loan to cover a year's fees. Probably better than selling up.' She forced a smile. 'But thanks, Clare. Thanks for asking.'

Clare gave Diane's arm a squeeze then she felt herself jostled. The runners were moving to the start line now.

'Shall we run together?' Diane said. 'I'm usually around thirty minutes.'

Clare hesitated. She wanted a fast time today. 'Erm…'

Diane laughed. 'It's okay. I know you'll be faster than me. On you go.'

'Buy you a coffee after, then?' Clare said.

'I'll hold you to it.'

They set off in a throng with Clare edging her way gradually to the front. There were a few spectators dotted around the course and volunteers at points where the course deviated. The sun was warm and she was glad when the route took them briefly into a shaded area. As she came back to the start at the end of the first circuit she checked her time. Seven minutes and two seconds. There was a ripple of applause from spectators at the start and she raised a hand in acknowledgement, digging in as she approached the short hill for the second time. As she crested the rise she looked across the park and the fuchsia-pink top caught her eye. Diane was just coming to the end of her first circuit. Clare ploughed on and, as the course levelled out her heart rate began to slow. She was neck and neck with a male runner who was obviously determined not to be beaten by a woman and she stuck on his tail. There was something familiar about him but, with his baseball cap and aviator shades, it was impossible to tell. Probably a regular.

Her second lap was quicker. Six minutes and forty seconds. She could hear the male runner's breathing become more laboured. He glanced over his shoulder at Clare and lengthened his pace. Clare matched him and they ran together up the hill for the last time. At the straight stretch he began pulling away. Clare was tiring now and she let him put a bit of distance between them. As they began the decline Diane's fuchsia top caught her eye again. Diane waved then punched the air. Clare looked ahead again. She could just catch him. The end of the race had a little rise and she was good on hills. She began to stretch out, closing the gap between them. He had stopped, looking over his shoulder now. Probably thought he had her beaten. Clare saw the finish post and reached in her shorts for her barcode. She was sprinting now and as the incline to the finish began she streaked past the male runner to cheers from the volunteers. She clicked her Garmin as she crossed the line and checked the time. Twenty minutes exactly.

'Good run,' a voice behind her said and she turned to see DCI Al Gibson, removing his sunglasses and cap. He ran a hand through his hair and squinted at his watch. 'I thought I had you back there.'

Clare drew a hand across her brow which was damp now. 'One second quicker and I'd have been under twenty.' She shook her head. 'Next time.'

They wandered up the path, out of the way of the steady stream of finishers.

'Coffee?' the DCI asked.

'I'm waiting for Diane Wallace.' She put a hand up to shade the sun from her eyes. 'I think she's just gone through the second lap.'

'Diane Wallace?' There was no mistaking the warning note in his voice.

Clare smiled. 'I didn't know she was coming here today. Matter of fact, I didn't know you were coming either.'

He had the grace to blush. 'Well – it's good to vary it sometimes. And, as I'm moving to Fife…'

Clare didn't press the point. 'Diane's a friend,' she said suddenly.

'I know. Just remember what Gayle Crichton said.'

'I will. All the same…'

'What?'

Clare shivered. She was starting to feel cold now. She unwrapped the top from round her waist and pulled it on over her head. Across the park she could see a fuchsia-pink figure moving along the flat stretch. 'She's not daft, Diane. She knows more about computers and networks than anyone I've ever met. What if she realises there's something going on? In my station? If she starts to ask questions, well I'm honestly not sure I'd know what to say.'

The DCI steered Clare over to a park bench. 'Clare, I'm not suggesting for a minute that Diane's involved in any leaks. But it could be someone she works with. Someone she knows really well. If you tell her about it, she might find it difficult to keep quiet.'

Clare thought of Diane and what she had said about her new member of staff but she said nothing about this. She could see the fuchsia top heading for the finish.

'It won't help either of you,' the DCI went on, 'if you blab to Diane. As an IT person she'd be in an impossible situation.' He touched her arm, softly. 'It won't be for ever. Maybe a week or so. Two at the most.'

The sun had gone behind a cloud now and the sky, so blue just an hour ago, was dotted with clouds, some threatening rain. They'd had the best of the day. Clare looked down at the DCI's hand on her arm, suddenly nervous. It was months now since she'd had any physical contact. Not since Geoffrey had left for Boston. Oh, she'd had hugs from her sister, even occasionally from her nephew James. But this was different. This was a work colleague – a senior one at that – and she wasn't at all sure about it. There was nothing sexual; nothing invasive. It was just a friendly gesture. So why did it feel unsettling?

And then, as quickly as he had touched her, he withdrew his arm and the moment passed. She looked across the park and scanned the throng, heading doggedly towards the finish. She rose from the bench. 'Come on. Let's cheer Diane along the last few steps.'

The fuchsia top was coming nearer. Clare cupped her hands and yelled to Diane who raised a weary hand in acknowledgement.

As she emerged from the finish cordon, Diane's face was the colour of her T-shirt. She was grinning. 'Twenty-nine minutes, forty, according to my watch,' she said, between breaths. 'First time under thirty minutes.'

'Well done you,' Clare said, slapping her on the back.

Diane stared at the DCI for a moment, her brow creased, and then a look of recognition crossed her face. She shot a glance at Clare, seeking an explanation.

The DCI saw this and he shifted awkwardly on his feet. 'Hello, Diane,' he said, meeting her eye and forcing his lips into a smile. 'It's er… good to see you again.'

Diane looked from Clare to the DCI then back at Clare again.

'Oh, he's just here to buy the coffees,' she said. 'Come on. I could murder a bacon roll.'

Sunday, 17 May

Chapter 9

'I hadn't forgotten, Jude. I'm looking forward to it.'

Benjy was running around in circles, chasing his tail, and Clare looked for something to distract him.

'Are you sure, Clare? I mean – James. He's not like other toddlers…'

Clare's eyes rested on a tennis ball and she picked it up. Opening the kitchen door, she fired it down the garden into a patch of – well, she wasn't quite sure what it was a patch of, to be honest. Benjy tore after it and Clare turned her attention back to her sister. 'I do know that, Jude. Just tell me what he likes to eat and do, and I'll take care of it. It's high time you and Frank had a break; and it is just the one night.'

'Oh Clare, I'm so looking forward to it.'

'And so you should.' She hesitated, then said, 'Jude – can I ask, I mean, has James – does he speak yet?'

There was a pause. Then Jude said, 'He may never speak, Clare. We keep trying but I've accepted now that it may not happen.'

Clare's heart ached for her sister. It was so difficult to know what to say. James's autism was new territory for them all. 'Oh Jude,' she said, at last. 'It must be so hard for you.'

Benjy reappeared and dropped the ball at her feet. Automatically, she bent, picked it up and threw it back down the garden again. He charged out the door, knocking over the kitchen bin as he went.

'Dammit. Look, Jude, I'll have to go. The dog's driving me crazy.'

'See you Friday, then,' Jude said.

Clare put down her phone and began clearing up the contents of the bin. Her phone rang again. Moira, her neighbour and dog walker.

'You know you mentioned needing a gardener, Clare?'

'You know someone?'

'My husband. Bill. He wouldn't want paying though. He just loves gardening and ours isn't big enough for him.'

Moira seemed set for a chat and Clare wandered through to her sitting room and parked herself on the sofa. Benjy had kicked the rug across the room and, as Clare stretched out her legs, she felt the familiar draught coming up from the gap in the floorboards.

'You don't know a joiner, do you?' Clare asked.

Moira said Bill usually did most of the jobs in their house but she would ask around. After a few more minutes of chat, Clare ended the call and pulled the rug back over the gap.

Her text message to Tamsin had elicited a simple *I'm fine* in response. Clare sent a similar message to Wendy who replied saying she had called in to see Tamsin that morning and would be back again late afternoon. Clare mulled that over. If she'd been running the operation she'd have had someone stationed with Tamsin, day and night. But Serious Organised Crime were in charge. She wondered if they'd have told her about Tamsin if she hadn't happened to be with the DCI on Friday morning. She also wondered how long that flat had been a safe house. Had there been witnesses living there before? With

73

the SOC parked outside keeping an eye on them? What else went on in the town that she knew nothing about?

She snatched up her car keys and, giving Benjy a quick ruffle behind the ears, headed out to drive the short distance into town. With such a powerful car, it was tempting to put her foot down and take the country road at sixty but it was a lovely day and she took time to glance left and right as she drove. The trees were in full leaf now and the landscape was peppered with fields of oilseed rape, a gaudy splash of yellow among the usual green and brown. The sky was dotted with clouds but it was dry and the temperature dial on the car was climbing steadily. She slowed for the roundabout at the south end of St Andrews, taking a right into Bogward Road. A few minutes later she drew into the police station car park, choosing a space well away from other cars.

She resisted the temptation to call into the station to *check on things*, choosing instead to walk along Pipeland Road past the bowling club. She stopped for a moment to watch the progress of a match. She wasn't quite tall enough to see over the hedge so she stood up on a low wall bordering the car park. She couldn't tell who was winning but it scarcely seemed to matter. The gentle sound of wood knocking into wood was followed by good-natured groans and laughs, and she thought there were definitely worse ways to pass a Sunday morning. Somewhere in the distance church bells began to sound, prompting Clare to step off the wall and carry on her way.

Passing along Kinnessburn Road something nagged at her. But she couldn't put a finger on it. The burn that had given the road its name was fast flowing today, the water level high after a recent rainy spell. She walked alongside it for a few minutes then took the footbridge over the burn and carried on, threading through the streets until she emerged into South Street. A stiff breeze was blowing and a carelessly discarded plastic sandwich box rattled along the pavement. Clare bent to pick it up, meaning to find a bin, but it was whipped away before she could reach it. Overhead the breeze was sending clouds scurrying across the sky, allowing shafts of sunlight to break through, warming the grey sandstone buildings. She walked on towards the zebra crossing, ducking out from the shade provided by the lime trees that were dotted along either side of the street.

A group of teenagers in school uniform was standing a little back from the pavement in Church Square. They were surrounded by half a dozen large black music cases and were in the process of setting up metal stands, securing their flimsy sheets of music with clothes pegs. Clare saw one of them remove a trumpet from a case. He smiled at her and she made a mental note to give them a few quid on her way back from Market Street.

The holiday season was in full swing, little groups of tourists perusing the shops and buildings at a leisurely pace. Across the road a steady stream of red-gowned university students was heading west and Clare realised they must be on their way back from the traditional Sunday Pier Walk. She stepped out of the way of the dawdling tourists and onto the road, opposite Tamsin's flat. She screwed up her eyes and scrutinised the windows for any sign of life. The blinds were closed and she supposed Tamsin was watching TV. There was precious little else for her to do. She must be bored out of her skull. Clare looked left and right, along the pavement below the flat for a sign of anyone hanging about. She had memorised Paddy Grant's face from his photo and she knew that he was tall and broad-shouldered with a head like a bullet. There was no one around who resembled him. But then she told herself he would be keeping a low profile – if he was still in the country. No. If Paddy Grant knew where Tamsin was, he'd have a couple of his men go after her.

A peep from a car alerted her that she was blocking a parking space. She stepped to the side and made her way across the cobbled street, taking up position a few doors along from the entrance to the flat. She took out her phone, tapped it then put it to her ear, pretending to take a call. Making the odd 'Yeah' into it, she scanned the opposite side of the road. As far as she could tell there was no one looking across at the flat, but she deliberately turned her head from left to right so that, wherever the SOC team were, they could see her face. There were cars parked in the diagonal spaces. Some had driven in but others, including two vans, had reversed in and were facing towards Tamsin's windows. The vans were both unmarked, one white, the other dark blue.

Dark blue.

Clare's mind went back to her journey from Perth, the DCI driving, Tamsin in the back. There had been a dark blue Transit van behind them for a couple of miles. But then it had peeled off, crossing Queen's Bridge over the River Tay as they had carried on ahead. She tried to recall how the van had looked in the rear-view mirror. Could this be the same vehicle? Admittedly there were plenty of blue Transits on the road but, all the same, it was quite a coincidence. And, if it was the same van, had Paddy ordered it to follow them from Perth? Had another car taken over when it had turned away from them to cross the river? Or could it even have been an unmarked Serious Organised Crime squad van? She had never heard of the SOC cops using unmarked vehicles to follow witnesses who were under protection but then Tamsin Quinn wasn't just an ordinary witness. She was the sole witness who stood between Phil Quinn and a heavy prison sentence and Clare knew the prosecution couldn't afford to lose her. And, if it was an undercover SOC van, had the DCI known about it? Or was she getting carried away again? Rattled by their Friday morning meeting with Gayle Crichton.

She cursed herself for not getting the registration at the time. Suddenly, the sun appeared above the buildings opposite and Clare had to shade her eyes to see across the road. There were no occupants in either van, as far as she could see, but that didn't mean there was no one inside. In fact, she hoped at least one of the vans did belong to the SOC cops.

She decided to check the numbers. With a quick glance for traffic, she began strolling across the road, pretending to tap at her phone. When she was close enough she took a photo of the front of the two vans and carried on her way, turning down Church Street, as she continued her pretend text message.

The brass players had set up on the corner of South Street now and were playing a rousing version of *Puttin' On the Ritz, their sheet music flapping in the wind against the clothes pegs.* Clare felt in her pocket and dropped a handful of coins into their open case. The trumpet player nodded in acknowledgement and she walked on past a restaurant with tables out on the pavement. A whiff of cigarette smoke reached her nostrils and she wondered – not for the first time – why it had taken her so long to give the habit up.

She strolled on along South Street and, as she approached the neo-Jacobean Madras College building, she heard singing. The buskers were certainly out in force today. A small crowd had gathered to listen and a pull-up banner proclaimed this was the university *Gilbert and Sullivan Society*. Clare knew little about music but, to her uneducated ear, they sounded very good. Especially for students.

And then she remembered why Kinnessburn Road had nagged away at her. That student Jim had been dealing with on Friday – Marek something. He had a flat in Kinnessburn. She wondered idly if his friend had turned up. Maybe it was something Jim could check with the university. She moved away from the singing students and headed down one of the many lanes that peppered South Street, back towards Kinnessburn Road. As she walked she dialled the station number. It went to the answering machine and she left a message instructing whoever picked it up to check on the two van registration numbers. Then she added a note on her phone to ask Jim on Monday to check on that student. She arrived at the station car park and, again, elected not to go in.

'I'm done with work for today,' she said to herself, clicking to unlock the Merc. The sky was empty of clouds now, thanks to the breeze, and she thought how lovely it would be to walk part of the Fife Coastal Path with Benjy. Maybe even stop at the Cheesy Toast Shack down the coast at Kingsbarns. And with that mouth-watering prospect, she pulled out of the car park and headed off to enjoy the rest of her day.

Monday, 18 May

Chapter 10

'So, what's with this Gayle Crichton person?' DS Chris West wanted to know. He was making short work of a bacon roll, a smear of ketchup on his cheek. Clare noticed he kept one eye on the door. No doubt watching for Sara, his colleague and girlfriend, who had recently decided that he could do with losing a few pounds.

'Just what I said in the email.'

'Yeah, I read that. But what does *Development of a New Comms System* actually mean? Are we all gonnae have to learn to use new software? Cos they can shove that where the sun don't shine.'

Clare pretended to read a text message for a few seconds. Then she glanced at Chris. 'No idea. All I know is I've been asked to make room for her and that's what I'm doing.'

'In Interview Room Three?'

Clare sighed. 'It's not like we use it. When's the last time you can recall us having all three interview rooms occupied?'

Chris shrugged.

'And wipe that sauce off your face.'

Jim appeared and Clare remembered the note on her phone.

'Jim, can you chase up that student please? The one who came in then disappeared? I think you had an address in Kinnessburn.'

Before Jim could reply the station door opened.

'Clare!' a voice said, and they all turned to see Gayle Crichton staggering through the door with a laptop bag in one hand and slightly larger padded case in the other.

Clare suddenly felt under-dressed. Gayle's dark green suit was impeccably cut, the jacket sharp and angular, the wide trouser legs swinging to reveal black patent Oxford brogues.

She dumped her two bags on the floor and came quickly towards Clare, all smiles. Clare held out her hand but she was surprised when Gayle stretched out her arms and embraced her.

'Clare,' she said again. 'How lovely to see you.' She surveyed the others. 'Hello, everyone,' she said. 'Gayle Crichton. Thanks so much for making some space for me.' Her eye fell on Chris. 'I'll try not to be a nuisance.'

Sara had come into the station behind Gayle but Chris was so distracted by Gayle's effusive charm that he forgot to hide the bacon roll. He blushed and Clare saw Sara's lips tighten. She and Chris had been what Jim quaintly termed *An Item* for over a year now, their relationship weathering the loss of their unborn baby when Sara was seriously injured. She had been good for Chris. Settled him down. Clare hoped he wouldn't make a fool of himself with Gayle and she resolved to keep him as busy as possible for the next week or two.

A clearly smitten Chris, having carried Gayle's bags into the small interview room, went to make her a coffee.

'I'll have one too,' Clare called, following Gayle into the room, but Chris affected not to hear.

Clare closed the door behind her and indicated the room with her hand. 'Well, here it is. It is a bit small, though.'

Gayle smiled. 'It's perfect. Thanks Clare – I appreciate it.'

Clare indicated a white panel on the wall. 'Data point there and plenty of sockets.'

Gayle tapped one of the black bags. 'I'll set up my own network,' she said, adding, 'Safer that way.'

The door opened and Chris appeared with coffee and a Wagon Wheel biscuit. Clare raised an eyebrow. No one knew where Chris hid his biscuits. Not even Sara. Clare had certainly never been offered one.

'Ooh, Gayle,' Clare said, 'you are honoured. Chris doesn't share his Wagon Wheels with just anyone.'

Gayle laughed. 'I won't, thanks.' She patted her stomach. 'Have to watch the figure, you know, er...'

Chris laid the coffee and biscuit down on the desk. 'DS Chris West,' he said, holding out a hand.

Gayle took the hand and held it for a moment. 'Firm handshake, DS West. I like that.'

Clare took advantage of this, scooping up the Wagon Wheel. 'Thanks Chris. I'll take this off your hands.' She nudged him. 'Come on, DS West. Let's leave Gayle to settle in.' She propelled a reluctant Chris back out into the main office. 'Let me know if you need anything,' she called to Gayle and she closed the door.

At the counter Sara, with one eye on Chris, was dealing with a report of a missing dog. Chris ambled over to pick up his own coffee but Clare forestalled him.

'Chris, can you check on a couple of van registrations I phoned in yesterday?' And, leaving him to do that, she took the opportunity to go out into the car park. At the far end, with no one else around, she dialled Wendy's number.

'Hi, Clare.'

'How are things?'

'Yeah, fine. I've brought in some more food and a couple of magazines for Tamsin. She's as nervy as hell, though. Keeps going to the window to peer through the blinds.'

'She's not to leave that flat, Wendy,' Clare emphasised. 'Not for anything. And she doesn't answer the door either.'

'Yeah, I do know that, Clare.'

'Sorry. I'm just a bit jumpy about this one. Listen, Wendy…'

'Yeah?'

'Can you keep an eye out for a blue Transit van please?' She reeled off the registration, pausing while Wendy wrote it down.

'Any reason?'

'Probably nothing. I saw one on Friday, in Perth – just after we picked Tamsin up. Then yesterday I was on Market Street and saw one that looked similar. It was parked opposite the flat.'

'Hold on. I'll look now.'

Clare waited while Wendy went to the window.

'Nothing, as far as I can see. There's a white one but not blue. I'll keep an eye out, though.'

'Not a word to Tamsin, mind,' Clare said. 'We don't want her spooked before she gives evidence.'

'Mum's the word.'

–

'Those registrations you asked me to check,' Chris said, as Clare walked back into the front office.

'Yeah?'

'One of them's ours.'

Clare was relieved to hear that. So the Serious Crime lads were keeping an eye on Tamsin. 'Which one?'

Chris ran a finger down his notepad. 'Erm... white Transit.'

An uneasy feeling was developing in Clare's stomach. 'And the other?'

'A red Nissan Micra. Registered in Doncaster.' He looked up. 'Did you think it was a van?'

'Eh? Let me see that number.'

Chris held out his notepad and Clare called up the photo she had taken. It was the same number.

'Check again,' she said.

Chris walked over to the computer. 'See for yourself.'

Clare followed him and sat down at the computer. She checked the number again. 'Dammit. False plates.' Her mind was racing. What to do first. 'Hold on here,' she said to Chris and she went back out the door into the car park, dialling Wendy's number as she went. The phone was answered on the second ring. 'Wendy – that dark blue Transit...'

Wendy cut across Clare. 'Hold on, Clare. I'll just pull in.'

'You're driving?'

'Yes. I'm heading back to Glenrothes. Why? Something wrong?'

'Get back to Tamsin and stick with her. She's not to be left, day or night. I'll get someone else to relieve you, later.'

'Right. I'm parked now. So, what's up?'

'Wendy, I can't tell you over the phone. Just trust me on this one. Get back there as fast as you can. And phone me when you arrive.'

'On my way.'

Clare's next call was to the DCI. 'Al, are you in the area?'

'Edinburgh. Why?'

'Can you get up here?'

'Is it important?'

'Yep.'

Clare ran back into the office and caught Chris by the arm, steering him into her office and closing the door. 'Don't ask any questions, Chris. I'm heading out for half an hour. Anything comes up – anything at all – get me on the mobile. Hopefully back within the hour.'

Chris stared at her. 'Clare, what the hell's going on today? First that woman tips up and takes over the interview room and now you're acting all weird. Enough of the secret stuff. Tell me!'

Clare hesitated. For a split second she considered telling Chris about Tamsin. And then she knew she couldn't. Someone had leaked Tamsin's location in Perth and yesterday a blue Transit van with false plates had parked outside the Market Street flat. She glanced at her computer. She had heard about hackers using webcams to spy. What else might they do? 'Not here,' she said, her voice low. 'And not now.'

'I'm supposed to be your DS.'

'Chris, I said not now.'

'Are you even going to tell me where you're going?'

'Nothing to tell,' she said, but she tugged at his arm and he followed her outside into the car park. She steered him away from the door. 'Look, when I come back, we'll talk. But not in there.'

'What, the station? What the fuck, Clare?'

'You'll just have to trust me, Chris.' She looked at her watch. 'I'll be half an hour. An hour at the most. Now get back in there. You're my eyes and ears.'

—

Market Street was a hive of activity, the tourists competing for pavement space with shoppers laden with carrier bags, and students carrying MacBooks. Clare abandoned her car on South Street, away from Tamsin's flat, and walked the short distance up Church Street towards the fountain. She hovered in a shop doorway, scanning Market Street. There was no sign of a Transit van, blue or otherwise. Even the white one was nowhere to be seen. Clare's mouth was dry. She didn't have a key to the flat and Tamsin had been told not to answer the door. If Clare rang, even called through the letterbox, she might scare Tamsin. Better to wait for Wendy. She checked her watch. Wendy would be here in ten minutes. She strolled up and down the street, pretending to glance in shop windows and chat on her phone. There was no sign of anyone resembling Paddy Grant. In fact, she couldn't see any sign that the flat was being observed. She sent up a silent prayer that the Serious Crime cops were concealed somewhere. A sharp toot alerted her to Wendy's arrival. She waved to Clare and drove on, past the flat towards North Street, presumably to park. A few minutes later, Clare saw her come round the corner of Union Street and she walked quickly to greet her. She steered Wendy over the road towards the fountain and positioned herself where she could see Tamsin's windows.

'That dark blue Transit van I asked you about...'

'Yeah?'

'False plates.'

'Shit.' Wendy looked up at Tamsin's windows. 'Do we tell her?'

Clare shook her head. 'I don't think so. Not for now, at least. They might not be watching her. Could be using false plates for any number of reasons. But I'm not taking any chances. I've asked DCI Gibson to come up. I don't want to do anything without speaking to him first. But he won't be here for another hour yet.'

Wendy nodded. 'Okay. Best get in and see she's okay then.'

Clare followed Wendy to the flat door. Wendy produced the key and, with a glance left and right, she slipped it in the lock. As she closed the outside door behind them she called up to Tamsin. 'Just me and Clare.'

There was a muffled response as they climbed the stairs.

'She's there, at least,' Wendy said, putting another key in the door at the top of the stairs. As they entered the flat Tamsin emerged from the kitchen, kettle in hand. The TV was blaring, Holly and Phil having another attack of giggles on *This Morning*.

Clare thought Tamsin looked tired, dark circles below her eyes. Hardly surprising, really, given the strain she was under.

'Just making a coffee,' Tamsin said, her voice flat. 'Want one?'

'Ooh yes please,' Wendy said.

Clare waved the offer away. 'I need to get back,' she said. 'Just popped in while I was passing.'

Tamsin looked at Clare for a moment, then back at Wendy, her expression clouded. 'Thought you weren't coming back till tonight. Is there something...'

Wendy's tone was bright. 'Afternoon appointment cancelled. So I might as well be here. Keep you company.'

Tamsin seemed to weigh this, then she managed a smile. 'I could certainly do with it. Being here on my own – well, time to think, ye know? Gets a bit…'

Wendy took off her jacket and jerked her head towards the door. 'Nice to see you, Clare,' she said. 'Maybe speak later?'

Clare took the hint. She had an errand to run anyway. Closing the outer door firmly behind her and checking the handle to make sure it was locked, she walked quickly down Market Street until she came to the shop she needed. She had to wait ten minutes to be served and it then took another twenty minutes to transact her business. Then she tucked her purchases into her bag and headed back to her car.

Chapter 11

If Clare had worried about what to tell Chris, on her return, she was saved the trouble. She saw the expression on his face.

'What?'

'It's a body, Clare,' he said. 'And it looks suspicious.'

—

'I can't believe it,' she said, as they drove along. 'I was just there on Saturday.'

'What? The park?' Chris asked.

'Yes. So was DCI Gibson. And Diane from Tech Support.'

'Eh? What was it – a works day out?'

'Just the Saturday parkrun. I decided to do it on the spur of the moment and it just so happened they were there too.'

'The DCI and Diane? I never had those two down as a couple.'

'Not together, you muppet. They both do parkruns and just fancied a change of course.'

'So exactly the same course on exactly the same day?'

'It's not like there are dozens of parkruns in Fife, Chris. Stop match-making and tell me about this body.'

'It's not actually in the park. Just off the main drive. There's a bit where the bushes are thicker.'

'And it's suspicious?'

'Looks that way. A couple out walking their dog found it. Or rather the dog did. Said the face was bloody.'

'Not mud?'

'It could be. SOCO are on their way so hopefully they'll give us an idea.'

'No cameras?'

'Nope.'

They passed Daisy Cottage and Chris said, 'How's the house now?'

'Yeah, it's fine, thanks Chris. Just one or two niggles to fix. Don't suppose you know a joiner?'

Chris slowed down as they approached the red sandstone lodge house at the entrance to the park drive. He signalled left and Jim, who was travelling behind them, did likewise.

'What you needing done?' Chris asked.

'Oh, nothing much,' Clare said. 'Some of the floorboards were a bit damaged when the central heating was upgraded. And the shed needs a new door. Gate's hanging off. Draughty window upstairs – actually, now I think about it, there is quite a lot to do.'

Chris turned into the park entrance, past the lodge house and up the long drive which led to the Dukes Golf Course and, beyond that, to the park itself. Ahead they could see a couple standing on the verge by a clump of dense foliage, a yellow Labrador at their side. 'This must be the couple that found it,' he said and he signalled again, pulling the car onto the verge a little short of the couple. Jim and Sara pulled in behind them and jumped out.

Clare and Chris began donning white forensic suits and overshoes while Jim set up a cordon.

Clare introduced herself and Chris, then asked the couple to tell them what they had found. The woman was visibly upset, the man white-faced.

'It's just in there,' the man said, pointing. 'The dog, you see. She was sniffing and barking and I called her but she wouldn't come. So I went in to see what it was…'

Clare thanked the couple and asked them to remain by the roadside. She moved along the verge a little, avoiding the route they had taken. Finding a gap, she stepped gingerly between rhododendron bushes into the trees beyond, Chris at her back. She made her way around and behind the body. It was maybe ten feet back from the verge and, looking at the ground between the body and the verge, she reckoned it had been dragged there.

'Not killed here, I reckon,' she said, indicating the disturbed ground. 'See where his heels have been dragged?'

Chris bent to look at the body. It was a young male, fully clothed, dressed casually in jeans and a hoodie. On his feet were blue and white trainers, the colour still visible beneath a covering of earth and leaf mould. 'Someone's not short of a few bob,' he said, standing up again. 'See his trainers?'

Clare looked at the shoes. Not a brand she recognised. 'You know them?'

'Jordans.'

'Should that mean something to me?'

Chris rolled his eyes. 'Michael Jordan? Greatest basketball player of all time? Godsake, Clare. Keep up!'

'Expensive then?'

'Could be. These look pretty retro. Hundreds, probably.'

Clare muttered something about a fool and his money and returned to her assessment of the body.

His collar-length hair was dark and he was clean-shaven. His clothing prevented them from seeing anything other than fresh bruising on his face and bloodstains on his temple. His eyes had rolled back in his head and his tongue protruded from bruised lips.

'He's been knocked about a bit,' Clare said, adding, 'Before death. But I'd guess not enough to have killed him.' She glanced at her watch. 'How long till SOCO arrive?'

'They were heading straight here. Should be any time now.'

'Right. Let's get back out and see if the couple can add anything.'

They retraced their steps. 'That's our way in,' Clare said to Jim who was driving posts into the ground to mark out the cordon.

'Want the park closed?' Chris asked.

Clare considered. In mid-May it would be busy, as would the nearby golf course. Clearing everyone out of the grounds would take more manpower than she had. And there would already have been a fair number of cars up and down the road, destroying any potential evidence such as vehicle tracks. 'Not for now,' she said. She looked along the road. 'Is there another way in?'

Chris shook his head. 'Not without setting up a huge diversion.'

'Okay. Let's extend the cordon a couple of feet out into the road and see what SOCO think when they arrive.' As she spoke, the SOCO van turned in past the lodge house and began making its way up the drive towards them.

Clare's phone began to ring – the station. 'DI Mackay,' she said.

It was Gillian. One of the uniformed cops. 'Sorry, boss. DCI Gibson has arrived. Said you wanted to see him urgently.'

'Dammit,' Clare said, 'I'd forgotten. Okay, Gillian. Tell him I'll be ten minutes. Fifteen tops.'

She hung up the call and waited while the SOCO van bumped up onto the verge. She was pleased to see one of the more experienced officers, Raymond Curtice, jump down, a white forensic suit in his hand.

'Raymond,' she said. 'Good of you to come so quickly.'

He smiled broadly. 'No problem, Clare. What do we have then?'

'White male. Possibly early twenties. Some injuries to his face but no other visible signs of a struggle. We think he's been dragged in,' she said, indicating the disturbance on the ground. 'Cordon's over here.' She pointed to the posts and tape Jim had set up.

Raymond glanced across and began pulling on his suit.

'Actually,' Clare went on, 'I've something urgent to attend to. Can I leave you with Chris?'

'Sure. We'll be a while anyway.' He looked back along the road. A car was approaching, driving slowly. Jim flagged it down and they watched as he spoke to the driver. He pointed up to the park and the driver said a few words in response. Seconds later it was on its way, driving slowly past, in the direction of the park. As Clare made to leave, Sara caught her eye.

'I've spoken to the dog walkers, boss. They don't usually come this way. Not been along the drive for a couple of weeks.'

Clare nodded. 'Okay, Sara. Names and addresses then they can go.' She looked back along the drive. 'We'll need another couple of cops here, please. Once they arrive, can you go down to the lodge house and speak to whoever's in there? See if they noticed any late-night activity.'

'Will do.'

Raymond was suited and booted now and preparing to make his way in to examine the body.

'Keep an eye on things, Chris,' Clare said. But as she made to leave, Raymond called her back.

'Bit of luck here,' he said with his usual cheeriness. He held out a small clear bag into which he'd dropped a plastic card. 'Student ID badge.'

Clare took the bag and scrutinised the card inside. The photo was of the young man whose body lay in the trees, there was no doubt about that. But it was the name that caught her attention.

Johannes Muller.

Chapter 12

The DCI was sitting in Clare's office drinking a cup of coffee and eating the Wagon Wheel she had purloined from Chris.

'I was looking forward to that,' she said but he just shrugged.

He drained his coffee cup and put it down. 'So what's all the urgency?'

Clare opened her office door and indicated for him to follow her. She led him out the side door, propped open by the painters. 'Mind your suit,' she said, stepping gingerly past the wet paintwork. Once they were safely out in the car park, she glanced round, then said, 'A blue Transit van. That's what.'

The colour drained from his face. 'Not Tamsin Quinn?'

Clare put a hand on his arm. 'It's okay,' she said. 'Wendy's with her and I've told her not to leave her alone.'

'Tell me.'

She glanced round again, then said, 'Remember when we were driving through Perth on Friday? Alongside the river – just at the point I told you to go straight on.'

'Yes...'

'Well there was a blue Transit van behind us. It had been following us for a couple of miles but, just as we passed the bridge, it turned to cross the river and we

95

carried straight on. I didn't think anything of it. But on Sunday, I took a walk past Tamsin's flat, just to check there was no one hanging about.'

'And?'

Out of the corner of Clare's eye she saw the station door open and Gayle emerge. She drew the DCI back out of view but it was too late. Gayle gave them a cheery wave and strolled across the car park, her trouser legs flapping in the breeze.

'Hello, you two. Is this a private party or can anyone join in?'

'I'm just updating DCI Gibson. I've a dead body out at Craigtoun Park.' She didn't dare look at the DCI but hoped his poker face was a good one.

Gayle looked suitably shocked. 'Oh God, how awful. Is it – oh, what's the word – suspicious?'

Clare nodded. 'I think so. The forensic guys are there now so we should know soon.'

'In that case, I'll drive with my doors locked.' There was just a hint of amusement in her expression. She began moving away towards her car, a red Audi cabriolet. 'Just off for some lunch. Byeee.'

Clare watched the car out of the corner of her eye. 'Just wait until she's out of the street.' She listened for the sound of Gayle's car starting. It roared away, out of the car park, a cheery toot as she went.

They stood watching until the car could be seen no more. Then the DCI said, 'So, Sunday. You were outside the flat…'

Clare gave an involuntary shiver. 'I don't know why she makes me so nervous. Anyway, I saw two Transit vans parked opposite the flat, one white, the other dark blue. Same type as the one that was behind us in Perth on Friday. Turns out the white one is Serious Organised Crime's van.'

'Anyone in the vans?'

'Not that I could see. I'm guessing they were sitting in the back, keeping an eye on the flat from there.'

'And the blue one?'

'False plates.'

The DCI swore under his breath. He stood thinking for a minute, then said, 'Think we need to move her?'

Clare's brow creased. 'I'm not sure. Every time we shift her we take a risk. At least in that flat we have her contained. One door in and out. The Serious Crime lads are across the road, Wendy in the flat with her.'

'What about Armed Response?'

Clare considered this then said, 'Probably not needed. I can't honestly see Paddy Grant being daft enough to try anything. Not here, at least. Probably just mind games. I think the real risk is when we transport her through to the High Court in Edinburgh. Might be worth having an armed escort for that. But let's wait and see what happens over the next twenty-four hours.'

'You sure? I can't afford to lose her, Clare.'

'If you could let the Serious Crime boys know about the blue van...'

'Sure. Will do.' He looked pointedly at his watch.

'Before you head back,' Clare said, 'I've something to give you.' Checking no one was watching she went to the boot of her car and clicked to open it. The boot rose up gently, revealing a pristine interior.

'It still has that *new car* smell,' the DCI said, a note of regret in his voice.

Clare was fumbling in the carrier bag she had brought back from the shop on Market Street. She took out two black boxes containing Alcatel mobile phones. 'Pay-as-you-go,' she said, handing one to the DCI.

He stared at her.

'Take it – before someone sees us. Look, Al, I'm paranoid about Tamsin. With what Gayle said about security leaks then that blue van with the false plates – well, I don't want to lose her because somebody, somehow has managed to hack my phone, or my email, or God knows what.'

'I honestly don't think it's that bad, Clare,' he said, looking at the phones.

'You think they're paying Gayle Crichton God-knows-how-much if it's *not that bad*?' She thrust the phone into his hand. 'Take it. I've put my number into yours and yours into mine. If we need to communicate about Tamsin, we use these.'

DCI Gibson regarded the phone in his hand. 'Okay, you win.'

'And you'll let the guys in the white van know about the blue one?'

'Yes, will do. Can I go now?'

'Just one more thing.'

He rolled his eyes. 'What?'

'You owe me a Wagon Wheel.'

Chapter 13

It was almost five o'clock when Jim, Sara and Chris returned from Craigtoun Park.

'You've left someone at the scene, yeah?' Clare asked.

Chris nodded. 'A couple of uniforms: Robbie and Gillian. The night shift will send another two over to relieve them.'

'Thanks Chris. Are SOCO still there?'

'Yeah but should be finished soon.'

Clare's mobile buzzed in her pocket. Raymond Curtice. 'Raymond, hi. Any news?'

'We're done here, Clare. Just packing up. Body's gone off to the mortuary and you're in luck. They're doing the PM now.'

'Any hints?'

'Not my field, Clare. But I'd say, judging by the bruising I saw around his neck, he was probably asphyxiated. No doubt they'll be in touch, though.'

Clare looked at the clock. 'I'll give them a couple of hours then call myself. Anything else?'

'Don't quote me, but I reckon he didn't die where he was found. There's a contusion on the back of his head with what looks like a grey sandstone mixed with blood and hair. The walls around the park are more of a red sandstone so it does suggest he was killed elsewhere. I'll need to get the samples to the lab to be sure though.'

'So he was pushed against a wall?'

'Something like that. There's a patch on his scalp where some hair has been ripped out. My guess is someone took a hold of him by the hair and hit his head against the stone. Then they knocked him about a bit and finished off by strangling him. But, again, don't quote me. The pathologist will know more. That's just my guess.'

Clare considered this. Raymond knew his stuff and was usually right. 'Okay, thanks Raymond. Oh, one last thing – do you think it would have taken a lot of strength?'

'Sorry, Clare. That really is out of my field.'

'Who's doing the PM?'

There was a pause, then he said, 'Neil Grant. You know him, don't you?'

She allowed herself a smile. If there was anyone she could push for a quick result it was Neil. 'Yes, I know him. Thanks Raymond. I'll give him a call.'

She hung up the call and looked across at Jim. 'Can you get me that lad Marek – what's his name? Can you get me his address?'

'Schmidt,' Jim said, moving to the computer. 'Was it not on the printout I gave you already?'

'Sorry Jim – it's somewhere on my desk. If you could just do me another quick print…'

'Aye, no bother.'

Clare turned to Chris. 'We'll call into his flat. See if he's at home. He might be able to ID the body.'

'And if he's not there?'

'Let's just see if he is, first.'

Jim handed Clare another printout of the missing person report for Johannes Muller. 'I'll get on to the university,' he said. 'Get an address and next of kin for the deceased lad.'

Clare snatched up a set of car keys. 'Come on, Chris. The sooner we find Marek Schmidt, the sooner we can find whoever killed Johannes.'

–

Kinnessburn Road was a jumble of houses, some very old, others added probably in the Sixties and Seventies. Judging by the number of bikes chained to lamp posts it was a popular street for student flats. Marek Schmidt's flat was at the west end of the street, just before the stretch where the narrow burn had prevented even the most determined builder from laying down foundations. Clare saw a space and pulled the car in. They walked along, checking door numbers and, after a few minutes, they found it.

There were two name panels, each with a buzzer. One read *G Morton* but the other was illegible, faded by the sun. She pressed the buzzer next to the illegible one, moving closer to the speaker. But they were buzzed in without further enquiry and she pushed open the outer door.

An automatic light flickered into life and they found themselves in a short passageway with two doors facing them. The door to the left was a modern, panelled type in a mahogany stain. A rush mat lay in front and there was a brass nameplate screwed to the door surround.

'G Morton,' Clare read. From the neat appearance of the flat door she didn't think this was the one they wanted. She regarded the other door and decided it was more likely to be a student flat. The red paint was peeling and there was a small hole where a lock had been. Securing the door was a newish brass Yale lock. 'This is ours,' she said. There was no sign of a bell so she rapped sharply on the door.

'It's open,' a voice called.

'Typical students,' Chris muttered. 'Leave the Yale on the latch then complain to us when they have their stuff nicked.'

They entered the hall which was illuminated by a Chinese lantern-style paper lampshade. The pendent was too long for the ceiling height and Chris had to duck to the side to avoid catching it with his head. The wallpaper was woodchip, painted cream at one time, now ripped in places, with an Extinction Rebellion poster covering most of one wall. On the other wall, next to the door intercom, someone had made a pyramid of business cards: take-aways, taxis, bicycle repair shops and the like. A door next to this was ajar and Clare could see a bath with a shower curtain drawn along its length. There were several other doors off the short hall but they were all closed. From somewhere within the flat music was playing but no one appeared to greet them.

'Hello?' Clare called. 'Police.'

The music stopped abruptly and for a few seconds there was no sound. Then a door opened and a girl appeared. She was about twenty, Clare thought. Pale-skinned, the only evidence of make-up the black kohl lines around her eyes. Both ears had multiple piercings and her nose bore a small stud. She was wearing tartan pyjamas and her long red hair was piled up on her head, secured by a clip. She looked from Clare to Chris, then back at Clare, glancing at her ID badge.

'I'm Detective Inspector Clare Mackay and this is Detective Sergeant Chris West.' Clare saw colour drain from the girl's face and she wondered what they might find if they rummaged through her bedroom. 'It's nothing to worry about,' Clare said. 'We just need to talk to Marek Schmidt. Is he here?'

A look of relief crossed the girl's face. 'Oh, Marek. Sorry. I've not seen him for a few days.'

She seemed disinclined to move out of the hall.

Clare gave what she hoped was a reassuring smile. 'Look, could we maybe...'

'Oh yeah, sorry. Erm, it's a bit of a mess though...'

They followed her into a sitting room. Every chair was piled high with clothes, books and carrier bags. A gateleg table bore the remains of several meals, judging by the number of dirty dishes, glasses and empty bottles. The girl began clearing the sofa.

'Sorry, not had much time for tidying. Exams soon, you know.'

Chris was staring round at the mess and seemed about to speak. Clare administered a sharp kick to his ankle.

'We're just the same, when we're on a case, aren't we, Chris?'

He looked at her then round again at the clutter. 'Yeah. That's right,' he said, his voice deadpan. 'Just like this.'

The girl flushed and avoided their eyes. She indicated the space she had made. 'You can sit down. I mean, if you want to.'

Chris hesitated, then slowly sat down on the sofa, perching on the edge. Clare squeezed in next to him. 'Can I ask your name please?' she said.

'Lily. Lily Keillor.'

'Well, Lily, we really need to speak to Marek as soon as possible so any information you can give us would be appreciated.'

The girl's eyes widened. 'Is Marek in trouble?'

'No, nothing like that. We just need to talk to him. Does he have a girlfriend?'

Lily shook her head. 'Marek's gay.'

'A boyfriend then?'

She shook her head again. 'No one special. I mean, sometimes he stayed out – all night, you know. But I don't remember him bringing anyone here.'

Chris looked round the flat. 'Who else lives here, Lily?'

'Paul. Paul Jessop. He's not here just now. I think he's in the library...'

Clare nodded. 'Okay. We'll need to speak to Paul. I'll leave my card for him to call me when he gets in.'

Clare fished a card out of her pocket. The girl took it but said nothing.

'How long is it since you've seen Marek?'

Lily sat back in her chair, thinking. Then she said, 'Friday. He was here on Friday morning because we were out of coffee and I accused him of using the last of it. I don't think I saw him after that.'

Friday.

Clare remembered that was the day Marek had come into the station to report Johannes missing. And he had left abruptly, before Jim could finish taking down the details. She made an effort to keep her tone light. 'And how did he seem? On Friday morning, I mean?'

Lily's brow furrowed. 'Actually, he seemed a bit upset. I thought maybe he'd had a fight with someone. You know – maybe someone he was seeing.' She began examining her nails. 'Suppose it didn't help me laying into him about the coffee.'

'Did he say anything that made you think he'd had a fight with someone?' Chris asked.

Lily turned to Chris. 'Not really. But he's quite sensitive, Marek. If someone had given him the brush-off or even been a bit sharp with him, he'd have felt it, you know?'

'Did you ever meet another student called Johannes Muller?' Clare asked.

They watched Lily carefully.

'Oh yes. That's Marek's friend. I think they know each other from school. They're both Swiss, you see. I mean, I don't see him that often. Our lectures are at different times. But he's nice, Johannes. They both are. Very polite. Nice manners, that sort of thing.'

'Could Johannes be Marek's boyfriend?' Clare asked, being careful not to use the past tense.

Lily frowned, then said, 'No, I don't think so. They're together a lot but not in that way.'

'Okay, thanks Lily.' Clare rose. 'Could you show us Marek's room please?'

The girl frowned. 'Oh, I'm not sure. I mean…'

Clare cut across her. 'Lily, we have reason to believe Marek may be in some danger so…'

'Danger? What danger?' Lily's hand went instinctively to her throat. 'What's happened to him?'

'That's what we don't know. So the more we can find out about him the better.'

Lily rose from her seat and led them back out to the hall and opened another door. 'This is Marek's room.'

Chris thanked Lily and they entered the room, closing the door behind them. The curtains were drawn and Clare moved to the window to pull them open. 'South-facing,' she said, as sunlight filled the room. She looked round. It was far tidier than the sitting room. 'Okay, gloves on. I'll start with the desk. You take the bed.'

Chris sighed. 'Why do I always have to do the bed? Why don't I do the desk and you do the smelly bit?'

'Because I'm the DI and you're the DS. Now get those covers off.'

They had barely started when Clare's phone went. Neil Grant.

'Hi, Neil. What you got for me?'

'Definitely murder, Clare, but I'm guessing that's not much of a surprise.'

'No,' Clare admitted. 'How did he die?'

'Asphyxiation. He was strangled, Clare. Not much evidence of a struggle. There's a contusion to the back of his head where I believe he was pushed hard against a stone wall. Bruising to the face, a cut above his eye. I think he was assaulted which would have made him woozy. Then a ligature was wound round his neck and pulled.'

Clare thought back to the body, dumped just off the drive that led to Craigtoun Park and, despite her years in the Force, she shivered, picturing Johannes's last moments. Then she gathered her wits. 'Type of ligature, Neil?'

'Rope. Most likely polypropylene. There's a pretty good imprint round his neck. If you pressed me, I'd say around eight or nine millimetres.'

Clare scribbled this down then asked, 'How long had he been there?'

'Hmm. That's trickier, Clare. He certainly didn't die there. Now I can't tell you when he was brought to the park but, in terms of when he died, rigor had subsided and there was some bloating.'

'Which means?'

'I'd say somewhere between four and six days, judging by the temperatures we've been having.'

Clare counted back. 'Could he have died on Friday?'

'Definitely not. Thursday at a push but more likely Wednesday.'

'Don't suppose you've done tox tests?'

'Clare! You know better than to ask that.'

'I know,' she said. 'Takes weeks. I just wondered if there was anything that might suggest he was a user.'

'There wasn't so much as a lager shandy in his stomach so he hadn't been drinking. And, if it helps, he was in excellent health so if he was a drug user I'd say he wasn't a serious addict. Certainly no track marks. And that's all I'm saying until the tox results are back.'

Clare thanked Neil and ended the call. She turned to Chris and began to relay the conversation then she saw that he was holding out a black and yellow Scarpa mountaineering boot. She peered inside the boot, taking in its contents.

'Get it bagged and let's see what else Marek Schmidt's been hiding.'

Chapter 14

It was seven o'clock by the time Clare returned to the station. She had sent a message to Moira, her neighbour, who had replied, saying she would feed Benjy and take him out for another walk. The bundle of ten and twenty-pound notes Chris had found stuffed in Marek's mountaineering boot were well-used and there would probably be too many fingerprints for the lab to analyse quickly enough.

'Even if they find a print from someone already on the system,' Chris said, 'it proves nothing. Think how many notes pass through our own hands.'

Clare had agreed but told Chris to count the notes with gloves on. 'Just in case.'

'Just over a thousand pounds,' he said, a few minutes later, placing the notes carefully back in the evidence bag.

Clare had requested sight of both Marek and Johannes's bank and credit card statements while a clearly frightened Lily Keillor had given a statement, denying any knowledge of the money.

Back in her office now, Clare picked up the mouse to bring her computer to life then stopped when there was a tap at the door.

Before she could call out it opened and Jim appeared. 'Clare—' he began.

'Jim! You should have gone home hours ago. You've been on duty since early morning. You know I don't have the overtime budget for this.'

He looked wounded. 'I wasn't expecting to be paid,' he snapped back.

Clare stared at him. In the year or so she'd been working at St Andrews there hadn't been so much as a cross word between them. Jim was the most placid and reliable of all her staff. 'Oh Jim, I'm sorry,' she said. 'Of course you weren't.'

He stiffened. 'I was waiting to have a word. But I can see it's not a good time.' He made to leave, his hand on the door.

'Wait,' Clare said, rising from her seat. 'Please, Jim – I'm so sorry. I shouldn't have said that.' She pulled a chair out from the wall. 'Sit down for a minute.'

He hesitated then he moved and sat down, his back still ramrod straight.

Clare pulled her own chair round the desk and sat next to him. 'Jim – I am sorry. You're the last person I should have a go at. To be honest, I don't know what I'd do without you here. You keep it all together. So – please – let's have that word. What's on your mind?'

Jim looked down at the floor for a minute as though wrestling with what to say. Then he found his voice. 'I'm wondering if it's time I should be retiring, Clare. Time I packed it in.'

Clare's eyes widened and her thoughts went immediately to Jim's wife who had suffered a debilitating stroke the previous summer. 'Oh Jim. What's brought this on? It's not Mary, is it? I thought she was doing a bit better now.'

Jim shook his head. 'Mary's fine, thanks, Clare. Her sister comes round most days when I'm at work and she goes to this group organised by the physio. A bit of exercise and a lot of cake, from what I can see.'

Clare smiled. 'That sounds quite positive. So – if it's not Mary…'

He hesitated, opened his mouth to speak but seemed to be struggling for the right words.

Clare waited. Better to let him say it in his own time.

Finally, he said, 'It's me, Clare. I don't think I'm as sharp as I used to be.'

'Rubbish! Jim, you know everything there is to know about this town. You're the best sergeant I've ever worked with.'

'You're very kind, Clare, but—'

'What is it, Jim? What's brought this on?'

'Well, it's that young lad – the one who came to report his friend missing.' He shook his head. 'I let him go, Clare. I knew there was something funny about him and I let him go. I should have put him in an interview room and talked to him properly. But I was busy – it had been a busy morning – and when he said he needed to go to the gents, well it was a relief, to be honest. I thought, while he was away, I could maybe deal with someone else in the queue. So I pointed him in the direction of the toilets – and then he never came back. Now you've found his friend murdered. Maybe he's in danger too, Clare. And I could have kept him here. Found out a bit more about him. And now, well, if something happens to him—'

Clare put a hand on her sergeant's arm. 'Jim, you couldn't have stopped him. It's a free country. If he chose to walk into the station then walk back out again, there's nothing you, or I, or anyone could have done to stop him.'

'I used to be good at it, Clare,' Jim went on. 'Persuading them to stay, sussing out when they were keeping something back. Working with them and getting them to trust me.' He shook his head again. 'I'm losing my touch.'

Clare met his eye. 'Jim, I won't have you blaming yourself for this. Even if he had stayed to complete his report he'd have left eventually. And then he would probably have gone… well, wherever he has gone.'

Jim inclined his head. 'Maybe…'

'Honestly, Jim, you haven't done anything I wouldn't have done myself. So please – let's hear no more about retiring. Please?'

He flushed and then he managed a smile. 'Och, I'm not that good, Clare.'

'Yeah, you're rubbish really. But you do make a decent cup of tea! Now, for goodness sake get yourself home to Mary.'

He rose and replaced his chair against the wall. 'If you insist. And thanks, Clare.' He turned to leave.

Clare suddenly remembered Johannes's body still hadn't been identified. 'Oh Jim – any luck with the lad's parents?'

He nodded. 'Flying in tonight. They're booked into a hotel in the town and I've said we'll send a car over for them in the morning.'

'Okay, thanks, Jim.'

He went out, closing the door, and Clare reached into her bag for the spicy chicken wrap she had picked up from Tesco on her way back from Kinnessburn Road. She took a bite from the wrap then, still chewing, went out into the main office. 'I need someone to get over to Johannes Muller's flat to go through his things,' she said, looking round. 'And we need a lock put on his bedroom door to keep the flatmates out.'

Gillian and Robbie, back from their vigil at the park, indicated they would do that.

'And look out for any stashes of money,' she called after them. 'Bag up anything remotely suspicious.'

With the pair gone, Clare began making a list for the following morning. Johannes's parents would have to be taken to the mortuary in Dundee to identify the body. Marek's other flatmate, Paul Jessop, would have to be interviewed. Then there was the press office, hounding her for a statement, and someone needed to speak to Johannes's flatmates. 'Chris, can you get Gillian on the phone please? Ask her to tell Johannes Muller's flatmates to be at home – let's say about nine, tomorrow morning. I'd like to interview them.'

Chris was in the process of shutting down his computer. 'No problem.'

'Then get off home,' Clare said. 'It's been a long day. I'll just update the night inspector then I'm off home myself. Back in at seven tomorrow, everyone.'

They didn't need to be told twice and the station emptied quickly. They were all tired and glad to be going home. Clare was tired too. She went back into her office and sat down at her desk for a few minutes, relishing the peace. Gayle had also left, back to her hotel, presumably. Clare wondered where she was staying. She hadn't mentioned it. No doubt somewhere expensive like the Old Course. Nice work if you could get it.

She tapped out an email to the night inspector then decided she could do no more. Out in the car park she smiled at the sight of the Merc. It was so lovely and she reminded herself this was one of the reasons she worked so hard. She climbed in and eased it out of the car park towards Daisy Cottage and the excitable Benjy.

—

In spite of his walk with Moira, Benjy was full of beans when she opened the door. He flung himself against her legs then ran round and round, making her progress to the kitchen hazardous.

She was still full of spicy chicken wrap and, frankly, too tired to cook anything. Her eye fell on the almost-empty bottle of red on the kitchen table and she poured the dregs into a glass. She took this through to the sitting room and, replacing the rug Benjy had again kicked across the floor, she put the wine down and took up her laptop. She sank back into the sofa and immediately noticed the absence of her favourite red cushion, a house-warming gift from her sister, Jude. She looked round the room and saw it over by the window on another chair. Benjy and those cushions! Usually he left them scattered on the floor but this was a new trick. She stood to retrieve the cushion and held it out to him. 'Leave it alone,' she said, trying to sound stern. He wagged his tail in response and Clare resumed her seat on the sofa, tucking the cushion in at her back.

She pulled the laptop onto her knee and clicked to open Facebook. Glancing at her news feed she saw that Geoffrey was eating swordfish in a harbour cafe. She read the caption:

Fish with friends

'Well, bully for you, Geoff,' she muttered, clicking on the search box and starting to type Alastair Gibson's name. There were no new updates since his parkrun on Saturday and she felt an odd sense of disappointment. She had enjoyed a peep into her DCI's private life, seeing another side to someone who, hitherto, had been no more than her boss. She was about to click on his photos when suddenly there was a ping. A private message from him. She felt her face redden. He couldn't possibly know she was browsing his profile, could he? Surely the message was just coincidence. Was she turning into a stalker, for goodness sake? Her finger hovered over the message but she didn't immediately click to open it. *Best not seem too keen*, she decided. And then she gave herself a shake. She was acting like a teenager, for God's sake. She drained the contents of her glass and clicked to read the message.

Quite a day. Hope you got home all right.

Clare sent a reply saying she was just home and, yes, it had been quite a day. She saw that he had read the message then she watched as the tell-tale dots indicated he was typing a reply.

Glass of red?

She typed back:

Of course!

Seconds later he replied with a wine glass emoticon. She stared at the screen for a few more minutes then the green dot beside his name disappeared. She sat back on the sofa, wondering how he was spending his evening. Was he likewise perched on his sofa, tapping away at his laptop, perhaps sending private messages to other colleagues? Did he even still have a sofa or had Alison taken that with her?

She clicked to close Facebook and felt vaguely unsettled. She began browsing the BBC News website and saw that the Phil Quinn trial had heard evidence about the cache of weapons recovered. Suddenly she felt uneasy and she wondered if Tamsin was still safe and sound in her Market Street flat. She thought about texting Wendy then decided she would leave it. If there was a problem she'd hear about it soon enough.

Her eye fell on the empty glass and she considered opening another bottle. But she was tired now and had an early start in the morning. She closed the laptop and rose from the sofa, carrying her glass into the kitchen. Then she opened the back door for Benjy to have a last pee in the garden. As he wandered back towards the house he stopped suddenly and his ears went back. His gaze was focused towards a neglected flower bed beside the fence that bordered the woods, and he gave a low growl. Clare looked across but it was dusk now and she could see nothing. Perhaps it was rabbits or some other snuffling creature beginning its night-time activities. Either way, she didn't want him taking off into the night. She gave a sharp whistle and he trotted obediently back into the house, settling down in his basket. She ruffled him behind the ears then turned out the lights and climbed the stairs to bed.

Tuesday, 19 May

Chapter 15

They gathered in the briefing room just after half past seven. The room, usually home to a handful of cops at one time, was busy with plain-clothes and uniformed officers occupying every available chair, some perched on the corners of desks. The blinds had been closed against the morning sun and, early as it was, the mercury was climbing. At the front of the room, on the whiteboard, Clare had pinned a photo of Johannes Muller. He was dark-haired with a swarthy complexion and he stared back at them, his blue eyes unsmiling.

'Johannes Muller,' Clare said, indicating the photo. 'Twenty-one years of age, a native of Lucerne in Switzerland. Student at the university here, studying…' She broke off.

'Physics,' put in Jim.

Clare nodded her thanks. She was relieved there seemed to be no sign of the self-doubt Jim had displayed the previous evening. She turned back to the photo. 'Cause of death was asphyxiation, probably with a rope. He'd been knocked about a bit then strangled. The pathologist and SOCO both think he was killed elsewhere, possibly somewhere in the town, but that's a guess, to be honest. After death he was transported, somehow, to Craigtoun Park and his body dumped a few hundred yards inside the park gates. It's a long drive, lined with trees and bushes, so plenty of opportunity to dump a body without being observed.'

Sara raised a hand. 'Nothing from the lodge house, boss.'

'Okay, thanks Sara.'

Gillian asked, 'Do we know when he was killed?'

'Not exactly. Probably the middle of last week, say between Tuesday and Thursday. But they can't be more precise than that. So I need you all to go through any reports of a disturbance last week.'

'He could have been held somewhere before being killed,' Chris suggested.

'Good point, Chris.' Clare glanced at her watch. 'I'm seeing the flatmates at nine this morning so they should be able to tell me when they last saw him alive and well. Once I have that we'll narrow down when he died. But in the meantime, go back to Monday last week and see if anything comes up.'

Chris caught her eye. 'The money, boss…'

'Yeah, thanks, Chris.' She moved along and indicated a second photo. 'Marek Schmidt. Some of you may have seen Marek last Friday. He called into the station to report Johannes missing. But he left before Jim had all the details.'

'Why?' someone asked.

Clare shot a glance at Jim. She hoped going back over Marek's sudden exit from the station wouldn't cause Jim to doubt himself again. She watched him carefully as he got to his feet.

'The lad seemed shifty,' he began. 'Worried-like. Kept glancing over his shoulder. I got as far as name and address for himself and Johannes, then he asked to use the toilet and that was the last I saw of him.'

'Jim, can you recall the last question you asked before he went to the gents?' Clare said.

Jim considered this. 'I think I asked him when he last saw Johannes.'

'So,' Clare said, looking round the room. 'Why would he leave? Was it cold feet or was there something in that last question that spooked him?'

'Guilty conscience?' suggested Gary, a PC in his mid-twenties. 'He might know something about his friend's death. Maybe an accident. Maybe he was involved in some way and he came in to report it to divert suspicion away from himself. Cover his own tracks.'

'And then he lost his nerve,' Sara added.

'Exactly,' Robbie said. 'He's tried to act natural by reporting Johannes missing but he couldn't carry it off.'

Clare stood by the board, considering this. 'What do you think, Jim? You were the one who spoke to him.'

Jim considered this, then said, 'I just don't know, Clare. He was certainly shifty, that's for sure. Right from the first minute I spoke to him. But, as to why, well, it could have been anything really. Something to do with drugs – or they might just have had an argument and he was feeling guilty about that. Or maybe it was genuine concern.'

'Not unexpected, if he was worried about his friend,' Clare said.

'Aye, but he was jumpy with it. And more than you might expect from a young lad reporting his pal missing.'

'Okay,' Clare said. 'Let's delve into the background. How did they know each other? Had they always been friends? Had they fallen out recently – that sort of thing? I'm going to release Marek's photo to the press so that may throw something up.'

'Is he a suspect, boss?' Robbie asked.

'Not at this stage. Let's call him a person of interest and one we need to speak to sooner rather than later.' Clare scanned the room again. 'Jim, could you chase up bank and credit card statements for both lads please? It's a murder enquiry now and we've a missing person. Any problems with the bank, refer them to me.'

Jim nodded and Clare looked round the room again. 'Chris, I want you with me this morning. First port of call is Johannes's flatmates. The rest of you, house-to-house, within three streets of Johannes's flat. Then we need university staff spoken to: tutors, any other staff he might have had contact with – classmates too. The university should have his mobile number. Get on to the phone company and go through the contacts. I want them all checked out. Anyone local – interview them. Then I want his calls, texts, social media – anything within the last two weeks. Again, if the phone company is sticky, I'll speak to them. Okay – that's it. Any questions?'

—

Clare had just finished telephoning the press office when Gayle put her head round the door.

'Goodness, Clare. It's a hive of activity this morning. Has something happened?'

Clare took in Gayle's appearance. She was wearing a soft grey sleeveless dress with a white cropped cardigan round her shoulders. How did she manage to look so effortlessly glamorous? Money, presumably. She smiled. 'It's that murder from yesterday. We had a young lad in the station last week to report the victim missing and now he's missing too.'

Gayle's smile disappeared. 'Oh, how awful. Then you'll not need me keeping you from your investigations. I was going to suggest lunch but...'

Clare searched Gayle's expression for any sign of an ulterior motive but she could detect none. Was Gayle simply trying to be friendly? She had to admit it would be lovely to step back from hunting Johannes Muller's killer for a couple of hours; but would a lunch with Gayle Crichton be the relaxing break she craved? She caught sight of Chris, hovering just outside her office door, and felt something approaching relief.

Gayle too saw him and she smiled again. 'Another time, perhaps.'

Clare suddenly felt guilty. Perhaps Gayle really was trying to make a connection. Perhaps she felt isolated, working alone in that small room during the day then back to her hotel at night. 'Let me see how I'm fixed later on,' she said. 'Maybe a quick run round the table, as my mum would say.'

'A what?'

'Sorry – family saying. It just means a very quick meal.'

'Ah I see.' She laughed. 'Let's try and fit in a *quick run round the table* then, as you say, Clare. We all need to stop now and again.'

As Gayle moved to the door Chris stood back to let her pass, earning himself a smile in return. He stood at the door, watching her for a few seconds.

'Oy, Romeo...'

Chris came in, closing Clare's office door behind him. 'She certainly brightens the place up,' he said.

'Don't you let Sara hear you saying that.'

'Course not! How's she getting on anyway – the news comms system, or whatever it is?'

'Not a clue,' Clare said lightly. 'It's all techno-babble to me.'

Chris rolled his eyes. 'I forget how old you are.'

Clare was so relieved that he hadn't questioned her further about Gayle's work that she ignored the barb. She rose from her chair. 'Ready to see these students?'

'Whatever you say, Detective Inspector.'

Chapter 16

Johannes Muller had lived with two other lads in a former council house just off Langlands Road, about half a mile from the station. They passed a small football ground on their way.

'Ever been in there?' Clare asked, seeing Chris looking across at it.

'Couple of times. The team's pretty good, for such a small town. Semi-pro,' he added.

Clare slowed now as she checked house numbers. 'Here it is,' she said, jerking on the handbrake.

The house was a two-storey block, divided down the middle with an entrance at either end. The outer walls had been pebble dashed at some point but clearly the damp had penetrated beneath the outer coating and it was easing away, here and there. The front garden was laid out in grass which had not been cut for several weeks, making Clare feel quite virtuous about her own garden. They mounted a few steps and followed a path round the left-hand side of the building. As they approached the door they could hear the strains of music and Clare felt sympathy for their adjoining neighbours. She rang the bell but there was no response. She rang again, this time keeping her finger on the button. A muffled cry came from within and the door was finally opened by a young lad dressed only in pyjama bottoms. He ran a hand through his hair and peered at them through sleepy eyes.

'Yeah?'

Clare marvelled that anyone could sleep through the drum beat of the music. She held out her ID badge. 'Detective Inspector Clare Mackay and Detective Sergeant Chris West.'

'Shit,' the lad muttered. 'Forgot. Er – come in. I'll just get Lloyd.' He pushed open a door to the sitting room. 'Just take a seat. Back in a minute.'

The lad disappeared and they heard another door open.

Clare put a hand to her head and massaged her temples.

'Stormzy,' Chris said.

She looked at him. 'How do you know this?'

He shrugged. 'I dunno. I keep up.'

The music stopped and they heard a low murmur of conversation. There was no sign of the lads appearing so she wandered round the room, taking it in. The sitting area was at one end with a dining table in the middle and a door leading to the kitchen at the other end. She poked her head round the kitchen door and saw the sink was full of dishes and the cooker in need of a good clean. The sitting room was little better, a messy mix of coffee mugs, computer games, half-dried laundry and take-away containers. There was the unmistakable odour of last night's curry.

'Christ almighty,' Chris said. 'And I thought Marek's flat was bad. Can none of them wash a dish?'

'Yeah, you're so tidy,' Clare said. 'I've seen your place.'

'Well it's a damn sight tidier than this.'

'Wouldn't be hard. Oh – I hear the patter of sleepy footsteps.'

The sitting room door opened and the pyjamas lad reappeared with another in tow. Both were now dressed in jeans and crumpled T-shirts. The first lad indicated the other. 'This is Lloyd.'

Lloyd came further into the room and perched on the arm of an easy chair. 'Lloyd McAinsh,' he said.

Chris noted this down then turned to the first lad. 'So you must be Tim – that right?'

The lad sat down on a wooden dining chair. 'Yeah, Tim Cole.'

Clare smiled. 'Sorry to drag you out of bed so early. I'm guessing you don't have morning lectures.'

They made no reply to this so Clare pressed on. 'You'll have heard about Johannes.'

The lads glanced at each other, then nodded.

Tim said, 'Yeah. Can't take it in. Suppose it's true? He's really dead?'

Clare said, 'I'm afraid so. And we're treating his death as murder so there are some questions we need to ask. And then,' she hesitated, 'we'll need to look round.'

There was no mistaking the look of panic that crossed the lads' faces. Lloyd flicked a glance at Tim but he was staring straight ahead.

'Look, lads,' Chris said, 'we're not interested in whether you've a stash of wacky baccy tucked away. Or anything else for that matter. I'm quite sure you know what's legal and what's not but that's not our concern today. We're here to find out about Johannes. That's all.'

The relief was evident. Lloyd tried a smile. 'Sure. What do you want to know?'

Clare began going through the usual questions. Did Johannes seem happy lately? Had anything changed? Was he doing okay at university? Any girlfriend or boyfriend? Anyone suspicious hanging around? For the most part the lads were clueless. Johannes was hard-working, studying physics, passing exams and generally seemed to be enjoying life. Yes, they had met Marek a few times and he was pretty sound too, but no, they didn't think he was Johannes's boyfriend. It was only when Clare raised the question of money that they hesitated.

Tim shot a glance at Lloyd. Then he said, 'He did always seem to have money, you know. Not running short like the rest of us.'

Lloyd nodded in agreement.

'Did he have a job?' Clare asked.

'No. I think maybe his parents were rich. He always had the latest phone, wore nice stuff and that. Talking about getting a car, wasn't he, Lloyd?'

Lloyd nodded again. 'Yeah. I guess his folks have money.'

After a quarter of an hour of questions, Clare felt they had learned all they could from the two lads and she rose from the sofa. 'We'll just go and look at his room now, then we'll be out of your way.'

Tim showed Clare and Chris to Johannes's bedroom door. 'Your other guys brought in a joiner. New lock,' he said, indicating the door.

'It's okay,' Clare said. 'We have the key.' She waited for him to leave and, after a few awkward seconds, he backed away down the hall, saying to shout if they needed anything.

Johannes's bedroom, by contrast with the rest of the house, was a model of tidiness. A single bed stood along one wall, the plump duvet neatly spread. The walls held a variety of posters, some obscure artwork Clare did not recognise and others of buildings she did: the bulbous, banded front of the Guggenheim Museum in Manhattan and the Sagrada Familia in Barcelona. Looking at these posters, she wondered what Johannes Muller had found in common with the two sleepyheads they had just met.

Beneath the window was a bookcase holding a variety of paperbacks. Chris picked up one or two and flicked through them.

'He liked to travel,' he said, replacing a Lonely Planet guide to Vietnam next to one for China. He bent to look at the next shelf, mainly crime thrillers.

'Check them all,' Clare said. 'See if he's hidden any money.'

'I know! You don't have to tell me.'

Clare ignored this and surveyed Johannes's desk. A slim MacBook sat to the front and she bent under the desk to remove the plug then slipped it carefully into a large evidence bag. To the back of the desk there was a small pile of physics textbooks and a notepad with three sharp pencils beside it. There was a coaster to the side of the MacBook, a Mondrian design with the distinctive thick black lines delineating rectangles in red, white and yellow. She thought suddenly of Geoffrey, with his background in sculpture and his knowledge of buildings. He would understand this room. This haven of order and design. Suddenly she felt an ache in her stomach and she longed to see him. Could she hop on a plane to Boston? Tie this case up quickly and take some leave? But, if she did, how would it be? Would she find him unchanged? The same easy manner she had known? Or would his experiences, his swordfish-eating friends, would it all have changed him? And what would they think of her, Clare Mackay? The Glasgow girl now living in a small Scottish town, spending her days rooting through students' bedrooms.

It wasn't exactly the glamorous life Geoffrey seemed to be leading. Chris was speaking now but she hadn't been listening.

'Sorry?'

'What is it? You found something?'

'No, nothing like that. Just thinking for a minute.' She turned to face him. 'What were you saying?'

'Nothing in the bookcase. And, before you ask, I've done the bed.'

'Okay. Just the wardrobe then,' Clare said. 'No money?'

'Nah. A few tenners but nothing like we found at Marek's flat.'

'Okay.' Having dealt with the desk, Clare moved to the wardrobe and began going through Johannes's clothes. They worked on, checking pockets and down sleeves. Clare picked up a pair of jeans from the floor of the wardrobe and held them out. 'See these?'

'Yeah, jeans. So what?'

'Bit tatty, wouldn't you say?'

'That's how they like them, these days.'

'No, I don't mean that. I mean they're well-worn. Look at the labels – faded so you can hardly read them.'

'So? He likes them. Maybe they're his favourites.'

'Yes, okay. But they're from River Island.'

'Clare – what's your point?'

Clare reached back into the wardrobe again and picked out another pair of jeans, the price label still attached. She waved the first pair in Chris's face. 'My point is he's been wearing these River Island jeans until they're almost falling apart and then there's these,' and she held up the other pair. 'These, Detective Sergeant, are Alexander McQueen. Now, I'm not an expert on men's clothing but there's a world of difference between High Street stores and designer gear. These haven't even been worn and take a look at the price.'

Chris peered at the tag then whistled. 'Two hundred quid. Jesus!'

'So, I reckon,' Clare went on, 'he's bought these recently. And, looking at some of the other clothes in here – Next, Primark, even – I'd say he's not always had money. It's like two different lives. The clothes he came with and the clothes he's been buying recently.'

She went out into the hallway, calling to the two lads. They appeared from the kitchen, coffee mugs in hand.

'Want one?' Tim asked, indicating his mug.

'No thanks. Just one more question. You said Johannes seemed to have money.'

'Yeah, so?'

'Did he always? I mean you must have lived with him at least since last September, if not longer. Has he always had cash to splash about?'

Tim shrugged but Lloyd weighed the question. Then he said, 'Actually, now you come to mention it, I'm not sure. It's maybe just in the last few months.'

'You reckon?' Tim said.

'Yeah. Think about Christmas. He was shopping around for the cheapest flight home. But when Easter came he flew to Cancun. And he didn't seem bothered about the price.' Lloyd nodded. 'And he bought that MacBook. Yeah,' he said again. 'I think it is a more recent thing. Why?'

Clare ignored this. 'Have either of you any idea where he might have been getting the money?'

The lads exchanged glances then Tim said, 'No, sorry.'

'Lloyd?'

Lloyd shook his head.

'Look,' Clare said, 'I'm up against it here, lads. Now, if Johannes was selling drugs, I need to know about it. And I will find out. You can bet on that. But if you can tell me anything that will save my officers days of searching, that would be a great help. And I certainly won't be coming after you two for using. That's a promise.'

Lloyd looked away for a minute, then said, 'Look, Inspector, everyone does a bit of cannabis. *Es* sometimes as well. They're everywhere. Not saying we do, mind you. But it's dead common.' He broke off.

Clare waited.

'But Johannes, well, I saw him take a puff of a joint once and he nearly puked. And, as far as I know, he wasn't pushing.'

Tim nodded. 'I agree. Johannes wasn't the type.'

Clare looked at them for a minute, then she said, 'Okay, thanks lads.'

Back in the bedroom, with the door closed behind her, she said, 'They reckon he's only had money to splash around in the last few months. Apparently he was shopping round for cheap flights at Christmas but didn't seem bothered about the cost at Easter.'

'And he doesn't have a job,' Chris said.

'So where was he suddenly getting all this money?'

Chris was silent as he considered this. Then he said, 'We've not found a bundle of notes like Marek's, though.'

'No, that's true. But look around you. He has some nice things. Pricey things. Maybe Johannes was spending it as fast as he was getting it.'

'You're assuming they were both getting money from the same source.'

'It's too much of a coincidence, Chris. Marek had a bundle of notes and Johannes a bundle of stuff. So, if they had both found some money-making scheme – what the hell was it?'

Chapter 17

They emerged into the May sunshine. Clare looked at her watch. 'I need to pick up Johannes's parents soon.'

'Want me with you?'

'No. Can you head back to the station and ask Jim how he got on chasing up the bank and credit card statements for the two lads please? We need them urgently, and the phone records as well.'

'Sure. Can you just drop me back?'

'It's half a mile Chris, if that!'

'Time is money, Detective Inspector.'

–

Clare watched Chris enter the station from the car then she took out her work mobile and called Wendy. 'How are things?'

'Oh hi, Clare. All fine here. Pretty dull, to be honest.'

'Dull is good. No sign of a blue Transit?'

'I did see one earlier this morning.'

'Doing what?'

'Nothing really. The engine stalled and it took a few minutes to get it going. Then it drove away.'

'Outside the flat?'

'Almost. Not directly.'

'Okay. But keep an eye on the street, please. Anything else?'

'Just a couple of calls.'

'Eh? Not for Tamsin, surely?'

'Yeah.'

'Jesus, Wendy! What's she playing at? She's supposed to have that phone switched off.'

'I know, Clare, I know! I've told her. She said she just switched it on to check her Facebook. I pointed out how dangerous that was and now the phone's sitting out on the table, switched off.'

Clare swore under her breath, then said, 'Who called her?'

'She didn't know. No one spoke. She thought it was maybe one of those computer-generated calls. You know, the ones in the middle of the night and no one's there?'

Clare was silent for a minute. Then she said, 'Wendy, if she so much as touches that phone again, you have my permission to stamp on it. Hard. I'll get onto the Serious Crime guys to find out why it's not been deactivated.'

'She's that important?'

'Yep.'

'When's she in court?'

'All being well, tomorrow. But I'll check with the DCI. He has someone in court watching the trial.'

Clare rang off and sat thinking for a few minutes. Then, taking the Alcatel phone with her, she stepped out of the car and went to her usual corner in the car park. She dialled the DCI's number. The phone rang maybe nine or ten times before he answered.

'Clare? Sorry, I had someone with me.'

'It's fine. Listen, Al, a blue Transit stopped outside the flat this morning. Pretended to have stalled. There for a few minutes then moved on.'

'Is that it?'

'No. The stupid eejit's had her iPhone switched on and, according to Wendy, she had two silent calls.'

There was a pause then the DCI said, 'She's what?'

He sounded, Clare thought, as though he was trying to hang on to his temper.

'That phone should have been deactivated on Friday,' he went on, his voice rising. 'And this is, what, Tuesday?'

'I know—' Clare said, but he cut across her.

'I take it that the SOC cop explained this to her?'

'He did, Al. And, to be honest, I thought she'd taken it on board. I suppose, being without social media for a few days – well, she's bound to be wondering what folk are saying, about the trial, I mean.'

'I'll give her trial,' the DCI fumed. 'Look, leave it with me. I'll get on to Serious Organised Crime and get it disabled immediately.'

'Thanks, Al. And, if you could drum up another couple of bodies to keep an eye on the flat… she's due to testify tomorrow and I'm worried they'll try something tonight.'

'Leave it with me, Clare. I won't have that lot messing this operation up.'

'Thanks, Al.'

Clare ended the call, thinking she wouldn't like to be in Steve Robins's shoes, when the DCI caught up with him. She checked her watch and realised the Mullers would be waiting for her at the Kenlybank Hotel and she jumped into the car and roared away.

Clare was glad to see Neil Grant's team had managed to make Johannes as presentable as possible. There was no mistaking the dark bruising on his face but the blood had been cleaned off and his eyes closed. Standing at the window, Clare asked them if they were ready and they nodded.

She felt she would never get used to this dreadful process. Johannes's mother wept quietly, leaning against her husband. He stood, ashen-faced, his back stiff, looking at the body of his only son. He put an arm round his wife and held her close. Clare saw his lips quiver and, once the identification had been confirmed, she withdrew to give them some time together.

The formalities completed, she took them to a nearby hotel where she ordered coffee. They sat in an alcove on high-backed upholstered chairs which seemed to envelop them and Clare thought, not for the first time, how grief could shrink a person. As they stirred sugar into their coffees she studied them. Johannes had been like his father, she thought. The same dark complexion and thick hair. His mother had finer features and her hair was blonde, the odd glint of silver threaded through. They would have made a handsome couple, had they not appeared so withered by their sorrow.

The coffee was strong and gradually the couple became more composed. They asked when they could take their son's body home, what would happen to his things, his flat…

Clare answered their questions as best she could and, when they seemed to have no more to ask, she said, 'I wonder if I could ask you about money?'

They exchanged glances then Herr Muller said, 'Of course. Ask anything you wish, Inspector.'

'Thank you.' Clare hesitated. 'How did Johannes support himself?'

'Oh, his fees were paid,' Herr Muller said. 'By the Government, you see. And he had a small grant too from a local charity. To help students study abroad, you know.'

'Was that all? Did he manage all right? Financially, I mean.'

Johannes's mother looked at her husband. 'We helped, where we could,' she said. 'Not a lot of course. My husband works in a bank and I help out in a flower shop. But we are not rich, Inspector.'

—

As she drove the Mullers back to their hotel, Clare mulled over their words. They were not rich. So how could Johannes suddenly afford to buy a MacBook and designer jeans?

'Team talk in five,' she said, as she entered the station. She went to hang up her coat and found Gayle filling the kettle.

'Time for that run round the table, Clare?' she asked. 'I've been to the baker and bought a selection of filled rolls.'

Dammit. She had completely forgotten. 'Oh Gayle, I'm sorry. I've just called a team briefing. Could we do it another day?'

Gayle smiled. 'Don't worry. Tell you what, take your pick of the rolls and you can buy them next time.'

Clare chose a turkey and cranberry roll and bit into it while she made herself a coffee. Then she carried her makeshift lunch into the incident room and perched on a desk at the front. Gradually both uniform and plain-clothes cops drifted in and, when the last of them had appeared, she began.

'Right. Thanks everyone and thanks to the officers who joined us from Cupar and Dundee. Your help's much appreciated.' She paused for a minute to let the St Andrews cops acknowledge this then went on. 'Links between Johannes and Marek – what do we have?'

Gillian stood and cleared her throat. 'They were friends, from school. Both came to St Andrews via modest sponsorship schemes from their local town. They didn't share flats but students we spoke to said they saw quite a bit of one another.'

Clare nodded. 'Have you spoken to Marek's other flat-mate? Paul…'

'Paul Jessop,' Gillian finished. 'Yes. Paul said Marek's a good lad. Good flatmate. No problems at all. Paul himself seems sound. Nothing on the Police National Computer.'

'Okay,' Clare said. 'So we've established they were friends. Now, money. Chris and I found over a thousand pounds in used notes, hidden in Marek's bedroom. By contrast, there was little in the way of cash at Johannes's flat but his flatmates said he had plenty of money to splash about, especially since Christmas. I've spoken to his mum and dad – understandably devastated – and they don't seem to have much money. So where was Johannes getting it from?'

'Job?' someone suggested.

'Nope. Didn't have one. And I don't think it's drugs either.' She turned to Chris. 'Any luck with those bank statements?'

'Sorry, Clare. Still don't have them.'

'What?'

'Yeah, bank being a bit sticky.'

'I'll give them sticky. Get right back onto them now and tell them I want those statements by first thing tomorrow, without fail. Remind them this is a murder enquiry and that they are obstructing justice.'

Chris rose from his chair and went to call the bank again.

Clare waited until he had closed the door then went on. 'Any disagreements between the lads and their friends here? Any problems with tutors?'

Heads shook. Robbie said, 'Both popular lads. Doing well on their courses.'

'Okay. So there's no obvious reason for Johannes to be killed. Except for that money. But we can't say much about that until we've seen details of their finances. So that leaves just one thing: we have to consider the possibility that Marek is responsible for Johannes's death.'

'Motive?' someone asked.

Clare spread her hands. 'Your guess is as good as mine.'

'Lover's tiff?' someone else said.

Clare frowned. 'I'm not sure. Marek was gay but apparently Johannes wasn't.'

'Maybe Marek fancied Johannes but got the knock-back,' Gillian said.

'It's possible,' Clare admitted. 'But none of the flatmates thought there was anything between them. So, for now, we continue to treat Marek as a person of interest in this enquiry. Finding him is our number one priority. He's either gone missing because he killed Johannes or he's frightened he might be next.'

Chris came back into the room. 'They've agreed. Should have them later today or tomorrow first thing, at worst.'

Clare nodded and turned back to the room. 'Right. Marek's photo is with the press office and should be on the evening news, earlier if we're lucky. So I need the phones manned for sightings. If he does turn up, try to get him to come in voluntarily for questioning. Arrest him if you have to but I'd rather not start the clock counting down on how long we can hold him, if we can get him to come in willingly.'

'What if he's not the killer, boss?' Gillian asked.

'Quite. At this stage we don't know why he decided to report Johannes missing then changed his mind. He may have fled because he believed he, too, was in danger. So let's look at recent prison releases, check up on known offenders living in the area. You all know the usual suspects. Anything remotely suspicious, I want to know about it.'

'Did he have any money on him when he was found?' Jim asked.

Clare frowned. 'I can't remember. Can someone look it up?'

Sara moved to a computer and navigated to the report on Johannes's body. After a few moments, she said, 'Black leather wallet, Bank of Scotland debit card, Mastercard, student ID card and forty pounds in notes.'

'So, robbery wasn't the motive,' Clare said. 'There must be some other reason Johannes was killed.'

'An assault gone wrong?' someone asked.

Clare dismissed this. 'Unlikely. He was killed elsewhere and dumped in the park. It was premeditated and organised so let's be thorough in checking on anyone with previous.' She looked round and there were nods and murmurs of assent. 'Right, that's it. Thanks, everyone.'

Clare's phone rang and she glanced at the display. Diane Wallace. She was about to click to take the call when Chris shouted.

'I've got the bank statements for both lads.'

Clare glanced at her phone again and declined the call. If it was urgent, Diane would leave a voicemail. 'Can you print them off?' she called to Chris. 'I'd like to look at a hard copy.'

Minutes later, Clare and Chris sat poring over the credit card statements. Marek's were unremarkable. A flight home at Christmas, a few purchases from Tiso and other outdoor shops while Johannes's showed larger purchases – the MacBook, an iPhone and those designer jeans.

'Pretty much matches what we found in their rooms. Marek watching the pennies, Johannes spending them,' Clare said. 'But where are the pennies coming from?'

They moved on to the bank statements. The debit columns showed the usual student stuff. Card payments at Tesco, various pubs and cafes plus regular cash withdrawals. Marek's statement showed he'd withdrawn four hundred pounds on Friday afternoon.

'Looks like he was planning to take off,' Clare said, pointing to the transaction.

'Half four in the afternoon,' Chris said. 'That was after he left the station wasn't it?'

Clare sat back and pondered this. 'He had over a thousand pounds in his room, hidden in that boot. Why not take that money?'

'Maybe he was keeping it for something,' Chris suggested. 'Saving it up.'

'But if you were planning to disappear, Chris, would you not take the money with you?'

'Yeah, I would. Maybe he went to report Johannes missing, panicked for some reason and decided to get out of St Andrews for a bit.'

'Which means...'

'He has to be in the frame for Johannes's death,' Chris said. 'He must be.'

'Honestly, Chris, I'm not so sure. Why go through the pretence of coming in to report him missing?'

'To make it look like he wasn't involved.'

'But what if he wasn't? What if he's gone because he thinks he's in danger too? Or what if we're too late?'

'Dunno.' Chris yawned. 'Come on – let's get this done.'

They returned to their perusal of the bank statements. And then they spotted it.

'See that?' Clare said.

'Yep.'

'So what do you reckon he was up to?'

Chapter 18

Clare decided to send Nita, a plain-clothes officer from Cupar, round to Johannes's flat to carry out a more thorough search of his bedroom. 'Take young Gary with you,' she said. 'You're looking for anything at all to do with money, banks, credit cards – that sort of thing. I've a feeling there's more to his finances than we've found out so far.'

That done, Clare made for the front door of the station but she was forestalled by Gayle.

'Time for a cuppa, Clare?'

Clare flushed. She had been on her way out to the car park to phone the DCI. Had Gayle somehow sensed this? Then she gave herself a shake. She was being ridiculous, letting this hacking business get to her. She smiled at Gayle. 'Quick one.'

Gayle produced a cafetière and began spooning coffee into it. 'I hope you like it strong.'

'I can't even offer you a biscuit,' Clare said. 'They don't last five minutes in here.'

'Just as well I have a secret stash, then.'

They carried their coffees into the small room Gayle was using. She bent to unearth a biscuit tin from beneath her desk and, as she did so, Clare's eyes went to Gayle's laptop. The browser was open at a webpage, a photo of a large building across the centre. She was just in time to see the name *Cadham Rest*. Gayle sat up again and pushed the biscuit tin across the desk to Clare, closing her laptop as she did so. 'Jaffa Cakes,' she said. 'My weak spot.'

Clare found it hard to believe Gayle had any weak spots but she took one of the cakes – or was it a biscuit? – and handed the tin back. 'How are things—' She broke off as Gayle tapped the side of her nose.

'It's going well, thanks, Clare. I'm making real progress with the comms system.' And she gave Clare a wink.

Clare wondered what the wink meant. Surely this room – one of her own interview rooms – surely it couldn't be bugged? Her eyes involuntarily scanned the walls, the ceiling, the floor, for any sign that someone might have planted a microphone but she could see nothing. She racked her brains for how to couch what she wanted to ask. Something noncommittal was needed. 'Have you made a breakthrough?' she said.

Gayle sipped her coffee, watching Clare carefully, then she smiled. 'Oh yes. I think I'm close to sorting out all the issues. With luck, I should be out of your hair by the end of this week.'

Clare wasn't sure what to think about this. On the one hand she was starting to become paranoid about being overheard. Having to keep Tamsin safe was bad enough without worrying that someone might be eavesdropping on her security arrangements. And then there was the leak itself – what had Gayle found? Was it somehow related to Tamsin's testimony? Was someone within Police Scotland tipping off the driver of the blue Transit van? Someone in Phil Quinn's pocket, determined to frighten Tamsin into withdrawing her co-operation? If that was the case then Gayle uncovering the culprit could only be a good thing.

She thought again about Gayle's reasons for choosing St Andrews as a base. Was it really so she could work undisturbed and unobserved? Or was it because she had known all along where the leak was and she'd chosen the station closest to it? And, if the culprit really was someone close to St Andrews, what would that mean for Clare and her team?

Suddenly the room seemed uncomfortably small. Clare bit into the Jaffa Cake but her mouth was dry and she took a drink of coffee to wash it down. She saw Gayle's eyes were on her and she made an effort to brighten. 'How's the hotel? Is it the Old Course?'

Gayle shook her head. 'No, I'm at the Fairmont. Know it?'

Clare did. A huge five star hotel set on cliffs south of St Andrews, as opulent as it was expensive. 'Nice.'

'Well, life's very short, Clare. And I've worked hard to get where I am so I don't intend to stint myself. Mind you…' She broke off.

'Problem?'

Gayle shrugged. 'Oh, I don't know. Sometimes you do get a bit sick of hotel life. There are nights when I'd gladly kick off my shoes and flop down on the settee with cheese on toast.'

Clare reckoned she could definitely give hotel life a go for a few weeks. No dishes to do, someone in the room every day to tidy up and meals at the drop of a hat. Instead, she found herself saying, 'I'm very handy with the toaster. Not that you'd want—'

Gayle's eyes lit up. 'Oh Clare – would you mind? I'd absolutely love an evening away from the hotel. It is lovely there but it would be so good to be in a real home, even for a couple of hours.'

'Oh – of course. I'd love to have you. Um, I'm not sure what time I'll finish tonight though.'

Gayle laughed. 'I wouldn't dream of imposing on you with just a few hours' notice, Clare. Anyway, I have a massage booked tonight.' She flexed her shoulders and put a hand up to rub her neck. 'Too much sitting over a laptop.'

Clare hoped the relief didn't show on her face. 'Tomorrow then? I'm in Edinburgh for the day but I should be home by early evening.'

Gayle beamed. 'Splendid. Shall we say seven?'

–

It was only as she was washing the cups that Clare remembered she had been on her way to phone the DCI when Gayle had forestalled her. She left the cups to drain in the small kitchen and, noting that Gayle's door was closed now, she went out to the car park. The painters were sitting on the tailgate of their van, enjoying a cup of tea.

'Afternoon,' one of them called to Clare, with a wink.

'Afternoon lads,' she said. 'Any idea when you'll be finished?'

'Should be tonight, all being well. Halfway through the last coat on the eaves.'

She smiled her thanks and walked on to the far end of the car park. Checking there was no one around, she took the Alcatel from her pocket and clicked to dial the DCI's number. He answered immediately.

'Just checking the arrangements for tomorrow,' she said. 'For Tamsin.'

'All in hand, Clare. The car will pick her up at seven.'

'And the security arrangements?'

'Two motorcycle outriders – one front, one behind.'

'Any armed officers?'

'Two in the car, plus the driver. And she'll be wearing a vest.'

'Names?'

The DCI reeled off the names of the armed officers and driver.

Clare recognised them. Good solid officers she could trust. That was something at least.

'Happy?' the DCI asked.

'Actually, Al, I've had an idea...'

–

Clare was just on the point of packing up for the night when Nita and Gary returned from Johannes's flat, clutching brown paper evidence bags.

'Bank statements and receipts, mainly,' Nita said. 'But we did find these.' She held out a small clear bag.

Clare took the bag and peered through the plastic at four bank cards, all from different banks. 'Where did you find them?'

'Under the bed,' Nita said. 'It was Gary who found them.'

'But we checked under the bed.'

Gary smiled. 'It was the carpet. He'd cut a tiny slit in it and slid the cards through that so they sat between the carpet and the floorboards. Then he'd fluffed it up again so the slit was hidden.'

Clare shook her head. 'Just when you think you've seen every trick in the book.' She saw Chris emerging from the incident room, heading for the exit, and she called him over. His face fell and he trailed across, one eye on the door. Clare ignored this. 'Chris, look – tomorrow's going to be busy. Can you take this stuff and go through it now please? It seems Johannes had multiple bank accounts and I want to know why. It's possible Marek had other accounts too. If so, we'd be better to get a warrant. As far as we know he's still alive so the other banks – if there are any –they might be sticky too.'

Chris yawned. 'Will it do tomorrow? I'm dog tired.'

'Nope. I need you for something else tomorrow. Look – if you phone the banks' fraud lines tonight and get the warrant requested, we might get the info for you to go through later on tomorrow or Thursday. Make the calls now and then I'll tell you about tomorrow.'

--

Clare opened the door of Daisy Cottage to an uproarious welcome from Benjy. He'd clearly had a busy day. Once again, her favourite cushion was placed over on the other chair while, in the kitchen, he had nudged the bin so it was blocking the door to the garden. 'You're not getting enough exercise,' she told him. She kicked off her shoes and ran upstairs to change into her dog-walking clothes then, moving the kitchen bin back to its rightful place, she picked up his lead and headed out into the evening sun. Benjy immediately made for the flower bed and fence he'd shown such an interest in the previous night, his nose to the ground as he followed a trail. As she stepped over the brambles once more she made a mental note to call Moira that evening about Bill's offer to help in the garden. She reached the gate and whistled to Benjy. He seemed reluctant to leave the fence, only giving up when Clare uttered a stern 'Benjy, come!'

They walked on through the woods, Benjy tearing around, investigating smells, marking his territory and generally having a wonderful time. 'We don't do enough of this,' Clare told him, clipping the lead on as they came to a single-track road.

Her thoughts turned to Gayle and their conversation earlier. What had possessed her to invite Gayle for supper? And in the middle of a murder investigation, to say nothing of keeping an eye on Tamsin.

Tamsin. With Johannes's murder to investigate, Marek's disappearance and then those hidden bank cards, she had forgotten about Tamsin. They were on their way back to the cottage now so Clare unclipped Benjy's lead and took out her mobile. But before she could dial Wendy's number it rang. She glanced at the display.

Diane.

Her finger hovered over the *Decline* button then she remembered Gayle's advice to act normally and she clicked to take the call.

'Diane, how are you? Sorry I missed your other calls. I'm up to my eyes just now.'

There was a hesitation; just long enough to alert Clare that Diane knew something was wrong. Then she said, 'Are you okay, Clare?'

'Of course. All fine. Just busy. We've had a murder and,' she broke off, wondering what to say, 'a few other things going on. You know how it is.' She hoped she sounded bright enough. But why was Diane asking? Had she spotted Gayle's activity on the network? Was Gayle not as clever at being covert as she claimed? 'Anyway, never mind me,' she went on, trying to deflect any concerns Diane might have had. 'How are things with you? Busy?'

'Are we ever anything else?' Diane said. She hesitated then went on. 'I heard there's a new comms system in the offing. I can't say I'm looking forward to that.'

Clare's mind worked quickly. Was Diane fishing? She must have spotted something. But Gayle had told her what to say and she had to stick to that. For all she knew, Gayle could have bugged her phone to make sure she didn't say anything about her investigations. 'Nor me,' she said, hoping she sounded convincing. 'Matter of fact, there's someone in my station this week, working on it.'

'Seems an odd place to be based. I'd have thought Gartcosh would have been better.'

She had a point, Clare thought. The Scottish Crime Campus at Gartcosh would have all the space and facilities Gayle could possibly need for her investigation. But then maybe it would be more difficult to work there covertly. 'Oh, don't ask me,' she said, attempting to sound bright. 'Something about needing peace to work. To be honest, Diane, we are usually quieter than most stations. I'm guessing she didn't bargain on a murder investigation happening while she was here.'

'It's a woman then?'

'Yeah. Don't see much of her, really. She just gets on with her work and I get on with mine.'

Diane seemed to swallow that. 'Oh well – as long as she doesn't get in your way. Anyway,' she said, brightening. 'I do have one bit of good news.'

'Oh,' Clare said, glad to change the subject. 'Is it your mum? Have you managed to find somewhere for her?'

'I wish. I've found a few nursing homes nearby though. I've made a list so I just need to start visiting them. And then I'll have to break it to Mum.'

Clare was prevented from replying by Benjy who had shot off after a squirrel. Thankfully the squirrel had retreated up a tree but Benjy stood at the foot of it, barking loudly. 'Hold on, Diane. I've a dog who's being a bit of a thug, here.' She clipped the lead back on Benjy's collar and dragged him away from the tree. 'Okay, sorted that. Where were we?'

'Oh, just me moaning on, as usual,' Diane said. 'Sorry, Clare.'

'Don't be daft. Offload to me any time at all. But did you say you had some good news?'

'Oh yes. My new assistant started on Monday and he seems pretty clued up.'

'Now that is good news. I'm so glad Diane.'

'You and me both, Clare. I had set aside some time to show him the ropes but he doesn't seem to need any help. He arrived on Monday and, after I'd shown him round, I gave him a couple of simple jobs that I thought would keep him busy for the morning. He did them in an hour and came looking for something else to do.'

'Wow! You'd better hang onto him, Diane.'

'I intend to. No one's poaching this one from me.'

'Where's he come from? Is he new to Police Scotland?'

'No. He's been at Gartcosh for the past five years. Do you know any of the techy guys there? His name's Craig Thomson.'

Clare searched her memory. The name didn't ring a bell. 'Don't think so. But I'm so glad he's working out well.'

Clare walked on, listening as Diane chatted on about Craig, about his skills, how he was a keen gamer, planning to develop his own games.

'What he doesn't know about coding...' Diane was saying.

'Did he say why he wanted a transfer through here? Surely there would be more opportunities for promotion at Gartcosh?'

'Yeah, I wondered about that too. But I think, reading between the lines, he wants more free time to spend developing his games. Plus he seems to have an on-off girlfriend in Fife so that may have something to do with it.'

Clare was at her back gate now and she opened it, unclipping Benjy's lead. He rushed up the path and stood waiting at the back door. 'Diane, I'd better go. Listen, it's been great to chat but let's catch up properly, yeah? Once this case is behind me.'

'I'd like that, Clare.'

As Clare closed the back door behind her and kicked off her shoes, Benjy began to bark. Seconds later the front doorbell rang. She sighed. It had been a long day already. All she wanted was to slam something quick and easy into the microwave and take a long, hot bath. Shutting an excited Benjy in the kitchen, she trailed through to the front door in her stocking soles. She opened it and saw DCI Alastair Gibson standing on the threshold holding a bottle of wine.

Chapter 19

'It's my birthday,' he said, by way of apology, de-corking the wine, as Clare went to fetch two glasses. 'And, to be honest, I could do with seeing a friendly face.'

Clare turned, glasses in hand. He looked tired, his shoulders hunched and his eyes, which were normally so alert, lacked expression. His jacket hung open and he had loosened his tie.

'Something wrong?'

He didn't answer immediately, but took the glasses from Clare and poured the wine.

'Just half a glass for me,' she said. 'In case something happens.'

He carried on pouring. 'I spoke to our lads outside the flat five minutes ago and it's all fine. Wendy's spending the night there, just to be on the safe side, and the Dundee inspector is on call.' He held out a glass for her. 'And I need this.'

Clare eyed him for a moment then she took the glass and led him through to the sitting room, pulling the coffee table over in front of the sofa.

He laid down his glass and sat, sinking back with a loud sigh.

Clare put her glass down and sat on the edge of the sofa, an elbow on the arm. She waited and, when it didn't look like he was going to speak, she said, 'So?'

He leaned forward and picked up his glass, taking a drink. Then he met her eye. 'I saw the Jag today.'

She thought she understood. 'I'm sorry, Al. Must be hard seeing Alison driving around in it.'

He drank again then, after a moment, he said, 'Wasn't her driving.'

Clare stared. 'She's sold it? Your lovely car?'

He shook his head. 'Nope. She was in the passenger seat.'

'So who was driving?'

He spread his hands. 'No idea. Some bloke. Looks like Tom – what's his name – from the *Avengers* films…'

'Hiddleston,' Clare said, reaching for the bottle and topping up their glasses. It was clearly going to be a long night.

'Yeah, that's him. All twinkling eyes and designer stubble.'

'He is very good looking.'

He stared at her. 'You've seen him?'

'Tom Hiddleston, not Alison's – whatever he is.'

He winced. 'Driving my car – the bastard.' He flicked a glance at Clare. 'I'm sorry. I shouldn't be bothering you with this, Clare. You've had a long day.'

She smiled. 'Forget it. It's a rotten thing to happen any day but especially on your birthday. Listen, Al – have you eaten?'

He shook his head. 'I was going to pick up a take-away on my way back to Edinburgh.'

'Fancy a curry?'

'Always.'

Clare rose. 'I've a menu for the local curry house somewhere. It's pretty good and they deliver out here.'

Forty minutes later they were sitting at Clare's dining table, sniffing at foil containers and setting them out on heatproof mats. 'I always order far too much,' she said. 'Look how much rice there is.'

The DCI tore off a strip of naan and dipped it into a tub of tandoori sauce. 'So, Clare, you've heard my tale of woe. How are things with you and...'

'Geoffrey? Oh, I don't know, Al.' She hesitated. Admittedly she now knew more than she might have wished about the Gibsons' marriage but did she really want to divulge the ins and outs of her relationship with Geoff? Did she even know what the ins and outs *were* any more?

'Sorry,' he said. 'I shouldn't have asked.' He picked up the wine bottle and emptied the dregs into her glass.

Clare rose from the table. 'I'll get another.' She went through to the kitchen, glad of the distraction. She bent to pull a bottle from the wine rack and checked it was red. Then she carried it back through to the table and began to remove the cork. She glanced across the table. He had taken off his tie and was now more relaxed than she could ever remember seeing him. And, as she refilled their glasses, she saw him drip tandoori sauce on his white shirt. 'Al – your shirt!'

He looked down and groaned. 'Oh God. It's a Paul Smith.'

'*Paul Smith?*' Clare was aghast. 'For a work shirt? Al! How much did that cost?'

He dabbed at the stain with a piece of kitchen roll. 'Don't ask!'

Clare rose. 'Should have gone to Tesco. Three in a pack – cheap as chips. Take it off. And stop dabbing at it, for God's sake. You'll make it worse.'

He stared at her. She wasn't sure if it was the suggestion that he buy his shirts from Tesco or the invitation to remove his, but he seemed disconcerted.

'Your shirt,' she persisted. 'Take it off and I'll soak it.'

He hesitated then began unbuttoning it.

She felt obliged to avert her eyes as she waited for him to hand her the shirt. But a quick glance told her he was as toned as she had thought at the parkrun. Just the right amount of chest hair, tending to grey. 'I'll soak it in a solution of vinegar and soap,' she said. 'Apparently glycerine is best for curry stains but who the hell has that in the house?'

'I do.'

She stared. 'You have glycerine in the house? Why on earth?'

'Alison uses it when she makes the Christmas cake – used it,' he corrected himself. 'Something to do with keeping the icing from going hard.' He watched Clare as she made up a solution of vinegar, liquid soap and water, then said, 'Do you mean to tell me, Inspector Mackay, that you don't make your own Christmas cake?'

'With my organisational skills, Chief Inspector Gibson, I'm lucky if I remember to *buy* a Christmas cake, never mind make one.' She spread the shirt out next to the sink and began working the solution into the stain. 'Right. We'll leave that to soak. Back to the curry.'

Sitting opposite her shirtless boss, Clare began to relax. He cut a comical figure, eating curry bare-chested. She sipped at her glass then picked up the bottle and perused the label. 'This is pretty good.'

'What is it?'

Clare scanned it. 'A Malbec. I don't remember buying it. Someone must have brought it.' She looked at the bottle. They had drunk more than half of it. 'Fourteen per cent. We should probably stop. Early start tomorrow and all that.' She rose. 'I'll make some coffee.' She swayed slightly as she walked. 'Oops. Just as well I didn't break out the whisky.' She filled the kettle and flicked the switch. The DCI appeared behind her in the kitchen, carrying plates, and she suddenly felt the kitchen was a lot smaller with two people in it. Benjy was sitting at her feet, gazing up hopefully.

'Definitely not,' she told him. She opened the back door and Benjy, seeing no titbits were forthcoming, trotted out to explore the garden. The DCI looked out of the window, following the dog's progress. The sun was low in the sky now but Benjy's activities had caught the security lamp and the garden was illuminated, strangely eerie in the half-light.

'I see what you mean about your garden. Look, I meant what I said when I offered to help, you know.'

Clare was starting to think there really was a decent human being, underneath his usual formality. She wasn't sure about letting him into her life outside work but she could see the offer was kindly meant. 'Will you not have enough on, with your new house?' she said, hoping to deflect the subject.

'There's always time to help a friend, Clare,' he said. 'And I like gardening.'

'Wait till you get your new house.' She tried to keep her tone light. 'Then see if you have any spare time.' She began loading the dishwasher, putting the leftovers in the fridge. Then she bent over the shirt and peered at the stain. 'I think it's going. But you'll probably have to put it out on the washing line for a few days. The sun will help bleach it out.'

He sighed. 'I'll have to learn all these things.'

She turned to face him, her hands on the sink behind her. 'Al, it will get better. Honestly. I promise. Just give it time.' She saw his eyes were moist and she realised for the first time that they were a piercing blue. She'd never noticed before. She put a reassuring hand on his arm. He looked at her hand then back at her. A sharp bark brought her back to her senses and she moved to open the door for Benjy.

She carried a tray of coffee and mugs through to the sitting room. 'I'll just give this a minute,' she said, indicating the cafetière. As they waited for the coffee to brew, they discussed the plan for the following morning.

'The extra car is all arranged. It'll be outside the flat at six thirty.'

'Good. Thanks for that, Al. Wendy will be there all night so she can be ready any time.'

'Good stuff.' The DCI yawned. 'I suppose I'd better get a taxi home now.'

Clare raised an eyebrow. 'All the way back to Edinburgh? That'll cost a fortune.'

He shrugged. 'Serves me right for turning up here and drinking your wine.'

'Don't be daft. You can have the spare room. I'll stick your shirt on a cool wash and tumble dry it for the morning.'

He looked at her again. His eyes really were blue. Why hadn't she noticed before? He said something but she missed it.

'Sorry?'

'I said, that's really kind of you. If you're sure I'm not imposing?'

157

'Course not.' She settled back down on the sofa and put her feet up on the coffee table.

'Mind if I take my shoes off?'

'Take your feet off, if you like,' Clare slurred.

The DCI kicked off his shoes and put his feet up on the table, next to Clare's. They sat, side-by-side, in companionable silence for a few minutes. Then he said, 'Can I tell you something?'

'Go for it.'

'I've always admired you,' he said.

She laughed at this. 'How very Victorian you sound, Chief Inspector.'

'I'm serious, Clare. You get results. You've a name for it. Did you know that?' He turned to look at her, blinking a couple of times as he focused on her face.

Clare's eyes widened. 'You're kidding.'

'Nope. There's not a DCI in Scotland wouldn't welcome you working for them. And – that hit-and-run case – remember it?'

Clare's mind went back to the time she and Chris had been hunting a serial killer, intent on running down five men. 'I remember.'

'And you stood up to me when I had a go at you.'

She flushed at the memory. 'How could I forget?'

'I thought then,' he said, 'that you were one of the finest officers I had ever met. You stood up to me and you got the job done, even putting your own life at risk.'

Clare felt a lump in her throat. 'Oh Al,' she said, putting her hand on his arm again. This time she didn't remove it. She could smell his cologne. Something woody. Expensive, probably. Instinctively her lips parted and she moved closer, finding his. After a few moments she drew back and rose, taking his hand in hers. She forgot Benjy. She forgot the cafetière full of coffee and she forgot the shirt soaking in the kitchen. She forgot everything else as she led him upstairs, flicking off the lights as she went.

Wednesday, 20 May

Chapter 20

Whether it was the wine or the strangeness of the man lying next to her she wasn't sure, but Clare slept badly. She had stayed awake long after Al Gibson had drifted into a deep sleep, listening to his breathing. She lay, looking at the ceiling. What the hell had just happened? What was she thinking? Al Gibson was her boss, for God's sake, on the rebound from his marriage break-up.

She glanced across at him, taking in his form as he slept. He lay on his back, one arm out of the covers, a muscular shoulder almost touching hers. She drew back and propped herself up on one elbow. A shaft of moon-light was shining through a gap in the curtains, giving the room a ghostly light and picking out his profile. She could see his chest hair, the stubble around his jaw, and she had a flashback to his arms around her just a few hours earlier.

And, as she lay looking at him, she suddenly remembered Geoff lying just where Al Gibson was now and a wave of nausea swept over her. What the hell had she done? For, despite all the photos of Geoff wrapped round the smiling blonde, for all her irritation at the wonderful time he seemed to be having, she never really believed he was being unfaithful to her. He just wasn't the type. But that was exactly what she had just done.

And what about Al Gibson? This man, lying next to her – the man whose wife had left him, presumably for the Jag driver he had seen her with yesterday. He must be so hurt and he had sought comfort in Clare's arms. But might Clare end up hurting him even more? He didn't seem like the one-night stand kind of guy.

She slid back down on the pillow and tried to sleep. She would worry about facing him in the morning. And then she remembered his shirt, still lying on the kitchen work surface.

She slipped out of bed and, pulling a dressing gown round herself, she stole downstairs to put it on a wash-and-dry cycle. Benjy wandered sleepily from his bed, his tail attempting to wag, and she led him back before climbing the stairs again, wearier than ever from the wine. A glance at her bedside clock told her she had only a few hours until she had to be up. She drank a glass of water in the faint hope of warding off a hangover then climbed back into bed beside the sleeping DCI.

When the alarm sounded just before five she wakened with a start. She silenced it quickly and crept out of bed. With one eye on the DCI she opened the wardrobe door quietly and took out a fresh set of clothes. She carried these through to the bathroom, setting them down as she waited for the shower to run warm. Last night had been one thing but she wasn't sure how she felt about dressing in front of DCI Alastair Gibson. Not when she was sober with a thumping headache, to boot.

When she returned to the bedroom he was switching off his phone alarm. He blinked a couple of times, as if trying to focus. 'You're dressed,' he said.

Clare stood awkwardly in the doorway, holding out a towel. 'I – er – I thought I'd get dressed and give you some space…' She tailed off, not knowing what else to say. She had no idea how to behave towards her boss the morning after sleeping with him. 'The – er – bathroom's down the hall. Shower's easy enough. Just turn the knob.' She gave him a smile and made to leave. 'I'll put coffee on.'

'Clare—' he said, but she was already running downstairs.

Over coffee and muesli he tried again. 'Clare, I hope you don't think I took advantage last night. The sob story about the Jag, my birthday. It wasn't my intention…'

She shook her head, not meeting his eye. 'Of course not, Al. We're both adults. We got drunk and then – well, we got carried away.'

He eyed her. 'I wasn't that drunk.'

Clare felt her cheeks flush. She was trying to ignore a voice in her head telling her she hadn't been that drunk either. She sipped her coffee, casting around for the right thing to say. 'Al – I – well, Geoffrey and I – I'm just not sure where we are…'

He put a hand across the table, covering hers. 'Clare, it's fine. I mean, I really enjoyed last night. All of it. I enjoyed your company, not just the sex.'

She bridled at the word and it didn't escape his notice.

'But, if you're not comfortable with – with what happened – well that's fine. I won't mention it again.' He picked up her hand and put it to his lips. 'But I *did* enjoy it.' He smiled and Clare saw those blue eyes again.

She let him kiss her hand then, gently, she withdrew it. A sudden image of them falling into bed the previous night flashed across her mind and she closed her eyes as she relived it. His hands beneath her sweatshirt, her hands loosening his belt; and, despite the lack of sleep, the earliness of the hour, she found she wanted him all over again.

But that couldn't happen and she opened her eyes, forcing the memory to the back of her mind. There was Geoff to consider after all, and Al Gibson was her boss. 'Al...' she began.

He put down his coffee. 'Yes?'

'Work – I mean, it might be awkward.'

He smiled. 'Clare, let's not get ahead of ourselves. We had a great time. Bloody brilliant, actually. And, yes, I would like to see you again. But I'm realistic enough to know you still have unfinished business with Geoffrey. I do know that. And work, well – we're both professionals. I think we can manage that. Don't you?'

Clare smiled back, wishing she shared his confidence. He made it sound so easy so why didn't it feel like it? Not knowing what else to say, she rose from the table. 'I'll get your shirt.' She moved into the kitchen and clicked open the washing machine. Carrying the shirt over to the kitchen window, she inspected it. 'I think it's nearly gone,' she called. 'It's a bit crumpled though. I could run the iron over it if you...' And suddenly she realised he was behind her. Standing so close she could smell her own shower gel on him. She closed her eyes, her head still thick from the wine. He took the shirt from her and folded it roughly.

'It's fine, Clare. I always have a spare in the boot of the car.'

She stood for a moment, looking at him as he moved about the room, collecting his shoes, jacket, wallet.

'I'll head across to the flat,' he said, perching on the arm of the sofa to lace his shoes. 'Just check everything's okay then I'll go back home. You're going to the trial?'

She nodded. 'I'll follow you over to the flat once I've cleared up here. I'll wait for them to leave then I'll travel behind Tamsin's convoy.'

164

'Let me know how she gets on,' he said, heading for the door. He hesitated as he reached it and seemed to be struggling for the right words. Then he said, 'Clare, thank you. For last night. For putting up with me. I really didn't mean to take advantage…'

She smiled. 'Of course not, Al. We're both adults. And I did enjoy it.' She took his hand in hers. 'I really did. I'm just not sure it's the right time – for either of us.'

He returned the smile. 'Maybe not.' And, with that, he opened the door and went out into the cool May morning.

Wendy and a clearly anxious Tamsin were waiting when Clare arrived just after six.

'We've had tears and tantrums already,' Wendy said, her voice low as she led Clare up the stairs. 'She's in a bit of a state.'

Clare put a hand to her head and rubbed her temple. 'She's still going to testify though?'

Wendy nodded. 'Yeah, I calmed her down. Then the DCI appeared and he was really good with her.' She glanced over her shoulder, then said, 'Matter of fact, I reckon he's at the capers. Judging by his appearance, he didn't go home last night.'

'Oh?' Clare tried to keep her tone light.

'Hadn't shaved and he looked as if he hadn't slept much either.' Wendy raised an eyebrow.

'Well, well,' Clare said, hoping she wasn't giving herself away. She followed Wendy into the flat and forced a smile for Tamsin's benefit. 'So, anything else I should know?'

'That blue van's been past a couple of times,' Wendy said. 'One of our lads made to approach it and it roared off. They radioed for another car to block the street off at one end in case it appeared again.'

'And did it?'

'Yes but it headed down Church Street this time.'

Clare moved to the window and pulled the blinds open just enough to look out. 'When was this?'

'Half five then again at ten to six.'

'Dammit. I must have just missed them. Did you see the occupants?'

'Yeah,' Wendy said. 'A big lad in front – bald head. Could be Paddy but it's hard to tell, looking down at a windscreen. There was a blonde woman next to him. White-blonde, from what I could see. Cropped hair. Maybe wearing something red.'

Clare looked at Tamsin. 'Does that ring a bell? The blonde woman?'

Tamsin nodded, her face lined with worry. 'Sounds like Paddy's sister, Rose.'

'Rose Grant?'

'I think so.'

'Does she have previous, Tamsin?'

Tamsin shook her head. 'No. She's too clever for that. Always managed to keep her nose clean, that one.' She shivered. 'But you wouldn't mess with Rose. If she's coming after me...'

'Okay, Tamsin. Now you listen to me: Paddy and Rose – they're just trying to scare you. But we'll keep you safe. Trust us on that, Tamsin. There's no way Paddy Grant can get to you.'

Tamsin shrugged. 'Maybe not today but what about after? After the trial?' Her voice shook and Clare saw she was clasping her hands to stop them shaking.

Clare went to sit down beside her. 'From what I can gather, you'll be given a new identity. A new life, away from here. No one will know where you are or even who you are.'

Tamsin didn't look convinced but she said no more.

'Time for a cuppa,' Wendy said, flicking the switch on the kettle. 'Tea or coffee?'

'Tea for me,' Clare said.

Tamsin waved this away. 'Cannae face anything.'

While Wendy dunked a teabag in each mug, Clare moved to the window again to peep out. As she looked, she saw Chris's red Golf GTi draw into the street and park opposite. 'Chris is here,' she said, checking her watch. She glanced at Wendy. 'Better drink up.'

Minutes later a Volvo saloon with the blue and yellow Police Scotland markings pulled into the street, the lightbar on the roof flashing. It drew into the kerb outside the flat and the lights were switched off.

'Ready?' Clare asked. Wendy nodded, picked up Tamsin's coat and pulled it on. Tucking her own hair inside, she put the hood up and headed down the stairs to the front door. Clare, watching from the window, saw a uniformed officer jump out of the car and hold open a door for Wendy who did her best to copy Tamsin's gait. The officer closed the door behind her, jumped into the passenger seat and the car roared away, siren blaring and lightbar flashing. Seconds later Chris pulled out and headed off in the same direction as the marked car.

Clare took out her phone and dialled Chris's number. 'Keep a fair bit back,' she told him. 'If they lose you they'll slow down till you catch up.'

'I have tailed a car before, you know,' Chris's voice said.

'And let me know the minute you get eyes on that blue van.'

'Wilco, Inspector.'

Clare ended the call and gave Tamsin a smile.

'You really think this will work?' Tamsin asked.

'Should do. If Paddy is tailing the car Chris should spot him soon.'

While they waited in the flat for another car, Clare helped Tamsin into a Kevlar vest.

'Is this really needed?' she asked.

'Probably not,' Clare said, hoping she sounded more confident than she felt. 'The chances of someone trying to reach you are so slim. But just knowing that you're wearing it can help. It's got me through many a sticky moment.'

Tamsin looked doubtful but she said nothing more as Clare checked the fastenings on the vest.

'Comfy?'

Tamsin did a few experimental moves with her arms. 'Suppose. How long do I have to keep it on?'

'Just till you're back here.'

'Christ. The whole day?'

'Afraid so.'

Clare took up position by the window. It was still early and, other than a couple of delivery men unloading cages from lorries, there were few cars around. Certainly no sign of a blue Transit van. After fifteen minutes of this vigil she saw another car pull up outside. A dark grey saloon, this time with no visible markings.

'We'll wait for the motorcycles,' Clare said. 'Then we'll get you out and into the car.'

Clare's phone began to buzz and she clicked to take the call. 'Chris?'

'Blue van appeared on cue. It just overtook me and cut in front. Had to slam on the anchors.'

'He's making no secret of it, then,' Clare said. 'Stick on his tail, Chris.'

She hung up the call and went to check the window again. The motorcycle outriders had just arrived. 'That's them here. Ready?'

Tamsin forced a smile. 'As I'll ever be.'

Clare led her down the stairs and, again, as she opened the door to the street, a plain-clothes officer jumped out of the car. Tamsin was stowed in the back within seconds and the first motorcycle moved ahead of the car and began riding along the cobbled street. It had been agreed that the car would take a different route from the decoy vehicle Chris was tailing. It was more circuitous and would take a bit longer. But, by the time Paddy Grant – or whoever was working for him – realised they were following the wrong car, it would be too late for him to catch them. Clare closed the door of the flat and headed for her own car. She passed a cafe advertising breakfasts and told herself there was no particular need for her to tail Tamsin's car. She had plenty of time. It had been a difficult start to the day and now she could feel the headache spreading round the back of her neck. She pushed open the cafe door and took a seat.

–

The cafe was empty, except for a young woman tapping away at an iPad and a couple of men in fluorescent jackets waiting for an order of filled rolls. The smell of bacon frying wrapped itself round Clare's heart and she ordered a full breakfast with tea. When it arrived she realised how hungry she was and she attacked it with relish. The carbs and fat did the trick and she began to feel more like herself. As she ate she thought about Tamsin – probably approaching the court buildings around now. How would she be feeling, as she prepared to give evidence against her husband? Would she have the courage to go through with it? To stand up in court and tell what she knew? Or would she bottle it? Clare knew how much the DCI was depending on Tamsin's testimony and she really hoped Tamsin wouldn't let him down. Keeping her safe had been an expensive exercise and, if Phil Quinn walked free, there would be hell to pay.

She was just mopping the remains of a runny egg off the plate with a slice of toast when Chris phoned again.

'He's gone, Clare.'

'You lost him?'

'Afraid so. We pulled off into the Newbridge Retail Park in Glenrothes and sat in the car for a few minutes. He hovered around the entrance then roared away. I went after him but he lost me.'

'Dammit.'

'But it's fine. I radioed the car Tamsin's in and they're on the Queensferry Crossing over the Forth now. They should be at the High Court in less than forty minutes. He'll never make it there before Tamsin.'

Clare ended the call and sent a brief text to the DCI letting him know Tamsin should arrive at the court in plenty of time. Then she looked at her watch. It was almost eight. She'd better get away herself. She rose from the table, paid for her breakfast and headed back to her car.

Chapter 21

By the time she approached the traffic backing up to cross the Queensferry Bridge, Clare had been on the road for an hour. She knew she should have left earlier and now she'd be stuck in this jam for another half hour at least. She switched on the radio, flicking through the stations until she found Radio Scotland. The morning news programme was running a feature on NHS waiting lists and Clare listened to the discussion, glad of the distraction. She checked her rear-view mirror and saw a BMW coming up the inside, signalling to move into Clare's lane. With one eye on the mirror, she saw the car behind edge forward to stop the BMW moving in. 'Get a grip,' she muttered, hanging back to leave a space in front of her. The driver pulled in, giving her a wave of thanks.

She had zoned out of the radio and when she began to listen again the presenters were discussing Phil Quinn's trial. Clare didn't want to hear it. She didn't want to think about the possibility that Phil Quinn might be found not guilty. What would happen to Tamsin then? And the DCI? He would be crushed. All his work and all the resources ploughed into the trial. In his present state of mind it would probably finish him. She flicked through the channels again until she found a station playing music.

Gradually the traffic edged along until, finally, she drove onto the bridge, its white fan-like cables gleaming in the morning sun. Glancing to her left, through the wind shields that kept the bridge open in even the strongest gales, she could see the tall suspension towers of the original road bridge, now reserved for buses and taxis. Beyond this stood the iconic cantilever rail bridge, with its famous red-oxide girders. Fifty metres below, the Forth was dotted with river traffic, sailing to and from the busy port of Rosyth, some two miles west of the bridges.

She cruised over the bridge then hit traffic again, making slow progress towards the city. She arrived in Edinburgh just after nine forty but there was still plenty of time. Tamsin wouldn't be on the stand much before eleven. More than enough time to park and walk to the Lawnmarket, home to the High Court buildings. As she weaved her way through the streets towards the eye-wateringly expensive Castle Terrace car park she mulled over Tamsin's appearance in court. She had declined the offer to give evidence by video link. Clare had pointed out that seeing Phil, her husband, in the dock might prompt a sudden rush of sympathy – fear, even – and that could affect her testimony. She had considered this and, in the end, agreed to give evidence in open court but screened from Phil's view.

'I'm not ashamed of speaking out against him,' she had said with a rare display of courage. 'He's gone too far now and he needs to be stopped.'

Clare turned into Castle Terrace and the stone edifice of Edinburgh Castle came into view, set high above the city on impenetrable rock. She pulled into the NCP car park at the top level and saw a car moving out of a space.

She locked the car and decided to walk along Castle Terrace, turning left to skirt round the high stone walls to the rear of the castle. As usual the parking bays in Johnston

Terrace were filled with tour buses and she walked past these quickly, admiring the elevated view south across the city. As the road curved up to the left she could hear the sound of traffic rumbling up and down the cobbled Lawnmarket. A steady stream of tourists was strolling between the castle and the souvenir shops that lined the street, and the strains of a piper playing a rousing reel were carried on the wind. So busy was the street that the tourists had spilled off the pavements and were ambling along the road, stepping aside for only the sharpest of toots from an impatient driver. Clare hurried along, dodging off the pavements to pass groups of shoppers collected round revolving stands of postcards and *See You Jimmy* tartan hats. Further down the road the pavements became wider, and she passed the historic Deacon Brodie's Tavern, named after the notorious eighteenth-century housebreaker. She was close to St Giles' Cathedral now, its gothic frontage standing tall and dark against the multi-coloured tide of humanity strolling past. Beyond St Giles, the Lawnmarket became the High Street, part of the succession of streets through the old town known collectively as *the Royal Mile*. She stood for a minute, watching the throng, then turned away from the cathedral and took out her phone. She sent a text message to one of the officers who had accompanied Tamsin to check she had arrived safely and received a brief reply that she had.

As she was not a witness for this trial, Clare entered the High Court building by the public door and found the court number for Phil Quinn's case. It was after ten now and it was likely the court was already in session. She entered the court room quietly and took a seat at the back of the public benches, slipping along to the far corner so she could observe the whole room. The area set aside for the Press was crammed with reporters, a reflection of the media interest in this high-profile trial, but there were a few members of the public too, watching the proceedings. Clare studied them, wondering if they had some reason for attending this particular trial. Was it just somewhere to go, or had they heard of Phil Quinn's reputation? Having spent many tedious hours sitting in court buildings waiting to give evidence, Clare couldn't imagine attending a trial unless she was compelled to. Court room proceedings, in her experience, moved at a snail's pace and certainly lacked the excitement found in TV dramas. But this trial had hit the headlines, particularly when it had become known that the accused's wife was a witness for the prosecution. And the prospect of closing down one of the largest arms operations Scotland had ever seen was one which had excited both the Press and public.

The atmosphere in the room was electric. Even the jury, several days into the trial, were paying close attention to the proceedings. An advocate was on his feet now questioning a witness Clare didn't recognise about the vehicles Phil Quinn owned. The door opened again and an elderly couple appeared. They hesitated, as if uncertain of their surroundings then, seeing Clare, they moved along the row, sitting in the centre, almost opposite the judge. Clare appraised them and decided they didn't look like associates of Phil Quinn. Probably just in for a nose around. She turned her attention back to the proceedings and studied the jurors. So important in a case like this. They were a mixed bunch – some young, others old. Hopefully they would recognise that the evidence against the accused was damning and return a swift guilty verdict. And then her eye fell on the man himself. He was clean-shaven, with a receding hairline and a sharp, chiselled face. His skin was tanned, the same leathery complexion as his wife. Clare had heard they had a property in Marbella and she wondered if the *Proceeds of Crime* team would be able to get their hands on it.

He was neatly attired in a grey suit with a faint stripe running through it. His shirt was pale pink, his tie mauve. Clare would have bet his socks were mauve too and his brogues brown. There was a glint from his tie that she thought must be a tip clip but he was facing slightly away from her, making it difficult to see. She reckoned he was probably wearing cufflinks as well. *How the gangsters love to dress up.*

Suddenly the witness was stepping down and a room divider was brought in. Clare found her palms were damp and she wiped them against her trouser legs. It took only a minute for the screen to be put in place then the door that led to the witness rooms opened again and Tamsin Quinn walked slowly into the court.

Months of work, hundreds of man hours, a network of undercover cops, and it all hinged on this nervous-looking woman. If Tamsin lost her nerve, if Phil Quinn's advocate managed to get under her skin and convince the jury she was an unreliable witness, then it would all have been for nothing. All the resources ploughed into this case would have been wasted. Clare held her breath as she watched Tamsin's progress through the court.

Tamsin stopped briefly, as if to orientate herself, then took her place in the witness box. Clare was glad to see she was still wearing the Kevlar vest. Not that it was likely anyone could smuggle a weapon into court but better safe than sorry.

Tamsin glanced at the screen, no doubt conscious that Phil was on the other side of it, then she stared straight ahead to take her oath. As she began to speak, Clare heard a door open. Her eyes were trained on Tamsin but she was aware of someone sitting down at the far end of the public benches, near to the door. As Tamsin swore to tell the truth, the whole truth and nothing but the truth, Clare glanced across at the newcomer and it was all she could do not to react. She was suddenly aware of her own heart thumping in her chest.

Tamsin had finished taking the oath now and she too had turned, her gaze fixed on the visitor. The woman, dressed in a red leather jacket, cut a distinctive figure in the otherwise sober surroundings. She was looking straight back at Tamsin and Clare watched in horror as the woman – very slowly – shook her head. The message was clear. Tamsin was being warned off. Clare saw the colour drain from Tamsin's face. The advocate was on his feet now, addressing her, but Tamsin's gaze was locked on the woman, and her white-blonde cropped hair.

For a moment Clare felt paralysed. She knew there was nothing she could do as long as they were in the court room but, if the blonde left, Clare would follow her out. She glanced back at Tamsin who was now attending to her advocate. She was listening to a question about her twenty-year-long marriage but her eye kept wandering back to the blonde. Was it Rose Quinn, Clare wondered? Paddy's sister? It had to be. That hair was too distinctive to be a coincidence. She took out her phone to send a text to the cop who had accompanied Tamsin into the court building.

> Possible associate of Paddy Grant in public gallery
> Trying to psych out Tamsin

Get to the door and stop her when she leaves
White-blonde hair, red leather jacket

As Clare clicked to send the message she realised the blonde was on her feet and heading for the door. Clare rose to follow her but the elderly couple were in her way. By the time she wriggled past and reached the door, the blonde was out of sight. She saw the cop she had texted standing a little way off, poring over his phone. Her message, no doubt.

'Did you see a blonde woman just now?' she shouted.

The cop shrugged and Clare ran for the front door. She emerged into the Lawnmarket, looking all round for the woman. And then she spotted the jacket, distinctive against the grey stone of her surroundings. The blonde was heading down the High Street, past St Giles now, towards a blue Transit van which was parked just beyond the distinctive arched entrance to the City Chambers. Clare could see fumes coming out of the exhaust and she realised the engine was running. She sprinted for the van as she saw the blonde dash round to the passenger door. Seconds later it roared away with a fresh plume of blue exhaust smoke. As Clare reached the City Chambers she screwed up her eyes in an effort to see the registration number but the van was moving too quickly. She stood to catch her breath, near the bronze statue of Adam Smith, the Scottish economist, and watched the Transit as it swung left onto North Bridge.

'Dammit,' she said out loud. 'Dammit to hell!'

She took out her phone to call Chris.

He answered within two rings. 'Oh, hi, Clare. You calling about the bank statements? I've got some interesting—'

'Chris, just listen: I want Wendy back at that flat on Market Street. Send a couple of cops in with her to make sure there's no one inside. And I want you to check that the guys doing the surveillance are still in situ. If not, get them back pronto.'

'Sounds serious, Clare. What's up?'

'Paddy Grant's sister appeared in the court room just as Tamsin was about to start giving evidence. Trying to warn her off.'

Chris gave a low whistle. 'They're not giving up without a fight, are they?'

'Nor am I.' Clare's tone was grim. 'Don't suppose you got the Transit's number this morning?'

'Yeah, picked it up on the dashcam. It's the same number you saw on Sunday.'

'That's something at least. Chris, can you check ANPR cameras from Edinburgh north please? See if they've headed back into Fife. Those two are dangerous and I want them under lock and key.'

'I'll get on it now.'

Clare ended the call and took a moment to control her breathing then she headed back into the court room, subjecting herself once more to the security rigmarole.

Tamsin looked across as Clare re-entered the court room and Clare shot her what she hoped was a reassuring smile. Tamsin held her gaze for a minute and the advocate turned to see what was distracting his client. Clare sat down quickly and the questioning resumed. From the answers Tamsin was giving, it seemed that the blonde's appearance hadn't been enough to scare her off. As Clare listened to the testimony, she could see why the DCI was so keen not to lose her as a witness.

In response to a direct question, Tamsin said that she had seen her husband handling handguns, rifles, stun guns and tear gas canisters. She identified photos of the weapons, confirming that they had been taken in her house. But when the advocate pressed her on her decision to give evidence she didn't immediately answer. Instead, she picked up a plastic cup of water and drank from it. She shot a sideways glance at the partition that separated her from her husband then she put the cup down and faced her advocate once more. 'I mean guns and that – well I thought it was just gangsters shooting each other. Saves the police a job, ye know? But then one night I heard him talking to Paddy…'

'That's Patrick Grant?' the advocate asked.

'That's right. Paddy works for Phil. Does all the organising and that.'

'So you overheard a conversation between the defendant and Paddy Grant?'

'Aye. Phil – he was saying *what the fuck was Paddy playing at?* And Paddy – he said he just did the deals. He didn't ask questions.'

Clare sat forward in her seat. This was the moment they had all been waiting for. Her heart was thumping so loudly she wondered if the elderly couple further along could hear it.

'And what did you take him to mean by that?' the advocate said.

Tamsin picked up the plastic cup of water and drank again. 'It was that case in Edinburgh. The family that was murdered.'

'You mean the Cleary case?'

'Aye.'

Clare remembered the Cleary case well. They all did. Brian and Elaine Cleary, gunned down in their own home. A dreadful case of mistaken identity. Gunmen had forced their way into the house, early one Sunday morning while the family slept upstairs. Brian must have heard the sound of the door being forced because they found him, shot dead at the top of the stairs. The youngest of the children, Ellie, had come out of her room and been caught in the crossfire. She was lying beside her father, a toy elephant still clutched in her hand. Then, the gunmen calmly ascended the stairs and forced their way into the twins' room where Elaine had attempted to barricade herself with the other children. Clare closed her eyes for a moment, reliving the photos. Those dreadful images of the crime scene. The bloodstained boot marks on the bedroom carpet, the bodies of Elaine and the twins, their Star Wars pyjamas dark-stained. One of the twins had fallen, his arms still round his mother, as if trying to shield her.

'Tamsin,' the advocate went on, 'can you please tell the court what the defendant meant by that remark?'

Tamsin took a couple of breaths in and out then she said, 'Phil imports the guns. Gets them through the Netherlands, mostly. Sometimes to order – if somebody wants guns for a job, ye know? But he always keeps a stash – for short-notice orders.' She paused to drink again, then ran her tongue round her lips. 'Paddy – sometimes he comes to Phil and says he has a client needing a few guns.'

'And this was such a case?'

'Aye. Paddy told Phil a couple of lads had asked him for guns. Just for a warning. Somebody owed them and they wanted paid. Said the guns would put the frighteners on them.'

'And did the defendant oblige?'

'Aye. Phil gave Paddy the guns and told him to sort it out. He said Paddy was to make sure he was paid up front and take a cut before giving Phil the rest.'

The jury were paying close attention now, and no wonder, Clare thought. It was compelling evidence and she found it hard to believe they wouldn't convict Phil Quinn – if they believed Tamsin, of course.

'And these guns – can you tell the court what they were used for?'

'The Cleary family.'

The advocate paused to let this sink in. Then he went on. 'You are saying the guns supplied by the defendant to his employee, Mr Patrick Grant, were then passed on to the men who gunned down and killed the Cleary family? Mr Brian Cleary, Mrs Elaine Cleary and their three children?'

'That's exactly what I'm saying.'

'But of course,' the advocate went on, 'it was a case of mistaken identity, was it not? The Clearys did not owe these men any money.'

'Aye.'

'And what was the defendant's reaction on hearing this?'

'He asked Paddy if the guns had been wiped clean before he gave them to the killers.'

Clare saw one of the jurors put her hand to her mouth. Another was looking down at the floor.

'And why do you think he asked that?'

'So they couldn't be traced back to us. Paddy said they were clean and not to worry. So Phil told Paddy to keep his head down for a bit and to make sure it never happened again.'

'The defendant didn't show any remorse? Or talk about giving the killers up to the police?'

Tamsin shook her head. 'No way. Phil would never do that.'

'And what did you think, Tamsin?'

There was a pause then Tamsin began to speak, slowly at first. 'I – that family – those wee ones. I suddenly made the connection – between the money we had and them lying dead, gunned down in their own house.' She turned to look at the partition that separated her from her husband. 'They didn't deserve it. None of them.'

Chapter 22

The court broke for lunch and Clare sought Tamsin out. She was safely ensconced in a room to the rear of the court building with two officers in attendance. She was regarding a packet of tuna sandwiches without enthusiasm when Clare entered.

'You did so well, Tamsin,' Clare said, sitting down beside her. 'Really well.'

'You think?' She seemed deflated and Clare hastened to reassure her.

'Definitely. You could have heard a pin drop in that court room. And I can tell you it's rarely like that. You made a real impression.'

She shrugged. 'Well, either way, it's done now. God knows what Phil will do if he gets off. I'll probably be dead in a ditch by the end of the week.'

Clare took Tamsin's hand in hers. 'That's not going to happen, Tamsin. After your testimony, I'll be amazed if he gets off. But, if he does, we'll look after you. New identity, new location and, wherever you go, the cops will only be a phone call away.'

'Aye, maybe.' She picked up the pack of sandwiches and began to peel off the plastic seal.

'About this morning…'

Tamsin looked up. 'What about it?'

'That woman who came into court just as you were about to start giving evidence. A blonde, in a red leather jacket.'

'Aye.'

'It was Rose, wasn't it?'

Tamsin sighed and put the sandwich box down again. 'Yeah. That's her.'

'She was trying to warn you off giving evidence, wasn't she?'

'She was. But, by that time – well, I was there, wasn't I? I mean I've burned my bridges with Phil now anyway. So I thought I might as well get on with it. Tell them what I knew.'

'That was very brave, Tamsin. Very brave indeed.'

Tamsin shrugged again. 'I just hope it's enough.'

–

Clare left Tamsin to her unappetising sandwiches and took the chance to wander down the Royal Mile. Her eyes were everywhere, looking for the blue van and its occupants, but they were nowhere to be seen. Tamsin's evidence for the Crown had been completed by lunchtime and she would face Phil Quinn's defence advocate in the afternoon. And then, with luck, it would be over. Clare fervently hoped the questioning would be completed today. She didn't fancy having to bring Tamsin back to the High Court again tomorrow with a repeat of the security arrangements today's journey had entailed. The sun was high in the sky and she elected to sit at a table outside a small cafe. She ordered a sandwich and a coffee which the smiling waiter said he would bring out. While she waited she tapped a message to the DCI.

Tamsin's evidence good so far.
Looks like Paddy Grant's sister turned up
in court trying to scare her but she went
through with it.
Defence this afternoon.
Should have her back in St A's this evening.
I've sent Chris and a couple of cops to check
the flat is ok.

She hesitated before pressing Send, wondering if she should add a personal message, then decided against it. This was work, after all. She sent the message then, a few minutes later, received a *Thanks* in reply. Thanks? Was that it? Maybe he was in the middle of something…

The sandwich and coffee arrived and she bit into it, realising how long it had been since that breakfast in St Andrews. As she chewed, she clicked to call Chris. It went to voicemail and, as she was preparing to leave a message, he cut in to answer the call.

'Hi Chris,' she said, her mouth still full of sandwich. 'What's new?'

'Your Transit van,' he said. 'Pinged a camera on the M90 but it left at the St Andrews junction and it's not been seen since. Probably keeping to the back roads.'

'Okay, thanks Chris. Just make sure that flat is still safe.'

'Yeah, on it. I still can't believe she's been there since Friday and you only told me last night.'

Clare hesitated. She had taken a risk telling Chris about Tamsin but she knew she still couldn't tell him there was a possible leak. 'Wasn't my decision,' she fibbed. 'Anyway, never mind about that just now. Any luck with those bank statements?'

'No warrant yet for Marek but we have the statements for Johannes's other accounts – the cards Gary and Nita found beneath the carpet and it's more of the same.'

'Right. I'll be back by teatime and we'll chat then. No sign of Marek yet?'

'Nothing.'

'Okay – get back on to the press officer and get another statement out. Let's say we're concerned for his safety. If he is out there and watching the news, that might make him more likely to come in.'

'Unless he is the killer.'

'There is that.'

–

The defence advocate's strategy was little more than an attempt to question Tamsin's integrity and the state of her marriage. She fielded the questions well, Clare thought, insisting that her marriage had been sound until the Cleary murders.

'Like I said, that was out of order. Decent family like that. But Phil – well, he said he'd sell guns to anyone. That he'd told Paddy not to be so fucking stupid in the future and it was all sorted now. Only, it didn't feel sorted to me and I knew I had to do something.' She straightened her back and glanced at the partition again. 'Some things are more important than a marriage.'

–

By half past three it was all done. Clare breathed a sigh of relief as she handed Tamsin over to the armed officers for the journey back to St Andrews. Chris had confirmed there was no sign of suspicious activity at the flat and that Wendy would be waiting to see Tamsin in safely.

'The Serious Crime guys are outside again. Different vehicle this time – a dark red Range Rover.'

Clare ended the call and made her way back to the car park. She was soon on her way out of the city and heading for the bridge. She was early enough to miss the worst of the teatime traffic and, before long, she saw the three towers of the Queensferry Crossing once more. As she drove onto the bridge she flicked the radio on and found herself singing along to Lady Gaga. She felt lighter now, with Tamsin's court appearance out of the way. All they had to do was to keep her safe for the next couple of days, until the verdict was returned. After that it would be over to the Serious Organised Crime lot to arrange her new identity and new life. She began to appreciate just how much of her waking hours Tamsin had consumed. She really should have been concentrating on Johannes's murder and she definitely hadn't given it the attention it deserved. That he deserved.

She looked at the car clock. Just after four. There would be time to go through Marek's bank statements with Chris. She set the cruise control to sixty and took her foot off the accelerator, allowing the Merc to coast back towards St Andrews.

Chapter 23

'Look at last month, for a start,' Chris said, moving the bank printouts across the desk for Clare to see. He pointed to the first statement. 'On the fourth of April he pays in £350 and…' he moved the next statement into view, '…on the same day he pays £250 into a different account.' He fished out another statement and indicated a transaction. 'See?'

'Let me guess,' Clare said. 'He pays money into all five accounts on the same day?'

'Nearly.' Chris pulled the other three account statements across the desk. 'See, in this one he does it on the third and the other two are on the fifth.'

'How much in total?'

'A thousand pounds.'

Clare scanned the statements. 'And then? Save me working it out, Chris. It's been a long day.'

'Take your pick. Some of it he transfers to other people—'

'Have you tracked down the recipients?'

He shook his head. 'No such luck. Abroad, mainly. Then there's one payment to a business in Delaware. Another to the Netherlands. Some of it he uses to buy stuff.'

'From?'

'Some from eBay, others I don't recognise.'

'Think it's legit?'

'I'm not sure. Judging by the number of transactions, I'd say no. But I can't see what he's bought – only the amounts – so I can't be certain.'

Clare yawned. After her sleepless night and early start she was fast running out of energy. 'So, of that thousand pounds paid in around the fourth of April, how much does he pay out?'

'Across all five accounts, nine-hundred-and-fifty altogether.'

'So he keeps fifty?'

'Yep.'

Clare leafed through the statements, scanning them. 'And he repeats this?'

'He does. Pretty much every ten days or so, although it varies from seven days to as many as eighteen. At least as far back as I've gone.'

'Which is?'

'January. It's enough to be sure there's a pattern.'

'Is it always a thousand pounds?'

'No. Sometimes a bit less, other times more. But always spreading it around the five accounts, I'm guessing to avoid raising suspicion with the banks.'

Clare sat back. 'And he always keeps back the same amount?'

'Five per cent, give or take.'

'So Johannes was a money mule.'

'Looks like it.'

Clare pondered this. 'Would the banks not have picked it up?'

'Maybe. But, from what I can see, he's been quite smart about it – no regular pattern – sometimes the money sits in his account for a week or two. One month he was withdrawing it fifty or a hundred at a time.' Chris leafed through the statements as he spoke. 'He's been pretty smart about it, Clare. It's well planned. There is a pattern but you have to look hard to find it.'

'Hmm. I wonder if we should call someone in. Someone with a bit of experience of this kind of thing.'

Chris nodded. 'Yeah, I think so. I've a mate over in Dundee – at Bell Street station. Specialises in fraud cases. I spoke to her earlier and she said more and more students are being tricked or persuaded into money laundering. I can ask her to come across, if you like?'

Clare rose, scraping her chair back. 'If you would, Chris.' She yawned again. 'I have to go home. I'm absolutely bushed.'

'Late night was it?'

She felt her cheeks redden. 'What makes you say that?'

'Calm down. I'm only asking. You've been yawning your head off, that's all.'

Clare avoided his eye. 'If you could call your friend in Dundee – it'd be good to talk to her tomorrow.'

As she went to get her coat from her office, Chris called, 'Oh, I forgot to say – I gave Johannes's laptop to Diane today. Thought she might be able to download the data for us.'

Clare stopped in her tracks. 'You were down at Glenrothes? At Tech Support?'

'No, actually. Diane was here when I got back from the decoy run.'

Clare made an effort to keep her voice level. 'Did she say what she wanted?'

'She had some new guy with her – Craig. Didn't catch his last name. I think she wanted to introduce him. Show him round – that sort of thing.'

Craig Thomson. Diane's new colleague. The one from Gartcosh who was shit hot at anything that came his way.

'What's he like?'

'Oh, usual techy guy, I suppose. Jeans, trainers, some band T-shirt. Nice enough. Seemed pretty interested in the set-up here.'

Clare wondered about that. 'Were they looking at anything in particular?'

Chris shrugged. 'Don't think so. I asked if he was something to do with this new communications system – the one Gayle whatshername's working on.'

Clare tried to keep her tone light. 'And is he?'

'Nope. Neither of them seemed to know much about it. They were both pretty interested, though.' His forehead creased. 'Call me paranoid, Clare, but does that not strike you as a bit odd? A new comms system and IT Services know nothing about it?'

Clare hesitated. She knew Chris wasn't the source of the leak. She didn't need Gayle Crichton to tell her that. She knew she could trust him. But could she rely on him not to give the game away if she did take him into her confidence?

He saw her hesitate. 'You know something, Clare. Don't you? Fucksake – don't you trust me?'

'Chris, I—' She broke off when the station door opened and Sara came in with a drunk in tow. She smiled. 'It'll keep.' And, leaving Chris to his suspicions, she walked briskly out of the station into the cool May evening.

–

As Clare drove home she mulled over Diane and Craig's visit. Could it be Diane suspected something? Or was it

Craig who had engineered the visit? Was there more to him than met the eye? Why would a young guy as skilled as Craig want to move from the very heart of things at Gartcosh to a small Tech Support office in Glenrothes? Could it actually be true that he wanted more time to spend developing computer games? Or resurrecting a relationship with some girl? Clare thought she would very much like to meet Craig to form her own opinion.

Or was she being too suspicious? Was Diane really hoping to catch Clare for a chat? She had seemed so down at the parkrun, talking about her mum. Maybe she just needed to talk. See a friendly face. Since her mother's dementia had worsened, Diane had aged ten years before Clare's eyes. 'Maybe I'll go down to her parkrun this weekend,' she said, out loud, as she turned the car onto the Craigtoun Road. And then she remembered she couldn't. She would be babysitting her nephew. It would have to be the weekend after. She decided to give Diane a call anyway, just for a chat. Surely Gayle couldn't object to that. 'And to hell with her if she does,' she said, slowing down as she approached Daisy Cottage.

She pulled into the drive and jumped out of the Merc. Benjy was barking behind the door and she opened it to let him out. In the kitchen, she went to the fridge to see what she could heat up quickly and saw the remains of the curry. That made her think of last night and of Al Gibson. What on earth had they done? She would hate things to be awkward between them, particularly as they had seemed to be getting on better, of late. She picked up her phone to send him a text. But what to say? Did she want to see him again – out of work? Admittedly she'd enjoyed his company last night and the sex had been surprisingly good too. Alcohol-fuelled no doubt but it had been exactly what they had both needed. Was it something she wanted to do again? Maybe. She was mentally composing a noncommittal message when her phone buzzed. She half expected to see it was him. Having the same thoughts as she was. Maybe suggesting dinner – at that steak barn they had passed on Friday, perhaps. She flipped open the cover and saw an unrecognised number. Then her heart sank as she read the message.

> On my way
> See you soon,
> Gayle x
> PS bringing a bottle!

Clare groaned. Between her fling with the DCI and trying to keep Tamsin safe to give evidence, then going over those bank statements with Chris, all on barely a few hours' sleep, she had completely forgotten about inviting Gayle over. What the hell was she going to feed her? She sent back a quick *See You Soon* and returned to the fridge. There was quite a lot of curry. Not enough for a meal on its own but if she baked some potatoes and opened a bag of salad…

She began stabbing potatoes with a fork then she coated them with olive oil and sprinkled the skins with chilli flakes. She shoved these into the oven, turning the dial up to the max and began spooning the curry into microwaveable dishes. Then she ran upstairs and stepped out of her work trousers, pulling on jeans and a jumper. Benjy began to bark, signalling Gayle's arrival, and she ran back downstairs to let her in.

'Clare…' she said, extending an arm to give her a hug. Then she drew back and presented a bottle. 'If in doubt, reach for the Prosecco,' she said.

Clare would have preferred a cup of tea but she didn't want to seem ungrateful so she fetched glasses while Gayle wandered round her sitting room, picking up paperbacks, photos and taking in paintings. 'I love this room, Clare,' she said. 'You have very good taste.'

Clare thought she was being over-generous with her praise but she accepted the compliment graciously. 'I hope you don't mind,' she said, 'but you did say you were fed up with fancy food so I'm doing baked potatoes with the remains of a curry.'

Gayle uncorked the Prosecco and said that sounded perfect. Clare passed her the glasses and she began pouring. 'Honestly, Clare, you've no idea how tedious hotel life is after a while.' She picked up one of the glasses. 'Cheers!' And she downed the Prosecco in one, reaching for the bottle to refill her glass.

Clare's heart sank. She really didn't want a house guest for the night. After the day she'd had she was in desperate need of a decent sleep.

Gayle saw her look. 'Don't worry, Clare. I wouldn't dream of imposing. I came in a taxi and the driver will come back for me when I'm ready.'

Clare hoped the relief didn't show on her face. 'Come on. Let's take these through to the sitting room while the potatoes cook.'

As they sat, Gayle chatted on about the jobs she'd had in the past. 'Some of the things I've uncovered, Clare – well, it would make your hair stand on end. Probably the most common thing is taking over a webcam or tricking someone into installing a keylogger to steal passwords – that sort of thing. One memorable case featured a prominent public figure whose website was hacked. The hackers uploaded photos of him in all sorts of compromising positions!'

'Really?'

'It was photoshopped, of course. But skilfully done. It's fascinating work but it does take me to the seamier side of life.'

As Gayle chatted on about her work, Clare noticed she said very little about her personal life. Emboldened by her third glass of Prosecco, she said, 'If you don't mind me asking, Gayle, is there anyone – I mean…'

Gayle raised an eyebrow. 'You mean do I have a significant other?'

Clare gave an apologetic smile. 'I couldn't think of a more tactful way to put it.'

Gayle traced a finger round the rim of her glass and it seemed for a moment that she might not answer.

Clare was suddenly mortified. She barely knew this woman, this woman who quite possibly was investigating Clare and her whole team. She had overstepped the mark. 'Gayle,' she began, 'I'm sorry—'

Gayle waved this away. 'It's fine, Clare. It's a perfectly reasonable question. But, sadly, the job, you know – well I travel quite a lot and, when I'm working on a job, it can be all-consuming. It doesn't lend itself to family life.' Then she brightened. 'But I don't think the same can be said for you, Clare – can it?'

Clare felt her cheeks flush. 'Oh…' she began then tailed off.

'And I'm not talking about that gorgeous man in the photo,' Gayle said, nodding at a small framed photo of Clare with Geoffrey. 'DCI Gibson – he has an eye for you, I think…'

Clare didn't reply.

'Oh, I'm sorry, Clare. Have I touched a nerve?'

The oven pinged and Clare rose. 'Saved by the bell,' she said. 'I'll just check on the food.'

Over dinner, they chatted about Daisy Cottage and the renovations Clare was having done.

'I had a new central heating system installed a few months back. Bit of a hassle at the time but I'm glad it's done now.' She looked round. 'Ideally I'd like to do the windows next but I'll have to wait till I can afford it.'

'And you have that fabulous car out there,' Gayle observed.

'Yes, there is that. It wasn't cheap.'

'Cars are your thing, then?'

'No, not really. I had an old Renault Clio for years. Practically ran it into the ground.'

Gayle raised an eyebrow. 'From a Clio to a Merc? That's a bit of a jump.'

Clare shrugged. 'Oh, you know how it is.'

'Impulse buy?'

'Something like that.'

Gayle put down her glass. 'Tell me to mind my own business, Clare but – well, I'm a pretty good judge of these things and you don't seem happy to me. The car – could it be you're papering over the cracks?'

It was the first time anyone had said it out loud. Her sister Jude, her parents – even Chris, her DS. They had all registered surprise when she had told them about the Merc. But no one had actually said what she knew they were thinking; what she herself was trying not to think. She looked at Gayle. 'You're very perceptive.'

Gayle looked back at Clare, studying her face. 'I'll tell you something else, Clare – you're afraid of me.' She put down her glass. 'You think my being here means trouble for you but you're not sure why.'

Clare stared at her. She had never come across anyone who was quite so direct.

Gayle carried on talking. 'You are worried I'm going to uncover something that will show you in a bad light – threaten your position.' She smiled at Clare. 'Aren't you?'

Clare closed her eyes for a few seconds. She could feel her head swimming a bit, thanks to a second bottle of Prosecco. Her judgement was probably impaired. Would she regret speaking her mind? Only one way to find out. She opened her eyes again. 'I'm asking myself,' she said, 'why it is that you've come to St Andrews. Why, with your office back in that… that place where we met, with all the offices you could have used at Gartcosh or in other police stations, why you have chosen to come here.'

'And what answers have you come up with?'

Clare swallowed and she avoided Gayle's eye. 'I think you are here,' she began, chasing curry around her plate with her fork, 'because this is where the problem is. Here, in St Andrews. I think you knew that much, when you summoned us to that place, last Friday. I think you have already found some kind of security leak here – or close to here – and you have come to ferret it out. And I'm worried it might involve someone I know – one of my officers.' She raised her eyes to meet Gayle's. 'They're a good bunch, Gayle. If someone's done something they shouldn't have – well, I'd like to be involved.' She laid down her fork. 'So, there you have it. You asked and I've told you.' She glanced at the second Prosecco bottle, almost empty. 'God, that's good stuff. They should market it as a truth drug.'

She was surprised to see Gayle's face soften. 'Oh Clare – have you really been worrying about it all week?'

'Yes I have. So, tell me, please – do I have anything to be worried about? Because it sure as hell isn't me.'

'No, it's not you, Clare. If it was, I wouldn't be here tonight, in this lovely house, eating your leftover curry. I'm not here because I suspect something's going on here, in St Andrews. I'm here because there isn't. I'm here because I know I can trust you.'

Clare looked at her. 'Can you, Gayle? How do you know that?'

'How do you think?'

Clare sat back in her seat and gave her head a little shake. She saw it all now. 'You've already checked me out, haven't you?'

'Weeks ago. And, as you know, you're clean. But, more than that, you are someone I felt I could rely on. Your reputation precedes you, Clare. You're a sharp cookie and straight as a die.' Gayle leaned forward, her arms on the table. 'Clare, I'm here *because* I trust you – not because I don't.' She sat back again. 'Does that help?'

'I suppose.' She forced a smile. 'Sorry, Gayle.'

Gayle smiled back. 'You know, Clare, I could do this job from my hotel room. I don't actually need to be in the station. It helps with security, of course, but I thought it might be nice to see a friendly face each day. Particularly one I can trust. But, if you really are uncomfortable with my being there – well, I'll go elsewhere.'

Clare was taken aback. 'You would do that?'

'Definitely. You only have to ask.'

Clare wasn't sure how to respond to this. The truth was she would love to see the back of Gayle but, if she took herself elsewhere, Clare would have no idea how the investigation was going. The old maxim of *keep your friends close and your enemies closer* came into her head. But was Gayle the enemy? She hoped not.

She regarded her now, sitting where the DCI had sat last night. She looked relaxed, glass in hand, a contented smile on her face. Clare decided she had nothing to lose. 'Well, since we're being frank with each other…'

Gayle raised an eyebrow. 'Oh God, Clare. Am I going to like this?'

'This leak – is there anything you can tell me about it?'

Gayle put down her glass. 'Strictly speaking, no.'

'But…'

'But we've had two bottles of wine and, as I said earlier, I know you're someone I can trust.'

Clare waited.

'Now, I can't tell you who I believe to be responsible, Clare. That *would* be unprofessional. But I can tell you a bit about the leak.'

Through the alcoholic fug, Clare tried to focus – take in what Gayle was about to say.

'Do you remember the people-trafficking case in Glasgow last year?'

Clare nodded. She remembered it well. Thirty-four Eastern European women smuggled into Scotland to be sold into prostitution.

'Then you'll recall that, while the police managed to find and free the women and arrest the men holding them, the couple who had organised the smuggling operation evaded capture. I believe they are still at large.'

Clare could see the faces of the women now, their haunted looks as they were led away from the hovel where they'd been kept prisoner. It had been a B&B for the homeless which the owners had sold cheaply when the estimated repair costs had exceeded the property value. 'They are,' she said, a harsh note to her voice.

'And the county lines drugs operation your DCI was overseeing?'

Clare began to understand. 'The dealers got away just before our lads raided the property.'

'I won't go into detail, Clare, but it's clear that, in both cases, the people heading up these operations were tipped off.'

Clare's mouth felt dry and she licked her lips. 'Oh my God, Gayle. Are you saying...'

'Someone in Police Scotland is tipping them off, letting the main culprits get away.'

'But – that would have to be...'

'...at the highest level,' Gayle finished for her. 'Either that, or someone with the skills to intercept communications. Someone with excellent IT skills.'

Clare sank back in her seat, processing this. 'But surely, if that was the case, an internal investigation, or even someone from another Force...'

'Too close to home, Clare. As soon as it was known there was going to be an investigation, email accounts would be wiped, documents shredded. No. A case like this needs someone from the outside. Someone with no connection to any Force.'

Despite the Prosecco, Clare's mind was whirling. She saw now why the DCI was so concerned about the Phil Quinn trial. Not only his own reputation to think of but a very real possibility of a leak that would see Phil get off. Perhaps that was why Paddy Grant had so successfully evaded capture. Had Paddy been tipped off when the arrests were planned? Thank God Tamsin had managed to give her evidence. But who the hell was leaking this level of information and why?

Gayle sat forward, her face suddenly serious. 'I probably shouldn't have told you this, Clare. But I feel I can trust you. It mustn't go outside these four walls though. Agreed?'

'Agreed.' She rose from the sofa, putting out a hand to steady herself. 'Coffee,' she said. 'We need coffee.'

–

Gayle trotted out into the night, calling her thanks and exhorting Clare to *drink a pint of water before bed*. As the tail lights of the taxi disappeared down the drive, Clare reckoned if she drank any more she'd throw up.

She cleared away the plates and glasses, loaded the dishwasher and climbed wearily up to bed, thankful at least that she didn't have as early a start the next morning.

But sleep eluded her and she lay awake long into the night wondering about the leak. Who on earth had been stupid enough to disclose details of operations and what the hell would the consequences be?

Thursday, 21 May

Chapter 24

Chris said that Corinne Sim, the Detective Sergeant from the Fraud Unit, would be with them by ten. 'I've given her a bit of the background and she said it's a familiar picture, these days.'

'Okay,' Clare said, her head still fuzzy from the night before. She really hoped no one would appear at her door bearing wine tonight. 'What about the warrant for Marek's accounts?'

'Yeah, got that now. Bank accounts, emails and a warrant to search his flat.'

'If Nita and Gary are available, send them over,' Clare said. 'They know what they're looking for now.' She groaned. 'God, I need coffee. Want one?'

'Please.' Chris followed her to the small station kitchen. 'Hope you don't mind me saying, Clare, but... you're looking a bit rough.'

'Oh, thank you very much! That's just what I needed to hear.'

'Sorry, but I'm only saying it because I'm concerned. You've not been yourself this week and... well, do you think you might be drinking a bit much these days?'

Clare raised both eyebrows as far as she could. 'Detective Sergeant West – are you having *The Talk* with me?'

Chris shrugged. 'Maybe someone has to. That's two days in a row you've rocked up looking like death's head.

And it's not gone unnoticed. If there's something wrong…
I mean, I know you must be missing Geoff but…'

Clare spooned coffee into mugs, stifling a yawn. 'By coincidence, I've had visitors turn up on my doorstep with bottles of wine, two nights running. That's all.' She lifted the kettle and poured boiling water into the mugs. 'Just because Sara's got you on a health kick, don't take it out on me.'

Chris lowered his voice. 'She's confiscated my stash of Wagon Wheels.'

Clare laughed out loud then regretted it and put a hand to her head. 'Got any paracetamol?'

Chris shook his head. 'It's poison, apparently.'

'Whaaat?' Clare handed him one of the mugs. 'She really is taking this seriously, isn't she?'

'Just a bit. You should see my lunch…'

'Mind you,' Clare said, appraising him, 'it is starting to work. You're looking quite trim around the middle – and it was much needed.'

'Cut it out, Clare. Or I'll tell her you have a drink problem.'

'You wouldn't.'

'Try me,' he said. 'Why should I be the only one to suffer?'

'Suffer from what?' Sara's voice said behind them.

Chris looked stricken.

Clare took pity on him. 'I'm threatening him with a night shift,' she said.

Sara opened her mouth to comment just as Clare's Alcatel began to ring. The DCI.

She didn't want to let them see the Alcatel, so she excused herself quickly and walked out of the newly painted side door towards her favoured corner of the car park. Thankfully the painters had finished and she didn't have to avoid them. As she walked she stepped out of the way of a car entering the car park. When it turned left into the staff parking area Clare watched it nose into a space. She didn't recognise the car. Maybe it was a member of the public choosing the wrong side of the car park. Perhaps they needed a bigger sign for visitor parking. The Alcatel was still ringing and, as she walked, she wondered why he was calling. Hopefully not about the other night. She had no idea what to say to him. What if he asked her out? Or said they had to talk?

She needn't have worried.

He got straight to the point. 'It's Phil Quinn.'

'What about him?'

'He's taken the stand this morning and has just accused Tamsin of running the whole operation. Says he was coerced.'

'Did he mention this when your guys questioned him?'

'Nope. He exercised his right to silence.'

'And now he's come up with this story?'

'Yup. And Tamsin's been given immunity from prosecution.'

Clare's mind was working overtime. 'Think they're in it together?'

There was a pause. Then the DCI said, 'You heard her evidence yesterday. Did she cast any doubt on his guilt?'

'Absolutely not,' Clare said. 'She dropped him right in it. To be honest, Al, I'll be amazed if the jury don't convict him, based on what she said, never mind any other evidence.'

She heard him sigh. 'Okay. Thanks Clare. I really don't want to lose the case at this stage.'

'Fingers crossed, Al.' Out of the corner of her eye she saw the car door open and a woman emerge. She was dressed simply in dark trousers and a knitted top, carrying a jacket over her arm. An ID badge swung on a lanyard as she walked towards the front door and Clare's curiosity got the better of her. 'Al, something's just come up. Let me know if there are any more developments.' She ended the call, relieved that there had been no time to move on to their recent liaison, and walked across the car park, following the woman in through the main door.

In the front office, she saw that Chris had come to greet the woman and she realised this must be Corinne Sim. Tucking the Alcatel back in her pocket she went to introduce herself.

—

Clare estimated Corinne Sim was in her forties. Her sleek dark bob was tucked behind her ears, revealing the odd liver spot on her temples and crow's feet at the corners of her eyes. Her no-nonsense manner suggested she knew her job inside out and Clare thought she was just the kind of officer she'd like to have on her staff. She scanned Corinne's badge and saw she was a DS. Not much chance of poaching her from the larger Bell Street station in Dundee, then.

'It's a common enough picture, these days,' Corinne was saying, as Chris placed three mugs of tea down on an empty desk in the incident room. 'Anyone with cash-heavy criminal activity is looking for a way to make the money clean. Sometimes there's so much cash that to pay it into an account would ring alarm bells at the bank. So they look for money mules to help them launder it.'

'And students are looking for easy ways to supplement their loans?'

'Yep. The universities do their best – lots of warnings about consequences – but some are still willing to do it. And, if they keep the account busy enough with lots of small transactions, the banks often don't notice.'

Clare pulled over the bank statements. 'Can you have a look at these please, Corinne? We've one student dead and another gone missing but no idea why. Is there anything you can glean from the statements?'

Corinne pulled on a pair of metal-rimmed glasses and began scrutinising the printouts. 'So here,' she said, after a few minutes, 'this purchase from Cesciland Corp in Delaware – that's almost certainly a shell company.'

Clare frowned. 'Which is?'

'Companies in name only. They're created to allow money to be shifted around through several companies, making it harder to trace. The reason they use Delaware is it's one of the two states in the US that allows companies to function, anonymously. Crooks set up multiple shell companies with fake orders and invoices and pass the money between them; and, because of the anonymity, there's almost no way to trace the owners. But the owners will be the same crooks who gave your student the money to pay into his bank.'

She studied the statements again then jabbed a finger at another transaction. 'See this?' she said. 'eBay. This debit card transaction for four hundred pounds. Then another for three hundred to PayPal a couple of weeks later.'

Clare's brow furrowed. 'But why would he use a debit card for eBay if he has a PayPal account?'

'Exactly. It makes no sense – unless you're trying to pay out a lot of money using different methods.'

Chris said, 'But, hold on – if they buy something on eBay, that's not laundering money. That's buying stuff. Or do they sell it on to someone else?'

Corinne shook her head. 'No, the stuff they buy doesn't actually exist. The crooks with the dirty money set up a series of eBay accounts, all through disposable email addresses. They then create a listing for a high-value item – say an iPad. They check prices of similar tablets and inflate the price – high enough to put off prospective buyers. Maybe they add on the maximum postage costs or list it as *Collection Only*. Our mule comes along and pays for it from his PayPal account. The money is transferred to the seller – your criminals – less the usual eBay and PayPal commission – et, voila. It's no longer dirty money. But PayPal get jumpy if you earn more than fifteen hundred pounds in a tax year so the mules use a variety of methods to pay for these non-existent iPads – or whatever they are.'

'So that explains why some of the payments are made direct to eBay and others to PayPal?' Clare asked.

'Yep. And it's not limited to PayPal, either. They can do direct bank transfers, or use other payment services – Nochex.com, CertaPay and so on. And then there are other vending sites they can use – not just eBay. There's even one called *ebuygumm*!'

Chris frowned. 'So, let me see if I've got this: the crooks give Johannes one thousand pounds which he banks, using his five different accounts – varying the amounts each month. He knows he can keep around five per cent so he withdraws some in cash, transfers some to businesses like the Delaware one and uses the rest to pay for bogus transactions?'

Corinne nodded. 'Pretty much.'

'And the purchases from the company in Delaware – the goods don't exist?'

'No. There will be a paper trail making it look as if goods have been sent but these companies are owned, anonymously, by the crooks trying to launder the money.'

'But what happens if another eBay customer buys the bogus iPad?' Clare asked.

'Simple. The seller cancels the transaction. Says it's developed a fault – something like that. eBay returns the money to the buyer and our crook simply lists it again on another eBay account, maybe increasing the price to put genuine buyers off.'

Chris sat back in his chair, processing this. 'They'd have to be pretty well organised to keep track of it all.'

'Which is why students are popular. They're generally tech-savvy and good at this kind of thing. It wouldn't surprise me if your Johannes's laptop had a detailed spreadsheet or something like that, keeping track of all these transactions.' Corinne jabbed at the statement again. 'Someone as organised as this is a dream to a crook with dirty money to launder.'

Clare fell silent for a moment. Then she said, 'Chris, we need to contact the university and get them to put out something to all students, warning them off this kind of thing.'

'I doubt it'll help much,' Corinne said. 'But it does no harm to remind the students of the potential penalties. They usually end up being kicked off their courses and can even do time for it.'

'In the meantime,' Clare went on, 'does any of this help us track down who Johannes was working for? I can't believe it's not connected to his murder.'

Corinne began leafing through the statements again. 'I doubt it, Clare. But if you give me copies of these I'll have a closer look. I wouldn't get your hopes up, though.'

Clare left Corinne and Chris discussing the statements and went outside to phone Wendy. 'How are things, Wendy?'

'We're okay, Clare. No more sightings of the blue van, thankfully, and the guys in the red Range Rover have been across the road so I think we're safe enough. But Tamsin's going stir crazy. Any word on the jury retiring?'

'Not sure, Wendy. Don't tell Tamsin but Phil Quinn's been on the stand and he's implicated her.'

'Hold on…'

Clare heard Wendy saying something to Tamsin then the sound of her running downstairs. Then she heard the noise of traffic. Wendy must have gone outside to continue the call.

'Phil Quinn's implicating Tamsin?' Wendy repeated.

'Yep. But there's no point in telling her. It'll only add to her worries. The time to worry will be if the jury believe him.'

'I didn't realise he'd lodged that as a defence.'

'He hadn't. And here's the thing, Wendy: Tamsin was given immunity in return for her testimony.'

'Whose decision was that?'

'The Fiscal's ultimately but DCI Gibson pushed for it.'

Wendy gave a low whistle. 'I wouldn't like to be in his shoes if Phil Quinn does get off.'

Clare was thinking the same thing. Al Gibson had taken a chance giving Tamsin immunity. Listening to her on the witness stand yesterday, Clare could well understand why he had done it. Her testimony had been damning. But, if the jury didn't believe it, Phil Quinn would get away scot-free. 'We'll know soon enough,' Clare said. 'Better go, Wendy. Not a word to Tamsin, mind.'

Clare ended the call and was about to head back into the station when her phone rang. Glancing at the display she saw it was DCI Gibson again. But why wasn't he calling her on the Alcatel? She swiped to answer the call. 'Hi Al—'

He cut across her, speaking quickly, his tone sharp. 'Clare, we have a problem.'

She wondered what on earth he meant and why his manner had changed from his last phone call.

'I've just been called out of Phil Quinn's trial to take a call from the Chief Superintendent.'

'Sounds serious.'

'It is. Remember that pro-am golf tournament you policed last month…'

'I do. The one sponsored by the Spanish sherry producer – on the Old Course.'

'That's the one.'

'That was all signed off, Al. I emailed all the forms over a couple of weeks ago.'

'Yes, you did. The only problem is they weren't right.'

His words stung. Clare prided herself on being particular with paperwork. 'Not right? How? What was wrong with them?'

'A small matter of the invoice for policing.'

She racked her brains. 'I think it was around eighty thousand – something like that. Have they not paid?'

'Oh, they've paid all right. Quickly too and I don't blame them.' He paused then said, 'Did you realise you missed a zero off the end?'

'Eh?'

'Clare – you invoiced them for eight thousand pounds. Not eighty. They must have thought all their birthdays had come at once. You've cost Police Scotland seventy-two thousand pounds.'

Clare's mouth felt dry. Could it have been some kind of printing error? But that didn't make sense – the amounts were always spelled out in words and figures. How the hell had it happened? 'Hold on, Al,' she said. 'I'm going back into my office to check.'

'Phone me back,' he said, his tone curt. And he ended the call.

In the office she wiggled the mouse to bring her computer to life and tapped in her password. She went to her documents and found the folder for the golf event. The invoice was there, among the documents, and she clicked to open it, tapping on her desk with a pen while she waited for it to load. After what felt like an eternity the document appeared in front of her and she looked at the total at the foot of the money column: eight thousand pounds.

Clare sank back in her chair. How could she have been so stupid? She had known full well it had been for eighty thousand. It had been such a busy few days. She must have been rushing to complete the paperwork and mistyped. She sat for a minute or two then picked up her phone again. The DCI answered immediately.

'Al, I don't know what to say.'

'So your copy says eight thousand?'

'It does. But I don't know how. I'm sure I made it out for eighty thousand.'

'Obviously not, Clare. And now I have to go and explain that to the Chief Superintendent who wants to know why we're seventy-two thousand pounds down on the event.'

'Al, I—'

'Look, Clare,' he said, his tone softening, 'it's not great. But maybe I can do something. I'll have a word with someone in Accounts – see if they'll issue a second invoice for the balance. Appeal to the company's better nature.'

'Think it'll work?'

He sighed. 'To be honest, Clare, I doubt it. But it's worth a shot.'

'Al – I should do it. It's my mistake.'

'Yes it is – and a bloody huge one too. But I have a bit more pull than you and I'd like to help if I can. Let me do this for you, Clare…'

Chapter 25

As Clare emerged from her office the cry went up.

'It's Marek,' Robbie shouted. 'Spotted in Tayport.'

She moved to a map of Fife on the wall. Tayport was a small but busy town eleven miles north-east of St Andrews. It sat on the south bank of the River Tay, looking across to Dundee and its popular suburb, Broughty Ferry. 'Whereabouts?' Clare asked.

'On the common. Early this morning.'

Clare scanned the map. 'It's next to a caravan park, right at the river,' she said to Robbie. 'Reckon that's where he's been staying?'

'Not sure yet, boss. Gillian's headed over there to speak to the park manager. But I gather it was a dog walker who spotted him.'

'Do we know where he is now?'

'No, but there was another possible sighting a couple of hours later at the cemetery. Woman who saw him wasn't sure but, from what she said, it sounds like him.'

Clare studied the map again. The cemetery was further west, almost out of Tayport. 'Just on the edge of the town,' she said and Robbie agreed. 'So where's he heading now?'

'If he's heading for Dundee he'll take the pedestrian walkway on the Tay Road Bridge. It's just a mile further on from the cemetery. Or he could carry on past the bridge into Newport-on-Tay. Or he could even cut across country further into Fife.'

Chris appeared at her elbow. Clare started to tell him about Marek but he interrupted her. 'That blue Transit van...'

'What about it?'

'It crossed the Tay Road Bridge last night. Heading for Dundee.'

'Time?'

'About half past eight, I think. Want me to check?'

'No, Chris. But is there any chance we could see the footage?'

'Leave it with me.'

Clare turned back to Robbie. 'I need every cop and car there is to head over to Tayport. And get onto Bell Street station in Dundee, too. If Marek's crossed the bridge he could be anywhere in the city. Is there CCTV on the bridge? Please tell me there is...'

Robbie nodded. 'Yep. Cameras at either end and another couple in the middle.'

'Good. So we should be able to see if he did cross the river. Robbie, can you do that please?'

'Anything I can do, boss?' Gillian asked.

'Yeah. Can you get on to the bus station, railway station and put a shout out to taxi drivers? If he's trying to put some distance between himself and the people he was laundering money for, we need to know where he's heading.' She scanned the room for Chris and saw him perched on a desk, next to Sara. 'Chris – can you co-ordinate the CCTV searches please? And make sure everyone knows to approach him with caution. For all we know he's responsible for Johannes's death and I don't want anyone else getting hurt.'

Having set them to work, Clare retreated to her office and sat down. She was already outstandingly tired and it was barely lunchtime. She put a hand to her head and rubbed her temples. Her phone buzzed and she took it out to read the message. It was from the DCI. Her heart sank and then she saw it was nothing to do with the golf invoice.

Judge summing up this afternoon.
Jury should retire after that.

She put the phone down and let her mind drift back to the court room and to the jury. A reasonable cross-section she had thought at the time. But who would they believe? Tamsin with her detailed descriptions of the arsenal Phil Quinn had amassed or would they accept Phil's assertion that Tamsin was the one behind it all? Clare was starting to wonder herself. Had Tamsin been pulling the wool over their eyes? She had said she was frightened of Paddy Grant. Was that because she had dropped him in it too? Clare hadn't seen all the evidence against Paddy but there must have been something for them to have issued an arrest warrant. If it was Paddy driving that blue Transit van, he must have good reason to risk being seen by the cops guarding Tamsin. Could Paddy even be innocent, the evidence against him concocted by Tamsin? Could Phil be telling the truth? Or were they all in it together?

A tap on the door brought her back to the present and she looked up to see Gayle. 'You look like I feel, Clare,' she said. 'Bit of a head this morning, I must confess.'

Clare forced a smile. 'I'll be fine.' She rose. 'Coffee? I could certainly do with one.'

Gayle hesitated, just long enough for Clare to notice. 'Something wrong?'

Gayle jerked her head towards the door and Clare followed her out of the station by the side entrance. The visitors' end of the car park was quiet and she walked across to the far end, Clare following.

Clare took in Gayle's appearance. She was neatly dressed, as usual, but her face was lined with worry, her easy smile gone. There was something more than a hangover here. Clare felt her palms become damp and she brushed them against her trousers. She wanted to ask Gayle what was wrong but, in truth, she was afraid of what the answer might be.

Gayle checked all round then turned back to Clare. 'Look, Clare,' she said, her voice low, 'there's something I would very much like to share with you – but I can't.'

Clare stared at her. 'What? Gayle! You can't just say that. What have you found?'

Gayle looked down. She seemed to be struggling with herself. Then she met Clare's eye again. 'I can't, Clare. I simply can't. I'm too close now. But what I want to say is, until I have filed my report and the person responsible for the leak has been taken into custody, you must trust no one.' She took hold of Clare's hand. 'No one, Clare. Got that?'

Clare wondered at the change in Gayle. She was a professional ethical hacker. Used to delving into the murky depths of company computers. Last Friday, when they had met in that secure unit, she had been utterly in command of herself. Aloof, professional and completely unfazed by the work she did. But here – now – this job – she seemed so *affected* by it. But what had she found? Who was it Clare shouldn't trust? Who would be stupid enough to jeopardise their career for a fast buck?

She thought of Chris and Sara – talking about saving up for a house together. Only the other day Sara was complaining they would need twenty thousand for the deposit. Had one of them been tempted? She put the notion right out of her head. She didn't even consider Jim, her solid, reliable sergeant. Not for one minute. Jim was as straight as a die and too near retirement to do anything stupid. The other staff – well, who could tell what they had going on in their lives? Hopefully nothing that would make them deliberately leak confidential information in return for a wad of cash. Most of them were lower ranks anyway and wouldn't have had access to information such as Tamsin's whereabouts. But were any of them so desperate for money that they would risk their careers?

And then it hit her like a sledgehammer. The one person who had been trying to get close to her. The person whose marriage had ended and who was trying to hang on to his very large pension. The person who had forsaken his beloved Jaguar for a Ford Focus. The person who she had spent the night with, just two nights ago. DCI Alastair Gibson.

Was that why he was so anxious about this trial? Had he given up Tamsin's locations in return for a payoff? Was he trying to have it both ways – see Phil Quinn put away and all the while leaking information that would put his star witness in danger? And was he the reason Paddy Grant was still at liberty?

A knot was forming in Clare's stomach. If she was right, Tamsin could be in even more danger once the trial was over. If Phil Quinn was convicted, would the DCI be straight on the phone to Paddy to let him know Tamsin would be leaving the Market Street flat? She thought she had done the right thing, giving him that Alcatel phone so they could discuss Tamsin's security without compromising her safety. But was she instead delivering Tamsin right into Paddy Grant's hands, via the DCI?

And then she gave herself a shake. What the hell was she thinking? The DCI was not the kind of officer who turned to the dark side for a few quid – was he? There was no getting away from the fact that someone had. And now Clare didn't know who the hell to trust.

–

'I've got that footage,' Chris said as she wandered back into the station.

'Eh?'

'The footage from the Tay Road Bridge last night. The blue Transit. Hello? Anybody there?'

Clare smiled. 'Sorry, Chris. I was miles away. Is it on the portal?'

He indicated for her to follow him and sat down at a computer, wiggling the mouse to bring the screen to life. 'Okay... I'll start it just a few seconds before the van appears and edge it forward, frame by frame.'

Clare watched the footage as the van came into view. 'Can you zoom in please?'

Chris zoomed in and they both peered at the screen.

'I'd say that's Paddy Grant,' Clare said.

'I agree.'

'But, where's his sister? According to Wendy, when she's spotted the blue Transit van the white-blonde woman was always in the passenger seat.'

'Well she's certainly not there now,' Chris said. 'Unless she's crouching down; and, given how visible she's been over the past few days, I can't see why she would do that.'

'So, Paddy's in Dundee and Rose is still in Fife,' Clare said.

'Looks like it. Are Wendy and the undercover guys still at the flat?'

'Yeah. They'll be there until the trial is over.'

'Well, that's something.'

'Chris – I wonder – I think I'll get the press office to put out Rose Grant's photo. Wanted in connection – something like that.'

'On what grounds, though, Clare? She's not done anything as far as we know.'

'I'll think of something. I could make a pretty good case for *interfering with a witness*, after her appearance at the High Court yesterday. I'm worried about Tamsin. Even if Phil Quinn does go away for a few years, with Paddy and Rose running around I'm not convinced she'll be safe.'

'Want me to phone the press officer?'

Clare smiled. 'Would you? I'm – well, I've a lot to think about today.'

Chris looked at her for a few seconds. 'You sure you're okay?'

She nodded. 'Yeah. Just a headache.'

'I'll nip out to the shop and get you some paracetamol,' he said, earning himself a grateful smile in return.

After he left, Clare sat in her office, trying to order her thoughts. Then she rose suddenly from her chair. 'To hell with this,' she said, opening the office door and marching out. 'Back shortly,' she called, heading for the front entrance. Outside, she walked past the car park and onto Tom Morris Drive, taking a left turn towards a row of shops where she guessed Chris would be. As she approached the Spar shop she saw him come out, eating a bag of crisps.

He saw Clare and his face flushed. 'Don't tell Sara,' he said. 'I just needed a treat. And you've no idea how good these taste.' He held the pack out to Clare but she waved it away. Then he reached into his pocket and withdrew a small box. 'Paracetamol.'

Clare took the box from him. 'How much do I owe you?'

'Forget it. Anyway, I said I'd bring them back. What's so urgent you've come to meet me? Has something happened?'

Clare glanced round. The street was quiet but she wasn't taking any chances. 'Follow me,' she said, leading him across to a large area of grass. 'And switch your phone off.'

Chris stopped in his tracks. 'Clare, what the hell is going on? You know, I've just about had enough of this. Either you tell me what's up or—'

'Just calm yourself down,' Clare said, powering off her phone. She nodded at Chris's phone. 'Off.'

He stood, watching his phone until the display went blank, then followed her into the park. 'This had better be good.'

The park was quiet. A man was kicking a soft football towards a pair of giggling toddlers and a woman with a tennis ball launcher was attempting to tire out an exuberant collie, but it was otherwise empty. Clare led Chris over to the far end where there were a couple of benches. She sat on one and indicated for him to join her.

He studied her face for a few seconds, then sat beside her. 'So? What's this all about?'

She hesitated, wondering for a moment if she was doing the right thing. Then she took a deep breath. 'Well, the first thing I have to tell you is that I'm probably for the high jump in the next few days. Might even get the sack.' She glanced at him then away again. 'It seems – and I'm not sure how – it seems I made a mistake with the invoice for policing that golf event. I undercharged the sponsors.'

'How much?'

'Seventy-two thousand less than I should have charged them.'

Chris whistled. 'Bloody hell, Clare. That's not like you.'

'I know, I know. I'm normally so careful, Chris. I could have sworn I made it out for the right amount.'

'Checked your own copy?'

'Yep. My copy's wrong so it must be my mistake.'

'Look, Clare, it's not the end of the world. Godsake – when you consider the size of the police budget it's a drop in the ocean. You'll probably get a bollocking and that'll be the end of it.'

She looked at him. 'You think so?'

'Yeah. I mean they might make you clean the lavs for a couple of weeks but that's about it. Anyway, would the DCI not put in a word for you? You and he seem quite chummy these days.'

'Eh?' Clare felt her cheeks flush. 'What do you mean, chummy? He's my boss, Chris.' She realised she had spoken more sharply than she had intended.

He held his hands up as if to defend himself. 'Okay, chill, Clare. Just a joke.'

'Sorry.'

'So, what else?'

'Eh?'

'You said that was the first thing. What else is on your mind?'

Clare didn't reply.

'Come on – you didn't get me out here for nothing so let's have it.'

Clare looked down at the grass for a moment, then back at Chris. 'Are you able – I mean, can you keep a secret from Sara?'

Chris indicated the half-finished packet of crisps. 'Obviously.'

'No, Chris. I mean a really big secret. Probably the biggest secret you'll ever be asked to keep.'

'Fucksake, Clare. Now I'm really worried. Just tell me. I won't breathe a word but *tell me*.' He stared at her then his face cleared. 'Hold on – it's that woman, isn't it? That Gayle person. I knew there was something up with her. All that bollocks about a new comms system. What is it then? She in the station to spy on us?'

Clare allowed herself a smile. He didn't realise how close he was to the truth. 'Okay, Chris. But this is strictly for your ears only – no one else. Promise? If she finds out I've told you, I'm finished. I mean *really* finished.'

'Okay, promise. So, go on. What's she up to?'

Clare met his eye. 'She's investigating a leak within Police Scotland.'

'You what?'

'I know. And what's more she's found it. Someone has been tipping off organised crime groups when a raid has been planned. She won't tell me who it is but she's said I've to be very careful who I speak to. And now I don't know who I can trust.' She could feel tears pricking her eyes. The strain of the past week – having Gayle in the office, hunting Marek, keeping Tamsin safe, sleeping with the DCI and that stupid mistake over that invoice – she felt as if it was all coming crashing down on her.

Chris was shaking his head. 'I can't believe you didn't tell me.'

'Chris, I couldn't. If you'd seen that place—'

'What place?'

'Last Friday. Remember the DCI cancelled our meeting? He picked me up and drove to this – this place. I don't know how to describe it, Chris. Middle of nowhere, like some kind of fortified bunker. Huge walls, cameras everywhere, body scanners – the full works. And that's where I met her. She told me about the leak and she threatened me with the Official Secrets Act if I breathed a word. So, frankly, Chris, if you're the leak, or you're working for her, then I'm stuffed. I might as well hand you my warrant card now.'

Chris looked at her. 'It was that bad?'

She nodded. 'Scared me shitless, to be honest. And, if she finds out I've told you, it really will be the end of my career. She'll see to it.'

'It's okay, Clare. I won't breathe a word. But – do you know who she thinks is responsible for the leak?'

Clare shook her head. 'She wouldn't say. But she implied it was someone I'm in touch with.' In spite of the May sunshine, she shivered. 'It's horrible, not knowing who to trust, or if my phone calls are being recorded. She even hinted there could be bugs – listening in.'

'Where?'

Clare spread her hands. 'Don't ask me. But since last Friday I've been too scared to speak anywhere except out in the open.'

'So that's why you didn't tell me about Tamsin Quinn?'

Clare met his eye. 'It just seemed safer to tell no one.'

'But someone knew. Someone's been leaking her locations.'

'I know.'

'Who knew where she was staying?'

Clare said nothing.

'Wendy?' Chris suggested. 'Surely not?'

Clare shook her head. 'I don't think so – as far as I'm aware, she didn't know about the safe house in Perth. There was a different liaison officer there. It's only when Tamsin was moved to St Andrews that Wendy was brought in.'

'Who arranged that?'

'The Serious Organised Crime lads, as far as I know.'

'It could be one of them.'

'Yes, I suppose it could be. But that's quite scary, Chris. To have a leak in the very department responsible for our most covert ops.'

'Certainly is. Then again…' He paused.

'Don't say it, Chris.'

'All I know, Clare, is that two people went to that bunker place, as you call it, last Friday. Now I know I trust you but…'

'You don't trust DCI Gibson?'

'Let's just say I have my doubts. And he has been hanging around here a lot, lately.'

Clare felt her cheeks redden again but said nothing. She was trying not to think of the uncomfortable possibility that the DCI's recent interest in her wasn't entirely romantic. Was she being played by him?

She glanced at her watch. 'Come on – we'd better get back and see if anyone's found Marek.' She rose from the bench. 'I'll go first. Follow me in after five minutes, and don't forget to switch your phone back on.'

Chris nodded and Clare began walking back across the park towards the station, leaving her DS to take in what she'd just told him.

Chapter 26

It was just after four when Clare's desk phone rang. Glancing at the display she saw it was Jenny, a Detective Sergeant from Dundee.

'Bit of a situation, Clare,' she said. 'You'd better get yourself to the Tay Road Bridge.'

–

It took Clare and Chris just twenty minutes to reach the car park at the Fife end of the Tay Road Bridge, eleven miles north of St Andrews. They had taken a circuitous route, avoiding the A92 dual carriageway that led directly onto the bridge, knowing there would be long queues of traffic, waiting for it to reopen. A uniformed cop waved them into the South Access Car Park that led directly to the pedestrian walkway between the bridge carriageways. Clare drove past rows of parked cars and bikes, and a kiosk selling snacks and drinks. The end of the car park, nearest the bridge, had been taken over by emergency vehicles and Clare parked as close as she could to the ramp that led to the walkway. The car park was illuminated by the flashing lights of emergency vehicles and out in the river she could see the orange lifeboat, scrambled from its shed across the river in Broughty Ferry. The bridge itself was empty of traffic, having been blocked off at both ends, and the air was eerily silent.

Jenny was waiting for them and she led Clare up a path that took them closer to the bridge legs. 'He's about a third of the way along,' she said.

Clare squinted up at the bridge as she followed Jenny. It towered above them, supported on a series of twin concrete columns which became shorter as the bridge neared the lower-lying Dundee end, and she thought how high it must seem to anyone up there, looking down into the fast-moving River Tay. She screwed up her eyes and scanned the bridge as they walked.

'See him?' Jenny said, stopping and leaning on the guardrail that bordered the path. She pointed up to the bridge, about half a mile along. 'He's standing on the outside of the barrier. We've a couple of negotiators up there with him now. Want a look?' She handed Clare a set of binoculars.

Clare took the binoculars and adjusted them until she could see Marek clearly. He was standing facing the bridge, his back to the water, holding on to the barrier with both hands. A few feet away were two uniformed officers, one female, one male. They seemed to be talking to Marek but he had his back to Clare, preventing her from seeing his face. She moved the binoculars down towards the river where the lifeboat was waiting. 'The boat will pick him up if he jumps, won't it?' she asked Jenny.

'It should do. But, at that height, if he drops and flails around, he'll hit the water pretty hard. He might not survive the fall.'

Clare handed the binoculars back to Jenny. 'I'd like to go up. Speak to him.'

'Sorry, Clare,' Jenny said. 'Look, I know you outrank me but the negotiators know what they're doing. They talk folk down almost every week. Rarely does anyone go into the water.'

'Jenny, I don't think he's a typical suicide. I think he's up there because he's frightened. Frightened of something he's done or of someone who's after him.'

'Explain please.'

Clare related the story of Marek coming into the station to report Johannes missing then taking flight. 'I think either he's killed Johannes and was reporting him missing to cover himself… or he's afraid whoever killed Johannes is coming after him. Either way, he needs to know that I understand – that we'll look after him.'

Jenny clicked her radio and spoke into it. Then the response came.

> He's coming back over.
> Wait till we give the say so then send the ambulance.
> No sirens, though.

She turned to Clare. 'Looks like it's finished. They've persuaded him to climb back over.'

Clare took the binoculars again and she saw the two officers, one on either side of Marek, helping him over the barrier. They had a firm grip on his arms and Clare saw the ambulance begin moving slowly along the carriageway, stopping short of the trio. Then Marek was led into the ambulance and he disappeared from view.

'Where will they take him?' she asked Jenny.

'Greystane.' She saw Clare's blank look. 'It's a psychiatric unit in Dundee.'

'Will he be admitted?'

'Oh yes. They'll probably issue an Emergency Detention Certificate. It'll let them keep him for the next three days while they assess him.'

'Would they let me see him?'

'Hm. Depends. If he's very distressed then probably not – unless it's an absolute emergency. You wouldn't be able to interview him though. Anything he said wouldn't be admissible in court.'

Clare stood thinking. If Marek had killed Johannes then at least he would be somewhere secure – for the next three days at least. She could put a police guard on his room to make sure he didn't leave. The staff would call her when he was fit to be questioned and, as long as she made sure a solicitor was present, she'd be able to take a statement. And, if he hadn't killed Johannes and was in fear for his own life, well, he would be safe in Greystane. She turned to Chris. 'I think we'll take a run over there. Just to make sure the medical staff know not to let him leave.'

'You want someone posted up there?' Chris asked.

'Yeah, I think so. Can you call Jim and ask him to arrange round-the-clock cover?'

–

Clare drove while Chris spoke to Jim.

The phone call done, he said, 'Why do you reckon he was up there?'

'Take your pick. Running from us, running from what he's done, running from someone else – who knows. Hopefully it won't be too long before he can tell us.'

'If he talks.'

'There is that.'

Greystane House was a modern building finished in a white render. It had been flat-roofed originally and, at some point, pitched roofs had been added. There was a barrier across the car park and Clare pressed a button on an electronic panel. A few seconds later a disembodied voice said, '*Yes?*'

'Detective Inspector Clare Mackay and Detective Sergeant Chris West. We'd like to speak to the duty doctor please.'

The voice made no reply but seconds later the barrier lifted and Clare drove through. They parked near the entrance and made their way through a huddle of smokers standing around the door.

'I thought this was meant to be a secure hospital,' Clare said, her voice low.

'I suppose they'll have secure wards,' Chris said. 'But I'm guessing most folk are here voluntarily.'

At the reception desk Clare explained their mission and they were asked to wait. After ten minutes she tried again. Eventually, a harassed-looking doctor appeared and Clare explained she would like to question Marek as soon as he was deemed competent.

'I'm issuing an EDC,' the doctor said. 'He has to be examined properly and that won't be tonight now. We'll keep him here for at least the next three days.'

Clare secured a promise from the doctor that he would let them know as soon as Marek was fit to be interviewed. 'And I'll be sending an officer over to make sure Marek doesn't leave,' she said. The doctor nodded at this and returned to his charges.

Outside, they made their way back through the fug of cigarette smoke and headed for the car. An ambulance was arriving and Clare wondered about the person inside. Was it another attempted suicide, like Marek? Or someone disturbed enough to be a dangerous? Whatever it was, her heart went out to anyone unwell enough to be admitted to Greystane House. Her phone buzzed as she clicked to unlock the car. She frowned at the display. A message from the DCI.

> Chief Superintendent wants to see us both on Monday.
> He's talking about disciplinary proceedings.
> I'll see what I can do with the Accounts folk before then.
> Leave it with me.
> A

Clare swore under her breath.

'Problem?' Chris said.

'Just my career going down the tubes,' she said, tucking the phone back in her pocket.

As they drove out of the car park they saw a police car heading towards them. Clare recognised the number plate and flashed the car, indicating it should stop. It was Sara. Clare explained the situation then left Sara to it, Chris giving her a cheery wave as they drove off.

'So,' he said, as they headed back down towards the bridge.

'No.'

'You don't know what I was going to say.'

'No, I am not stopping for chips on the way back. Just because Sara's going to be occupied for the next few hours doesn't mean I have to be complicit in you breaking your diet. You've already had a bag of crisps today.'

'You've got really boring in your old age, Inspector.'

As they approached the bridge they joined a slow-moving queue.

'I thought this would have cleared by now,' Clare said.

Chris glanced round at the traffic. 'Dunno. Could take a while, I suppose.'

After a few minutes they joined the bridge, gradually picking up speed.

'Do you think he'd have gone through with it?' Chris asked, looking at the barriers. 'Jumped?'

Clare considered this. 'I'm not sure, Chris. Until we find out why he disappeared, it's hard to know how far he might have gone.'

'We really need to speak to him, Clare.'

'I know. But it's the doctor's call. If we did force the issue, he could claim anything he said was given under duress.'

'Yeah, okay. So what about our star witness then? What happens to her once the trial is over?'

Clare hesitated. She had no idea if their car might be bugged. Was she being ridiculous? She decided she couldn't take the chance. 'Actually, Chris, I meant to call Jenny back. You know – the DS in Dundee who was at the bridge this afternoon? Could you get her on the phone please?'

Chris looked at her for a minute and then he seemed to understand. He picked up her phone and found Jenny's number. He dialled and put it on speaker.

'Hi, Clare. How's the lad?'

'He seems okay, thanks, Jen. They're keeping him for the next three days, as you said, but I'm hoping we'll be able to question him sooner than that. Your guys did a good job, talking him down.'

'Yeah, they're pretty good. They get plenty of practice these days. There must be something in the air tonight though – they've just brought another one off.'

'What – tonight?' Clare was shocked. 'Seriously?'

'Yep. A woman this time. In fact, she must have been arriving just as you were leaving. We've only just cleared the bridge.'

Clare remembered the ambulance. 'I think I saw them arrive.'

'Yeah, could be. Mind you, it's a busy place in the evenings.'

She ended the call just as they were approaching Guardbridge.

'I really am hungry,' Chris said.

Clare was pretty peckish herself. The chip shop was just off the roundabout they were approaching. She glanced at him. 'If you breathe so much as a word to Sara about this, I'll kill you. I'll kill you and I'll get away with it because I know how!'

'Scouts honour.'

–

Clare insisted they eat their fish suppers outside. 'I don't want anyone to smell chips in this car,' she said.

Chris indicated a low stone wall next to the chip shop and they sat down to eat. 'I'd forgotten how great this tastes,' he said, munching on a crispy piece of batter.

'Yep. Pretty good. All the same, don't go undoing all that good work.' She studied his waistline. 'It has made a difference, all this healthy eating.'

Chris nodded. 'Yeah, I know. And Sara – well, I get it, Clare. After she was attacked last year, all that time in hospital, it made her much more conscious of her health. The doctors said she had recovered so quickly because she was fit and healthy. And, after all she went through, well if this is what she wants to do, then I have to support her.'

Clare licked her fingers, wiping them on a tissue from her pocket. 'She's good for you, Sara.'

Chris smiled. 'Yes, Clare. I think she is.'

Friday, 22 May

Chapter 27

Diane sent a WhatsApp message while Clare was having breakfast.

> Parkrun tomorrow.
> Fancy coming down to Lochore?

Clare tapped a message back to say she was looking after her nephew but would definitely join Diane the following Saturday. She added a line asking how Craig, the new assistant, was working out. Diane replied, saying he was great, that he just got on with things and she was catching up with the backlog.

Clare sent a message back saying she was really pleased and would hear all about it next Saturday at the parkrun. Diane replied that it was a date, and Clare rose to clear away her breakfast dishes. As she loaded the dishwasher she considered the day ahead, wondering if there would be a verdict in the Phil Quinn trial. She really hoped he would be convicted but you could never tell with juries.

Her thoughts turned to the DCI and she wondered about his attitude to that mistake with the invoice. Any other boss would have torn her off a strip but he seemed almost eager to help. Was it because they had shared something the other night? Something more than a drunken mistake? He had said – what was it – that he *had always admired her? But could he honestly go on admiring someone who had made such a blunder? Perhaps, underneath that stiff work persona, Al Gibson really was a decent guy.* What was it Robert Burns had written? *The rank is but the guinea stamp?* He was right about that.

But was the DCI helping her out of misplaced loyalty? Gratitude for her sleeping with him? Guilt, even? And had she now blown this potential relationship like every one that had gone before?

She thought about Tom – her ex back in Glasgow – he had wanted to move up to St Andrews to be with her. Marry her, even. But Clare couldn't forget that when she had needed him most he hadn't been there for her. When she had been under investigation for shooting dead a young lad in a hostage situation she had asked him to be with her at the inquiry. But there had been a conflict of interest with Tom's employer and he had put work before Clare, leaving her to face the inquiry alone. No, Clare couldn't forgive or forget that. And now Tom was marrying someone else.

Then Geoffrey Dark had come along – a chance encounter when she was investigating a series of hit-and-run murders. His expertise in wood carvings had helped her track down the culprit and a relationship had blossomed. She had thought they were in it for the long game and then he had announced he was moving to Boston for a few years. Admittedly he had asked Clare to go with him but the ease with which he dismissed her ties to St Andrews had been a wakeup call for Clare. Perhaps the beginning of the end – or so she was starting to think.

And now Al Gibson – the DCI – he had appeared on her doorstep at just the right time and they had sought comfort in red wine and sex. But now, she had put him in an impossible situation with the Chief Superintendent.

She was starting to wonder if she had a self-destruct button when it came to relationships. An impulse seized her and she picked up her phone, tapping a quick message.

Fingers crossed for the right result today

Minutes later the DCI replied with *Thanks Clare*, and a fingers-crossed emoticon. Clare looked at it and felt faintly disappointed. But then what had she expected? This was work, she told herself, and they were both busy. There would be time enough to see where they stood when things calmed down a bit.

She put him to the back of her mind and considered Tamsin. She would be glad to be rid of her. And Gayle too, for that matter. Actually, it wasn't so much Gayle herself, rather the uncertainty over who was leaking information. It was unsettling to be regarding every officer she knew with suspicion. She thought back to her drunken conversation with Gayle a few nights ago. It was oddly comforting to know that Gayle too lacked someone in her life. 'Not so perfect, after all,' she told Benjy, gathering up her work bag. She ruffled him under the chin and went out to the car.

To her annoyance it wouldn't start. She left it for a couple of minutes then tried the ignition again but it was completely dead. 'Six hundred quid a month and it won't bloody start!' She reached over into the glove box and fished out the warranty documents. Then she called Chris. 'Bloody car won't start. Can you pick me up?'

Chris said he would be round in ten minutes. While she waited, Clare called the dealer who said they would have the car collected that morning. 'Probably just an electrical fault,' the salesman said. 'Should have it back to you within the day.'

Clare told them she would leave the key at the station and she ended the call. Then she walked down the drive to wait for Chris.

The news that Marek had been taken to Greystane House had spread round the station and there was a sense that the investigation was winding up. DCI Gibson had telephoned and suggested Clare charge him with Johannes's murder sooner rather than later. Clare wasn't sure about that but she'd know more once they were able to interview him. A constable from Dundee had kept an eye on Marek overnight and Gillian was there now. Sara was back at her desk, ploughing through a pile of paperwork.

At ten o'clock Gayle tapped on Clare's office door. She indicated her cafetière. 'Coffee, Clare?'

Clare glanced up from perusing Marek's bank statements. He too had multiple bank accounts with a similar pattern of transactions. It looked like they were both helping someone to launder money. The question was who? Hopefully the medical staff would give the go-ahead for them to interview Marek in the next day or two. But could she persuade him to talk? Maybe find out if that was the reason Johannes was killed?

She looked at the cafetière. Perhaps a break would help clear her thinking. She rose from her chair. 'Thanks, Gayle. Coffee would be lovely.'

Gayle produced a box of cakes from Fisher & Donaldson, a bakery on Church Street. 'It's my last day here,' she said, 'so I thought – why not.' Then she patted her stomach. 'I'll have to go on a diet after this week. There are just too many lovely food shops in St Andrews.'

Clare helped herself to a custard tart while they waited for the kettle to boil. 'So your work's finished?'

Gayle smiled. 'Yes, all done now.'

Clare studied her face for any clue as to what she had found but Gayle just continued smiling.

'You'll be given a redacted version of my report in due course but I'm afraid I can't give you any details, Clare.'

'Nothing at all?'

'Afraid not. All I will say is… well, I hope they'll treat the culprit with… with some understanding.' She picked up the kettle which had boiled with a cloud of steam and began pouring water into the cafetière. 'It might seem glamorous, what I do, Clare – exciting, even. The reality is quite different. Sometimes people feel compelled to do things by circumstances. Sometimes, life – well, it kicks you in the teeth, doesn't it? These cases I investigate. They're not always driven by greed, you know?'

Clare wondered what she had meant by that. Had she discovered some sad story in the life of one of her officers? Someone who had a desperate need for money? Then suddenly she remembered seeing a webpage on Gayle's laptop – just a glimpse before she closed it. *Cadham* something. She was racking her brains to remember what was on the webpage when Sara appeared at her shoulder. Clare turned to offer her one of Gayle's cakes then saw the worried expression on her face. 'Sara? Something wrong?'

Sara hesitated, then she said, 'Boss – I probably shouldn't ask – but it's just that I saw you and Chris talking yesterday – in the park.'

Clare was suddenly aware of Gayle's presence. She was stirring the coffee, her head bent. But before Clare could stop Sara she carried on.

'I know you didn't see me. I was out on patrol – coming along Tom Stewart Lane and I looked across. You were sitting on a bench in the park. Looked like you were deep in conversation. And I started to worry. Chris and I, well we had this awful row...'

It was the smallest reaction. Almost nothing at all. But it was there. Whether it was in Gayle's shoulders or her back, Clare wasn't sure but, in that moment, she knew Gayle understood. She understood that Clare and Chris had left the station to walk a short distance to the park to have a private conversation. And there could only be one reason for that.

She felt her face flush and she turned back to Sara. 'I'm sorry, Sara – what were you saying?'

'It's the mortgage, you see. I said to Chris we should be saving for the deposit and he said we needed a holiday. And, well, when I saw you talking, you both looked so serious. And I started to worry that he's getting fed up with me nagging. I know I can be a bit...'

Gayle had stopped stirring now and was replacing the lid on the cafetière. Clare looked at Sara's face, creased with worry, and she wrestled with her conscience. It would be the easiest thing in the world to say in front of Gayle that they *had* been speaking about Sara and Chris's row. But, horrified as she was at being caught out by Gayle, Clare couldn't do that to her young PC. Sara looked miserable enough as it was.

'Honestly, Sara – it was just work stuff. I wouldn't dream of discussing your private business with Chris.' She smiled, seeing Sara's face clear. 'Tell you what, once this murder enquiry is behind us, why don't we three sit down together and try to work out if there are any schemes that might help you both?'

Sara smiled back at Clare. 'Thanks, boss. That would be great.'

Sara went off to answer the phone and Clare turned back to the coffee, examining the mugs to find the least grubby ones. There was an awkward silence and she racked her brains for something to say. Eventually, she said, 'Staff, eh? Worse than a bunch of kids.'

Gayle raised an eyebrow. 'I'd say, Clare, that it's probably just as well my work here is almost finished.' She formed her lips into a smile but her eyes didn't follow suit. 'Wouldn't you?'

And, with that, she plunged the coffee and began to pour it into mugs. 'Think I'll take mine in my room.' She flicked a glance at Clare. 'Still a few loose ends to tie up, you know.'

Clare felt sick. She remembered Gayle's warning and wondered if she'd carry out her threat to have Clare arrested. Her phone started to ring and, glancing at the display, she saw it was the DCI. What the hell now?

She left her coffee behind and went into her office, closing the door before she took the call.

'The jury came back ten minutes ago.'

'And?' She held her breath.

'Guilty.'

'Oh, thank God. Sentence?'

'He's been remanded in custody, pending reports. But the judge did say he should expect a lengthy term.'

Clare felt a huge sense of relief that the DCI's gamble giving Tamsin immunity had paid off. Had it really been just two days since Tamsin had stood up and given evidence against her husband? It felt like a lifetime to Clare. 'Any sign of Rose Grant in court?'

'No, nothing. Nor Paddy.'

'So, what now for Tamsin?'

'I'll call the Serious Organised Crime lads. They'll take it from there.'

'Should I call Wendy? Let her know?'

'I'd leave it to them, Clare. It's their show now. They'll let her know soon enough.'

After the call had ended, Clare sat back in her chair, processing this development. Phil Quinn was going to jail – that much was clear. But Rose and Paddy Grant were still at large. She wondered what that would mean for Tamsin. Would they still come after her? And would the DCI continue heading up the hunt for Paddy? It didn't seem fair that Clare's mistake on the invoice should affect him. And then she knew she wouldn't let that happen. She would tell the Chief Super it was all her fault. The DCI had been through enough lately.

She forced her thoughts back to Tamsin before she was tempted to question her own motives for wanting to protect the DCI. She hoped the SOC lads would move Tamsin quickly from St Andrews. She was looking forward to waking up, knowing that Tamsin was no longer her problem. Admittedly her evidence had helped convict Phil Quinn but that evidence had been bought with immunity from prosecution. And, as far as Clare was concerned, that made her every bit as guilty as her husband.

Having Tamsin out of the way would allow her to concentrate fully on finding Johannes's killer – unless, of course, they had already found him. She wondered how soon she would be able to interview Marek. It might be worth trying later today, if the doctor's assessment was favourable. She really hoped he would be fit to be questioned. He might confess to murdering Johannes. But Clare didn't share the DCI's view on that. She couldn't see what he had to gain by killing his friend. From what she could tell, they were both laundering roughly equal sums every week or so; probably as much as they could without drawing attention to themselves. They were both careful about it, spreading it over a variety of accounts and sending it on to different recipients. They had probably worked on it together and she couldn't see them falling out over that. Certainly not enough for Marek to murder Johannes. According to their respective flatmates they had been good friends. One straight, the other gay so a lovers' tiff didn't seem likely either. She couldn't think of any reason Marek would have killed Johannes. But if he hadn't, then who had?

She sat back in her chair, going over the day Marek came into the station to report his friend missing. The day Clare had arrived with Tamsin in tow. She hadn't paid him much attention then, but maybe it was worth revisiting it now. She rose from her chair and went in search of Jim. She found him at his desk, poring over policing requests for another golf tournament.

'I can't see how I can do this without cancelling leave for at least six officers,' he said, rubbing the back of his neck. 'We just don't have the manpower in the middle of summer.'

'See if we can beg a favour from Dundee,' Clare suggested. 'They'll probably have a few bodies to spare.'

Jim nodded at this then put down his pen. 'Was there something you wanted, Clare?'

'Yes, if you don't mind. Jim – could you find me the footage from the front desk, the day Marek came to report Johannes missing? No desperate rush but I'd like to view it before I interview him.'

She left Jim to look for the video footage and stood checking her phone for messages. Nothing from the garage yet. Admittedly it was still early. She'd give it another couple of hours then call to see if they'd found the fault with the Merc. She couldn't call Wendy either – the DCI had been quite clear about that. There was a pile of paperwork in her office, that had accumulated while she'd been busy dealing with Tamsin and the two students. The prospect filled her with dismay but the sooner she started…

As she passed by the small interview room she saw the door was slightly ajar. Gayle was tapping away on her laptop. Clare wondered what was going into her report. If the leak had come from someone based in St Andrews, what would that mean for them all? Would there be an enquiry? And what would Gayle do about Clare's indiscretion? If the leak had been found, maybe it wouldn't matter that she'd told Chris. She could always deny it. There was no way their conversation could have been recorded. She could prime Chris to say they were talking about something else – anything but the leak. And anyway, Gayle had said she was leaving today. Maybe she'd let it go…

She closed her office door and sat at her desk, shaking the mouse to bring her screen to life. She thought about the crime statistics report she should be compiling. But she couldn't settle to it. There were so many things up in the air today.

On an impulse she picked up her phone and dialled the number for Greystane House. It was answered after a few rings. Clare introduced herself and explained to the operator that she wished to speak to whoever was assessing an attempted suicide from the previous night.

The operator asked her to hold then, after a few moments, she spoke again. 'Miss Grant, was it?'

Clare started to reply. 'No, it was a young man – Marek... sorry, what name did you just say?'

'Grant,' the operator said. 'A Miss Rose Grant.'

It took her a split second to react. Then, trying to keep her voice level, she said, 'Listen carefully to me, please. I believe one of your patients is in danger from another patient. Serious danger. Write this down: Marek Schmidt – S-C-H-M-I-D-T. Young man, early twenties, dark curly hair. I need two members of staff to go to him immediately and to stay with him. I have an officer on site and I'll be sending more along. And when you've done that that I want the same supervision organised for Rose Grant. Rose is potentially dangerous so you'll need two members of staff keeping an eye on her at all times. Do you understand?'

The operator said that she did and Clare rang off.

'Chris?' she yelled, heading out the door.

He followed her, grabbing his jacket. 'Where's the fire?'

Clare pushed open the station doors and made for the car. 'Rose Grant managed to get herself admitted to Greystane last night. I'll drive. Can you get on to Bell Street in Dundee and get them to send a couple of cars up there now? I want that hospital locked down. Then get on to whoever's there...'

'Gillian—'

'Get on to Gillian and warn her. Tell her to stick to Marek like glue.' She jumped into the car, immediately switching on the lightbar and siren, and they roared out of the car park.

Chapter 28

She abandoned the car outside the barrier and ran past the police cars that had come from Bell Street, through the front entrance towards reception, holding her ID badge in front of her. Two uniformed cops met her.

'Marek?' she asked.

One of the cops shook his head. 'Not in his room.'

'Oh God.' Clare felt sick. She was already imagining his bloodied body hidden in a sluice room or a cupboard somewhere. 'What about Rose Grant?'

'Can't find her either.'

'Dammit. Right. We need more cops. I want this whole place searched and the perimeter secured. Rose Grant to be arrested on sight. Close-cropped white-blonde hair.'

'That's a lot of ground, Inspector,' the cop said.

'And?'

The cop wisely made no reply and began speaking into his radio.

Clare turned to Chris. 'Let's check the kitchen first.'

'Kitchen?'

'Knives, Chris!'

A charge nurse led them to the kitchen where staff looked round, surprised to see them.

'You can't come in here without—' a woman in a white coat began, walking towards them, but the charge nurse waved this away.

'Check your knives,' Clare said. 'Any missing?'

The white-coated woman stared.

'Now, please,' Clare said. 'A man's life is in danger.'

After a moment's hesitation the woman began moving round the room, speaking to staff and opening drawers. After a minute or so, she came back to Clare. 'I can't be absolutely sure but I don't think there's anything missing.'

Clare turned back to the charge nurse. 'Do you carry out any medical procedures here?'

'You mean operations?'

'Yes. Anything that would require sharp tools.'

The charge nurse shook his head. 'Nothing like that.'

Clare's mind was whirling. Where could Marek be? Had Rose got to him or was he hiding from her? 'What about laundry?' she asked. 'Is it done here?'

'No. It all goes up to Ninewells.'

'Okay, then. Let's be methodical. Every cupboard, every toilet, every single room. I want to search them all.' Clare's radio crackled. The cop at reception.

'Boss, we have cars at as many points as we can round the perimeter; and a dozen cops out searching the grounds now.'

'Make sure every fire exit is manned and keep in touch.'

–

They found Rose first.

'Heading over a fence into the woods at the back,' the voice on the radio said. 'I reckon she heard the police sirens and realised we were onto her. No sign of a weapon. She's cuffed and in the back of a car now.'

'Right. Hold her there until I think where to send her. Get her cautioned. Then ask if she knows anything about another patient. Radio me if she tells you anything at all. But do not mention Marek by name. Got it?'

They carried on searching in silence until Chris said, 'The thing that's worrying me is…'

'Yeah, I know. If Rose was trying to escape, what's happened to Marek?'

'Clare…' Chris stopped, as if trying to order his thoughts. 'What if there isn't a connection between Marek and Rose Grant? I mean, why would there be? There's nothing to suggest they know each other. What if Rose is just a bit unhinged, or high on drugs even? She might easily have wandered onto the bridge and been mistaken for a suicide.'

'Not very likely,' Clare said.

'But I can't work out why she would be chasing after Marek. In fact, we don't even know if she was. She might have another reason for getting herself admitted, assuming she's not a genuine suicide case.'

Clare spread her hands. 'I've no idea, Chris. Maybe Paddy and Rose were the ones running the money laundering scheme. Maybe they killed Johannes – I just don't know. But it's too much of a coincidence, for my liking. We have to find that lad alive. If we lose him, we lose any chance of identifying Johannes's murderer.' Clare began walking again and Chris followed. She pushed open the door labelled *Store*. As soon as she entered she felt there was another person concealed somewhere. It had to be Marek. But was he still alive?

She looked round at shelf upon shelf of towels and bed linen, large rolls of toilet paper, wider rolls for examination couches, packs of blue paper towels and bottles of chemicals. 'Marek,' she said, 'I am Detective Inspector Clare Mackay and I have Detective Sergeant Chris West with me. Charge Nurse...' She glanced back at the nurse, still in the corridor, outside the door.

'Gerry Donaldson,' the nurse said.

'...Gerry Donaldson,' Clare went on. She held her ID badge out in front of her. 'I know you're frightened but we're going to take care of you. The woman who came here to find you has been arrested. So you're safe now.' She held her breath, listening for any clue as to where he was concealed. There was a slight movement behind a stack of white towels. 'Come on out, Marek,' she said, her voice soft. 'It's all over.'

The towels shifted again.

Clare moved slowly towards the shelf. 'Marek, I'm just going to move these towels out of the way. Okay?'

There was a muffled sob and Clare stepped forward, gradually removing one towel at a time until she could see a pair of frightened eyes. 'It's okay,' she said. 'It's okay. You're safe now.'

The duty doctor, after examining Marek, agreed that he could be interviewed, providing a nurse was in attendance. But when Clare raised the possibility of taking him to St Andrews for interview he was less keen. 'We'd really like to keep an eye on him here,' he said. 'There is an Emergency Detention Certificate in place.'

Clare considered this. She didn't believe Marek would be safe at Greystane. They might have arrested Rose, but Paddy Grant was still at large. 'I think he went to the Tay Road Bridge in desperation,' she told the doctor. 'I think he was chased onto the bridge and that he ran along the carriageway to draw attention to himself. It's a busy bridge so there would have been plenty of witnesses – to say nothing of cameras – enough to put off someone trying to harm him. If I can show that, will you let me take him over to the station? We've far more chance of keeping him safe there than you have here.'

The doctor agreed and said that he would sit in on the interview. As it was taking place away from the station Chris set up his phone to record the proceedings. While he was doing this, Clare took the chance to have her first good look at Marek. He was around five foot nine, his build average. He was dressed in dark blue jeans and a faded grey sweatshirt, with blue Adidas trainers on his feet. His skin was olive but he was pale now with dark circles beneath his eyes. Clare guessed he hadn't had much sleep since taking off from St Andrews and she gave him what she hoped was a reassuring smile.

She began by asking him if he needed an interpreter.

He shook his head. 'I'm fine with English,' he said, with a slight accent.

'And you're sure you feel well enough to be interviewed?'

'Yes,' he said, his voice flat. 'I'm just tired.'

'I understand, Marek. If, at any time, you feel you can't continue, please let us know and we'll suspend the interview.' She glanced at the doctor who gave a slight nod. She went on to caution Marek and he indicated that he understood.

The formalities out of the way, Clare told Marek that she was investigating a money laundering scheme and that she would be questioning him about it. 'We will provide you with a solicitor before discussing that but please remember you are under caution.'

Marek nodded at this and Clare pressed on.

'Marek, before we discuss any possible offences you may have committed, I'd like to ask you about last night. Can you tell me why you found yourself up on the Tay Road Bridge please?'

He took a moment to answer then said simply, 'I was frightened.'

'Frightened of what?'

He looked at Clare. 'That woman. The one with the short blonde hair.'

'Why were you frightened of her, Marek?'

He met Clare's eye, his expression clouded. 'It's difficult to explain...'

'Okay, Marek,' Clare said. 'How about you tell us what happened yesterday – in your own way.'

Marek nodded. 'I'd been staying at the caravan park. In Tayport. I needed to get out of St Andrews – I knew something bad must have happened to Johannes – so I caught a bus out of town and got off in Tayport. The caravan park looked pretty nice and it was tucked out of the way on the edge of the town. So I went to the office and spoke to the manager. Asked if he needed any odd jobs done. I said I was good with my hands and I'd be happy to work in return for somewhere to stay. He said there was an old van he couldn't rent, that I could have that if I worked for him. So I made myself useful and he seemed pleased with me.'

'And then?'

'It was yesterday morning,' Marek said. 'I was in the laundry, washing the floor. And when I went back to the main office they told me a woman had been asking for me. And I was worried, then. Because I hadn't told anyone where I was.'

'Did she ask for you by name?' Clare said.

Marek nodded. 'Yes she did; and she said she had a message from Johannes.'

Clare sat forward. 'Johannes Muller? Your friend?'

'Yes. And I knew that couldn't be right because – well, I'd seen on the news, about Johannes…' He tailed off, his eyes brimming with tears.

'And what do you think she meant by that, Marek?'

He spread his hands. 'What would anyone think, Inspector? I thought she had killed Johannes and now she had come to kill me too. So I decided to leave. Get the hell out of there before she found me.'

'And where did you go?'

'The common. It's next to the caravan park and quite open so I knew I'd be able to see her coming.' He shivered. 'I was keeping near to the river and I'd nearly reached the end of the common when I saw her. She was a bit away – the other side of the pond – but I could see she was looking at me. Watching me.' He shook his head. 'I… had seen her before, you see. That white-blonde hair – it's unmistakable.'

'Where had you seen her?' Clare asked.

He hesitated. 'You said I could have a solicitor…'

Clare smiled. 'Yes, that's fine, Marek. We'll leave that for now. If you could go on, please? You recognised this woman. What happened next?'

'She watched me for a minute and then she started running across, towards me. So I started to run too. As fast as I could. I'm pretty fast, you know. And, after a few days walking around, I knew the area.'

'Where did you run to?'

'Along the beach. And then round by the harbour. There are little lanes between the houses, and paths along the beach. I didn't think she would know that so I ran through them, keeping off the roads as much as I could.'

'And then?'

'I came to the cemetery. I hoped I'd be safe there. Not many people around, you know. I stayed there for a while, just to make sure she hadn't followed me. And then I saw the bridge in the distance. I thought, if I could get to Dundee, well, it's a big city so maybe I could lose her there.' Marek drank from a plastic cup of water then continued. 'I started walking to the bridge and I got to the grass beside it and then she was there again. From nowhere. She must have realised I'd head for the bridge and she was there, waiting for me.' His face was pink now, his hands shaking.

Clare sensed the doctor was becoming concerned. 'Would you like to take a break, Marek?'

He waved this away. 'No, I want to tell someone.' He met her eyes, his voice almost a whisper now. 'It's a relief to speak about it; and I've been so frightened.'

Clare smiled. 'I understand.' She waited for him to continue.

'So I ran,' he said. 'Up to the car park and over to the ramp. I thought if I was up there I would be safe, with all the cars. That she wouldn't try to follow. But she did. I was running along the walkway, you know – between the two roads. And I could see her coming up the ramp. So, the only thing I could think of was to jump onto the carriageway, in front of the cars. I dodged through a couple and then the next car put on its hazard warning lights and slowed down. The driver offered to take me off the bridge but I didn't know if I could trust him. I was too frightened.'

'And the woman?' Clare asked. 'What did she do?'

'She hung back. I could see her watching me and the car driver – waiting to see what would happen. So I climbed over the barrier to make them think I was going to jump.'

The doctor caught Clare's eye and she gave him a nod.

'Marek,' the doctor said, his voice gentle, 'did you think that you might jump? Was it a real possibility?'

Marek looked at the doctor and shook his head. Then he turned back to Clare. 'It was so cold out there, you know? The wind. My sweatshirt was flapping and, when I looked down at the water, it was black. So black.' He closed his eyes. 'I imagined myself plunging down, hitting the water and going down, down and maybe not coming up.' He opened his eyes again. 'I couldn't do that,' he said. 'I haven't the courage.'

Clare leaned forward. 'I think you're very brave, Marek,' she said. She caught the doctor's eye to check he was happy with Marek's response and he nodded. 'Go on,' she said.

'When the police came, she disappeared. I've no idea where she went. And I was so glad to see them. And the ambulance. When I saw that I knew I was safe.' He shivered again. 'Or I thought I was…'

Clare asked Marek again if he was happy to continue and he said that he was.

'Can you tell me when you next saw the woman?' she asked.

Marek swallowed. 'This morning. I was having break-fast. There's a table in the ward and we all sat round eating. And something made me look up. I saw her outside the door. She was watching me and I knew she'd come to kill me.'

'What made you think that?' Clare asked.

'She'd followed me all yesterday – in Tayport and then up to the bridge. And then she was here. In a psychiatric unit. Why else would she have come?' His eyes were swimming with tears now. 'I thought she was going to kill me,' he whispered.

The doctor reached over to a cupboard and took out a box of tissues which he passed across to Marek. He took one and wiped his eyes then blew his nose. 'Sorry,' he said eventually. 'It's just horrible, remembering…'

Clare met his eye. 'You're doing so well, Marek. You really are.' She paused for a moment to allow him to blow his nose again then she went on. 'If you're happy to continue, maybe you could tell me what you did – when you saw her watching you?'

Marek flicked a glance at the doctor. 'I told one of the other men that I wanted a bit of privacy, you know? I winked and he said *Had I got someone lined up for a quickie?* I said it was something like that and he said he knew just the place. I then said the girl I was seeing had a friend on her ward who was jealous and that we had to avoid being seen by her. I said she had white-blonde hair. He laughed and said leave it to him. He went out and checked the corridor for me and he led me to the store room. And that's where you found me.'

Clare's phone began to ring. She cursed herself for not having it on silent. She nodded to Chris to pause the recording and looked to see who was calling. Jim. It wasn't like him to interrupt her unless it was urgent. 'I'm sorry,' she said, 'I'll have to take this. Chris, could you stay…'

Chris indicated that he would and she left the room. In the corridor she swiped to take the call. 'Jim?'

'Something I need you to see, Clare. I'm going to send you a short video clip.'

Clare ended the call and waited for the clip to arrive. After a few minutes her phone pinged and it began downloading the video. She could see it was about thirty seconds long and that it was part of the footage from the camera covering the public enquiry desk at the station. She watched Marek and Jim in conversation, Jim's head bent as he wrote down the details of Johannes's disappearance.

And then she saw herself coming into shot, with a clearly nervous Tamsin in tow. Marek glanced across at them, first at Clare, then at Tamsin. And then Clare saw why Jim had sent the clip. She saw Marek's eyes fixed on Tamsin and hers on him. She held his gaze and his brow clouded as if he was confused by her presence in the station. And then his expression changed to one of fear.

Chapter 29

She called Jim back immediately. 'It's hard to be sure on my phone, Jim. The screen is so small. But do you agree Marek recognised Tamsin?'

'Definitely. And what's more, he was frightened of her. You maybe can't see too clearly on your phone but on the monitor here there's no doubt about it. That explains why he shot off. I didn't realise it until I reviewed the footage.'

'Okay, Jim. I need to think what to do next. Leave it with me.'

She sat thinking for a minute then called the DCI. He answered immediately, his 'Hi Clare' a little stiff and formal.

'Al, I've no time to explain. We need to bring Tamsin in for questioning.'

'Impossible. She has immunity.'

'From dealing arms. But I've reason to believe she knew our murder victim and his friend. You'll have to trust me.'

'Clare, we'd have to go through Serious Organised Crime.'

'Then could you please do it? Please, Al?'

He sighed. 'You'd better have a bloody good reason.'

'I do. Trust me. Just get them to bring her in.'

Chris eyed Clare as she came back into the room but she said nothing, resuming her seat. Chris restarted the recording and the doctor looked pointedly at his watch.

'I do have ward rounds, Inspector...'

Clare nodded. 'I'd like to ask Marek a few more questions, if you can bear with me, and then, I'd like to take him to St Andrews – for his safety.'

Marek stared at her, his eyes wide. 'What is it, Inspector?'

Clare took out her phone and opened up the video footage which she had paused at the moment Marek's expression had changed on seeing Tamsin. But she didn't immediately show it to him. 'Marek, first of all, I must remind you that you are still under caution. Do you understand?'

Marek said that he did and Clare went on.

'I'd like to ask you about a woman called Tamsin Quinn.'

The colour drained from Marek's face but he said nothing.

'You do know Tamsin, don't you?'

Again, Marek said nothing.

Clare pushed her phone across the desk to show Marek the still from the station camera. 'This is you, last Friday. The day you came into the station to report your friend Johannes Muller missing. Do you agree that this photo shows you speaking to my sergeant?'

Marek nodded.

'For the tape, please, Marek.'

'Yes, that's me.'

'Thank you. Now, Marek, at this point in the footage I entered the station with Tamsin Quinn. This recording has been viewed by Sergeant Douglas who you spoke to and both he and I are agreed. We believe, from your expression, that you recognised Tamsin Quinn. I also believe that you were frightened enough by seeing her there that you left the station without completing the missing person report. Is that correct?'

Marek was looking at the floor now.

'Marek?'

He raised his head. 'Where is she – Tamsin?'

'Let's not worry about that for now, Marek. But I think, with the doctor's permission, that I'd like to take you back to St Andrews Police Station where you'll be placed into protective custody. You'll be far safer than you could be here.' She glanced at the doctor who inclined his head.

'I'll write a prescription for a mild sedative and send it to the pharmacy.'

Clare rose. 'If you give it to me, we'll have it dispensed in St Andrews. It'll be far quicker and we do need to act without delay.' She turned to Chris. 'Will you accompany Marek to his ward please, Chris, and help him get his things together? The sooner we're on our way the better.'

–

They drove back to St Andrews in silence, Clare and Chris in the front, Marek in the back with Gillian. Clare had called ahead to arrange a duty solicitor for Marek and she saw the solicitor's car pull up behind them as they arrived. Once they were safely inside the station, Clare detailed Robbie and Gillian to stay with Marek at all times.

'Except when he's speaking to his solicitor. Otherwise, I don't want him left on his own. Get young Gary to nip out for some sandwiches but do not leave his side. He goes to the loo, I want you in there tearing off the toilet paper for him. Got it? I'll be in to question him as soon as I can. Meantime, stick to him like glue.'

Clare sought out Jim next. 'Can you get on to the cops holding Rose Grant and tell them to send her to Cupar please? I don't want her in the same station as Marek. If he sees her he might clam up.'

Jim went off to make the call and Clare took Chris into her office. 'Sorry I've not had the chance to let you see this, Chris. But I needed to get Marek back here for his protection. Have a look at it now,' she said, handing him her phone.

Chris viewed the clip a couple of times then shook his head. 'All this time – we've had Tamsin in protective custody and she's the reason he legged it.'

'Yup.'

'Do you know why?'

'Not yet but I plan to interview him shortly. I just need to gather my thoughts.'

'You think he's been laundering money for her? Or Phil?'

'Could be. Or maybe there's some other reason he's frightened of her. Who knows what she's been up to. She's certainly no angel. I've spoken to the DCI and asked him to bring her in.'

'But she has immunity, doesn't she?'

'Yes, for the arms charges. But if there's something else going on – something that involves Marek – we could legitimately charge her with that.'

'You reckon Serious Organised Crime will let you near her?'

'They'd better, Chris.' Clare's expression was grim. 'We have one dead student and another almost killed. I'd bet my eye teeth Tamsin's involved.'

'You're not planning to bring her here, are you?'

'No way. Can't risk her running into Marek again. Not until we have his statement. We can send her to Cupar or Dundee, even. They'll have room.' She checked her watch. 'Come on – let's see what he has to say for himself.'

Marek seemed more relaxed in the police interview room. 'I feel safe here,' he said, giving Clare a smile.

She returned the smile and began the tape, reminding Marek that he was under caution. He confirmed that he understood the caution and the interview began. Clare started by asking him what his connection with Tamsin Quinn was.

'We were in a pub one night, Johannes and I. Just chatting and this woman approached us.'

'Can you identify this woman?' Clare said. 'For the tape?'

'It was Tamsin Quinn. She sat down and said she was a businesswoman looking for some extra help. She said she thought we were students and that she was looking for someone good with numbers; that it was tricky work and she needed someone intelligent and reliable.' He smiled. 'I suppose we were flattered – that she'd chosen us.'

'Go on,' Clare said.

'She said in her kind of business she needed to move money around different accounts but that the banks wanted to charge her for each transaction. She said it was cheaper to do it with non-business accounts but that she already had several and the banks wouldn't allow her to open any more.' He paused to clear his throat then went on. 'So Johannes asked what kind of transactions she meant.'

'And what did she say?' Clare asked.

'She said she represented small start-up companies. That they had limited capital and she helped them to make short-term investments that earned better interest than they'd get from the banks. She said if we were interested in helping these businesses they'd pay us a commission.'

Clare had to admit Tamsin certainly knew how to put a positive spin on a criminal activity. 'Go on,' she said and Marek continued.

'She said that everyone needs a leg up at some point and that these were small local businesses who would be so grateful for the help.' He looked from Clare to Chris. 'She made it sound such a positive thing to do.'

'Marek, bearing in mind you are still under caution, were you aware that Tamsin was asking you to assist in laundering money? That to do so is a criminal offence and that the money had, in all probability, come from other criminal activities?'

He shook his head. 'Not at first. But by the time we realised what we were doing it was too late. She said we were in it up to our necks and if she went down she'd drag us down with her. And – you know – the money she was paying us for doing it came in handy. Made a change from watching every penny. So we talked about it and decided we'd do it till the end of the year then stop. We thought if we went away for the summer she'd find someone else.'

Clare nodded at this. Then she said, 'Did you ever see the woman we believe to be Rose Grant when you met with Tamsin? She's the woman who you claim chased you onto the Tay Road Bridge and who you later saw at Greystane House.'

He nodded. 'Yes. The first time Tamsin gave us money to pay into our accounts she was there too.' His brow clouded. 'I still don't know how she found me.'

Chris said, 'You've an iPhone, haven't you?'

Marek said that he had.

'Did you ever hand it over to her?'

'Yes. But only for a few minutes. She said she had to put a few numbers into our phones. Hers and Tamsin's. Maybe someone else – I can't remember.'

'I'm guessing you have Find My installed?'

Marek shrugged. 'Maybe. I think so.'

'She's probably gone to Location Services and turned on Sharing Your Location. It can be set to Indefinitely. Once you disappeared she'd be able to track you to within fifty metres, if the Wi-Fi and GPS were strong enough.'

Marek shook his head. 'I never thought to check.'

Clare glanced at Chris, wondering if her own phone had the location shared. She made a mental note to check this later then turned her attention back to the interview. 'Marek, let's move on from that please. At some point in the future I'll question you again to compile a detailed account of your transactions for Tamsin. But I'd like to turn to Johannes now. Can you tell me when you last saw him?'

Marek didn't speak for a minute. Then he said, 'Two days before I came here to report him missing.'

'And what did you think had happened to him?'

Marek began to fiddle with a loose thread on the cuff of his sweatshirt. 'I wasn't sure – he said he was going to speak to Tamsin. Said we were doing a lot of work for just five per cent. He wanted more.' He shivered at the memory. 'I said he shouldn't. Said we didn't know what she might do but he laughed it off. He said we knew too much about her. That she'd have no choice but to agree. He was going to tell her it was ten per cent or he'd go to the police.'

Clare groaned inwardly. Stupid naïve lads. They had no idea what the likes of Tamsin would do. Life was cheap in her world.

'I think it was the Wednesday,' Marek said. 'He was going to see her on the Wednesday night. Make her an offer she couldn't refuse. At least that's what he said. I tried to persuade him not to but he said I'd thank him when we were raking in twice as much. And so I waited. Waited for him to call. Tell me how it had gone. But he didn't call. And the next day he wasn't at his lectures. I saw Lloyd and Tim in the union coffee bar and I asked them if they'd seen him but they hadn't. So, on the Friday, I thought I should report him missing. And – well, you know the rest.'

From within her pocket, Clare's phone began to buzz. She slipped it out and glanced down at the display. Moira, her neighbour. What on earth did she want? She ended the interview and excused herself, leaving Marek with his solicitor. 'Moira? What's up?'

Clare could tell from the sound that Moira was outdoors.

'Oh Clare, I'm so sorry but it's Benjy. He slipped his lead while I was walking him and he's running along the road. I can't catch him and I'm worried he'll be run over – or cause an accident.'

Clare swore under her breath. Benjy! Of all the days.

'Bill has the car today,' Moira went on, 'or I'd drive after him.'

'Don't worry Moira. I'll come and round him up.' Clare ended the call and put her head round the interview room door. 'I'm sorry, Marek – something urgent's come up. I'll have to leave you here. I'll be back as soon as I can.'

He waved this away. 'It's fine, Inspector. I'm relieved to be here.'

Clare indicated to Chris to follow her out of the room. 'I need a lift, Chris. Now, please. Can you get the car keys and I'll explain as we go?'

While Chris drove her along the Craigtoun Road, keeping an eye out for Benjy, Clare tried the DCI again. She had to make sure they detained Tamsin before she set off for her new life. She tried three times and each time the call was declined. 'Well fuck you,' she said, hanging up after the third attempt.

Her phone rang almost immediately but she saw that it was Diane.

'Clare, I need to speak to you,' Diane said. 'It's pretty important. I—'

Clare cut across her. 'Diane, I'm sorry. I can't talk right now. I'm right in the middle of something. Look, I'll call at the weekend. Okay?' She ended the call without waiting for an answer.

'There he is,' Chris said, spotting Benjy trotting along the side of the road. He pulled the car into the verge and Clare jumped out, whistling to the little dog. Benjy turned, delighted to see her, and scampered back towards the car, flinging himself against her legs.

'You are a very bad dog,' she said, taking him by the scruff of the neck and shoving him into the back of the car. 'Can you take me home please, Chris? And if you hang on I'll put him back in the house then we are going to pick up Tamsin Quinn and to hell with the Serious Organised Crime squad.'

As Chris reversed the car into Clare's drive she saw that her own car had been moved. 'Oh, it's back,' she said. 'They must have fixed it. Look, Chris, time is against us. You head for the Market Street flat now and keep Tamsin there. I'll follow on in my own car.'

Clare jumped out, opening the back door for Benjy, and Chris roared away towards Market Street. Inside the house she retrieved the spare car key and, giving Benjy a quick rub behind the ears, she locked the front door and jumped into her car. Thankfully it started first time. There was a service sheet on the dashboard and she tucked it into the glove box to read later. 'Right, Tamsin Quinn,' she said to herself. 'The show's over.' And she pulled out of the drive, putting her foot to the floor.

Chapter 30

Chris was waiting for her at the door to the flat as she arrived on Market Street.

He jerked his head up at the windows. 'Too late,' he said. 'She's gone.'

Clare looked across the street to where the dark red Range Rover had sat for the past couple of days but it too was gone. She took out her phone and called Wendy. It was answered immediately and it sounded as if she was driving. 'Wendy,' she said, 'when did you leave Tamsin?'

'About half an hour ago, I think.'

'Do you know where she was heading?'

'Sorry, Clare. The Serious Organised Crime boys arrived and told me to leave. They had a suitcase which I'm guessing was a change of clothes. They walked me to the door and I saw them watch as I drove off. Was there something you needed her for?'

'You could say that. Look, Wendy – I don't suppose you still have a set of keys?'

There was a hesitation. Just enough to let Clare know that she did. 'Clare – I know I wasn't meant to but I had an extra copy made. Just in case. Obviously I couldn't tell the SOCs. It's a serious breach. But I didn't want to risk not being able to get in so...'

'Wendy, you are a godsend. Look – where are you now? Could you head back here and let me into that flat?'

'I can, Clare. But I'm nearly at Glenrothes so it'll be another half hour at least.'

'Just as quickly as you can, Wendy. And thanks.'

Clare ended the call and immediately tried the DCI again. It went straight to voicemail. 'Come on, Chris,' she said. 'Let's find a cafe and wait for Wendy.'

They crossed the road to a small cafe with a view of the flat and ordered mugs of tea. Chris looked longingly at a tray of cakes but Clare steered him away, telling him to find a table.

He chose a table in the window, away from the other customers, and took out his phone. As Clare sat down beside him he indicated the phone. 'Presume you want this switched off?'

She shook her head. 'Frankly, Chris, I'm past caring. I'm pretty sure Gayle knows I blabbed to you and, anyway, this is her last day. Between that damned invoice, me telling you about the leak and Tamsin slipping through our fingers, I doubt I could be in any more trouble.'

Chris put his phone back in his pocket and they sat in silence, waiting for the tea. When it arrived and the waiter had moved away, Clare said, 'Okay, let's try and get this clear in our heads.'

Chris picked up his cup and took a sip. 'You're thinking Tamsin organised the money laundering scheme?'

'Yes, I think so. I believe she recruited Johannes and Marek, and probably plenty of other students too. Maybe a few housewives – anyone she thought would be happy to earn a few quid without asking too many questions.'

'But where's the money come from?' Chris asked.

'Probably from Phil Quinn's illegal arms dealing. Don't forget she only turned against him when he supplied the guns that killed the Clearys.'

'So she says.'

'Well, yeah. Anyway, she has all this money that she wants to make legitimate. So she recruits the two lads. All goes well until Johannes gets greedy. I reckon he went to meet her that Wednesday night and she – or someone – was waiting for him, knocked him about a bit then slipped the rope around his neck. Then they threw him in a van or the boot of a car and drove him to Craigtoun Park where they dumped his body.'

'Hold on, though,' Chris said. 'It can't have been Tamsin who killed him.'

'Why not?'

'Think, Clare – this arms case against Phil Quinn. It's been going on for two weeks now. Tamsin was in protective custody all that time and probably for a good while before the trial began. She couldn't possibly have met Johannes to kill him.'

Clare slapped her forehead. She'd forgotten Tamsin had been in the Perth house before coming to St Andrews. 'Of course, Chris.' She ran through the possibilities in her head then said, 'She must have told Johannes she would meet him – somehow…'

'Burner phone?'

'Yes, it must have been. The SOC guys would have been monitoring her own phone.' She ran a hand through her hair, then said, 'Okay, Chris. She has a phone they don't know about. Probably used it to keep in touch with her money mules. She realises Johannes is getting greedy and calls someone to get rid of him.'

'Pretty extreme,' Chris said. 'You reckon she has it in her? To have Johannes killed?'

'Listen, she's married to Phil Quinn. She's no stranger to violence. He's had some pretty dodgy characters working for him over the years so she wouldn't be stuck for someone to do it. I'm guessing our Tamsin only has to pick up the phone and Phil's heavies are only too happy to oblige.'

Chris shook his head. 'Those young lads, Johannes and Marek – they had no idea who they were dealing with.' He picked up his teaspoon and began stirring his tea, idly. 'Thing is, Clare – even if you do track Tamsin down, what could you charge her with? I doubt we can prove she arranged for Johannes to be killed.'

'Depends. I'm pretty sure Marek's evidence will be enough to get her for money laundering. And I'll have a bloody good go at charging her with *Conspiracy to Commit Murder*.'

'Bit of a long shot, though, isn't it?'

Clare nodded. 'It is. Proving it won't be easy. She'll have covered her tracks, that one.'

'But we do have Marek, thank God. That was a good call, finding out Rose was in Greystane.'

Clare smiled. 'Bit of luck, really. And we have Marek's phone now. So, maybe...' She broke off when she saw Wendy's car draw up outside the flat. 'Chris, get Gillian on the phone and ask her to get Tamsin's number from Marek's phone. Then get hold of Johannes's phone records and see if there's a match. That should help us pin the money laundering on her.'

'You're assuming he'll be happy enough to give us his phone.'

Clare reached down to pick up her bag. 'We haven't time to wait for a warrant so he'll have to help us. If necessary, remind him that Tamsin's still roaming free and that it's in his interests to help us find her. And if the solicitor is minded to be arsy about it, tell Gillian to say we need it to track a criminal and that it'll be noted when we decide whether to charge Marek with any offences.' She rose, scraping her chair back. 'And, once you've got the number, get on to the phone company and find out if Tamsin's phone has pinged any masts since she left St Andrews this morning.'

She left Chris to make the calls and went to meet Wendy.

'Not a word about this key to anyone, Clare,' she said. 'Or I'll be for it.'

'Of course. Just make sure you get rid of it safely.'

Wendy nodded. 'I have a coarse file at home so I'll grind it down tonight – unless you think you'll need it again?' Wendy put the key in the lock then hesitated. 'The SOC boys have probably wiped the place down. Do you have gloves, Clare?'

Clare opened her bag and produced two pairs of gloves. Wendy pulled on a pair and opened the door. They climbed the stairs and Wendy took the other key, opening the door at the top. The flat was little changed from Clare's last visit except that Tamsin was no longer there. There were coffee cups on the draining board in the kitchen and a pile of magazines lying on the sofa. Clare went into the bedroom and opened the wardrobe. Tamsin's clothes hung there and draped across the bed was the coat she had worn when they had brought her from Perth. 'Looks like they've given her a new wardrobe,' she said to Wendy. 'Probably a whole new identity.'

'Yeah. It's a high-profile case,' Wendy agreed, 'and, with Paddy Grant still at large, it's safer that way.'

Clare sat down on the sofa. 'It makes me so angry, Wendy. She's done such damage. One student dead. Another driven almost to the point of suicide, frightened for his life. And all that money she's laundered. She turns evidence against her husband and she walks away with a new life.'

'I know, Clare. But sometimes it's the lesser of two evils. At least this way Phil Quinn is off the streets.'

'I suppose.' Clare glanced at her phone as it buzzed. A text from the DCI. 'A bit late, Al,' she said to herself, swiping to read the message.

> Sorry, Clare.
> Tried my best.
> SOC wouldn't let me anywhere near Tamsin.
> She's left now with a new ID.
> Sorry again,
> Al

'Tell me something I don't know,' she muttered, putting her phone back in her pocket.

A loud rap at the door made Wendy jump. Clare rose. 'It'll only be Chris,' she said, going down the stairs to let him in.

'Got the number,' he said. 'Jim's tracing the phone company then he'll check if she's passed any masts. He's also asked for a list of contacts from Tamsin's phone. Might help us trace more of her money mules.'

'Thanks, Chris.' Clare glanced at her watch. 'Fancy a trip over to Cupar?'

The police station in Cupar was in a modern block built mainly in honey-coloured stone. It sat on the aptly named Waterend Road which bordered a narrow section of the River Eden. They had travelled separately, Clare unwilling to leave the Merc parked on Market Street, and managed to find the last two spaces in a car park to the side of the building. They walked back round onto Waterend Road towards the front door of the station.

Clare looked at the river. 'It's quite high, isn't it? I'm not sure how confident I'd be leaving my car parked here all the time.'

'It has burst its banks in the past,' Chris said. 'Flooded all along here.'

At the public enquiry desk Clare introduced herself and Chris and said they would like to interview Rose Grant.

'She's asked for a solicitor,' the desk sergeant told them.

Clare clicked her tongue. Typical of the likes of Rose. Keep them waiting as long as possible while the clock ticked down. 'How long before you can get one here?'

'Could be half an hour – if we're lucky.'

The sergeant took them through to the staff rest room. It had a kitchen area at one end with the usual kettle, microwave and fridge, and an assortment of easy chairs at the other. The desk sergeant offered to make them coffee while they waited but Clare waved this away. When he had gone she closed the door behind him and sat on one of the chairs.

'Let's think about Tamsin,' she said. 'Now, I'm not familiar with the Serious Organised Crime squad's operations. You?'

Chris was wandering about, reading notices that had been Blu-Tacked to the wall. 'Eh?'

'The SOC, Chris. Have you had any dealings with them at all?'

'Nope.'

'You know what?' Clare said. 'I'm sick of this. I'm going to phone Steve Robins.'

'The cop from SOC?'

'That's him.' Clare took out the business card Steve Robins had given her on Monday and tapped in his number. He answered immediately. Clare asked if he remembered her.

'Yes, Inspector. What's this about?'

'You had a witness,' Clare said, choosing her words carefully. 'The woman we met on Monday. I need to—'

'Let me stop you right there, Inspector. That is information you do not need and we are not having this conversation.'

'I only want to—'

'I'm ending this call now and you will not contact me about this matter again. And that's an order, Inspector.'

Clare began speaking again then she heard the three short beeps that told her he had ended the call. 'Dammit.'

'He's not for talking?'

'Nope.' Clare put the phone back in her pocket. 'So, if they won't tell us what they've done with Tamsin, we'll have to work it out. So let's put ourselves in their shoes.'

'Okay.' Chris stopped reading the notices and took a seat opposite Clare. 'First of all, she'll have a new location. Might be in Scotland – maybe not. So how do they get her there?'

'Drive her,' Clare said. 'Except...'

Chris waited.

'Put yourself in Tamsin's shoes,' she said, at last. 'She was living in a safe house in Perth and the location was compromised. Then she comes to St Andrews and, again, someone finds out where she is and passes that information to Paddy Grant.'

'Yeah, we know all that.'

'Chris, think about it. That information has to be coming from inside Police Scotland.'

'The leak Gayle Crichton was investigating?'

'Yeah, could be. So, if you were Tamsin, with a new identity and location organised by the police – would you trust them?'

'I see your point.'

'If I was in Tamsin's shoes, Chris, I'd be making my own travel arrangements.'

'You think they'd let her?'

'She's a free woman. They couldn't stop her – if she was determined enough. And I'd say she was.'

Chris rubbed the back of his neck. 'Godsake, Clare. If that's true then we haven't a hope of finding her.'

'Well we have to try. So get thinking. How might she have got herself to a new location?'

'Taxi and train?'

Clare nodded. 'So we're looking for any taxi firm who sent a car to Market Street this morning. Find out where it went. We need the CCTV from the local railway stations – check Leuchars, Dundee, Cupar and Kirkcaldy. She could have gone to any one of those. Ladybank, even, if she was being cautious enough.'

Chris scribbled this down.

'Car hire,' Clare went on. 'She could have hired a car to go – well, who knows where? So we want any car hire company that sent a car to St Andrews. And if that doesn't throw up any results, check all hires out of Cupar and Dundee – any destination. Get the registrations and see if any of them have pinged any ANPR cameras on the way to St Andrews.'

'That's a hell of a lot of work, Clare.'

'Draft in as many cops as you can. I'll authorise the overtime. But see who's around first.'

The desk sergeant appeared and said that the duty solicitor was with Rose Grant now. Clare and Chris followed him to a small interview room. She hesitated outside the door, oddly nervous. The closest she had been to Rose had been in the High Court in Edinburgh and now she was coming face to face with the woman who had tried to scare Tamsin off testifying and who had probably tried to murder Marek Schmidt.

Chris glanced at her. 'Ready?'

She nodded and put a hand on the door. 'Come on. Let's see what she has to say for herself.'

Chapter 31

Rose Grant was sitting behind the desk, a middle-aged woman in a dark suit next to her. The woman looked up as they entered and gave them a nod, but Rose's expression was not encouraging. They took their seats opposite and Chris began fiddling with the tape recorder while Clare took her first proper look at Rose. She found it hard to work out how old Rose was. She could have been anything from late twenties to early forties. She was tall and wiry and her hands, crossed in front of her, looked strong. She wore no make-up on her face which was long and angular. Her hair was her most distinctive feature, white-blonde, as Clare had seen that day in the High Court, with the beginnings of dark roots starting to show. It was shaved close at her neck and spiked on top. Her eyes were a steely grey and her gaze penetrating. Clare realised now why she had felt nervous outside the door and she marvelled at Tamsin's ability to give evidence after Rose's unscheduled appearance in the court room.

Clare introduced herself and Chris and delivered the usual caution. Then she asked Rose how she knew Tamsin Quinn.

Rose's response was a terse 'No comment.'

Clare couldn't quite work out her accent. She wasn't a Dundonian, nor a Glaswegian. Maybe somewhere between the two – central Scotland, probably. She asked why Rose had been seen in a blue Transit van in St Andrews over the past week and received the same reply. She tried again, asking when Rose had last seen her brother Paddy Grant.

Rose yawned and made no reply.

Clare changed tack. 'How do you know Marek Schmidt, Rose?'

'Never heard of him.'

'Are you sure?' Clare persisted. 'Because he told us you chased him onto the Tay Road Bridge. That you had followed him through Tayport to the bridge and that you put him in fear of his life. And we'll be checking the CCTV that covers that end of the bridge.'

'No comment.'

Clare sighed. 'Okay, Rose. Why don't you tell me why you found yourself on the Tay Road Bridge yesterday?'

Rose met Clare's eye and stared at her for a few seconds. Her eyes seemed to bore into Clare and it was all Clare could do to hold her gaze. Then Rose said, 'I was gonnae kill myself, wasn't I?'

'Really?'

'Really.'

'Mind if I ask why?'

Rose shrugged. 'Life gets a bit tough, sometimes. Just thought I'd end it all.' There was the hint of a smirk, at odds with what she had just said.

Clare reckoned there wasn't the remotest chance that Rose Quinn had contemplated ending her life. Sitting there, just a few feet from Rose, she thought it was no wonder Marek had been driven to run into oncoming traffic on the bridge. She was making Clare pretty uncomfortable so she must have scared the life out of the young student. 'Do you deny you tried to intimidate Marek Schmidt, one of the patients at Greystane House?'

'Me?' she said. 'You've got me mixed up with someone else.'

'He says you were watching him through the door when he was having his breakfast this morning.'

'I was having a wander about. Stretching my legs,' she said. 'Or is that a crime now?'

Clare ignored this. 'Why were you found running away in the grounds?'

'Pfft. If you'd been in one of those places, Inspector, you wouldn't have to ask. All that touchy-feely stuff – psychologists asking you how everything makes you feel. Does my fuckin' head in. I'd had enough so I legged it.'

Clare tried a few more questions then she ended the interview.

Rose's solicitor said, 'Inspector, I cannot see you have any reason to hold Miss Grant any longer. She has answered your questions. There are no grounds to charge her with anything.'

'Oh, I'll think of something,' Clare said. 'Let's try *Interfering With a Witness*, and *Threatening Behaviour*. I'd say that was enough to detain your client, pending her appearance in court.' And, with that, she swept from the room, Chris following in her wake.

Outside, he said, 'She's not going to be an easy one to crack.'

'Nor am I, Chris,' Clare said, her expression grim. 'Nor am I.'

In the car park Clare said, 'I'm going to head back to see Marek. Can you check on those possible transport links please?'

Chris went to his car to start making phone calls. Clare jumped into the Merc and headed back along Waterend Road, turning towards St Andrews. As she drove, she called Jim, switching the phone to speaker.

'We've got Tamsin's phone number, Clare, so they're checking masts now. Meantime there are lots of numbers stored. We're working our way through them as fast as we can. There could be more money mules among them or who knows what else.'

'Good work, Jim. I'll be back soon to speak to Marek. Let me know if anything else comes to light.'

She was out of Cupar now driving through lush countryside as she approached Dairsie, a small village built mainly around the road that ran through it. A tractor with a forage harvester attached was making its way along the field next to the road, cutting grass for silage. The field on the opposite side was dotted with sheep, their heads bowed as they grazed. Clare slowed for the twenty miles an hour speed sign and drove carefully through the village, past the low-built houses that bordered the road. Beyond the village she carried on past the roundabout towards Guardbridge. A mile further on the road and verges widened, and she saw the flagpoles at the entrance to Clayton Caravan Park. Marek had believed he would be safe at the caravan park in Tayport but Rose Grant had still found him. Having witnessed first-hand how intimidating Rose could be, Clare thought it was no wonder he had taken flight. Poor lad. He was paying a heavy price for his stupidity.

She had gone through Guardbridge now, passing the chip shop where she and Chris had enjoyed the furtive fish suppers the previous night. She had to hope Sara never found out about that! She drove on and was just passing the Balgove Steak Barn when Jim phoned again.

'I think Tamsin Quinn must be driving west,' he said. 'She's pinged a mast near Balmullo. It's on a small hill above the village called Lucklawhill.'

'Where do you reckon she's heading, Jim?'

'Well, Balmullo would take her on to Cupar, although there are more direct ways of getting there. But, beyond Cupar, she could go south to Edinburgh or even over the Clackmannanshire Bridge towards Glasgow.'

Clare ended the call and drove on, lost in thought. Something in the far reaches of her mind was niggling. If only she could think what it was.

And then she remembered.

Chapter 32

Clare dialled Chris's number again, cursing her own lack of local knowledge. It was more than a year now since she had transferred from the busy Maryhill Road station in Glasgow and she knew her way around St Andrews all right. She was familiar with the little villages that peppered north-east Fife too. But when it came to the network of narrow roads that ran between the villages she still occasionally struggled.

He answered after a couple of rings. 'I'm just about done here, Clare. I'll be heading back in a few minutes.'

'Never mind that,' she said. 'What do you know about a place called Lucklawhill?'

'The hill near Balmullo?'

'That's the one.'

'Not very big. Nice walk with good views but there are masts that spoil the look of it a bit.'

'Where do you walk from?' Clare asked.

'Depends. If you're coming from the west you'd take the A92 then turn off at the signpost for Logie. It's a tiny hamlet a few miles south of the road. There's a place where you can park just before the village. Depending on how fast you want to go, the walk to the top might take twenty or thirty minutes.'

Clare considered this then said, 'What about if you were coming from St Andrews?'

'Much easier. Head for Balmullo and, as soon as you enter the village, take the first right. Hayston Park, it's called. Follow this along until you pass the school then, at the junction, turn right again. Carry on through the village until you see the Quarry Road going up to the left. There's a mast up ahead – if you see that you're on the right road.'

'There's a quarry?'

'Yeah. You've heard of Balmullo chips? The pink gravel for driveways? Decent parking at the quarry too, if you don't mind a few potholes.'

'Is that where the road ends?'

'No – it carries on past the quarry, round the side of the hill. It comes out at the other end – at Logie. Clare – why are you asking this?'

'Because Tamsin Quinn has pinged that mast you were talking about.'

'You got her number from Marek?'

'Yep. So she's either at, or passing through, Balmullo. And, so far, she hasn't pinged any other masts. So I think she might still be there.'

'Unless her phone's switched off.'

'That's true.'

'Clare,' Chris said, 'why would she hang about? If she's involved with the money laundering and Johannes's death, don't you think she'd want to get as far away from St Andrews as possible? I certainly would.'

'Agreed. But there's one other thing…'

'Which is?'

'Her mother. She used to take Tamsin up Lucklawhill to watch the air displays at Leuchars when she was little. She told me that when we first brought her to St Andrews.

What's more, she scattered her mother's ashes on Lucklawhill. So, if she is heading off somewhere for a new life…'

'She could be up there now, saying goodbye.'

'Exactly.'

Clare heard the sound of Chris starting his car engine.

'So how do you want to play it, Clare?'

'Can you call the desk sergeant at Cupar and ask him to send a car round to Logie please? You can explain the location better than me. Any cars parked near the hill itself, I want them checked against the list of taxis, hire cars and sales of new cars. If we get a match, we've found her. And, if they do find her, they need to close the road and call for reinforcements. I'll head for Balmullo and make for the quarry. If we can block the road off at either end we can stop her going any further.'

'Clare – you should wait for reinforcements.'

'I can handle Tamsin Quinn,' Clare said. 'Don't worry about that.'

'It's not Tamsin I'm worried about,' Chris said. 'Think – who's been dogging her footsteps all week?'

Clare swore under her breath. Paddy Grant. She had forgotten him.

'If Paddy somehow has managed to follow Tamsin,' Chris went on, 'he won't let you stand in his way. Think about this: why has Paddy been sticking around?'

'To frighten Tamsin. Stop her testifying against Phil. But that's all over now.'

'Not necessarily,' Chris persisted. 'Think about it, Clare: Paddy took a huge chance, making himself so visible these past few days. Do you honestly think it was all out of loyalty to Phil?'

'You think he was worried Tamsin would testify against him too?'

'I'd have thought so. He knows there's an arrest warrant out for him but, if Tamsin was out of the way, it could be hard to make charges stick.'

'But Tamsin has a new identity now, and a new life. And, given Phil was the main prize, I doubt they'd risk her safety by bringing her back to testify against Paddy. Oh wait...' She tailed off as light dawned. 'Phil doesn't know that – her new identity. He doesn't know she's heading off for a new life...'

'...so he's still after her,' Chris finished. 'And Paddy's going to see to it there's no new life for Tamsin.'

'Then it's even more important we get to her first,' Clare said. 'I want her put away for what she's done.' And with that, she ended the call. She saw a farm gate up ahead and hit the brakes, performing a swift three-point turn. She was going to Balmullo to find Tamsin Quinn and she meant to get there before Paddy Grant.

Chapter 33

It didn't take Clare long to reach the village and she slowed as she approached the *Welcome to Balmullo* sign. A glance to her left gave her a view across Leuchars to the Eden Estuary where the river met the North Sea, not far from St Andrews. She could only imagine the views from the summit of Lucklawhill would be even more impressive. She was looking out for a right turn – *Hayston Park*, Chris had said. Luckily it was signposted for Lucklawhill and she swung the Merc round into a residential street. It curved gently and, despite the urgency of her mission, she slowed her speed for fear of causing an accident. At the T-junction there was no further sign for the hill but she turned right as directed by Chris. The road narrowed and began to rise up and she knew she was on the lower slopes of the hill itself. A horse rider was up ahead, astride a magnificent chestnut animal, and she slowed to a crawl. The rider glanced over her shoulder and steered the horse into a driveway to allow Clare to pass. As she did so, the houses began to thin out and she approached a crossroads. A blue and green cycle path sign pointed up to the left and a road sign sunk into the verge read *Quarry Road*. Clare took a left and headed up the road in search of the quarry. She immediately saw the mast up ahead and knew she was heading in the right direction.

It was a single-track road, with passing places, and she met a few cars as she climbed up towards the quarry. She scanned the drivers' faces carefully as they passed but none of them looked anything like Tamsin. There were one or two houses dotted along the left-hand side, the hill itself to the right; and then the road began to level out as it skirted round the side of the hill. There was a sign for the quarry up ahead and, as she approached the gates, she reached a large clearing, surfaced in pink gravel from the quarry. A line of cars was parked to the back of the clearing and, judging by the tyre marks, it was also used to allow lorries to turn. Up ahead the road carried on, to Logie presumably. It seemed to become even narrower with a fair sprinkling of potholes and Clare decided she would take the Merc no further. In her rear-view mirror she saw the familiar blue and yellow markings of a police car and she pulled off into the gravel parking area to await its arrival.

Sara drew in alongside Clare's car and jumped out, Robbie in the passenger seat beside her.

Clare explained the situation. 'I'd like this road closed, now. Any cars wishing to proceed are to be searched and the occupants faces checked against the photos we have of Tamsin. She has a new identity now so names and addresses are pretty meaningless.'

'What if we do find her, boss?' Sara asked.

'Certainly no heroics,' Clare said and Sara flushed, recalling an incident earlier in the year when she had ended up seriously injured after tackling a suspect. Sara's actions had helped arrest the culprit but she had almost paid too high a price. She nodded and, seeing this, Clare continued.

'If you do think you've found her, tell her there's been an accident further along the road, depending on which direction she's coming from. Then radio me and ask how long it'll take to clear the accident. As soon as I hear that message I'll know you have her and I'll send reinforcements. Okay?'

The pair nodded and Clare walked over to the line of parked cars. Then she took out her phone and called Chris.

'Any luck with those cars?'

'Getting there. I've spoken to the taxi firms in the town. Only two taxis did runs to the railway stations and both customers were males.'

'Still could be Tamsin,' Clare said. 'Doubtful, I know. But we can't chance it. I bet taxi drivers don't look at their fares too closely. Get the railway station footage for up to an hour after pick-up. Anything else?'

'I've still to do sales of new cars. But I've done the hire cars – not many. Two from Dundee, one from Cupar and two from Kirkcaldy.'

'Okay, Chris. I'm going to reel off registration numbers for the cars parked up at the Balmullo quarry. Can you check them against your hires please?'

Clare worked her way along the row of parked cars but none of them matched. 'Any word from the Cupar cops at Logie?'

'Yeah, one car parked. A silver Nissan Juke. Doesn't match any of the numbers we have for hire cars but Jim's running it through the DVLA records to check if it changed hands in the last few days.'

'Okay, Chris. Can you get back onto the Cupar cops and tell them I want the Logie end of the road blocked off please? Every car coming through is to be checked.

Any female occupants, get them to check against Tamsin's photo. Any doubt at all, get hold of me and I'll drive over and take a look myself. Or, better still, draft Wendy, the FLO, in. She knows Tamsin better than anyone.'

'Will do, Clare. Is that it?'

Clare stood, looking out over the Fife countryside, the sound of quarry works grinding away behind her. Had she covered everything? There was certainly no sign of Tamsin here. 'Has she pinged any more mobile masts?'

'Nope. So either the phone is off or she's still in the area.'

'Okay, Chris. Can you give me the details of the five hire cars please? It's probably worth checking them against ANPR cameras too.'

Chris reeled off details of the five cars and Clare noted them down. There was a blue Ford Focus Estate, a black Vauxhall Corsa, a dark blue Renault Captur and two Hondas: a white CR-V and a red Jazz. None of the cars in the car park matched these and, with a wave to Sara and Robbie, she climbed into the Merc and circled round to head back down the single-track road to Balmullo. As she drove, she stopped at the gateways of the houses she passed to check their vehicles but she could see none that resembled the list of hire cars Chris had given her.

As she reached the end of the single-track road she turned back towards the village. A bell was sounding, somewhere distant. For a minute she thought it was a burglar alarm and then she realised it was the local primary school. She glanced at the car clock and saw it was three o'clock. The end of the school day. As she approached the T-junction once more she saw the children, spilling out onto the pavement, some dawdling along, others wobbling on bikes, with outsize helmets. Clare slowed down, as she had for the horse and rider, giving the brave few riding on the road as wide a berth as she could. They seemed so happy and carefree and she thought about her nephew James. Coming to stay tomorrow! Goodness, she'd better get organised for him. It didn't look as if she was going to be able to tie up this investigation for the weekend. But she had booked the time off and arranged with one of the Cupar inspectors to cover her area so she would just have to walk away and concentrate on her family for a change.

She reached the end of the road and sat, her engine idling for a few minutes while she tried to decide what to do: head back to St Andrews or hang about here on the off chance of seeing Tamsin. And then she remembered there was a Spar shop further along the road. It had been a long day and she could feel herself flagging. Maybe some chocolate would give her a boost. She pulled out into the main road and began driving along towards the Spar. And then her stomach lurched and she hit the brakes. A car behind her gave an angry peep and pulled out to overtake, giving her the finger as he went. But Clare saw none of that.

She only saw the red Honda Jazz parked outside the village shop.

Chapter 34

Clare's fingers trembled as she swiped to find Chris's number, one eye on the red Honda.

It only rang twice before he answered but it seemed like an eternity.

'Clare?'

'Chris, I need a couple of cars and as many bodies as you can get blocking off all roads in and out of Balmullo.'

'You've found her?'

'Think so. There's a red Honda Jazz sitting outside the Spar shop in the village.'

'Which way is it facing?'

'Towards Cupar. I'm behind it, near Hayston Park.'

'Checked the reg?'

'Yep. It's one of the hire cars from the list you gave me. It's too much of a coincidence, it being in Balmullo. Chris, it's Tamsin. I know it.' She listened as she heard Chris on the radio, requesting cars at either end of the village. After a minute or two he came back on the phone.

'Cars on the way but they'll be five minutes at least. The Cupar car's closer so should be a bit quicker.'

'That's fine,' Clare said. 'I'm sitting at the other end.'

'You could call Sara down from Lucklawhill.'

Clare considered this, her eyes firmly fixed on the red Honda. There was no sign of it shifting. It was hard to see from where she had parked, but she was fairly sure it was empty. Was Tamsin in the shop? Or had she abandoned it and picked up another car? If that was the case they'd have no idea where she'd gone. But, unless she'd switched off her phone or left it behind in the red Honda, she was still in the area. Was it worth the risk, moving Sara and Robbie from their post at the quarry? She decided it wasn't. 'I'd rather not, Chris. Just in case I'm wrong about the red Honda. It could be a coincidence and, if she is on the hill, I don't want her escaping.'

'Okay,' Chris said. 'Look, the Cupar lads should be with you in three or four minutes now. St Andrews cops maybe five minutes behind them. Just keep an eye on the car till they get there. I'm on my way too.'

Clare put down her phone, her eyes trained on the Honda, and reversed her car further into the side, keeping the engine running. She was taking a chance, sitting there. Had Tamsin seen her driving the Merc? Parking it outside the Market Street flat? And, if she came out of the shop now, would she recognise it and take off in the other direction before the Cupar cops arrived to bar her way?

But what if she wasn't in the shop? Where else might she be? Maybe she had friends in Balmullo and was visiting them before going off to her new life. There were houses here and there, along the main road. If Tamsin was in one of those and she heard the sirens, she could be out the back door and over the fields before they could possibly check all the houses. Clare doubted she'd have the manpower to search them anyway, let alone get a warrant in time.

A boy of about ten wobbled past on his bike, a shaky hand stuck out as he signalled to pass Clare's car. On the pavement a couple of girls whizzed along on micro-scooters followed at a more leisurely pace by two young women, carrying schoolbags. Mothers? Or childminders?

Clare thought it was hard to tell. It was a distraction she didn't need. In fact, she hoped they would all be along the road and safely out of the way before the police cars arrived. And then the shop door opened and Clare saw a woman emerge, a green carrier bag swinging from her wrist. The clothes were different, the hair tied back. But she had spent enough time with Tamsin over the past week to know it was her. 'Gotcha,' she said softly. And then she swore under her breath. Tamsin was not alone. And, unless Clare was much mistaken, the man who had come out of the shop behind her was Paddy Grant.

For a brief moment, Clare assumed Tamsin was under duress. That Paddy had found her and coerced her into taking him with her. Automatically, her hand went to the gear level as she prepared to tail the Honda. And then she saw that she was wrong. That she'd been wrong all along. There was no coercion there. No intimidation. The sight of Tamsin's hand briefly touching Paddy's arm before he went round to the passenger door of the car told her all she needed to know. 'Cunning bastards,' Clare said under her breath. Tamsin had held out on the lot of them. Paddy Grant hadn't been driving past that Market Street flat to frighten Tamsin. It had all been for show. And all the time Tamsin had pretended to be afraid of Paddy, she was secretly planning a future with him.

'I'm going to have you, lady,' Clare said to herself. 'You and your bullnecked boyfriend.'

She dialled Chris's number, putting it on speaker-phone, and started the car.

'I'm on my way, Clare,' he said. 'Five minutes, tops.'

'Chris, just listen. Tamsin is in the car now and she has Paddy Grant with her.'

'Paddy? What the fuck?'

'It's all been a put-up job. They're in it together. He's not been scaring her. They've been playing us.' As she spoke, she saw the brake lights come to life on the red Honda and then they went off again. The indicator light started to flash.

'They're pulling away,' Clare said, flicking the indicator on the Merc. And then she heard the siren. It was distant, but coming closer. She sent up a silent prayer of thanks. There were no other roads out of the village. They had them covered. And then she realised Tamsin and Paddy must have heard the siren too. Tamsin was executing a swift three-point turn in the road. And from the screech of tyres, she wasn't hanging about. Clare glanced in her mirror and saw to her horror that a group of children on bikes had just come out of Hayston Park and were cycling along the road towards her. She couldn't risk the Honda hitting them. It was speeding up now, as the sirens behind it came closer.

It was a split-second decision – one she would have to account for several times in the days to come – but it was never in doubt. Clare turned her car – her beloved Merc – broadside across the road to stop the Honda going any further. The road was narrow enough, with hedges either side, leaving the Honda nowhere to go. Then she jumped out of the car and ran down the road, yelling at the children and their parents to get back. They froze for a second but when she carried on yelling they turned and began running back towards Hayston Park. A girl in a pink anorak began to cry and seemed rooted to the spot. Clare ran towards her, scooping her up and popping her quickly over a low garden wall. A woman pushing a double buggy, hung with schoolbags, did a swift about-turn and joined Clare in yelling at the children. Bikes and scooters were abandoned and in seconds the road was clear of children. The sirens were coming closer as the Honda screamed towards them.

Clare stepped into the road, her hand held up to bring the Honda to a halt. She could see the police car approaching from Cupar now and she knew she had them. And then she realised the Honda wasn't going to stop. With seconds to spare, she leapt for the same garden wall she had dropped the child over, clearing it just in time. The child, seeing Clare leaping towards her, fell over, screaming in terror as Clare landed beside her. There was no time to comfort the child as she heard the Honda strike the side of her beautiful dark blue Mercedes, spinning it round with the sickening sound of twisting metal. Clare looked up in horror at her car which now had a red Honda firmly planted where the front passenger door had been.

The Honda revved, Tamsin crunching the gears as she tried to back it away from the Merc but they were twisted together. Clare saw Paddy struggling with his door but it too had buckled on impact and was stuck fast. Tamsin's door opened and she staggered out. Paddy began crawling over the front seat to follow her as one of the cars from Cupar arrived. Two officers leapt out, one of them closing the Honda door to prevent Paddy escaping. The other set off after Tamsin but he wasn't as quick as Clare. Driven by fury at the fate of her beloved car, she found a speed she didn't know she possessed. She reached Tamsin and brought her down. Clare landed on top of her and grabbed Tamsin's hands, twisting them behind her back. The other officer arrived and snapped his handcuffs round Tamsin's pudgy wrists.

With her knee still in Tamsin's back, Clare caught her breath then began, 'Tamsin Quinn, I am arresting you on suspicion of money laundering, contrary to The Proceeds of Crime Act 2002. You do not have to say anything—'

Chris appeared at her side. 'Jesus, Clare – your car…'

Clare continued to deliver the caution and, when she had finished, she handed Tamsin over to Sara and Robbie who Chris had radioed. She rose to her feet and surveyed the wreckage of her Merc. 'Might need a lift,' she said to Chris who, seeing the tears in her eyes, put an arm round her shoulder and steered her towards his car.

Chapter 35

'So Tamsin and Paddy Grant set Phil Quinn up?' Chris asked.

'Looks that way.' Clare was cradling a mug of coffee, the shock of the events in Balmullo starting to recede. She was nibbling on a Wagon Wheel Chris had secreted away *for emergencies*.

'I thought Sara had confiscated these?'

'This is my emergency stash,' he said. 'Only, you mustn't tell her about it.'

Clare smiled. 'Where do you keep them?'

Chris tapped his nose. 'I could tell you, Clare, but then I'd have to kill you.'

'Okay, no more questions.' She bit into the Wagon Wheel again then, through a mouthful of marshmallow, she said, 'You know, I reckon Tamsin could see that Phil's days were numbered. She must have realised we were getting close to him and decided to bargain for her own freedom.'

'And Paddy and her?'

'Probably carrying on behind Phil's back for years. It explains why the cops couldn't find Paddy when they arrested Phil and the others. I reckon Tamsin would know we were about to arrest Phil and warned Paddy to clear out.'

Chris shook his head. 'So much for *honour among thieves*.'

Clare laughed. 'Was there ever?'

Chris shrugged. 'Maybe not. Reckon we'll get them for Johannes's murder?'

'I'm hopeful we'll get Paddy. Depends on DNA, though. Has anyone taken samples?'

'Yeah. We took a sample from Paddy. It should be at the lab within the hour. I spoke to Raymond Curtice and he's promised to rush it through. Hopefully we can recover the blue Transit van as well – the Dundee cops are keeping an eye out for it over there. And when we do get it I'll bet my pension we find Johannes's DNA in the back.' He picked up the Wagon Wheel and broke a bit off. 'There's always Rose – Paddy's sister. She might give us something on Tamsin.'

'I doubt it. You saw how she was when we interviewed her. A tough nut, that one. All that psyching Tamsin out at the trial – it was all for show.'

'Maybe when she's staring a sentence in the face,' Chris suggested.

Clare shrugged. 'Yeah, maybe. But I'm not convinced we'll be able to pin anything on Rose. If we build a case based on Tamsin and Paddy being in it together, then Rose intimidating her at the trial doesn't stand up.' She sipped at her coffee again then said, 'We can charge her with *Threatening Behaviour* towards Marek but a clever defence counsel could easily destroy that. The Fiscal might decide to drop the charges against her and concentrate on Tamsin.'

'But if none of them talk? If they all stick to the same story,' Chris said, 'and if we don't get a DNA match, we could end up losing all three.'

'Frankly, Chris, I'd rather not think about that. Although I have had an idea…'

'Yeah?'

'Phil Quinn. He sat in court listening to his wife destroy him – giving enough evidence to send him down for years. So I'm guessing he won't feel much loyalty towards Tamsin. After all, he did try to pin it all on her when he was cross-examined.'

'You think he'll testify against her?'

Clare nodded. 'He pretty much already has, at his own trial. He's nothing to lose. And if I was his solicitor, I'd be advising him to do all he can to minimise his sentence.'

'True. Fingers crossed, then.'

Suddenly Clare remembered Marek. 'What have you done with the lad?'

'Nita spoke to the DCI and he's been bailed, subject to surrendering his passport. Corinne Sim's going to come back and help us review the money laundering charges. With the Gruesome Threesome in custody, there didn't seem any need to keep him here.'

Clare nodded and they fell silent for a few moments. Then Chris said, 'What about your car? Reckon they'll write it off?'

'God, I hope not. I'm pretty sure it'll be worth fixing. I just hope the insurers aren't sticky about it.'

'Think they might be?'

Clare shrugged. 'Maybe. I mean, I did park it broadside across the road. They could argue I took an unnecessary risk.'

Chris's eyes narrowed. 'If they try anything like that, we'll make such a bloody noise on your behalf.'

Clare forced a smile. 'Thanks Chris. Suppose I'd better get to the form filling.'

There was a tap at the door and Gayle's head poked round. Her expression was grave. 'Clare – I heard what happened. Are you okay?'

'Yeah, I'm fine, thanks. Just glad we picked that pair up. Hopefully we can make the charges stick.'

'Goodness, I don't envy you this job – not one bit.'

'Easier than yours, I suspect,' Clare said.

'How's the new comms system coming along?' Chris asked.

Clare's eyes widened at his barefaced cheek. She didn't dare look at Gayle, focusing instead on her coffee mug.

Gayle met Chris's gaze, one eyebrow raised. 'Very well, thank you. In fact, I'm done here. All finished. I just came to say I'm leaving now.'

Clare threw Chris a look and rose, steering Gayle out into the front office. Jim was at the desk while Sara and Robbie were in the incident room, writing up their account of the events in Balmullo. 'Your – work… you say it's all finished?'

Gayle nodded. 'As I say, Clare, my report will be submitted. You may see some ripples in the next week or two as a result. But I'm done here.' She gave Clare a smile, the frostiness from earlier all gone.

Clare hoped it had been forgiven and forgotten. It certainly seemed that way. 'I wish I hadn't been so busy,' she said. 'It would have been nice to have spent a bit more time together.'

Suddenly Gayle pulled Clare towards her and gave her a hug. Clare felt the soft wool of Gayle's jacket against her neck. Her scent wasn't one Clare recognised. She tried to put a finger on it. Was it bergamot? Or a spiced orange? It was intriguing. Like Gayle.

Then she pulled back, holding Clare at arm's length. 'You don't get rid of me that easily, Clare,' she said. 'We're kindred spirits, you and I. Let's keep in touch.'

Clare smiled. 'I'd like that.'

Then Gayle picked up her work bags and, tossing her scarf over her neck, walked out of the station.

'DCI on the phone,' Jim said, cutting across Clare's thoughts.

Her heart sank. She hoped he wasn't going to have another go at her about the invoice for the golf event. She'd had quite enough for one day. She turned and made for her office. 'Can you put it through, Jim?'

She sat down behind her desk, suddenly dog tired. The phone buzzed and she picked it up.

'Christ's sake, Clare,' he said. 'Do you realise the risk you took?'

'Good afternoon to you too.'

There was a pause then a sigh. 'Sorry. It's just... well, you could have been hurt. I mean, what if you hadn't got out of the way in time? And your car!'

'Ach, it's fine, Al. I did get out of the way and maybe it's nature's way of telling me a Mercedes is out of my league. Maybe I should join the Ford Focus club.'

'Hah, touché. Look, Clare...' He hesitated, his voice softening. 'Do you want to grab lunch some time? Have a proper catch-up – now that things are calming down a bit. I mean, only if you want...'

Clare's lips began to form into a smile. He hadn't even mentioned that mistake with the invoice. 'That would be nice.'

'How about this weekend?' he said. 'We could do the parkrun and maybe grab a bite to eat after.'

Clare glanced at her watch. Shit! She had completely forgotten her sister, brother-in-law and nephew were coming that evening. 'Al – sorry, just remembered. I can't do this weekend. In fact, I need to get away. My sister—'

'Yeah, okay, Clare…'

'Honestly, Al. It's been arranged for weeks. But next weekend for sure.'

'It's fine, Clare. Don't worry. Look, I'd better go. Paperwork, you know.'

And with that he ended the call. Clare put the phone down slowly, mulling this over. He was so quick to take offence. Maybe it was just too much trouble. Maybe it would be easier if they kept their relationship strictly professional. But part of her thought that would be a pity.

There was a tap at the door and Chris came in, holding a set of car keys. 'Your insurers have sent a hire car. It's just been dropped off in the car park.'

Clare looked up, without enthusiasm. 'Don't suppose it's another Merc?'

'Ford Focus, I think the guy said.'

Clare laughed. It would be. She took the keys from Chris and pushed back her chair. 'I've had enough for one day, Chris. I'm going home. I'm off this weekend but, if there are any issues with Tamsin and Paddy, just call.'

—

Clare's sister Jude, brother-in-law Frank and her toddler nephew James had already arrived by the time she reached home. Benjy, beyond himself with delight at all these visitors, ran round and round, chasing his tail, sending the TV remote control skidding across the wooden floor. Clare saw that they had put the mail on the dining table and she scanned the letters and flyers quickly, establishing there was nothing that couldn't wait. A flyer on top caught her eye. *Cadham Rest Care Home – a few miles outside Glenrothes. Where had she seen that before?*

'We let ourselves in,' Jude said, holding her arms out to give Clare a hug. 'Hope you don't mind?'

Clare thought Jude had lost weight. Her pale pink jeans were loose around the legs now and her blouse seemed to hang straight down. She left the letters and went to embrace her sister. As she pulled her into a hug, she felt there was nothing of her. Jude was so thin now that Clare felt, if she hugged her sister too hard, she might break her bones. 'Don't be daft,' she said. 'I told you to use the key in the box.' She grinned at her brother-in-law. 'How are you, Frank? How's the world of education?'

'Oh, you know, Clare. Same old same old. Mostly fine, though.'

Clare turned and knelt down next to her nephew who was standing uncertainly, one arm clutching his mother's leg. He wasn't a baby any longer. She smiled at him and took his hand. 'And how's my James? Looking forward to staying with Aunty Clare?'

James stared back at Clare, unsmiling.

'He's packed a big bag of toys,' Jude said, indicating a blue child's backpack on the floor.

Suddenly Clare had a flashback to the children making their way along the road in Balmullo, their backpacks hanging off their shoulders – or from their mothers' arms – and she shivered at the memory of what might have happened, had she not screamed at them all to get away from the Honda. Then she put these thoughts to the back of her mind. 'Can I see?' she said to James.

He moved towards the bag, his eyes fixed on Clare, and he reached inside, taking out a blue Thomas the Tank Engine train. He held it out for Clare to see. She took it carefully and began to wheel it along the floor. James bent and took the train back from Clare and replaced it in the bag.

'You are honoured,' Frank said. 'It's not everyone who gets to touch his trains.'

Clare smiled. 'We're going to have fun this weekend, aren't we James?'

Over dinner, they told Clare about James's progress.

'They're not keen to label him while he's still so young,' Jude said. 'But they seem fairly confident the diagnosis will be autism.'

Clare looked at her sister's face, lined with worry, and wished she could do more to help. 'What does that mean, Jude? For his future?'

Jude spread her hands. 'We simply don't know, Clare. It's such a variable condition. His limitations will only become apparent as he gets older.'

Clare hesitated, then said, 'And there's nothing they can do to help him speak? Speech therapy or something like that?'

They both shook their heads. 'Nothing at the moment,' Frank said. 'We just have to hope he finds his voice, in his own time.'

Clare and Frank washed up while Jude put James to bed. When she was sure her sister was out of earshot, Clare said, 'Is Jude okay, Frank? She's very thin.'

Frank sighed. 'She is thin. She's not eating enough and she doesn't really sleep. Always one ear open for James.'

'I noticed she rather picked over her dinner. And she didn't have much to start with.'

'I'm keeping an eye on her, Clare. Hopefully having a night away tomorrow will give her a bit of a break. I can't tell you how grateful we both are to you for keeping James. There's no one we'd trust more with him.'

Clare put a rubber-gloved hand on Frank's arm. 'It's my pleasure, Frank. I should do more...'

He shook his head. 'Your work, Clare – we know how it is. But we're so happy to see you settled here. You like it?'

'I do. It's a lovely station and the town is so beautiful. You must come and stay longer next time.'

—

When they had all gone to bed, Clare lay awake, running over the day's events: from learning that Phil Quinn had been convicted to the discovery that Tamsin, far from being afraid of Paddy Grant, was planning to start a new life with him; and then there was Marek – Marek who had been working for Tamsin Quinn and was close to being killed by Paddy Grant's sister Rose. Perhaps it was Rose who had killed Johannes. They'd have to check her DNA too. Then she remembered that mistake with the golf event invoice. She knew it had been eighty thousand. So why had she charged them eight thousand? Perhaps she was losing the plot. Missing Geoffrey and losing focus.

And then there was her car. Her beautiful sleek Mercedes.

It felt like the events of a month, packed into a single day. No wonder she was tired. In spite of this, sleep eluded her and she lay awake until past two in the morning. She heard her sister pad through a few times to the little room where James was sleeping, and she was glad that Jude and Frank would be in a lovely hotel tomorrow night. Clare didn't care if she sat up all night with James as long as it put a bit of colour back in her sister's cheeks.

The moon was bright outside her bedroom window and, through the unlined curtains, it cast an eerie glow about the room. The air was thick too with a heady perfume. Was it the honeysuckle growing below her bedroom window? She thought she should get out of bed and close the window but she was too tired. Funny she hadn't noticed the smell before…

As her eyes roved round the moonlit room, Clare noticed that a dark grey shift dress was hanging on the outside of her wardrobe door. Or was she imagining it? She reached across and switched on her bedside lamp and there it was. How long was it since she'd worn that dress? It had been at the back of her wardrobe since she moved into Daisy Cottage. Deliberately put at the back because she didn't want to recall the last time she had worn it: the final day of the Fatal Accident Inquiry into the death of the young lad Clare had shot and killed when she was a firearms officer. The lad had been toting a replica weapon identical to the real thing and it had been accepted by everyone that the threat to life had been real and imminent. Everyone except the lad's family, of course. Clare had been exonerated and she had put the dress to the back of her wardrobe, never to be worn again.

She probably should have thrown it out, or given it to a charity shop, but somehow she never did. And now she wondered, lying in bed looking at it, if there was something in her subconscious stopping her from getting rid of it? As though keeping it reminded her that, even with the best of intentions, she could sometimes get it wrong.

So why was it there now, hanging on the outside of her wardrobe? Had she taken it out, meaning to give it to a charity shop and, in the mayhem of this past week, forgotten she'd done it? Perhaps she was sleepwalking. It was not something she was ever aware of having done but she had a vague recollection of Jude doing it a few times when she was younger. But how on earth would she know if she was sleepwalking? With the exception of that ill-judged night with the DCI, there was generally no one there to tell her she was doing it. If it was the case then she really needed to do something about her stress levels.

'Oh, what the hell,' she said to herself. 'It's only a dress.' She switched out the light again and pulled the duvet over her head.

Saturday, 23 May

Chapter 36

Jude and Frank chatted happily over breakfast about their planned overnight treat.

'We're going to have afternoon tea then head to the spa for a swim and sauna,' Jude told Clare.

'Then dinner and a few whiskies, to round off the night,' Frank added.

Clare was glad to see them looking so happy. In spite of her sister's disturbed night, Clare thought she seemed brighter today. Hopefully the break away from home and worries about James would put some colour back in her cheeks. From his highchair, James looked on, stony-faced, munching on a slice of toast and marmalade. She glanced down at her phone which had buzzed. A message from Diane.

> Hi Clare.
> I know you said you couldn't make the parkrun.
> Fancy a cup of tea instead? This afternoon, maybe.
> I could come up your way.
> I've a favour to ask.
> D x

Clare looked at the message for a few minutes, trying to decide how to reply. Gayle had gone now, her work done.

But Clare knew her report on the leak probably hadn't been read yet. If that was the case, there was no way she could say anything to Diane about it. If she could just keep out of Diane's way for a few more days…

She tapped back a quick message.

> Got my nephew here all weekend.
> Sister and husband going to hotel.
> Sorry x

Clare sent the message then saw immediately that Diane was typing a reply. It arrived a minute later.

> Ok, yeah, you said. Sorry!

Clare's conscience pricked at her. She had known Diane for years and she would trust Diane with her life. Yet all week she'd been avoiding her, on the say so of Gayle Crichton. Gayle who, despite her promises to keep in touch, would probably be here today, gone tomorrow. She tapped back another message.

> What's the favour?
> I'll help if I can.

She saw that Diane was typing a reply. Then the typing stopped for a minute before resuming. And then the message flashed up.

> Need to look at nursing homes for mum.
> One near me looks promising – Cadham Rest
> Would you have time to come down this way?
> Help me look it over?

Cadham Rest. It rang a bell. And then Clare remembered seeing the flyer with her mail when she had come in the previous night. But it had rung a bell with her last night too. Had Diane already mentioned it? Or was she starting to imagine things? Overthink them? Had that eighty thousand pounds mistake shaken her confidence? Was she starting to question everything? *Clare, you need a holiday*, she told herself. Maybe a trip to Boston would be a good idea. See if she could sort out her relationship with Geoffrey. If they still had one…

'Is that okay?' Jude was saying. 'Clare?'

She realised her sister had been speaking and she hadn't heard. 'Sorry, Jude – I missed that.'

'I said, would it be okay if we went about twelve? We can check in from two but it's such a lovely day. We could dump our bags and go for a walk.'

Clare laughed. 'Go now, for goodness sake! James and I will be fine.' She turned to her nephew. 'Won't we?'

James stared back at Clare and held out his piece of toast to her. She took it solemnly, pretended to nibble then handed it back.

-

It took Frank several attempts to get Jude into the car. 'Honestly, Jude,' he said, rolling his eyes at Clare. 'Will you stop nipping Clare's head? She already knows everything to do with James.'

Jude pulled her seat belt on. 'I know. It's just—'

Her words were lost as Frank drove off quickly, before she could think of another reason to run back into Daisy Cottage.

Clare stood waving them off, James in her arms and, when they had gone, she set him down. 'So, young man – what about a country walk?'

The sun was out, casting a warm glow on fields of grass, wheat and brilliant yellow oilseed rape. With James strapped securely into his pushchair, Clare set off along the road, heading away from St Andrews. There were no pavements on this section so she walked quickly, soon approaching the sign for Craigtoun Park where Johannes's body had been found. As the red sandstone gatehouse and pillared entrance came into view, she deliberately averted her eyes, trying not to think about Paddy Grant in that blue Transit van, looking for somewhere to dump the young student's body – if it was Paddy who had killed him. She wondered if the DNA results were through yet. She couldn't remember if she'd asked Raymond to hurry them up. Maybe she could send him a quick email…

It was warm now. She steered the pushchair into the verge and stopped to unzip her hoodie. As she took it off she felt the spring sun on her arms and she wondered how warm it would be in Boston at this time of year. The idea of visiting Geoffrey was appealing more and more. She tied the hoodie round her waist while James sat, kicking his red Hunter wellies against the footplate, his favourite Thomas the Tank Engine clutched in his hands. Maybe when James was having a nap she could look online for flights. He twisted his head round to see why they had stopped and she saw that his nose was running. His tongue was poised to explore this and she quickly fished a tissue out of her pocket and gently wiped his nose. She tucked the tissue back in her pocket and began walking again, her head filled with plans for Boston. A couple of cars flew past, a bit too close for Clare's liking, and she picked up the pace, keen to find a quieter road.

A little further on she came to a single-track road which climbed up towards the villages of Peat Inn and New Gilston, and she stopped to unstrap James who was kicking his feet more insistently now. She lifted him out and he steadied himself before setting off up the slope, still clutching his toy train. It was a quiet road and they walked on, Clare wheeling the empty pushchair, until James's little legs began to tire. There was a gap in a stone dyke and Clare took his hand, leading him through the gap into a field, recently ploughed. She stood looking at the view, down across the land that gave onto the Eden Estuary. It was the same land she had viewed yesterday but now she was looking north instead of east from Balmullo. She remembered that the estuary was a nature reserve. Perhaps she could take James there on Sunday.

A car was coming up the hill, its window down, music blaring from the radio. Clare listened as it came closer. It was a Scottish country dance band playing a reel – one she recognised from her schooldays, those agonising lessons where the boys were made to dance with the girls. Clare loved a ceilidh now but, as a ten-year-old, having to dance with the boys was mortifying. And then she remembered the tune – it was Cadham Wood. One of a medley the teacher would put on when she attempted the near impossible task of teaching the class the Eightsome Reel. Clare listened as the car passed, enjoying the memory, and then for some reason she suddenly felt uneasy. Cadham. That name again.

She recalled her teacher telling the class that Cadham Wood was near Kirriemuir, a small town north of Dundee. But the flyer delivered with yesterday's mail was for a different Cadham: *Cadham Rest*, the nursing home near Glenrothes. Was that the same one Diane had said she was considering for her mum?

With one eye on James, she took out her phone to check Diane's message and she saw that she was right. *Cadham Rest*.

But something still was nagging away at Clare. She had seen the name *Cadham Rest* somewhere else.

And then she remembered – and it was like a hammer blow to the chest.

It had been on Gayle Crichton's laptop that day they had shared a cafetière of coffee with Gayle's stash of Jaffa Cakes.

James was stomping about contentedly, kicking earth from the furrows. Clare sank down on the edge of the stone dyke to think. Diane was interested in *Cadham Rest* for her mother and Gayle had been looking at the nursing home website. Could it really be a coincidence? Gayle hadn't mentioned having any elderly relatives herself. So why was she looking at Cadham Rest on her laptop?

And then Clare thought about that invoice. As much as she'd had to concede that her copy showed eight thousand, she knew she had made it out for eighty thousand pounds. So who had changed it and how had they managed to change Clare's own copy? Was it really possible that someone could bill the golf events company for eighty thousand pounds and replace the invoice on the system with one for eight thousand, pocketing the difference? It would take considerable skill to do that – and to get away with it. Someone with a high level of IT skills. The kind of skills found in the staff at IT Services.

And Clare knew that no one would question the IT Services team accessing staff accounts online. Monitoring online traffic was part of their job, after all. What was it Gayle had said? *She hoped the culprit would be treated with some understanding.* What had she meant by that? Or, rather, *who* had she meant? Clare felt sick just thinking about it.

They resumed their walk up the hill but, as they reached the tiny Hamlet of Denhead, James was starting to drag his feet.

'Home for lunch,' Clare said, strapping him back into his pushchair. He put a thumb in his mouth and lay back, his eyes becoming heavy.

By the time they reached Daisy Cottage he was fast asleep. As she trundled the pushchair across the gravel Clare noticed something on the doorstep. Drawing nearer she saw that it was a magpie. It lay there stiff, its eyes long gone, courtesy of crows, no doubt. But how had it got there? She squinted up at her front windows to see if there was any sign of it having struck the glass but she couldn't tell.

'Poor thing,' she said, picking it up. It was as light as air and she went quickly to the bin to put it in before James wakened. There was no sign that a cat (or, thank goodness, Benjy) had attacked it. She looked at the upstairs windows again. Surely if it had struck one of them it would have fallen onto the gravel – not under the front door porch. She felt faintly uneasy about this. Had someone left it there? Was this some quaint country custom she didn't know about? Maybe Moira would know. But wasn't there something unlucky about a single magpie?

James began to stir and she went to unstrap him. She removed his wellies, knocking them together to dislodge the earth from the ploughed field, and led him indoors.

She chatted to him while making his lunch and he appeared to be listening attentively. After they had eaten she read him a story and, gradually, his eyes began to close and he was soon snoozing. Clare settled him on the sofa, tucking a blanket round him, and began clearing up lunch. She mulled over what they might do in the afternoon. Another walk perhaps or maybe he would be happy playing with his trains. She wondered what Jude and Frank were doing now. Hopefully Jude was relaxing, perhaps finding her appetite over a tempting afternoon tea. Looking forward to a few hours in the hotel spa. Maybe she could set aside one weekend a month to take James and let them have a break. If this weekend went well she would suggest it.

The doorbell rang, sudden and shrill, cutting across Clare's daydreams. She glanced at James to see if it had disturbed his sleep but he snoozed gently on, his long lashes resting on pink cheeks. She went to the door, wondering who it might be. Living in the country meant few callers. She pulled it open and saw Gayle standing on the doorstep, bearing a bottle of Prosecco.

'Clare,' she said, her smile warm. 'I'm sorry. This is really bad of me. I know you have your nephew to stay this weekend. But I don't check out of my hotel till tomorrow morning and I thought you might like another pair of hands with the wee one. I mean, tell me to go away if you like but I do love children. Lots of nieces and nephews and I'd love to help.'

Clare regarded her visitor with a mix of emotions. On the one hand, she felt hugely relieved that Gayle seemed to have forgotten her indiscretion over the leak. And, if she was being honest, she was flattered that someone like Gayle wanted to spend time with her, especially now their working relationship was at an end. But this was to have been her time with James. A chance to get to know her nephew a bit better so she could lift some of the load from her sister's shoulders.

Gayle must have sensed that Clare was conflicted. 'Oh, Clare – I'm sorry. It was rude of me, turning up unannounced. I'll leave you in peace. Forgive me?'

Her smile was so appealing that Clare relented. What else could she do? She stepped back to admit Gayle, closing the front door behind her. In the sitting room James snoozed on. Clare looked at the Prosecco doubtfully.

Gayle followed her gaze. 'Oh, don't worry,' she said. 'I didn't think you'd want to drink when you're babysitting. But this is for you. Have it when everyone has gone. Drink it all yourself.'

Clare laughed. It was a tempting thought. 'Cup of tea then?' she said.

'Yes please.'

She turned for the kitchen, Gayle following her, bottle in hand. And then something blinding and sharp shot through Clare's head and blackness overtook her.

Chapter 37

Clare was dreaming. She was in Provincetown with its gaily painted clapboard houses. She was going from house to house, looking for Geoffrey, but she couldn't find him. And then she did see him, standing on a jetty with the toothpaste-advert blonde. She waved to him but he didn't see her. And then DCI Alastair Gibson came walking towards her asking for eighty thousand pounds. She wanted to explain but her lips wouldn't move. She tried again to talk but, for some reason, her mouth was incapable of forming the words. What was wrong with it? She tried waving to Geoffrey again but this time her hands wouldn't move. They seemed frozen – her legs too. Someone was speaking to her. That voice – she knew it but she couldn't place it. And then she realised. It was Gayle. Gayle Crichton was in Provincetown with her. What on earth was she doing there?

'Hello, Clare,' Gayle was saying. 'Can you hear me now?'

With an enormous effort of will she opened her eyes. The houses were gone now. From somewhere distant she could hear barking. Benjy. Where was he? And where was she? Her eyes darted back and forth and then she realised she was at home. She was in the sitting room at Daisy Cottage. Gayle stood before her.

'Well, you took your time, coming round,' she said. 'I was starting to think I'd have to throw a glass of water in your face.'

Clare tried to open her mouth to ask what was going on. And then she realised there was tape across it, preventing her from speaking. She looked at Gayle, uncomprehendingly, and then down at her feet which were tied to the legs of one of her dining chairs. Her hands were tied behind the chair back and she found she couldn't move. Not a single inch. Her head ached and she blinked once or twice in an attempt to focus.

'It was quite a knock,' Gayle said, indicating the bottle of Prosecco. 'I thought I'd killed you, for a minute.'

Clare's eyes searched Gayle's face for any indication of what was happening.

Gayle raised an eyebrow in response. 'Confused?' she said. 'I bet you are. Well sit back, Clare, and I'll enlighten you.'

Clare suddenly remembered James and her eyes flitted round the room for any sign of him.

'You're looking for the boy, are you? Don't worry. He'll be safe with me, Clare.'

Even in her confused state, a fury began to take hold of Clare. What the hell did Gayle think she was doing? She tried to rock the chair back and forward but it was solidly made and it barely moved.

'Stop that,' Gayle said, her tone sharp. 'Unless you want me to give you another smack with the bottle.'

Clare did as she was told and studied Gayle's face. The effusive smile, the bonhomie – it was all gone now. She saw that Gayle was perhaps a little older than she had realised. There were lines around her eyes and her mouth.

And there was a coldness to those eyes that Clare hadn't seen before. And then a smirk began to form on the face.

'I said you wouldn't get rid of me that easily. I also think I told you to trust no one. I'd have thought a police officer with your experience would have realised that meant *no one*. But you didn't think I meant me, Clare, did you? Well perhaps I should explain.'

She was fully conscious now. Her head ached somewhere round the back. Instinctively she tried to put a hand to it to feel if there was a lump and then she remembered she couldn't move. Her thinking had cleared and she saw that she was Gayle's prisoner. Entirely at the mercy of this formidable woman. But why? What did she want? And why had Gayle bound and gagged her?

'I told you at our first meeting,' Gayle was saying, 'that I'm an ethical hacker. This is quite true. I studied computing at university and did a postgraduate course in ethical hacking. And over the years I've built up a reputation as one of the best, if not *the* best. I can name my price, Clare, and I do.'

A strand of hair fell across Clare's face and she tried to flick it out of her eyes. Gayle moved forward and brushed it tenderly behind Clare's ear, a gesture somehow at odds with Clare's plight.

'There,' she said and she backed away, perching on the arm of Clare's sofa. 'Now, where was I? Oh yes – the wonderful thing about being an ethical hacker is that it gives you the skills, if required, to be an *unethical* hacker. And, my dear Clare, that's just what I did. You see, there was never a leak in Police Scotland.'

Clare's eyes widened.

'Nope. Not at all. I made it all up. As a matter of fact, it's one of the hardest hacks I've ever done. Police Scotland should be proud of their security. I, however, am not just any old hacker, Clare. I am an exceptional hacker. I plug away, biding my time, waiting for the inevitable vulnerability – human error, usually. There's always one, if you're prepared to wait long enough. And that's when I sneak in. And once I'm in, well, anything is possible.' She laughed then went on. 'And when I did gain access, I did two things: I set up some rogue communications, making it look as if someone within the organisation was leaking information. That was such fun. Those operations where the main culprits got away – just bad luck. The kind of people who head up criminal enterprises have an instinct – they have timing. They clear out at just the right time, leaving someone else to carry the can. It's the very reason they rise to the top. An officer of your experience should know that.

'Anyway, once that was done, I made sure that any searches for registered ethical hackers threw up my name and my glowing testimonies. After that, it was only a matter of time before they approached me.' She laughed again. 'Wasn't it clever, Clare? I made them choose me.'

Gayle rose and began walking round the room. 'They even gave me an office in their most secure location. That place, in the shadow of Ben Cleuch, with all its walls and cameras. They actually offered me an office there. Can you believe it, Clare? That's when I knew I was home and dry.

'I chose St Andrews, of course. Once I had found out where you were—' She broke off as she saw Clare's expression change. 'Oh yes, Clare. I knew you had worked in Glasgow. In fact, I know a lot about you. But I'm getting ahead of myself. Once I found out you were here in St Andrews it was easy enough for me to say I wanted to be based there. That way I could observe you. See what your new life was like and get as close to you as I could.

'All that hogwash about it not being safe to speak within the police station – did you seriously think anyone could bug the entire place? All the offices? Cars?' She laughed. 'Honestly, Clare – and you're a detective, too. You were so easily persuaded!

'I will admit I hacked into your mobile, and your email. Played about with it a bit too. That invoice for eighty thousand pounds – it was a cinch to change it to eight thousand. I bet you thought you were going mad!' She smiled again. 'It's actually been a lot of fun, Clare. I've really enjoyed myself.'

Gayle moved to the sofa and picked up the red cushion. She held it out for Clare to see. 'Did you like my little tricks? Moving the cushions? The wine I left? You must have wondered when you bought it. I hope you enjoyed it – I guessed you'd appreciate a decent Malbec.

'And then the dress – I remembered the dress. Right at the back of your wardrobe. Out of sight but definitely not out of mind. Well, not out of my mind anyway. Do you remember that day? You must, Clare. The day you attended the Fatal Accident Inquiry to hear you'd been exonerated? It must have been quite something to learn that no further action was to be taken; that you had shot and killed a boy – a lad who only had a replica gun – and no charges would be brought. You were even commended for your quick actions. Oh yes – I couldn't resist hanging that dress out to make you remember.'

She moved close to Clare now. Clare could smell her perfume and she realised with dreadful clarity that it hadn't been the honeysuckle she had smelled that night in her bedroom. It had been Gayle's perfume. That same orange fragrance she had smelled when Gayle had given her what she thought was a goodbye hug.

And then she saw it all. Gayle had been here. In Daisy Cottage. Not just that night she came round for supper. She had been here when Clare was out – God knows when or how often – when Clare was working, perhaps – chasing all over Balmullo, trying to find Tamsin Quinn. Gayle had been here, going through her things, moving cushions, looking for that shift dress. Was that why Benjy had growled that night in the garden? Had Gayle been watching her, concealed in the dusk? What else had she done? And what was she planning to do? Clare tried again to rock on the chair and earned herself a slap across the face for her trouble.

Gayle rubbed her hand. 'Don't do that, Clare. It won't help.' She sat back down again. 'I had you going with that witness woman, too. Tamsin – you thought someone in Police Scotland was leaking information. And so did the Serious Organised Crime lot. I could have saved you all that work. Tamsin herself was leaking her location to that big lunkhead she went away with. But you probably know that now. Still – it's a bit of fun, isn't it?

'Oh,' Gayle said, as if remembering something suddenly. 'Did you like the magpie? I bet that was a shock to come back to this afternoon. One for sorrow, I believe the rhyme goes, Clare. Well I'd say that was about right, wouldn't you?'

Gayle began walking round the room, her arms folded. Then she turned back to Clare. 'We've both had our sorrows over the years, Clare, haven't we? Everyone does, I suppose. But you – well, you took a life, didn't you? And you didn't pay for it.' She stopped for a moment, her

326

eyes looking past Clare, into space. And then she drew her gaze back to Clare and her eyes narrowed.

'But, what you don't know, Clare, is that the life you took – the boy you killed – he was my nephew.'

Clare could feel a buzzing in her ears and the room began to swim before her. She blinked, trying to force her mind back to the present. Her head throbbed and she felt herself slipping into unconsciousness. She blinked again a couple of times and made an effort to control her breathing. What had Gayle just said? She was the aunt of the boy Clare had shot and killed when she was a firearms officer? This had to be a dream – a terrifying nightmare. But there was no waking up from this bad dream. She continued drawing breaths in through her nose, as deep as she could, trying to calm the thumping in her chest. A trickle of mucus began to run from one nostril but the tape prevented her from licking it away.

'Ugh,' Gayle said. She tore a tissue from a box on the coffee table and wiped Clare's nose roughly. The gesture reminded her of James. She had wiped his nose that very morning – was it the same day though? She had no idea how long she'd been tied to this chair. And where was James now? What had Gayle done with him? She moved her head left and right again, looking as far round the room as she could, but there was no sign of him.

'Oh, I know what you're thinking,' Gayle was saying. 'How could someone like me possibly be related to a boy like Francis Ritchie? A fifteen-year-old lad who goes around robbing shops? Well I'd tell you not to be so bloody judgemental. Anyone can go off the rails, Clare. My poor sister. She fell in with a bad crowd. That was her only mistake. It happens so easily. Next thing we know, she's having a baby with one of them and that was that. I'm sure you've seen it often enough in your line of work. The benefit trap. No job, no hope. Just an endless cycle of Job Centre visits to sign on with all the other no-hopers.

'We all tried to help her. Gave her money, offered to get her another house, away from that dreadful scheme, pleaded with her to come home. But there was no reaching her. She had become part of that crowd. They were her tribe and she couldn't see a life outside of them. And Francis's father – well, there was no way he was letting *his laddie* be brought up by someone else, especially us.'

Her lips tightened and she fell silent for a moment before going on. 'When I saw the life my sister had, bringing up Francis in that grotty flat...' she gestured round the room, '...a million miles from places like this, well I determined to make something of myself. Save myself from falling into the same dead-end lifestyle my sister had. And I did. I did it in style. So, while my sister was picking daffodils from roadside verges to put by her son's pathetic little gravestone, I was shopping in Harvey Nicks and turning down five-figure contracts.

'And even after you killed Francis – even after all that – we still couldn't reach her.'

Gayle seemed to be looking past Clare now, lost in her memories. And then she turned back to face her. 'Do you know what it's like, Clare, to want so desperately to help someone and realise you can't? I offered to buy her a flat, you know. Nice part of Glasgow – away from Francis's dad and the rest of them. But she said she couldn't see the point. Not without Francis. She was such a lovely girl, once, and she had become this husk of a person, consumed by grief and guilt.'

She shook her head at the memory. 'It was a dreadful moment when I realised there was nothing more I could do for her.

'Nothing, except this.

'And so you see, Clare, here's how it works: you took my nephew's life. It seems only fair that I take yours, in return.'

Clare felt she might be sick. Her stomach lurched and she feared she would choke. Somehow she managed to swallow back the bile that had risen in her throat but there was no stopping the trickle of pee that was starting to run down her leg. Tears of embarrassment pricked her eyes and she tried to blink them away as the urine began to pool on the floorboards.

'Oh dear, Clare,' Gayle said in mock horror. 'We appear to have peed our pants.'

Clare looked at Gayle, her eyes swimming now, but Gayle just laughed.

'Oh yes, Clare. I'm going to take your life in exchange for Francis's. That seems fair, don't you think?'

Somewhere distant, Clare heard Benjy bark. She turned her watery eyes on Gayle in question.

Gayle shrugged. 'Dunno. Might kill the dog. Might not. I'll see how I feel. Don't worry about the boy though. Unlike you I'm not a child killer.'

Gayle smiled. 'I think I'll make a cup of tea. For me, obviously – you're a bit indisposed at the moment. And when I've drunk it I'll tell you what I'm going to do.'

Chapter 38

'You'll be wondering about my report,' Gayle said, sipping a mug of tea. 'I've sent it off now. They'll be reading and digesting it over the weekend.' She dipped a biscuit into her tea and bit off a corner. 'Your friend Diane – she was the one who worried me. You're right about her. Straight as a die and sharp with it.' She sipped her tea again. 'Shame she'll lose her job.'

Clare's eyes narrowed at this.

'I needed a fall guy,' Gayle explained. 'I could have made it you but Diane was just too good. I had to get rid of her. As you know her mother's gone gaga now...'

Clare winced at the expression.

'Oh, I'm sorry,' Gayle said, an expression of mock horror on her face. 'Was I not being PC enough for you? I'll rephrase it – her mother's suffering from dementia and poor Diane has to find the money for a care home. Your eighty thousand error is going to land at her door, I'm afraid. I've buried copies of both invoices – the original one and the fake one for eight thousand –deep in her hard disc. Unless she knows they're there she won't see them. But I've pointed out the location in my report. She'll be out on her ear by Monday morning and up on a fraud charge.' Gayle seemed lost in thought for a minute. 'It grieves me, Clare, to do the dirty on someone as skilled as Diane, but needs must.'

Gayle stood and drained her mug. She put it down on the dining table. 'Don't worry about DNA,' she said. 'I made sure your colleagues knew I'd come round for dinner the other night. So my DNA and prints will quite legitimately be all over this house and no one will think anything about it.' Her eyes twinkled. 'On the other hand, your colleague, the DCI, well, no one knows he was here, do they? You two kept that very quiet.' She shook her head. 'Honestly, though, Clare – he's no ball of fire, is he? You could do so much better. Not that it matters now...'

She moved to the side of the sofa and lifted a backpack. She placed this on the sofa and opened it just wide enough to show Clare a breathing apparatus set, similar to the ones she had seen used by firefighters at large blazes. Clare felt her stomach lurch again and she fought to control her breathing and calm the heaving in her gut. Was Gayle going to burn the house down? With her in it?

'No, not fire,' Gayle said. She looked round the room. 'It's such a lovely cottage, I couldn't bring myself to do it. And anyway – someone might see the smoke and call the fire brigade. Then you'd be rescued and I couldn't have that.'

She reached into her pocket and withdrew a small pair of forensic gloves which she began pulling on. 'No, Clare – I'm going to poison you. You should be glad, really. It's quite a nice way to go. I'm just going to loosen the housing on your boiler flue – where it meets the outside wall, you know? Just enough to let the fumes escape into the house. I'll come back this evening with my trusty gas mask, once I'm sure you're unconscious, and I'll untie you. And it'll look like a dreadful accident.' She smiled again. 'Clever, don't you think?'

And, with that, she moved quickly into the kitchen, screwdriver in hand.

Clare heard her working at the boiler housing and then the sound of the boiler firing up as the heating was switched on. Gayle came back into the room a moment later, all smiles. She picked up her backpack in one hand and James's car seat in the other. Clare eyed the car seat, terror in her eyes, wondering where Gayle was taking James, but Gayle ignored this.

'Well, goodbye, Clare,' she said. 'The next time I see you, you'll be pinking up nicely with the carbon monoxide. Ciao!' And, with that, she swept out of the room, leaving Clare desperately wondering how long she had before she would lose consciousness. There was a pain in her chest, when she thought of James – what Gayle might do to him, where she might take him. A pain so acute and commanding that she felt her chest might burst with it. She imagined her sister – frantic with grief at not knowing where her precious boy was – and the ache spread to her stomach. It was everywhere and it was agony. Was this what love really felt like? If so, Clare had never been in love like this.

She heard the front door bang and the sound of a car engine starting up. Gayle was leaving and she was taking James. Clare knew she had to get free. If she could just get to a phone and call 999, or Chris even. He could be there within minutes. She looked frantically round the room for anything that would help but, tied to the chair, it was all out of reach. She saw her mobile phone sitting on the table, an agonisingly long distance away. She tried to wriggle to free herself but the tape was strong. She could feel her breathing becoming faster, her heart racing, her chest tight and she knew she had to control the rising panic. The gas was odourless but common sense told her it was too soon for it to have filled the room. The constriction in her chest was pure anxiety. She closed her eyes and began breathing slowly in and out until she felt her heart rate return to normal. And then she started to think. It was years since she had undergone emergency fire training but it had to be there, in the far reaches of her mind.

And from nowhere she remembered: carbon monoxide was lighter than air. If she could only get down low she might have a chance of surviving. But for how long? She had to try. With a supreme effort she tried rocking the chair forward again but to no avail. It was simply too heavy. But what if she tried rocking it to the side – or even backward? Her legs were taped high up the chair legs so it was difficult for her feet to touch the ground. She tried stretching her toes out as far as they would go and screamed through the tape as one foot cramped. She wiggled her toes desperately to relieve the spasm then tried again and found she could just reach the floor with her toes, and she began pushing with all her might to try and dislodge the chair.

It took a few attempts but finally she felt the chair move and, as it rocked, she threw her head backward creating just enough momentum to send it falling towards the floor. At the last moment she tucked her head forward and felt the jerk as she hit the floorboards. She groaned through the tape as her arms, pinned behind her, took the brunt of the fall. Pain shot through them and she felt they must be broken. The weight of her body resting on her arms was unbearable and tears sprang to her eyes. She lay there, for a few moments, like a beetle on its back, trying to work out what to do next.

Despite the pain shooting through her arms, her hands found the floor. She balled them into fists and pushed them down. The sound of Benjy barking came again and she imagined him, perhaps trapped in an upstairs room. The gas would reach him as it rose and the barking would gradually cease. And James – where was he? What had Gayle done with him? What if they never found him again? It would destroy Jude and Frank. It would absolutely finish them. From somewhere, she found the extra strength to force the chair over through ninety degrees until she was lying on her side.

The force of her fall had dislodged the rug that sat in the centre of the floor and suddenly Clare felt her prayers had been answered. That draught – that bloody wonderful draught that came through the floorboards, damaged when the central heating had been upgraded. It had driven her crazy every time Benjy dislodged the rug that sat across the gap. And now, that same gap in the floor might just save her life – until help came.

The weight of the chair was all in the back, and now that she was lying on the side she found it was easier to turn it through another ninety degrees until she was face down on the floor. Her knees were touching the floorboards now and, although her hands were still firmly lashed behind her, she managed to make slow progress across the floor, sliding her knees and forehead alternately. She grimaced as a splinter burrowed into her skin but that draught – that blessed draught was coming ever closer.

Whether it was the result of the knock from the Prosecco bottle, the fall or perhaps the carbon monoxide that was starting to fill the room, she wasn't sure. But she could feel her head becoming muddled. She must stay focused. She must get to that gap in the floorboards before the gas overwhelmed her. The pain in her arms was unbearable but, somehow, she kept going – going towards the draught.

And then she was there. All her weight – and the weight of the substantial dining chair – was through her knees and her head now. She knew they were aching, that her arms were in agony, but she felt detached from the pain. As though it was happening to someone else. She had to get her nose as close to the gap as she could before the gas overtook her. Planting her forehead, she shimmied her knees round until she was facing the widest part of the gap. It was just large enough to cover her nostrils and, with the most enormous relief, she allowed her shoulders to sink down and she breathed the fresh cool air from the crawl space below Daisy Cottage. She had made it. She closed her eyes and gave in to her fate, whatever it was to be. She could do no more.

Chapter 39

Clare was dreaming again. She knew, in the back of her mind, that she shouldn't be sleeping, but the dream was irresistible. She was sitting on a chair and they were all passing before her. Her parents, Jude and Frank, little James who was calling out 'Aunty Clare, Aunty Clare.' She stretched out to try and touch them but they were just out of reach. She tried to rise from the chair but her legs wouldn't obey. Jim was there, drifting past with his usual cheery smile, then Chris and Sara, hand in hand. Robbie, Gillian, Jenny, the DS from Dundee – they were all there. And then she saw Tamsin and Paddy, laughing at her. Diane appeared next and she was calling to Clare. Calling and calling. Clare leaned forward to try and hear what she was saying.

'Clare – Clare...'

The voice became more urgent and Clare tried to open her mouth to tell Diane everything was okay but her lips wouldn't obey.

'Clare... oh my God – what's happened to you?'

She felt a tugging at her face – someone was pulling her hair. Then suddenly there was a ripping noise and her face stung with a sudden burning. She gasped in air and opened her eyes.

'Diane...' She was back in the room. But she was sitting up now, still bound to the chair, and Diane was there in the room with her. For a moment she was confused and then she remembered. 'Diane,' she gasped. 'Boiler – windows – open windows…' She started to cough and she saw Diane looking at her blankly for a moment.

And then realisation dawned and Diane ran to the windows, forcing them up. But the weights were missing from the sash and case mechanism and the panes slid back down. Desperately, Diane looked round and then, seeing a pile of books, she forced the window back up again, propping the books on the sill to prevent it from closing. Then she ran to the sitting room door and threw it open. Clare heard the sound of the front door opening. Then Diane ran back into the room and through to the kitchen to open the back door. Clare felt a draught run through the house and her heart lifted. Diane was behind her now, dragging the chair over to the window, and Clare gulped in lungfuls of fresh, clean air. Diane stuck her own head out of the window and breathed in and out then, taking an enormous breath in, she ran for the kitchen and returned with a knife. She set about the ties securing Clare's hands to the chair, stopping every few seconds to breathe in fresh air through the window.

It felt like an eternity to Clare as every cut of the knife seemed to rebound off her arms. She was screaming inside her head but her breathing was too shallow to call out. Then, at last, she was free of the ties and she staggered on cramping feet, with Diane supporting her, out into the fresh air, and collapsed on the ground. She gasped and wheezed as she heard Diane's voice.

'I need ambulance, fire and police. Daisy Cottage, Craigtoun Road, St Andrews. Carbon monoxide poisoning. One adult female, now in fresh air but needs medical attention…'

Clare's eyes were heavy and she let them close. And then she remembered. 'James?' she gasped.

Diane was bending over her now, tucking a throw from the sitting room round her. 'He's safe, Clare. Sleeping peacefully in your car in his car seat. Once the fire brigade arrive we'll find the keys and let him out.'

Clare closed her eyes again. And then she heard a sound that brought tears to her eyes once more. Benjy was barking. She opened her eyes but found she couldn't form the words to ask.

'He's safe too, Clare. In the back garden. I'm guessing she couldn't bring herself to let him die.'

'She?' In Clare's confusion she registered that Diane seemed to know who was responsible for almost killing her. Who was it? It was a woman but she couldn't quite… had they caught her? Thoughts swam round her head but she couldn't make sense of them. She was so tired now.

She could hear the ambulance drawing nearer and she allowed her eyes to close again. It was so much easier than trying to keep them open. The siren was deafening now and then she heard tyres crunching on gravel. Diane was speaking and there were other voices. Male? Female? She couldn't tell. They were calling her name now and something hard was being placed over her mouth. She felt her lungs fill and had the sense of something good spreading through her head. And then she was being lifted up, doors were closing and she felt herself swaying as the ambulance backed out of the drive and roared away. She saw a woman in green. Her lips were moving and Clare tried to focus on them but it was too difficult. She could hear a siren and wondered briefly where it was coming from before the weariness that had overtaken her won and she drifted off into unconsciousness.

Chapter 40

Clare was in a room she didn't recognise. The walls were white and there was a smell of something she couldn't identify. Was it that spiced orange perfume? She didn't think so. Something from her past – the swimming pool maybe. She used to go every morning before work when she lived in Glasgow. Was she back there now? Was that why the walls were white?

She raised her head and gazed round the room then she felt pain shoot through her left arm. She looked down and saw it was wrapped in some kind of brace, with a strap going across her chest to the other arm. Had she hurt it? And, if so, who had put the brace on?

She looked round the room again, trying to work out where she was. There was some kind of screen on the opposite wall. When had she done that? Her TV in Daisy Cottage sat on a stand she had bought from a second-hand furniture shop. What was it doing on the wall? To her right was a window which looked out onto a concrete wall with large square windows. There were chairs beside her and she screwed up her eyes, trying to focus. Jude was sitting on one of the chairs. But that wasn't right. Jude should be in her hotel, relaxing in the spa. Or having dinner and those whiskies Frank had been looking forward to. She was speaking to her. 'Clare,' she heard her say. 'Clare…'

She blinked a couple of times then she realised she didn't know where she was. A sudden terror overtook her and she struggled forward.

Jude was at her side instantly, a hand placed gently on her head. 'Clare,' she said, 'you're safe now. Everything's all right and you're safe. Just lie back. The doctor says you have to rest.'

Clare stared at her sister. She tried to speak but something was over her face. She remembered the tape. Tight across her mouth. Was it there again? In a sudden flash of something – fear perhaps – she remembered Gayle. The glamorous woman who had been working in the station all week. Something about an investigation… Her eyes darted round the room, looking for Gayle. Was she there?

'Clare,' Jude was saying, 'listen to me: you are in hospital and you're safe. Everyone's safe – James and Benjy – they're all safe and sound. That woman who was working with you – Gayle something – she tried to poison you by rigging your boiler. But Diane from work – she found you and you're safe in hospital.'

She was starting to remember. Gayle had been in Daisy Cottage. Clare's brow furrowed as she struggled to process her thoughts. How had Gayle come to be there? Had Clare let her in? She couldn't remember. And how had she come to be tied to a chair, gaffer tape across her mouth? She tried to retrieve the memories from the back of her mind but they were stuck in a kind of fug.

She remembered Gayle saying that Francis Ritchie was her nephew. Francis Ritchie, the boy Clare had shot and killed. Could that really be true? And the leak in Police Scotland – the one that had Clare and the DCI talking on cheap phones, to avoid their conversation being overheard – was it all untrue? Had she really managed to get past the high-level security at Police Scotland and install herself as an ethical hacker, chasing down non-existent leaks? It all seemed too far-fetched. She looked at her sister's face, lined with worry, and then she remembered James. She realised now that it was an oxygen mask over her face and lifted her other arm to pull back on the elastic, raising it from her mouth long enough to whisper, 'James?'

Jude smiled. 'He's fine, Clare. He's here. Frank's taken him down to the main concourse for a snack, then he'll be back.'

Relief flooded across Clare.

'Benjy's safe too,' Jude went on. 'Your neighbour – Moira, is it? She has him and she says she'll keep him just as long as you need her to.'

Clare pulled back the mask again. 'Your weekend...' she said, tears in her eyes.

Jude gently replaced the mask over Clare's face. 'Don't you worry about that. It's all worked out fine. When the hotel heard what had happened they found us a family room and put a cot in for James. They sent us flowers and gave us a voucher for fifty pounds towards another stay. I think they're hoping for some publicity out of it!'

The door to the room opened and a woman in a pink blouse and grey trousers entered. She had an ID badge clipped to the pocket of her blouse and a stethoscope hung round her neck. The woman smiled. 'Well, Clare. You gave us all quite a fright yesterday.'

Clare raised an eyebrow but didn't speak.

The woman went on. 'I assume you understand a little about carbon monoxide poisoning, given the nature of your job?'

Clare gave a slight nod – as much as she could manage.

'The firefighters who attended, after you were brought out of the house, assessed the levels there as lethal – and that was after the doors and windows had been opened. I'm not sure how you survived that level of exposure but I'm very glad you did.'

Clare raised the oxygen mask from her face once more. 'Draughty floorboards,' she whispered. 'Got my nose into a gap.'

The doctor smiled. 'Very resourceful. Getting down to the floor and finding a source of fresh air almost certainly saved your life.' She picked up a clipboard hanging from the end of Clare's bed and scanned it. 'Your carboxy-haemoglobin levels are still a bit high but everything else is improving.' She smiled again. 'Your arm will be pretty sore for a few weeks. Broken humerus, I'm afraid. You must have given it quite a crack. But you're fit enough so I'm confident it'll mend well. I think we'll keep you here until tomorrow and see if we can reduce the oxygen in the next twenty-four hours. If we can do that, we'll send you home.'

Clare wanted to protest but, in truth, she was too tired. She let the oxygen mask fall back over her face and closed her eyes.

When she opened them again she saw that Frank and James had returned and were sitting by her bed. James was clutching the blue Thomas the Tank Engine with one hand, the thumb from his other firmly lodged in his mouth.

'Look, James,' Jude was saying. 'Aunty Clare's awake now.'

James turned a solemn gaze upon Clare. She stretched out a hand to touch his. Lifting the mask from her face she said, 'Hello James.'

He looked at her, his dark brown eyes hooded with thick lashes. He held out the train for her to take.

Clare took it and ran it slowly along the bedclothes. James's eyes never left her face. And then he opened his mouth and said, 'Antyclare.'

Chapter 41

'We've picked her up,' Chris said, 'but I've no earthly idea where to start with the charges.'

'Might I suggest attempted murder?' Clare said, glad to be free of the oxygen mask for a few minutes. She was sitting up in bed now, supported by pillows, her left arm still immobilised by the brace.

'She's clearly breached The Computer Misuse Act,' Diane said. 'I'll get Craig to crack on with that, first thing on Monday.'

'How on earth did you find her?' Clare asked.

A nurse entered and looked pointedly at the oxygen mask. 'Ten minutes, we agreed.'

'Just a few more minutes – please?' Clare said and the nurse nodded.

'See she puts it back on again,' she said to Chris and Diane who assured her they would.

'So?' Clare persisted. 'How did you track her down?'

Chris inclined his head towards Diane. 'Our resident tech whizz here.'

'It was Wednesday,' Diane said. 'When you were at court.' She glanced at Chris. 'I was already concerned about her so I asked Chris who she was. Why she was here. Something about what he said didn't ring true. I don't think you believed it either, did you, Chris?'

He shook his head. 'I did think there was something odd about her. I just wasn't sure what it was.'

Diane went on. 'I knew that story about a new comms system was rubbish. The way budgets are these days they'd have had us doing all the work to save money. So I ran a check on her. I have a friend down in Edinburgh who's an ethical hacker. Works all over the country. She hadn't heard of her. So I put out some more feelers and they all came up blank.'

Clare's breath was becoming laboured again and Chris rose to put the oxygen mask over her face. She waved him away but held the mask close to her nose. 'But – her references?' Clare panted. 'She must have had pretty good ones for Police Scotland to engage her, surely?' She lay back on the pillow, exhausted by the effort of speaking, and allowed Chris to replace the mask over her nose and mouth.

'All fake,' Diane said. 'That's the beauty of being a hacker. You can place documents anywhere you like, providing you can breach the firewall. And if you choose a large enough company, the HR department won't remember names and faces. They'll just search the records and send an appropriate reference. If you make a fake employee's record authentic enough people actually start to think they remember them.'

'So was she not an ethical hacker?' Chris asked.

'Oh yes. And a good one too. But she hadn't worked for the government agencies she claimed on her CV. My guess is that most of her work is for large international corporations, possibly abroad. But to be employed by Police Scotland she needed to have done work with UK organisations. Civil service departments – that kind of thing.'

The nurse opened the door a little and, seeing Clare was now wearing the oxygen mask, she let the door close again.

'But how did she persuade them there was a leak?' Chris said.

'I'm not absolutely sure yet. There will be an enquiry without a doubt. But I'm guessing once she'd found her way into the system she set up a ghost IP address using a virtual private network. The software's freely available and if she used that, plus a browser like TOR that doesn't keep track of internet activity, she'd be able to mimic hacking attacks from within Police Scotland itself.'

Clare shook her head.

'In a way,' Diane went on, 'she's done the Force a favour by exposing their vulnerabilities. Bit of a crap day at the office for you, though, Clare.'

Clare rolled her eyes and Diane went on. 'Anyway, once I knew there was something dodgy about her I put a tracker on her car.'

Clare's eyes widened and Diane laughed.

'I attached it to the inside of the wheel arch. And, once I did that, I could see where she was at any time. She was at your cottage a lot, Clare.'

'But how did she get in?' Chris asked.

Diane shrugged. 'No idea. But she was there one evening I think. For dinner?'

Clare nodded and Diane went on.

'She might have taken an impression of the key then, maybe if you went to the loo. She could have used that to make one using a 3D printer. Or, if you have a spare key she probably found that.'

Clare groaned inwardly. It had all been far too easy. She had let her guard down and she had almost died as a result. She pulled back the oxygen mask. 'But what made you suspect her in the first place?'

Diane smiled. 'She made one mistake, Clare. She chose me as her fall guy. I think she considered making you look responsible for the leaks. But she probably knew you didn't have the skills to carry out a plan like that. So she looked round for a target that was close to you. Any IT technician worth his salt would be capable of setting up a ghost IP address and leaking a few documents, if they wanted to. I could certainly do it and she would know that. And, as we were friends, she chose me in order to get close to you. I'm guessing she warned you off speaking to me about the supposed leak – am I right?'

Clare flushed then gave a nod. She pulled the mask back just long enough to say 'Sorry, Diane. It all seemed so official.'

Diane smiled. 'Don't be daft, Clare. I can imagine how it must have been. Anyone would have been taken in by someone like her.'

'You weren't, though,' Chris said.

'No,' Diane admitted. 'I received an email that didn't look quite right. When you've been in IT as long as I have, you have a nose for that kind of thing. There was an attachment and I suspected it was malware. So I scanned it and realised it was a backdoor attack designed to access my emails and my work account. Now that always interests me. Why has someone sent it and what information are they after?

'So I opened up an old laptop, created a quick clone of my account with an email address so similar to my usual one that no one would notice the difference. I populated it with enough emails and files to make it look genuine and forwarded the rogue email to that. I then downloaded the attachment and went offline to stop it spreading. After that I deleted the original copy in my real account so whoever had sent it wouldn't know I'd forwarded it. All I had to do then was to set up a redirection for any email coming from that sender to my new, slightly different address.'

'But how did you work out it was Gayle?' Chris asked.

'I didn't – not at first. But she was new in the station and I didn't believe a word about the new comms system. So I thought it was worth trying her before I looked elsewhere. I started creating emails on different topics, feeding information to whoever was spying on my machine. Then I waited to see what would happen. And I didn't have to wait long. *Cadham Rest*, for instance, Clare?'

Clare's eyes widened and Diane smiled.

'I thought as much. I knew Gayle would be sowing seeds of doubt about me in your mind. I wondered if she might say something about *Cadham Rest*. I've no intention of sending my mother there. I just wanted to see if Gayle would bite.'

Clare removed the oxygen mask completely now. She had too many questions for Diane. 'It was up on her laptop,' she said. 'One day when she invited me for coffee – in the room she was using at the station. The website for *Cadham Rest* was up on the screen and, now that I think back, she left it there just long enough for me to see it before she made a pretence of shutting it down in a hurry.'

Diane grimaced. 'Yes, she set it all up beautifully. And it wasn't long before I discovered the rogue invoice for eight thousand pounds, plus a copy of the genuine one hidden away on the hard disc of the dummy laptop I'd set up. I knew as soon as I saw them she was out to get you, Clare. What I didn't know was how to stop her.'

'And I played right into her hands,' Clare said, shaking her head. 'I'm so sorry, Diane. I should never have doubted you. But she said she'd have me suspended if I breached her confidence. And, if you'd seen that place where we first met her… well it was all pretty scary.'

'Forget it, Clare. She was a formidable opponent.'

Clare's brow creased. 'She must have had access to my computer account too. I found the eight thousand pounds invoice in my documents on the network and I know I didn't put it there.'

Diane nodded. 'She sent you the same piece of malware she sent me, only when you downloaded it, you gave her access to everything on your account. I could see from the network that there was some unusual activity. Your account was being accessed from different locations, including that hotel on the coast road out of town. I looked at the times and knew it wasn't you who had accessed it because you were in court that day and that confirmed my suspicions. That's why I tracked her car.'

Clare's eyes were bright now. 'I owe you my life, Diane,' she said, her voice shaking as she spoke.

'Don't be daft. You'd do the same for me.'

—

Later, when they had gone, Clare lay on her bed, turning over the events of the past few days. She'd made the rookie error of assuming the leaks Gayle claimed to be investigating were linked to Tamsin's locations being compromised; that whoever was leaking information was also leaking Tamsin's whereabouts to Paddy Grant. 'Stupid mistake, Clare,' she told herself, clutching her aching left arm with her right hand. 'Stupid.'

Jim had phoned towards teatime. 'We've charged her with attempted murder,' he told Clare who breathed a sigh of relief. 'The fire brigade confirmed the boiler flue had been tampered with and their calculations put the time the escape began to within an hour of Gail's car being tracked to Daisy Cottage. Tech Support are examining her laptop now and they seem pretty confident they'll find evidence that she accessed both your and Diane's accounts.'

'Are they allowing Diane to work on gathering the evidence?' Clare asked.

'No. She's volunteered to take a week's leave to avoid a conflict of interest. But her whizz kid assistant Craig's working on it round the clock. And there's no question of anything being laid at her door. She's probably in line for a commendation.'

Clare allowed herself a smile at that. If anyone deserved a pat on the back it was Diane. Tech Support really were the unsung heroes of the Force. 'Thanks Jim,' she said. She was tired now after a steady stream of visitors and she just wanted to sleep. And then a thought struck her. 'Did she make any reply to the charge, Jim?'

There was a hesitation, just long enough for Clare to know that she had.

'Tell me…'

'She said that it didn't matter. That she'd get you next time. But Clare – that's all rubbish. She'll go away for years. You know that.'

Clare saw, in spite of the heat in her hospital room, that she had goose pimples on her arms and she pulled the covers further up the bed. 'I know, Jim,' she said, hoping she sounded more convincing than she felt. She was about to ring off when she remembered Tamsin Quinn. 'Any further forward with Tamsin and Paddy?'

'Yes. Good news there. We've recovered the blue Transit van. Oddly enough it wasn't burned out, as we might have expected. I'm guessing as Tamsin was leaving with a new identity the plan was to wipe her DNA from the system. Fortunately we were able to access it before that happened. Paddy has pre-cons so his was on the database anyway. We have a match for Paddy on Johannes's body and both Johannes and Tamsin's DNA has been found on a blanket in the back of the Transit van. So, although Tamsin was in the safe house in Perth, we've charged her with *Conspiracy to Murder* and Paddy with *Murder*. Johannes's blood is there too. So I think we can be sure they'll both be convicted. And, with a bit of luck, we'll get Rose for *Threatening Behaviour* too.'

'No problems with the Serious Organised Crime lads muscling in?' Clare asked.

'Nope. The DCI stepped in and said the lad's death was an unrelated charge and that if SOC had a problem with it he'd be happy to set them straight. Oh, he sends his regards by the way.'

'Oh!' The exclamation was out before she could stop herself. 'Please say thanks from me,' she said, hoping she hadn't given herself away. She had been watching the door to her room all morning, wondering if he might visit. Obviously not. The doctor appeared at the door and Clare ended the call.

'Good news,' the doctor said. 'Your carboxy-haemoglobin levels have dropped to within the normal range and your lung function is much improved. We'd like to keep you in overnight just to check this progress is maintained. If the levels are as good tomorrow, I'll be happy to let you go home. Let's say early afternoon.'

Clare sent a message to Jude to let her know. The reply pinged back almost immediately.

> Fantastic news
> We'll be in to collect you.
> Just say when.
> James keeps saying your name!
> Love of love,
> J xxx

Clare smiled at that. Wee James was such a darling. And his first words had been her name. Once she was feeling a bit better she'd have him to stay again. Give Jude and Frank a proper break this time. She sent a message back saying not to worry, that she'd get Chris and Sara to pick her up.

Jude sent back a *You sure?* and Clare replied with a thumbs-up. She yawned and leaned back on her pillows. She was outstandingly tired now. Yesterday's events seemed so far away. She just wanted to forget. She closed her eyes and allowed herself to drift off into a deep and dreamless sleep.

Sunday, 24 May

Chapter 42

Clare wakened early to the clattering of breakfast trolleys. Her door burst open and a cheerful nurse entered, bearing a tray which she put down on the table next to Clare's bed. She then opened the curtains to reveal the window streaming with rain.

'Not so nice this morning,' the nurse said. She helped Clare sit up and propped her pillows behind her. Then she swung the table across in front of Clare and lifted the covers off the plates.

Clare looked without enthusiasm at a bowl of muesli and a triangle of toast. A small tub of olive oil spread and another of marmalade lay next to the toast.

'Tea?' the nurse asked.

'Please. Milk, no sugar.'

The nurse went back out into the main ward, returning moments later with a small catering-sized cup of milky tea which she placed on the tray beside the toast. Clare picked up her spoon and made an attempt at the muesli.

After breakfast – or what she could face of it – she texted Chris again to check he was okay to pick her up. *Doctor says any time after 2*, she added.

Chris replied with a thumbs-up and Clare put down her phone. She thought about work, wondering if she'd be fit enough to return on Monday. Her arm was still pretty painful but she was sure they'd give her some decent painkillers. There was such a lot of paperwork to be done and she'd have to give a full statement on what she could remember of Gayle's attack. She shivered at the memory of it and wondered if she should leave the gap in the floorboards unfilled. It felt like tempting fate to have it filled in. Would she ever be free of the legacy of Francis Ritchie's death or was he to haunt her for ever? Perhaps she should take that trip to Boston – once her arm had healed. See how she liked it. Maybe go to the place on the postcard – Provincetown, wasn't it? That was assuming Geoffrey still wanted her, of course. Maybe he'd already made a new life for himself out there. Him and the toothpaste blonde.

'Perhaps I'll go and find out,' she said to herself.

'Beg pardon?' the nurse said, coming in to check Clare's blood pressure.

Clare shook her head. 'It's nothing. Look – when you've done all this – can I get dressed?'

The nurse hooked Clare up to the blood pressure monitor then stuck a digital thermometer in her ear. As she waited for the results from the machines, she checked Clare's pulse. After a few minutes she smiled and picked up the chart from the end of the bed.

'You look pretty fit to me, Clare. I'll speak to the doctor and see if he'll sign you off. Then I'll help you into your clothes. Just make sure you take it easy for a few days. No aerobic exercise – nothing strenuous that'll put a strain on your lungs. And definitely not back to work for a couple of weeks.' She gave Clare a severe look. 'Take my advice. Or you'll end up back here.'

Clare assured her she would follow all the advice she was given. She picked up her phone and thought about messaging Geoffrey. And then she decided there was no point in worrying him. Once she was home and back to normal, she'd let him know what had happened. Or maybe she wouldn't…

She was surprised the DCI hadn't been in touch, other than messages via Chris and Jim. She hoped that business with the eight thousand pounds invoice would be forgotten now. Hopefully the Chief Super would accept it hadn't been Clare's doing. And then she remembered her house. Swarming with firemen, Chris had said. Would it be safe to return to? Or would the fire brigade have declared it uninhabitable? She sent him another quick message:

> Just wondered about the house.
> Can I go back home?
> Fumes all gone?

The reply came quickly.

> Yes, all fine now.
> They checked it again this morning.
> Boiler fine and fumes gone.
> Off out for a run now with Sara. God help me!

Clare laughed. She thought how lucky she was to have friends like Chris and Diane. Coming to St Andrews had definitely been a good move. She was longing to see Benjy again and she opened up the photos app on her phone to watch some videos of him tearing through the woods behind Daisy Cottage.

And then there was her car. What would happen about that? Would the insurance company pay up? No doubt they'd take their time deciding and would probably choose to be difficult about it. Well she'd be ready for a fight.

She'd survived Gayle Crichton's worst efforts. She could definitely take on her car insurers.

She eased herself off the bed and looked at her clothes. Following advice from the nurse, Diane had brought Clare a large man's shirt and she contemplated this now, trying to work out how to put it on without knocking her arm. Finally she gave in and buzzed for the nurse who promised to come and help her as soon as she was free. She had been told she wasn't allowed to have a shower for at least two weeks and Diane had brought in a pack of baby wipes. She set about trying to freshen herself up with these while she waited for the indignity of the nurse coming to dress her.

Once she was dressed and her belongings gathered together she had nothing to do but sit and wait on Chris and Sara. She flicked through TV channels but it was all news, politics and cookery shows. Clare thought it would be quite some time before she could even lift a frying pan, let alone cook exciting meals. Not that she cooked much anyway…

The time ticked slowly by as she waited for Chris and Sara to arrive. She had been dressed for hours and even the doctor had popped in with a bag of medication. She played Candy Crush and Solitaire on her phone with one eye on the clock.

And then the door opened, tentatively at first, and Clare stared at the figure in the doorway. Instead of Chris and Sara, it was Alastair Gibson. She suddenly felt self-conscious and wondered what her hair was like.

'Clare…' he said, then he broke off. He shook his head. 'I can't believe it. I'm so ashamed of myself.'

'Al… I was expecting Chris…'

'I told him I'd collect you.' He came forward and sat on the bed facing her chair. 'I warned him not to tell you

– in case you wouldn't let me come. And I wanted to see you so much, Clare.'

She looked at him and he returned her gaze.

'I can't believe I let you be in such danger. That I was taken in by – that woman.'

'Al – we both were. Let's face it: the highest levels in Police Scotland were taken in by her. She was bloody good.'

'Diane wasn't.'

Clare smiled. 'No, she wasn't. And thank God for that, Al. We both owe her a big drink.'

'And some.'

There was an awkward silence and Clare broke it first. 'So you've come to take me home?'

He nodded. 'Yes, if that's okay. If you'll let me, I mean…'

Clare smiled. 'I'd like that very much.'

He looked down at her free hand and, very gently, he took hold of it.

Clare watched as he began tracing a pattern across her fingers with his thumb and she sat for a moment enjoying the sensation.

'And maybe,' he went on, breaking the spell, 'I mean once you're feeling better, maybe we could do something? Go out, somewhere? Just if you want to, of course…'

She noticed he was avoiding her eye, as he continued exploring her fingers with his.

'And your garden…' he said, glancing at her empty shirt sleeve. 'I was thinking – you're not going to be able to do any gardening for most of the summer. So, I could come over – cut your grass, do a bit of weeding, that sort of thing. God knows, it needs someone to sort it out.' He broke off, as though he had run out of things to say, and he raised his gaze to meet hers. Those blue eyes again.

'I think I'd like that,' she said.

The door was pushed open again and a nurse stood in the doorway. 'You're going to be spoiled for choice today,' she said.

Clare glanced at the DCI then back at the nurse for an explanation.

'*Two* handsome lads vying to take you home, Clare. Now how often do we see that?' And she stood back to let a suntanned Geoffrey Dark walk into the room.

'Clare!' he cried, striding across to her. Clare immediately let the DCI's hand slip from hers.

He rose awkwardly and moved back to allow Geoffrey to greet Clare.

'It's so good to see you,' he said. 'I've been so worried.'

Clare gaped at him. 'But how did you know...'

'Jude telephoned me on Friday night. It's the start of summer recess and I was planning a trip up into Canada but, as soon as I heard, I jumped on the next plane. Oh Clare...' He sat down next to her and took her gently in his arms, avoiding her broken arm. 'I'm so sorry, my darling. What you've been through.'

The DCI was hovering awkwardly near the door and Clare hurried to introduce the two men. They shook hands and Geoffrey said how good it was to meet Clare's boss.

'You must have been so worried about her,' he said to the DCI, and Alastair Gibson nodded.

He indicated the door and, with one eye on Geoffrey, he said, 'Maybe I should go, Clare...'

Clare looked at him. 'No, please stay,' she said. 'I mean, I'd like you to...'

A nurse bustled in, a pile of clean linen in her arms. 'Oh, I'm sorry,' she said. 'I thought these handsome gents had taken you home.' She smiled at Clare. 'So who's the lucky chap then? Which one gets to drive you, Clare?'

Clare looked from one to the other.

Which one indeed?

And, for the first time in her life, she had absolutely no idea what to do next.

Acknowledgements

As ever, I am indebted to a growing band of friends whose technical knowledge has been invaluable. In particular I would like to thank Alan Rankin, Angela Nurse, Donald Jenks, Richard Renwick, Tom Darbyshire, McIsabel and, of course, my amazing family, Iain, Stuart, Kenneth and Peter. Your requests for a share of royalties have been noted…

To my wonderful editor, Louise Cullen, who makes every single word better, and to her lovely colleagues Fran and Siân, my most grateful thanks. Thanks also to Deborah Blake for her skilled copy-editing and for bearing with the fact that I cannot spell *focused*! And to Hannah Weatherill, my incredible agent who fields my long emails with such patience, a very special thank you.

Finally, my apologies once more to the residents of St Andrews for bringing murder and mayhem to their streets. And I hope Police Scotland will forgive the ills I have done them in this book. In my defence, I did give you DI Clare Mackay to sort it out.

CANELOCRIME

Do you love crime fiction and are always on the lookout for brilliant authors?

Canelo Crime is home to some of the most exciting novels around. Thousands of readers are already enjoying our compulsive stories. Are you ready to find your new favourite writer?

Find out more and sign up to our newsletter at canelocrime.com